La Maravilla

Alfredo Véa, Jr.

A PLUME BOOK

PLUME
Published by the Penguin Group
Penguin Books USA Inc., 375 Hudson Street, New York, New York 10014, U.S.A.
Penguin Books Ltd, 27 Wrights Lane, London W8 5TZ, England
Penguin Books Australia Ltd, Ringwood, Victoria, Australia
Penguin Books Canada Ltd, 10 Alcorn Avenue, Toronto, Ontario, Canada M4V 3B2
Penguin Books (N.Z.) Ltd, 182–190 Wairau Road, Auckland 10, New Zealand

Penguin Books Ltd, Registered Offices: Harmondsworth, Middlesex, England

Published by Plume, an imprint of Dutton Signet,
a division of Penguin Books USA Inc.
Previously published in a Dutton edition.

First Plume Printing, April, 1994
20 19 18 17 16 15 14 13

Excerpt from "A Process in the Weather of the Heart." Dylan Thomas: *Poems of Dylan Thomas*. Copyright 1939 by New Directions Publishing Corp. Reprinted by permission of New Directions Publishing Corp.

"Five Feet High and Rising" (Johnny R. Cash) © 1959 Chappell & Co. (Renewed)
All Rights Reserved. Used By Permission.

Ⓟ REGISTERED TRADEMARK—MARCA REGISTRADA

LIBRARY OF CONGRESS CATALOGING-IN-PUBLICATION DATA
Véa, Alfredo, 1952–
      La maravilla / Alfredo Véa, Jr.
         p.   cm.
      ISBN 0-452-27160-6
      1. Mexican Americans—Arizona—Phoenix Region—Fiction.   2. Boys—
Arizona—Phoenix Region—Fiction.   3. Phoenix Region (Ariz.) —
Fiction.   4. Grandparents—Fiction.   I. Title.
PS3572.E2M37   1994
813'.54—dc20   93–31582
                                                                       CIP

Printed in the United States of America
Original hard cover design by Eve L. Kirch

ALFREDO VÉA, JR., was born in Arizona. He lived the life of a migrant farm worker before being sent to Vietnam in 1968. After his discharge he worked at jobs that ranged from truck driver to carnival mechanic as he put himself through college and law school. Currently he is a criminal defense attorney in San Francisco. The author says of his first novel, *La Maravilla*, "The flesh of the book is fiction; the bones are real."

Dedicated to the memory of Jack Beery . . . the best
high school teacher there ever was.

Thank you,

Chris Gauger and Theresa Ordonez, Cynthia Marcopulos, Joseph Billingsley, Flynn Bradley, Harold Rosenthal, Christine and Timothy McDaniel, Norma Paz Garcia and Bert Feuss, Robin and Bob Mayer, Newton Lam and Hon. Maria James, Robert (Beau) Garcia and Janet Franchi, Michael (Miguelito) Sivila, Raj and Vicki Lynn Chabra, Doug Hergert and Elaine Anderson, Earl J. and Sue Waits, Dovia Shexnayder, Patrice McElroy, Ed and Sarah Clancy and especially Edmundo Vasquez and Tami Miller and
above all, Susan Breall
for support and encouragement.

Sandra Dijkstra, for seeing something there.
Rosemary Ahern, for making the editing process so painless.

Manuel y Josephina, for haunting me still . . .

Contents

A process in the weather of the world
Turns ghost to ghost; each mothered child
Sits in their double shade.
A process blows the moon into the sun,
Pulls down the shabby curtains of the skin;
And the heart gives up its dead.

Dylan Thomas
from *"A Process in the Weather of the Heart"*

Prólogo

I died some time ago. Soy mujer de historia. I passed away. No, no, don't be sad. Those words have lost their meaning for me. I could just as easily have said that I've changed my mind. Really, all that happened was that I changed my mind.

I certainly can't be sure when it happened—the exact moment. If you've ever swum beneath the surface of a pond that's been allowed to go still . . . if you could hold your breath long enough (and I have no problem with that now) so there were no waves on the surface, you would be hard-pressed to tell whether you were beneath the surface or above it. You could reach above your head to touch the margin between air and water and see your own reflection reaching. Then you could fragment it, touch the surface, make the margin chaos. Are you above or below? It does no good to look around because things are moving with you. It gets even more complicated when you realize that neither man nor woman is the measure of all things. I, for one, certainly can't be sure, even now.

Did I tell you that I am convinced that when Christ walked upon the waters, He made the very same statement: that there is as much below as above; that there is as much before as after?

Imagine the same still pond with yourself standing on it, not even breaking the surface tension; on it like a breath, with the softness of a maidenfly. Beneath your feet are your feet, and below that, your face. All of you—and your universe beyond that. An absolute sym-

*metry. Which is real? As far as you are concerned, both are. Now, I
don't mean to be condescending, but human language is as limiting
as human eyesight or human thought. Think about it, how much of
the light spectrum can you see? Not much. How much of the spectrum
of ideas can you understand or speak? Far, far less.*

*Oh, there are people who are pretty damn conversant. It's sur-
prising who they are. Almost invisible people, people who have never
been fashionable . . . far from it. I knew it before. Or, at least, I felt
it even if I could never admit it. Those Yaqui Indians and those black
people at the Mighty Clouds of Joy!*

*But it's a strange thing, human knowing. Most mortals have a
mind-closing function that works so much better than the mind opener.
Really, it's useless to try to explain it to you in this way. I don't
speak anymore. Remember, I died. I passed on, or whatever you wish
to call it. I'm lying on my back . . . at least those huesos of mine,
those old bones that once dragged themselves all the way from Andalusia into a desert in America, are lying in a cemetery in Phoenix,
Arizona. The only reason I can speak to you now is because I've
hovered around my grandson's head for so long, nagging at him. I
tease at his mind, coax him with images. He struggles to know and
translate the fields I generate when I'm near him. He believes my life
required some act of closing.*

*To tell you the truth, I can't actually tell if I desire an act of closing
or prefer to simply live in the same moments, always. My grandson,
Beto, finds these moments in his dreams and in his memory and sets
them down. There is a difference. Perhaps I am just a terrible irony
that has become part of the organic fabric of things: a set of waves on
the pool, a weave in the cloth. Perhaps I am still in the past and
looking forward. To foresee is to foresuffer.*

*I do know that I finally fell down full of arthritis on a day when I
could barely hear Dinah Washington's voice on my electric phonograph. I thought perhaps a vacuum tube was dying. I dragged down
a whole dish rack of plates and spoons, and my altar came down on
top of me. I saw the statue of the Holy Virgin tumbling down the
steps of my home, and I felt hot candle wax on my skin. I pulled them
down and we all fell soundlessly.*

*The fall was such a relief in a way. I'd spent my last few years
walking so carefully, mincing around, taking care not to tumble. I
had become too brittle, you see. People who hugged me thought I felt*

like a small bag of popcorn. Dios Madre, I'll tell you, that last fall was a glory! I dove into it thankfully.

For two dark days no one found me, and it must've happened somewhere in that time. It must've come as I dreamed. Subtly, at the core of it, I dreamed in one direction that all at once I was dreaming in another. Just like that! I poked my finger through the surface tension. It is the waves that create and obscure.

Some things remain clear. I know that my precious bag of medicines and cures was given to the proper person before the day I collapsed and that the bodies of Wysteria and her dogs were thrown yards from the freeway.

I hear all the Chinese words that have come between me and my Manuel. God help us all, they are so lonely.

And yes, I know about the Tet Offensive, and I've seen the helicopters spitting flames and spinning out of control above the Perfume River. I've seen my grandson apologizing for the world into the ear of a hopeless, faceless man with the morphine needles dangling from his skin. But I see the candles, too. I see my children coming.

I saw and I see these and many things thereafter. I saw many such things while I still lived. You see, nightmares are sometimes the price of vision.

I know there was a burial. I saw it firsthand. Dios mío! What a horrible day that was! What a tragedy! God forgive me, my own funeral was unbelievable.

Well, the blame for it all lies with me. I know it now just as I know that Manuel heard my apology. Now that I have a mattress of grubs and a blanket of marigolds.

How he and I—our dust—lay for eternity is my fault; our separation, my true penance. How we lived . . . no, how we live, is another story.

Oh yes, one last word. Hay gente en esta página conmigo.

There are people with me on this page.

1

Abuela

The woman in black looked up into the high, endless sky. The skin of the hand that shaded her eyes was browned and softened by the tannins of her life.

"I have a husband that does not await the Resurrection."

She pulled off her mantilla. Slowly and purposefully, she shook back her long hair and it was as if black curtains were let loose, as obscure as burned cornsilk. She reached up and pulled the tan butcher paper back even farther in the deep window to let a flood of white light pour into the room. For a sharp moment the dark was driven out and the interior of the adobe house was made visible: a colored shawl proudly flashed its bright red warp and green embroidered flowers; raven hair held out courses of gray; hoops of silver with turquoise stones on a single finger; a wrist, and at the place where the heart echoes, a hammered silver crucifix hanging next to a small sealed jar of oils, herbs, and lizards' toes—its tiny, brown cork waxed over. The woman considered the depth of sky, then let her mind go out, catching the first faint sense that her spirit beckoned to her. It had been warmed suddenly as it called her to a familiar vision of the Alhambra—the tiled walls and a cool, hidden garden she and her sister had found so long ago.

Behind the mossy fountain, behind the door, was a garden

unexpectedly filled with silent, lounging cats; the green lawn strewn with bright fish bones and glassine shrimp skins. Entering this vision was so easy. Tails up, the cats rushed over for petting. It was a well worn and comfortable path in her mind, a thought-rubbed groove, and she sent her spirit to it often. She smiled as beads of sweat gathered in the small of her back, above her hips, a memory of childbirth. Her mind's eye dilated; another vision pushed forth with old schoolmates whose young faces were now erased and irretrievable in the same timeless, unchanging monument—the Alhambra.

Years ago she had suffered distress after distress as each name fled beyond recollection and then took the countenance with it. The silent adobe room was filled with a cacophony of now nameless children's voices bounding and rebounding off the dark Moorish tiles and echoing again behind her eyes. She saw the huge brown portals once again and tiny Adelita between them wearing her dark blue school uniform, her hair in two perfect braids meeting at her flowered crown.

Adelita. Where was she? Could she see the Tagus from a similar window? Does hers have glass? She ran off on a hazy Tuesday evening when she was all of seventeen and married a Portuguese man, to Mama's eternal shame, then disappeared into Lisboa. She had waved sheepishly, looking back, her beautiful hair let down. Such a slight action was a wave, she thought wearily. She felt again the sharp disappointment of a planned evening between sisters ruined forever by a planned life between lovers.

Do all things happen on a day of the week? Such a grievous gesture, that little wave. She had known it then but had clung to every hope and every letter. It was long years before she knew that her knowing had finality to it. Adelita never wrote now, not for many years. Her last few letters even had Portuguese words in them.

"Adélita," she said softly to the window.

"I married a Yaqui," she said softly to herself.

"My husband does a dance with cocoons on his pants."

Like a jump rope rhyme.

"My husband does a dance with cocoons on his pants."

She winced at the old, painful irony.

"So far from Andalusia, both of us."

The woman shifted her eyes one degree of arc in the Phoenix sky and thus turned an airy page that caused her to shiver in the heat and plant her feet below her as if to receive a blow she knew would come. She felt it waiting on her spirit's route, waiting out there like the sober, white crosses painted on the roads in Mexico. She was chilled again by the same waking dream.

"Is someone on my grave? Has a spirit passed here and heard me and answered me in a dream?"

She knew that some dreams can't be controlled; after all, they exist whether or not there is someone to receive them. There is no human will involved in that case, but the future or the past or the other world demanded to be present, regardless, and it was she who was so often chosen as witness to it all.

In the dream Manuel is beside her, but not. His face is completely still, yet moving toward her. What age is he? Where are we? She felt restricted, claustrophobic, as she saw what was not there. She knew she was trapped by the dream once more, and she knew it would have its way with her till it ran its course. She could not hope to change it or wish it away. She sought only to understand it. His mouth was closed but opening, the desire to speak painfully clear in his eyes. There was a tide of incoherent phrases.

She reached out her other hand to steady herself on a wall she could not see. A flood of Yaqui words she once thought, things about the singing tree or *otra cosa, quién sabe*. But nowadays she knew better. She had heard the words at the market: the Chinese words. An eternal flood of Chinese words.

"Cantonese? A village called Longchuan."

She experienced a longing that came in smells and feelings that she could not fathom.

"What does it mean?"

Years ago, before the war, she had dreamed about the yellow pigeons feeding on blue carrion and knew the Japanese emissaries in Washington were not to be trusted. Hadn't she dreamed the crippled pinta woman, too? The speckled woman knocking soundlessly at her kitchen window not two days before *pobre* Maria was sprayed with pesticides in a field near Glendale?

She had seen the silk covering Eugene's face, felt the tug of the risers long before her son·joined the Airborne and took her blood into the sky above Korea; she had been jerked out of bed by it, her bed sheets billowing overhead. She had drifted from the belly of an airplane like *pan dulce* sliding from a baking sheet.

She had dreamed weddings and births and accidents for everyone *en la comunidad*. She had believed those meanings even if no one had listened to her at first. Hadn't she made a living from the meanings? But Chinese? The longing, the pain in that dream was horrible, palpable. Home. To be home.

She was frozen by the fear of it, just as she had been the day before and so many different days before that. As suddenly as the vision came to her, it slipped away, and she was once again aware of the deep sky and her spirit, done with fetching, came quickly back to her.

She dropped her hand slowly, and the paper folded back down to allow only a hard, narrow shaft of light into the room.

"*La boca del diablo*, the devil's muzzle," she said with a mixture of contempt and distraction.

"That's what they call it, Beto, when all the goddamn air over Buckeye Road falls up."

She looked back into the room where the boy was sitting quietly at the feet of his grandfather, her husband.

"Things are backward here."

She raised her hand slowly as if to follow the path of the accursed air. A gesture that began in disdain and ended with resignation as the hand dropped and she walked across the floor toward the kitchen, her black dress rustling. She'd shed the emptiness with those words aloud.

The stillness down on the ground didn't show it, and the heat waves above the road didn't show it, but the torrents of hot air piled, pushed and shoved upward crazily, gray with humming gnats and red with gnashing beetles—a wide living shaft cut into again and again by angling bats.

La boca del diablo. It flooded over the hills and swirled into cottonwoods which moved when nothing else did so that it seemed a hundred green *marionetas* were forever dancing and drying on the ridges behind the *ramada*. The cicadas' song sent it up on its way. The faraway wail of the wistful freight trains sent it up. A thousand quiet people fanning themselves sent it up. It was an ocean of crimson-edged swells, sweltering heat, wilting leaves. Heaving, spinning vortexes of splashing heat, it escaped when people couldn't.

It burned them all. It laughed at those below and left them there. It lapped at the canyon rims and far mesas and held them all torpid in the vacuum, just before it left for the moon.

It was the same in 1958 as it is today and as it was when Manuel's father, the boy's great-grandfather, walked north with his changeling tribe; walked away from the Yoris and their wars and their God; walked away from the slave camps in the Yucatán. Like so many times before, the peaceful nations of Sonora and Chihuahua were forced to transform their self-image; men who knelt by the water as farmers and hunters saw homeless guerrillas staring back at them. They saw only sadness in their own reflection.

The Yaquis turned north in 1910, as did the slender Mayos, the husky Huichols and the square-faced Fuertes, bringing their burros and goats, their *pascola* masks and their shamans.

The river people had been told by the gentry that their ten thousand years on the land meant nothing in the new order, that Spanish markings on sealed papers meant everything. The river people chose to fight just as they had four hundred years before when they turned from fighting the Aztecs to fighting the Spanish.

The *revolucionarios* came next and told the Yaqui nation that the land did not belong to the gentry; that, in the new order, it was being seized in the name of the people for land reform. The river people, once the best soldiers of the revolution, now fought them all.

Hunted like wolves and conscripted by both sides, they left skulking packs of guerrillas behind in the foothills, packs to descend on their pursuers and to win back the land.

"We were not the *Aztecas*," they howled. "Now, we are not you."

The river people poured north out of Mexico, leaving their sacred waters forever.

The boy sitting on the floor watched without looking and could see his *abuelo* riding on that hot air outside. Yes, the old man was rocking in his chair, the furrows on his salty brow irrigated and shining; but the tension clear on the stretched eyelids indicated something else.

Beto watched the old man turning on his own thermal path and using it to rise up above the creosote and manzanita; rise above the darting, frenzied bats, the nagging blackbirds and the catclaw trees till the dirt road below dimmed yellow and brown, as though time had turned back to his own father's time, his father's desert, a desert without fences, without rails. A desert *sin fronteras*.

He rose till the mesas beyond appeared and the redtail was near. He floated on the fringe of the wavering air, his tips spread and his neck down toward lost Sonora, the homeland—the lodestone. And following the trace through the valley that brought the people so long ago, he flew back into himself, the high, crazed call in his throat piercing everything, hanging everywhere, freezing small frightened animals in their paths and forcing bent, working men to turn and look.

The boy had seen him flying like this just once before, and one day he would go along with him. Once, in the desert and down a dark hidden wash, a hard narrow shaft of light would thrill him, pierce him with the sight of the long line leaving the Yoris' revolution behind, the gunfire of the Ba-catete hills in their ears. He would see them leaving the Span-iards and their hard churches behind. He would hear the prideless *Federales* scream as the Yaqui rear guard fell on them, stripped them and sent them back south through the desert with the soles of their feet hacked off. He would see the flesh and blood baton passed on. Something passed down.

He would see the flashing deer from far above and decipher

the whispers of the lizard below, and he would have speech
with the wolf.

"Ay, *mijo*, don't get too close to him when he's flying
around like that. The fool is with his witch again, *la puta*."

It was her holy posture, her hands planted firmly on her
hips. The boy had seen it many, many times before.

"And please don't hold your breath," she said while quickly
crossing herself.

The boy saw her staring at him from the kitchen and then
down at the old man. She was a small, thin woman with
more wrinkles than seemed possible for a face that did not
really seem old. Her cheeks were angular one moment and
rounded the next. She possessed a sharp nose to complement
her tongue and a rounded chin to go with her smile and her
deep black eyes seemed to have no pupils—doe eyes.

She walked in from the kitchen and stood in the archway
leading to her bedroom. Behind her, on the dresser, stood
her photos, encased in silver frames. Stiff city people with
canes and felt hats. A gray man and his small wife. Severe
faces that presented little evidence that they were once ever
young.

There was one of herself taken on some grassy place long
forgotten that showed a whitewashed dance pavilion in the
background. Her skin had been white as marble and her
fingers slender. Another showed her with her little sister,
years before meeting the Portuguese or the boy's grandfather,
Manuel. Both girls had worn long lace gloves to their elbows.

"If you hold your breath, he could wander with those lazy
ancestors of his for days, *y entonces*, who the hell would work
to feed all of us?"

As his grandmother returned to her enormous cast-iron
stove, the boy exhaled slowly, the musk of adobe in the
shadow mixed with the deep, pungent scent of chorizo. A
small web on his grandfather's chair shivered with the breath.
In the dark a tortilla resumed its flight between his *abuela*'s

hands while her face hung in the air above it like a spirit.

Behind her and lighting the Sacred Heart, three votive candles in red glass burned in a *nicho* scooped into the adobe. Her white ivory comb, like a dove, floated above her face.

"Don't bother him. If you knock him even a little off his balance, he might not be able to come back home," she whispered, her eyes widened with the import of what she was saying.

She indignantly flapped a tortilla onto the *comal*, then crossed herself, kissed the crucifix that hung on her wrist.

"He was stuck out in a flash flood once when Tía Julia bothered him."

She nodded toward her sleeping husband.

"Julia held her breath to take a *pastilla* and he stayed a gila monster for three days, tasting the air with his tongue and crawling on the cracked bones of his heathen fathers . . . and he couldn't get back here."

She turned again.

"It's like waking a sleepwalker, I think. He's dreaming but it's sure not a dream. It's more dangerous than a dream. It's that godforbidden Yaqui tea again. You can love your *abuelo*, but remember that Yaquis are strange. They say the Yaquis once burned witches!"

This time she spoke with indignation and some anger.

"You see, the whole living family must breathe together. All of us. He almost drowned out there in a flash flood." Her hand pointed out somewhere past the cesspool.

"Fool! *Pendejo Indio* . . . and Doña Juana sat with me for most of a day and a night before we got him back. We both sang the sacred songs and burned more candles than his skinny Yaqui ass will ever be worth. *Gracias a Dios*, the Holy Virgin interceded on our behalf and in he came, right back to us, safe and sound and without so much as a scale on his skin or a solitary word of thanks."

She looked down at him with disdain and affection.

"Do you know how we met, me and the flycatcher over there?"

This was not a question meant to be answered. Though he had heard the story before, the boy still shook his head no.

"Long ago, when I lived in Denver, I took a job in the evenings just to get out and see the town and the people. I was very gregarious then, and in those days men and women would get all dressed up just to walk downtown and promenade in the parks. We all wore hats. In my Spanish clothing I created quite a stir."

She pulled at her sleeves and lifted her chin proudly.

"*Válgame Dios*," she said, looking backward in time with obvious pleasure.

"I had a job in the most magnificent theater west of Nueva York! Do you know what I did?"

The boy knew. His mind had been seeded and tended by both of his *abuelitos*, and the interior of the now-demolished Downtown Lumiere Theater was as real to him as the Yaqui wars. He could feel the soft restriction of the velvet rope and the cool brass latch where it terminated.

"I played the piano for the silent moving pictures that they used to show. Oh, how I loved it! I loved the smell of teacakes and lemon. None of that popcorn and soda water stuff like today. It was civilized then, I'll tell you! You had an intermission *con* live *música*." She bowed gracefully and lowered her eyes with a smile. "The people would file out into the lobby to have their refreshments and to smoke. Each seat would have its hat and its coat. You didn't have to worry about thieves back then. The men who preferred pipes or cigars were allowed to stand out in the side exits where they might comment on the night sky and flip their ashes between the pavers. And all the while I would play."

She ran her fingers over invisible keys.

"But even this was not the best part. I saw the great Rudolph Valentino as the Sheik over two hundred times including matinées and practice sessions. Can you believe it? Me in a theater all alone with the man of my dreams, practicing *la música* that would breathe even more life into his images? Just the two of us.

"Oh, of course there was that old crippled wino projectionist—*pobre borrachín*. I was so young then that I couldn't see that he was choking on his own clay.

"At first I had to read *la música* from the sheets, but soon enough *la música* became such a part of me; the heart beating in Agnes Ayres's breast seemed to beat in mine. Ay, *Dios mío,* how I hated her stupid *gavacha* reticence! How I burned at her spoiled, grudging compliance! Each night I rose and I fell upon those keys below the light striking the silver screen.

"Do you know that after a while I ignored the sheet music altogether? Every sad scene was Bessie Smith and the love scenes . . . only Carlos Gardel! No two shows were the same. I don't think anyone ever knew the difference unless, of course, they came more than once. I tell you, when I left, that theater lost money."

Her hands came together at this point. They always did.

She sat silently a moment before resuming the story at the customary place.

"One day the *pendejo, idiota* projectionist was smoking *cigarros* up in the booth where he had a little bunk and one of his *pinche* matches set the films on fire. He burned up half the booth and most of himself before the fire brigade came. The firemen said that the old drunk burned like Sterno. *Pero, una cosa más importante,* he had burned up our only reels of *The Sheik. Qué pena,* no? How I cried! We waited three long weeks for a new copy to come in from Los Angeles.

"Oh, I would play anyway. With tears in my eyes I would play to a black screen and an empty theater. Little did I know that I was really crying because the man who was bringing the film in from the railroad depot would see to it that I, Josephina Valenzuela de Castillo, would be happy for the rest of my life.

"Perhaps not a strictly pious life, mind you. Perhaps he has doomed me to everlasting purgatory . . . that remains to be seen."

She raised her voice, hoping that the flying, sleeping man would hear.

"Perhaps Redemption will be denied me in the Last Days and I will turn on a spit of eternal fire because of his heathen ways. But happy."

She waved her finger at the boy.

"Do you know how handsome that man was? An *Indio* with green eyes! *La mierda,* he's still *muy guapo.* He came into the

theater with that *mujeriego* Salvador and a couple of nervous
Pimas. When they started up the film the Pimas were frightened to death by it and ran up to the lobby to hide behind
the curtains, but the Yaquis had a look on their faces that
said '*y qué*' "—she shrugged—"so what?"

Josephina was smiling now.

"There was something about this man that drew me to him,
pulled me to him. That lustful Salvador kept eyeing me, but
your grandfather would have left right then and there without
another thought of me or of Rudolph Valentino. At that very
moment the Holy Mother spoke to me and told me exactly
what I had to do. I walked over to the piano and began to
play. Somehow I knew it would keep him there. Somehow I
knew the notes would pierce his rough and sunburned heart.
Have you seen his hands, *mijo?* The strength in his hands?
That very day he became *mi cielo*, my sky."

She seemed far away once more.

"I told my mother he was Catholic! I told her in the letters."

She clenched her small hands into fists.

"I played music he had never heard before, pieces from
Harlem. I played a tune called 'Willow Tree' for him. Oh, he
was some kind of Catholic all right! But not like any Catholic
I'd ever known. All his people are only Catholics in the day-
time. *Con fraude*; false pretenses! The rhythm method meant
absolutely nothing to him! You should see how he's ravaged
my belly with stretch marks!"

She placed her hand on her womb.

"*Dios mío*, when the change of life finally came, I called
Virginia and Ana and the others over to my house and we
had a farewell party! Farewell to the curse! We stole *viejito*'s
precious whiskey and drank the whole bottle. Then we
burned a big box of Kotex sanitary napkins right out there.
You know, the giant size."

She spread her arms out to outline the dimensions of the
box.

"You could see the flame for miles."

There was a silence in the adobe as the dancing flames died
away in the old woman's eyes. The momentary rapture of
the Kotex fire was quickly replaced with a look of concern.

"You see, the evening of the flash flood, it was the Holy Trinity that rescued him from his *yoan-ya*, his crazy religion. *La verdad*. It still holds him." She crossed herself twice.

"His dead heathen father even came to us right here in this very room, where you sit now, to stop us from our prayers."

She closed her eyes and sighed.

"He was hiding behind his burial mask or whatever it was on his head. I think they call it a *máscara chapayeka*, a Pharisee mask. But to me it looked like an owl, a *tecolote*. And there was a second mask hanging down his back and tied around his neck by a leather thong. It was as black as death with red paint on the lips and long white hairs above the eyes and below the chin. What earthly good is a mask that faces backward?

"His face was frozen in death, but I knew it was him. Two masks couldn't fool me. I recognized the scars *aquí y aquí*." She pointed to her stomach and right thigh.

"*La verdad*. I knew it was him. Jealous because I'm from *Españe*."

She turned her indignant face heavenward, then batted her eyelashes imperiously.

"Jealous because of the power of the Trinity and the power God gives to me. He didn't even know who Duke Ellington is, or Sarah Vaughan!"

She turned away for a moment, the scorn obvious.

"I remember him at the wedding. *Cabrón*, he couldn't even bring his heathen ass into the church to see us joined before a proper God. But I showed him. I refused the Yaqui part of the ceremony." She raised her chin imperiously. "I refused.

"Can you see someone like me, Josephina Valenzuela de Castillo, celebrating my wedding day with sweating, brown pagans wearing deer antlers and ribbons? Do you know what they do at a wedding? The betrothed are escorted to separate family feasts. They are chaperoned everywhere. Then the groom's people capture the bride and carry her to him.

"Finally, they stand separately, surrounded by their respective sponsors and their families. While the clown dancers mock them and jeer at them, they are pushed toward each other, and, at last, when they alone are facing one another, they join hands and say to each other: 'Only you.' That's all there is to it!"

She rolled her eyes in derision.

" 'Solamente tu.' It's certainly not a Catholic ceremony!"

She shook her head disgustedly.

"Can you see me being kidnapped by his sweating family? By the mercy of God I was spared that indignity."

She shuddered at the thought of Yaqui men tossing a blanket over her, capturing her and carrying her off to Manuel's hiding place.

"I was born Catholic and I'll die Catholic. I curse him and all the *rio* Yaquis, and those Mayos, they just came for the food. I swear they're worse than Okies. Christians on the outside but *moreakame*, bad witchcraft, in here," she said, placing her finger to her heart.

"You see, the Yaquis were so isolated, so belligerent, they learned nothing from the Conquest. Did you know, they resisted first the Aztecs then the Spanish with force? Then they fought the *Federales* and Pancho Villa at the same time! Strange, resistant people. I've read that at the turn of the century there was a Yaqui insurrection in Mexico just about every twenty years. *Cabezudos!* Hardheaded people!

"But *Jesus Santo*, the food was good at the wedding! *Carnitas y tamales. Pozole y albondigas y birria.* And the Yaquis made this deer meat *adobada, qué sabrosa!*"

She was lost for a moment in the memory. The boy sat between the two of them, the only one whose thoughts were anchored in the present.

"You would think that a man who loves good food as much as your grandfather does could refrain from eating six-legged creatures. *Su abuelo* there still eats insects, *mijo*. To this very day."

She turned away to scrape the *comal*.

"*Todos tipos de insectos*. He'll deny it, but I catch him at it all the time. Moths and flies, too. Sometimes *grillos* even though I tell him it's bad luck. Even the *Chinos* say it's bad luck to hurt a *grillo*, and you know the *Chinos* will eat anything. Watch him sometime from the corner of your eye, and you'll see him eating flies.

"But be careful you don't look too far in the corner of your eye," she warned with a lowered voice, pointing her finger at him. "You'll see spirits that don't want to be seen; that don't want their names to be called. *Espíritus, hijo,* coming and going and even burning up like a passion finally vented. They can sit in the same chair with you, and neither of you will ever know it. Under you, on you, you won't know it. You'll feel a chill or look around for someone who's not there, but you may never know. Remember that."

She stopped for a moment to consider the impact of her words on the boy. He seemed to be listening intently, and it pleased her. None of her own children listened anymore. They're grown now, she thought, and flying away from us as fast as they can. Even Mona, my youngest, is leaving the desert. She wants a house with stucco on it. A thin-walled house with electricity and an inside toilet.

She pointed a bent finger at the boy again and laughed as she shuffled from the shelves to the iron stove. "Please stay away from those Yaquis. Listen to these rules! And don't ever disturb a Mexican graveyard. I know you and the Okie kids have found it. In Mexico, *mijo,* the dead have their own holidays. People cook food for the dead and invite them into their homes. Mexicans seem to bury everything but the past. Don't play around over there. Mexican graveyards are alive."

She turned away, shaking her head.

"The only house in all of Phoenix, Arizona, without flies."

The stack of steaming tortillas grew behind her as the pile of dough balls diminished, each ball in turn flattened by her fingers and turned on the *comal* until half cooked. They would be thrown back onto the *comal* just before they were eaten. The sight and the smell of it soothed them all, soothed Buckeye Road and the endless desert. The sound of it, the flap of the flying dough was a chant; the scent of chorizo an incense.

The drowsy boy thought about what his *abuela* had said. The pictures in his descending dreams were of whispering gila monsters and black masks fringed with white goat hair. He imagined the frightening double visage of his great-grandfather; then slow darkness came. But just before he dozed off, the boy, his head canted into the reddening dust glory and slowly bobbing with the rise and fall of his chest, saw a bright flash in the corner of the room, in the corner of his eye.

2

A Compass in the Blood

Hours passed. Beto had been sitting quietly with the wiry mahogany man who was his grandfather ever since his *abuela* last had spoken. The boy on the ground wore only shorts while the man wore tattered Ben Davis pants and a solid blue shirt from J. C. Penney's. There was a sliver of a bright silver ring like a new moon on his left hand. Arthritis had come just recently and trapped it on the finger, swallowed it up as a tree will swallow up barbed wire.

A sadness crept over the boy as he watched the old man. The feeling came like a cast shadow so he looked around the room, as his *abuela* would, to see if it had come as a man or an insect or possibly a snake. There was nothing to be seen, so perhaps it had come over him as a spirit.

The palpable sadness deepened, and he realized that it had to do with his relationship with the man in front of him and the woman behind him in the kitchen. That relationship had changed within the last few days, though the precise how and why still evaded him. The milestone was reached the moment he realized that people, grown-up people, did things for reasons other than those they gave; they did unreasonable things. This moment coincided with his mother, Lola's last visit.

Lola had been gone for four years now and had returned

to Buckeye only twice in all that time. Each visit came on a summer evening, and the crunch of tires beneath a slow, heavy car had been the harbinger—a tentative driver, not a friend. When she came back it was always with a new man, a grinning, handshaking *payaso* calling himself "Daddy" or "Uncle." And each time she returned there was a new car to admire and a flurry of new plans to be enthusiastic about.

"Raymond has some experience welding so we figure that if we moved to Stockton he could get something in the shipyards."

All eyes would move to the man with welding experience, who would then look down uncomfortably. Next Lola would modestly, gingerly reach into the Pontiac or the Kaiser Manhattan to pull out a little squirming bundle. The only moment of real civility and seriousness would come when she introduced the boy to a new brother. Now there were two little brothers, both mestizos like himself. One for each husband.

His mother and his grandmother had argued about this the last time she came to visit. There had been screaming in the adobe while another "uncle" waited in the car, impatiently arranging the shoulder pads of his clay-colored double-breasted.

"Don't you understand the vows? Till death do us part? I raised you in the church! I raised you in the church! You were baptized before God! Now two divorces *y Madre de Dios*, a baby without even getting married. You are shameless! *Sin vergüenza!* Nobody asks for your hand, nobody comes to us to ask for you, and so there is no proper courtship. I don't even know his family. Where is his family?"

The old woman covered her face with her hands, then walked slowly into the kitchen, where she sat down. Her seething daughter followed her in. A child in a woman's clothing, she cursed the dirt floor that made walking in high heels impossible. Balancing in the doorway, she removed one shoe then the other. A strange sigh escaped with her breath as each foot touched the earth. A disturbed look came over her face that quickly tensed into anger as her mother continued her lament.

"You act like you don't understand that a marriage is not

just for you. It is for *la familia*, too. You are no one's *novia* and I am disgraced in Phoenix. Look at you! You wear makeup like some *puta!*" Josephina reached out and smudged the rouge on Lola's left cheek across to the bridge of her nose. "And you marry a man who beats you . . . and in some city hall over in California! Why didn't you talk to me? Why didn't you ever talk to me?"

The old woman wept while the young woman screwed her pretty face into a sneer.

"You are sickening people. Sickening, old, superstitious people. You still live on mud and you shit down holes in the ground and you're telling me how to live my life! I got out of this place. *Sal si puedes*, right? In my house I'll have three sliding aluminum windows with real glass and I'll have a refrigerator. And I'll have a real toilet where I won't have to kick the side to scare the spiders. No more goddamn spiders! I can't believe you talk about disgrace. Look where you live, in this junk heap of a town. I'm an American now. I can go where I want and I'm not stuck out in some desert."

Meanwhile "Uncle," pacing in the dusty yard, made it clear that he was unhappy about this time wasted in a foreign language, prompting Lola to change her screaming into English to show him that she was not backing down.

"Not English," Josephina cried, "not between *la familia*."

"It's English from now on," Lola said, turning on her heel and heading for the car. "Get used to it. I'm going back to Stockton. It's a real town."

Abuela cried for hours after. Manuel tried to calm her, but his presence only seemed to sadden her more.

"*Malinche, Malinche*," she sobbed, invoking the name of the traitorous Indian woman who betrayed the entire Aztec nation for the love of Hernan Cortés—the only word strong enough to express the faithlessness of a daughter.

On this last visit, there had been only the barest cordiality. Each time the car drove away, punctuating all those promises and curses with the exhalations of the shock absorbers as they met the ruts on the way out, the boy waved to his brothers only. The adults had their reasons, their own agendas. The promises his mother made were always nothing, vaporous.

She always arrived in a whirlwind and left the same way, and the boy had no lasting impression of her, save that he resented what she had done to his grandparents.

Before, they had just been Abuela and Abuelo, and he had been *mijo*. Now, those two feisty, willful souls seemed world-weary and uncertain. The two pillars of his existence were shaken in this sorrow.

For the first time in his life, the boy felt a deep flux beneath him and above him. The feeling rose in his nostrils now like vinegar, like the aether.

It was no miracle that a child could sit so long and be so still. Red desert evenings kept Buckeye Road still, the only cool of the day when the scent of wild sage and rosemary can venture out without being sucked up into space. It mixed with the scent of *frijoles* on the small breeze and smelled better to Beto than star jasmine.

He had been sitting and dozing below the amber light that came through the window holes in the adobe. Two feet thick—and more in places—the walls held back the wavering heat that simmered the cesspool and silenced the vociferous *Chinos* at the market and had shoved the cackling, laughing *Negritos* back into their game room or under their tar-paper lean-tos.

But come evening these same walls held in the cooling air while Buckeye stirred to life; the asphalt streets were only now walkable for the shoeless; the upholstery and skins of dead Cadillacs touchable for the homeless. Outside, the tar-paper walls and roofs hardened up and the sun-bleached soda-pop thermometers hanging everywhere rested from their sweet proselytizing, their thin, red hearts visibly sagging.

Buckeye Road was not Phoenix, not even a part of Phoenix, not a suburb or an outskirt. When streetlights went on in Phoenix, Buckeye stayed in the dark. For Buckeye, the lights of Phoenix were only a constellation, low on the horizon, one that did not move with the seasons.

Buses stopped at the main road, two miles from Buckeye,

and no taxicabs would dare come in. There were no street
names or street signs, no boulevards or cul-de-sacs; no houses
had numbers. Mail was sent to the Rainbo Market. Everyone's
mail was sent there, and the *Chinos* charged a penny per piece
of mail for the service. Even people from Tar-Paper, people
"*en las casas de cartón*," received their mail there. It was less
than unincorporated, it was unknown.

There were other towns like Buckeye on the spreading
fringe of Phoenix, small squatter communities forced outward
into the desert by malls and convalescent homes and peewee
golf courses for the retired old gringos who had come down
for the air.

For Indians who once lived alone in this desert, the ap-
proach of the squatters was the first sign that it was time to
move on.

Manuel and Josephina had built their adobe ten miles from
the nearest telephone pole, and in three years Buckeye had
crept up on them again. It had no sidewalks, no landlords,
no solicitors. Only Harold, the Jewish Fuller Brush man, and
the Jehovah's Witnesses bothered to knock on tar-paper
doors. Every outhouse was stocked with *Watchtowers* as a
supplement to the usual Fuller Brush catalogues. The Jehovah's Witnesses didn't care how the paper ended up as long
as it was read first.

The Mormons had come once, but only once. Four of them,
blond men in blue suits with crucifix cuff links and tiepins,
looked around slowly, then climbed back into their Rambler
Ambassador with its tinted windows and continental tire kit
and drove away.

Phoenix acknowledged Buckeye in only one way: each
morning at four o'clock its *jefes y potentados* sent buses and
flatbeds rumbling down Broadway past the tract homes and
into the desert to load on workers by the hundreds. Pickers
for Glendale and Paradise Valley, Arizona's two miracles of
modern irrigation.

Cauliflower pickers waited over by the tire dump, brussels
sprouts lined up at the church, cotton at the side of the store,
and rice across from the bus stop. Roofers would come for
Mexicans to work the ovens on days when the sun alone

would melt the tar plugs together by midmorning. Construction companies would come for Indians to work as lumpers, setups, hod carriers, and screeters. Local 23 came for dishwashers, and the motels from the main highway wanted young, dark-eyed maids and old janitors. The Liquid-Ox plant came for men to clean up and bury the chemical spillage. They handed out impressive, new white cotton gloves and paper masks to attract their workers.

The early morning was always quiet with scattered coughing and shuffling and the rubbing of eyes that strained for the first sign of the headlights. The men stood or leaned or squatted on their hams, but rough benches had been made for the women: black women, Indian women, Mexican and Okie women, some with their infants on their laps. Breasts long hidden to all but one man were now lifted up and flopped out to quiet small mouths.

Sometimes Beto and his Arkie friend Claude would wander in and out of the waiting groups selling Josephina's special *café con canela* from a large thermos jug.

"*Café con canela!*" Beto would cry out.

"Mexican coffee!" Claude would echo.

For a hundred yards glowing cigarettes flickered in the dark, were stomped out and lit elsewhere. Black and brown facial features flashed on then off as each Ohio blue tip flared then died. Two, three faces, for an instant, shared the same rising flame. Voices carried. Incomprehensible Pima words made someone in the dark laugh. Apache curses began a sudden fight. The quick gust of attackers and restrainers in cowboy boots attracted almost no attention.

In small groups, maids passed a single bottle of no-buff white shoe polish in preparation for the other world, and young Mexican busboys practiced pronouncing "May I take your plate, sir? May I take your plate, sir?"

Down near the Rainbo Market the Cheungs' food wagon was being loaded with hampers of vegetables, meat and rice for the chop suey that would feed the field-workers. One of Cheung's boys was busy bolting on a new propane tank.

Otherwise, Phoenix stayed away. Its police cars, its fire department, its ambulances all stayed away.

Buckeye Road was truly transformed at sunset, became bewitched at sunset. It came alive. Cars that never, ever moved could now pretend to have just parked, their rotting tires invisible, their touring occupants only here for a visit. The omnipresent veneer of fine red dust seemed to disappear with the light. The makeup on whores that was nightmarish at noon became alluring at night.

In the evening, the buses and trucks rumbled back from the fields and hotels to disgorge a lighter load than they left with, the weight difference in someone's pocket far away. Guts empty and dehydrated, muscles buzzing with fatigue, the peculiar light-headed laughter that comes with exhaustion and relief is laughed at every doorstep. A common laugh then, another day had been purchased with ligament and muscle. Life bought with life, children rushed to greet their tired fathers or mothers. It was the signal to start the frybread or the chitlins or refry the *frijoles*.

At sunset Vernetta's yellow light came on. At Josephina's insistence, the only white prostitute in Buckeye Road had agreed not to use a red light.

Down the road the Lees, the rich *Chinos*, climbed into their car and drove out of Buckeye after barricading the Rainbo for the night, their children staring out of the back window of the car for a last glimpse of their friends.

The Cheungs, the poor *Chinos*, camped on the edge of Tar-Paper next to their kitchen on wheels. In the evening the Cheungs cooked for themselves. It was gratifying for all the field-workers in Buckeye to know that the Cheungs ate no better or worse than they served. And for the first time all day, Mister Andre's do-shop did a real business as his lofty hairdos held up in the cooling air and his fetid lye-based preparations and relaxants properly congealed.

Awaking from his short sleep, the boy watched small glories of dust cutting across the room and moving slowly with the sun. He was as quiet as the small icons in the altar. Quieter than the doomed fly gliding near his grandfather's face. He looked at his grandfather's feet and down at his own and knew that his would, be just as gnarled one day, toenails like potato chips, opaque and striated. Indian feet, his grandmother called them. One of them, the right one, pushed against the red dirt floor in the amber light and quietly drove the old rocker back again and again. It went without him with only a flicker of will at two-second intervals.

He watched the long muscles slide under the skin below the old man's knee, like brown sisal rope beneath canvas, his kneecap the pulley. Driving the chair back, he was working even at his rest, eyes closed. The boy took comfort in the mere presence of the chair in the room. Comfort in its movement. It was dry from years in the sun and bent from infrequent rain, and only in the last few months had Manuel seen fit to bring it inside with the family.

One morning, without a word, he dragged it in to a chosen spot and draped his red blanket over it, before leaving for work. It was monumental somehow. It was important and the boy felt it, though he didn't know if it was a good sign or bad.

His grandfather's chair was now on a flat tin and mud floor. His chair rocked under a roof instead of in its rightful place, its spirit place between the lean-to and the cesspool. The spot near the goats. The spot that faced the east and the sunrise.

The lean-to was a small wall about six feet from the adobe with a slant tin roof. Manuel called it his *fogón*, his caboose. Beneath the tiny roof was an army surplus cot with a thin mattress and three or four Navajo blankets on top, one acting as a pillow. There were antlers, large racks nailed to the adobe wall above the carved *nicho* that held Manuel's shaving mirror and his straight razor. His tobacco tin was there with his favorite knife—his special place in the wall with the miraculous jar of small black bones and ebony rocks. Manuel kept his precious gloves there. Real cowhide leather, ancient, red-stained; ten small work-worn caves for his stiffening fingers.

He stored his mystery things there, too. Secret things were stashed under his mattress and in old tins sandwiched be-

tween Brilliantine and Tres Flores bottles, behind Spam cans
full of nails, from spikes to sixpenny. His whiskey was there
alongside his bottle of good tequila. Irish whiskey only.

"Tequila for celebrations, whiskey for contemplations," he
always said.

All of his things were out there still, yet here he was living
inside. For three years he had slept in the lean-to, staying
with his wife in the early evening, then going outside at night
to sleep. For three years the boy had slept outside with him.
It had been the same when the family lived closer to town
and before that. Always the old man kept his sleep from being
walled in. But now he was within the walls, and Josephina's
sadness was noticeable and had spread to Beto and the whole
community. Dinners were larger lately, and somehow that
was a sad thing, too.

She cooked *nopales* for him now, even though she had never
missed an opportunity to show her disdain for eating cactus.
She even bought from the dusty Mescaleros and let him eat
the cooked *mescal* meat, but only after a proper dinner. She
peeled the *tunas* for him; she had always delegated that odious
task to a daughter. She even brought the red-fleshed fruit to
him now on a plate with a small, folded *servilleta*. He would
take the plate and look at her in a way that Beto had never
seen.

She criticized him less and called him pagan or heathen
only when she couldn't stop herself. And when she said it
you could see the pain, the years of habit obscuring the affection. She even dressed quietly on Sunday mornings and
left for church without cursing him, walking the two miles to
the bus stop alone.

His things were still out there, the pieces of his life. The
boy had come in to see him, to watch him for a clue to the
sudden change. So he sat quietly, poised, his mind once
layered only by a child's appetites and dreams now agitated
with concern.

"She loves me in her way."

The boy had no way of knowing how long the old man
had been awake or if he had ever been asleep.

"Do you want a soda, *hijo?* Do we have a soda?" he asked in a loud voice.

"She's just afraid I'm trying to influence you. She could give a shit about the other ones, *hijo.* I don't know why. Maybe it's because you've got the *pelo chino* like me," he said, laughing.

Slowly he ran his fingers through his graying, curly hair. "And like my own father," he concluded.

"You look like me; it scares the old woman. I like the Mission Orange *y cómo se llama la otra?"*

"Bubble Up?"

"*Sí*, the Bubble Up. She's afraid you're more Yaqui than you are Yori."

He used the Yaqui word for Mexican, a word full of disdain and defiance. "I've told her you won't always sleep outside and she knows it's true. She's dreamed you ten years from today and ten years from that. And now that I'm in here with her you should stay inside too. And besides," he said slowly after a quiet pause, "soon your mother will be coming for you, and then how the hell can I have influence on you? You will go off to L.A. or El Centro and then forget all about the old man, *el viejo su abuelo.* I tell her, Beto, that soon you won't even remember me."

"I will always remember you, Grandpa," the boy said, "and besides, I won't go with my mother. I can stay here in Buckeye with you, can't I? I don't like her. I don't like my father. I won't go."

"That man last year was not your *padre, hijo.* And he was not your *tío.* I don't care what nobody says."

He reached into his pocket and gave the boy a silver dollar.

"When you go out, get me a Bubble Up and get whatever you want. Shit, these people think lying to you will make you feel better or it's good for you some way. That man is not blood. He's some *pendejo* your mother picked up somewhere near Needles or Boron. Get me a real cold one, *hijo.*"

He paused thoughtfully. He hoped that he had not hurt the boy's feelings.

"But your mother is your mother, and if she comes here

and says you got to go, your *abuela* and me, we got to let you go."

As he spoke he slipped from Spanish to Yaqui and back with an occasional English word. It wasn't because he ran into a thing he could not say in one language. It was because that specific tongue could not say the thing he wished to say.

Beto had long since grown accustomed to his grandfather's speaking in this fashion. So much so that he was no longer sure which words went with which language.

When with his Yaqui *compadres*, Manuel's thoughts were in Yaqui; otherwise he had difficulty thinking in Spanish and only translated into English with conscious effort and great difficulty. The differences in color and texture and perspective of the other tongues gave him trouble, not the words. Even Josephina, who was perfectly bilingual, almost never thought in English, except when she sang. Neither Manuel nor Josephina was the same person in their different languages.

English could not speak to the shared tribal compacts of Manuel's past any more than Yaqui or Pima can speak to modern contracts with their conditions precedent and third-party beneficiaries. Like many tribal languages, there is no true "cousin" in Yaqui, only relatives and generations. Someone is family or he is not. If not, he is a brother in the tribe. All Yaqui are kin.

As precise as English is, only Spanish could meet Manuel's and Josephina's need for a rounder and softer language. A language with many more words for skin or soul or pain or love, familial and sensual honorifics. Manuel's Mexican Spanish embraced *cariñosos* that were holdovers from the ancient Nahuatl tongue. To Josephina, its conventions are more indulgent and endearing than English; it's an affectionate, impressionistic tongue. Mexican Spanish can sound petty and gossipy or angry in a way that only black English or Cantonese can match. Only English as it's spoken by the Irish can echo the irony of Spanish, and only the Welsh singsong resembles the cadence in the streets of Guanaguato.

Yet for the old man neither Spanish nor English was enough when it came to speaking with his grandson. To say his family was poor would be accurate enough but not really true. In

Spanish *pobre* would be true but, in his mind, not very accurate. In Yaqui to be *kia polove* is to be without desire for "things." There is no concept of "poor" for a noncomparative, communal society. A Yaqui is only poor when he deals with the whites or the Mexicans. When he is forced to pay taxes on land he has always lived on or when the laws of Arizona require that he buy a tombstone, then he is poor. Then he must reach outside his language for the word.

When the old man reached an idea such as poor, his mind leafed through the three languages for the one that contained it the way he meant it.

"When a gringo brags that his house is on a quarter acre, now that is poor. Beto, when a Yaqui has nothing but his hands and the horizon, that is *kia polove*."

The old man was a different man in each tongue, and so he was a different man to his tribesmen, to his wife, and different to his grandson. The Yaqui man needed fewer words. The idiom was of the soil and the sinew and the budding beauty of dark-haired girls. In Manuel's idiom, withering both followed and preceded turgidity in fields and ideas and in men. The idiom was of the singing tree and the dancing stories of the deer. An old Yaqui could be by himself, but he was never alone. The paths, even to the sky and to the findings of things, were well worn.

The Yaqui idiom, the Yaqui ethos, had no words and no thoughts to deal with a fierce daughter in a Pontiac car and three sons from three fathers. The man who spoke Spanish spoke it haltingly as its relative complexity, like English, opened onto concepts that were immaterial to the Indian. Yaqui spoke of "being by one's self," but Spanish and especially English widened out into "alone" and from there into "loneliness."

There is no Yaqui word for the kind of loneliness that is found on the crowded sidewalks of Phoenix. A gringo will go to the edge of his city to look "out" into the desert, while a Yaqui will go to the edge of the desert and look "out" into the city.

Mexican sociologists who were scrambling to develop a jargon to describe the anomie of their largest swelling cities found themselves borrowing from English, the language that blazed the path to modern loneliness at the beginning of the industrial revolution.

The old man who spoke English seemed to lack confidence and seemed a little slow. Where he worked in downtown Phoenix, at the construction sites, he was just a friendly mule. But he was easygoing and quick-witted in Spanish. In Spanish he tried to reason with his hard-headed wife and his angry daughter, but he was always ignored.

"They are too much alike," he explained to the boy. "The love and the hate are the same size with them."

In Yaqui he was a repository of his people's history and a sage, as his fathers were before him. With Spanish and English he groped about desperately to paint Yaqui pictures in his grandson's mind.

"Your mother she is not *muy inteligente porque* . . . she is a child without much experience. How could we keep her here in this *kari, esta casa?* The children these days are so different now."

His eyes took on a distance as he groped between tongues. His mind recalled his beautiful daughter, Lola, her young mouth forming the Anglo-Saxon words *fuck you*, then the tongue hurling them at his wife. Yaqui did not countenance a child running off with an older man in a new Pontiac.

"*Tu abuela*, your grandmother was brokenhearted when she ran off to Nuevo Mexico with that fool man. She was just thirteen, a baby still. They ran off at night or I would have caught him and asked the council how he should be hurt. God, I could've hurt him. Forgive me, *hijo*, he is your father. But I hate him for what he has done. A man should have more honor than that. But that's water past the village now. That was two husbands ago. I think she's now someplace in Los Angeles. I'm sure she's afraid you will forget her, and I know she loves you. No, she will come and the decision will be made."

"What should I do, Abuelo? I don't want to go with them," the boy protested.

"Those decisions are made. I have seen you far away from

here. But you will come back. *Soy un guante para ti.* A glove
for you when you look for things that fit."

Manuel closed his eyes to consider his words.

In the pause, the boy thought of his mother and for all of
his effort could not conjure up a vision of her, her face or
eyes. He could only recall clearly the look in the faces of men
as they sought approval in her eyes, as they responded to
her beauty. It was the clearest reflection of her that the boy
possessed.

"Don't think we are too crazy, your *abuela* and me. We are
old spirits and these new times have no room for us."

He looked in the direction of his wife, well aware that she
heard every word.

Beto smiled.

"When I met her she was a child too, *pero una mujer también*.
We married for love, you know. We were too different to do
it for any other reason. Shit, I was always half creosote then,
up to my *huevos*, a railroad man. She was a criolla beauty
with enamel skin and a will of her own."

He quietly enjoyed the memory for a second or two.

"Love can be a big goddamn mistake," he grinned.

"A big goddamn mistake. But God always does things like
that to the people. At the time that a *niño*, a baby, produces
the most shit and the most noise is when God makes them
the most cute. It's no accident. So it's easy to clean his little
ass. Everybody is pretty when they are eighteen so God makes
them crazy at that age. How many forty-year-old people do
you see running out there that are pretty? Not too many! God
gives you the urge to choose a mate before people get to
looking how they're supposed to look. Love cripples the brain,
como fiebre, and then you go and make the most important
decision of your life in that condition. *Qué raro, no?*

"Your mother and us, we are all crippled by it. *Mutilados*.
But we all mean to do right."

There was silence in the room. He seemed to slip back into
his sleep, but this time the rocking was more forced. There
was a concern before him, and he seemed to hove into it over
and over as if bucking a head wind. Finally, in a voice barely

audible, he asked, "How many times has she baptized you now?"

"Four times," answered the boy.

"Three that her Catholic church doesn't recognize, four I don't recognize," the old man laughed.

"I should build her a damn shower. *Pobrecito*, you must think that every time you take a bath someone has to pray over you," he laughed loudly.

"She's afraid you won't be a Mexican and she doesn't even like Mexicans. She's just so far from Spain now, and to her, Mexican is better than Yaqui. *Qué rara, ella*. She should stop fighting me through you. She should just stop this war. It's gone on too long."

He exhaled the words slowly.

"Now, let's see, after your first baptism in the Catholic church it was the Jehovah's Witnesses next, then the Southern Baptists and now the *Negritos'* church down the street. When I found out she had taken you to the river for a baptism with *los Negros*, I could've hit her, but of course I didn't. But don't let her confusion confuse you, *mijo*. She just wants to make sure her own witchcraft doesn't hurt you somehow."

Beto began to feel the chill of Josephina's cold stares from the kitchen—as did the old man.

"She's a *bruja*, you know, a witch. But not like on Halloween. A curing witch. She's a healer. A *curandera* but with a special understanding of signs and spirits. It's not Catholic. It's definitely not Catholic, and that makes her feel very guilty. Whenever someone gets sick or has bad dreams, she is a *bruja* first and a Catholic second, and she knows it."

"That's where the guilt comes from. So I guess she's taken to cursing me and baptizing you to even things out. The women in her family got it from the Moors, you know. The Spaniards took hundreds of herbs and medicines out of the soil of Aztlán and brought them back to Spain. Now she's brought them back where they belong. It's crazy."

He looked at Beto reassuringly.

"Don't worry, all those baptisms just cancel each other out, like making one section gang dig a hole and then having another one fill it up. I've seen it happen." He smiled.

"Don't baptize the boy no more," he yelled abruptly across the house at his wife, who quickly turned back to her cooking.

"My mother had me baptized, too," whispered the boy a little awkwardly. "It was in a big tent."

"God, I guess it runs in the family. They are all so scared that Christ will turn out to be Quetzalcóatl. Well, that baptism is canceled out too." He smiled, drawing his finger across his neck.

"The women in this family are all crazy, I tell you." He sighed and slapped the boy on his shoulder.

"Will we eat soon, *mi amor?*" He winked. "The boy is starving."

"Soon," came the answer from the kitchen, "but first he has to go to the store."

"Make it a Mission Orange instead," he said, feigning secrecy, "the big bottle."

"Abuelo," the boy interrupted, "is it true I am an American? Vernetta says I'm a Mexican but also an American."

"Yes, you are American, but not in the gringo sense."

"How do you become Mexican or American?"

This opened the old man's eyes and the chair froze suddenly in midrock.

"You are Spanish and Yaqui, you are a mestizo from Aztlán, this land, right here where the Nahua people began." He stamped his foot into the packed earth.

"That is what a Mexican is. But you were born here in America, *también*, and that's what a Chicano is. You don't become nothing. It's only the gringos that become! They are Xipe," he said, referring to the ancient god of new growth beneath the old, the god the Aztecs distorted into the God of the Flayed Skin. It was Manuel's word for those people on earth who do not know where they belong.

"They become other religions like choosing a hat and become other names and have no connection to places they live. They become the things they own or the cars they drive. They say that they are one-third this and one-quarter that and their ancestors came from such and such, but they don't know nothing about them. They have no stories. They have no tribe. Their camp fire is the goddamn television. You"—he pointed at the boy now—"you know where your blood has been for the last ten thousand years, *mijo*. There are words and songs, *palabras y canciones*, that tell and explain to you.

"You do not become American, no, no. Shit, no. America becomes you, *mijo*."

He closed his eyes, inhaled deeply through his nose, then pointed over his shoulder.

"Do you smell that, *mijo*? The tortillas and the *frijoles* and the chorizo? No matter where you go, to places I know I will never see, when you walk past a doorway or a window and one of those smells hits you, you will come back here to this place and this time. Always. And that is just smell. There are things far deeper than smell."

"Are you American, Abuelo?"

"No. I am not American, I am not Mexican. In fact, I think I am no longer Yaqui. Shit, I can't tell you nothin' for real. I'm nowhere, now."

He leaned back, the anger in his leather face subsiding, and he exhaled slowly, a small hitch near the end of it caused by an old drawn-out affair with Chesterfield nonfilters. Like a ghost, his pain had come into the room. Josephina by the stove felt it and stopped her moving. She stood silently looking for an insect or a snake, on her face a mixture of distress and resignation.

"You see, boy, these people up here around us are so mixed up now that no one belongs, even though this is their country, our country. Do you see?"

"Leave him alone, Manuel," Josephina said in a hissing voice.

"You can be in the wrong place," he continued in spite of her warning.

"Your whole life, all of it, you can be in the wrong place and not know it because you've lost the power to know where is right. It's a hard thing to say. I can't explain."

He sat back again, composing himself and considering, then nodding to himself. He leaned forward and spoke thoughtfully.

"Someone is in a bus that sways a little on its way up and down the streets, and that person is pleased and gets comfort

by the swaying." He moved his dark hands slowly back and
forth. "It is so comforting that this person takes the bus even
when he has nowhere to go. He just rides and rides. Sometimes he stands up and lets the bus roll underneath him.

"*Entiendes, hijo?* That person, if he had the power, would
know that his ancestors were sailors, *marineros*, and that the
sea is calling to him. The sea is trying its best. It's not just
ruts in the road or a bad shock absorber, the sea is calling.
The sway of the boat is a small thread of blood, *la sangre*, that
comes up and ties him even when the flesh has fallen away
from his dead fathers.

"It's *una brújula en la sangre*, a compass in the blood, and
it's a dim command in the blood. And in decades and generations the power to hear it is bargained away in small decisions and small concessions. So he leaves the bus on the
street corner and sits at a desk and suffers from something
he will never understand. The *curanderos* will tell him he is
depressed or needs a special ceremony or a vacation or something like that, but that's not it.

"He'll drink from bottles and sometimes throw things and
maybe hit his wife. But at night his spirit throws out the net,
and in the morning it's pulled back torn. And at night the
sound of the highway makes him stay awake. It is not the
loud rush of the highway." He pointed the index fingers of
both hands at the boy for emphasis. "It's not the cars or the
trucks . . . it's the waves, the sound of the sea and the simple
people on it. He has forsaken himself by forsaking the sea.

"So many others have forsaken even the land. They live
on cement and carpets and make marks on paper for a living.
They hunt in stores when their blood longs to hunt the mesas.
Even more have forsaken ideals. Sea birds who once dove
into the ocean's muscle to rise with a living cell flapping in
their beaks, now they circle the piers for a wage. You see,
mijo, the Papagos' truck is a pony," he said slowly and with
frightening intensity. "Those flatbeds loaded with Pimas and
Apaches you see in the morning headed for the cauliflower
fields in Glendale, they are a war party."

He fell silent suddenly.

"When I leave to go to work in the morning and I cross

that shitty overpass on Black Canyon, it's the *rio* Yaqui. In another world, like two different spaces folded one on top of the other"—he placed a dark right hand flat on the left—"at the very same tick of the clock my skin is almost black with the sun and my feet are touching the dirt like a moving root. I fish the river and till the dirt and I need to buy nothing. I am standing at both places, in this hard world"—he rapped his fingers on the armrests of his chair—"and in the world where my soul belongs, my body cannot be found.

"And in this world where we buy meat from the *Chino's* store and pick our fish from the ice truck, my soul keeps flying off."

He was quiet now.

"To lose yourself is the greatest mutilation."

He turned his face away from both of them.

"*Mexico* is an old word, *mijo*. It means the navel of the moon."

The old man used the heels of both hands to rub his eyes. The boy knew that his grandfather had been drinking.

"To the gringo immortality means from today forward, *mijo*; each gringo wants to live forever. That's what they want from their God, that's what they want from their medicine. To a Yaqui immortality can also mean from today backward to the beginning. The future is no longer than the past. They are the same distance no matter where you stand. The Yaqui people have lived forever."

The look on his face told the boy that no more would be said today. To the obvious distress of his wife, the old man reached behind his chair and grabbed his bottle of Irish whiskey. It had been on the floor, hidden behind the red blanket on the backrest. Tequila was for happiness. Whiskey for sadness. He leaned back and began to sing "The Rising of the Moon."

The boy rose and walked into the kitchen, where his grandmother, though shaken, had resumed her cooking. She tasted the beans while he watched, then added salt.

"There's four bits on the dresser, *hijo*. Go to the Rainbo when it gets cooler and get some more *mantequilla* and you can buy a soda. *Pero, solamente una!*"

She raised her voice to a shout in order to drown out her husband's singing.

"I wish you would not say things like that to him, Manuel," she shouted. "And I wish you would not drink."

He looked up at his wife, the drink still glistening on his lips.

"You of all people should know better than to wish, *mujer*."

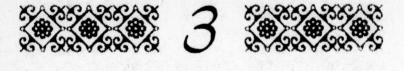

3

La Cometa

Within the walls of the adobe there was always a pocket of perfect calm beneath the wilting heat of the day. A soft-edged anodyne in the comfortable movements of kin in the kitchen and the living room. A quiet that would seed the boy's bloodstream with permanent pangs for the crumble of dust and the cool of shade and the scents of life at ground level.

Abuela hummed contentedly in the kitchen, recovered from the upset of her husband's rare and unseemly outbreak of words. The old wringer clothes washer complained in rhythmic, chugging cycles of work, its agitated bearings grinding and scraping in a greaseless race. Abuelo, in two different worlds, rocked back and forth between them.

Nine-year-old Beto spent that September day much as any other. He sat between the shafts of dusty light that were his grandfather's preference and the flicker of the red votive candles that was his grandmother's. Unaware and unresisting, Beto became part of the flux that radiated between the two magnetic poles that were his *abuelitos*. He quietly turned the pages of volume K–L of his precious *New World Book Encyclopedia* and drank a lime cola that bore no thermal evidence of its morning in the icebox.

Four years before, the boy had been carried back to the desert. After going places he would never remember, he had

been returned to his place of birth. His mother had swept
into town and back out again like a perfumed dust devil,
depositing the boy at the old house.

"Just for a few weeks," Lola had said four years ago.

"You flew in like the milkweed," Abuela would say to him
often. Fearful that he would feel abandoned, she attempted
to displace a small torment with planted, laughable memories.
"I guessed a gypsy's name and they presented you to me as
a prize! I touched a midget's hump for good luck and the next
day there you were . . . the answer to my prayers."

The three of them had lived in the old adobe house, the
one closer to town, where all eight of Josephina's own children
had been given light. Phoenix had been sleepy and small
and miles away when Josephina and Manuel had first moved
into it.

"In Spanish, to give light is to give birth," as the old woman
had so often explained.

That adobe had been built by another family, people from
New Mexico who built tiny rooms and doorways. They had
dragged their building techniques down from the red cliffs of
Pojoaque onto the desert flatlands. Manuel had always
wanted a bigger house of his own, one built by his own hands.

"Now that there is only one child, you want a bigger house?
You don't sleep inside anyway," his wife had complained.

She had refused for years to even speak about moving.
There were just too many memories in the little house.

"I will sleep inside someday" had been his response to her.

It was a statement she never wanted to hear from him, in
any language. Then one morning Apache disappeared.
Apache was Josephina's famous messenger dog who sported
a distinctive red bandanna. She could put a note into the
bandanna and the German shepherd mix would deliver the
note to whomever's name she whispered into his ear.

"Take this note over to Doña Juana's," she would say. "And
don't stop to play with that collie bitch!"

The day that Apache disappeared Josephina had suddenly
demanded that they move. In one of their few moments of
agreement, the old woman and the old man had decided that
civilization was getting too close and that it was time to move

on. The telephone poles had crept up on them; at night they could hear the thin wail of sirens in town.

Josephina, every red evening before the house was vacated, would sneak out to the desert to conjure against her dog's return and to pray he would not follow them. For good measure she'd circled the house three times, sprinkling the ground with black pepper.

The new house was now three years old. It had been hand-built by Manuel, two of his sons and some of his old friends. Tío Eugene had driven in from Yuma in his brand-new Pontiac with his new redhead wife in tow and Tío Jorge drove his Nash Rambler in from Camelback.

There was still no glass in the windows, and any small breeze moved the butcher paper back and forth and sometimes brought the foul smell of the goat pens or the cesspool with it.

The old man had promised glass for the windows, but it never materialized. "Don't *ventanas* mean wind?" That was always Manuel's response to Josephina's complaints. "Don't windows mean wind?"

But then again there was never rain, only floods now and then, so the old woman seldom complained. The butcher paper filtered a yellow light into the rooms, the kind of light that fills Mexican churches.

"This house is cooler than the old one was, but still, that goddamn iceman has got to come everyday when the temperature is like this," Josephina called from the kitchen.

"I can't keep wasting good *queso y mantequilla* on the goats and pigs. No, not yet," she said upon catching her grandson's imploring glance. "It's still too hot to go to the store. Only *Indios* and *Negritos* run around in heat like this. Your old grandfather's orange soda can wait."

She tossed another package of melted cheese into the swill bucket as she spoke.

All of a sudden, from across the lot, Vernetta's voice boomed out angrily just as a bad starter motor was beginning to grind violently into the teeth of a flywheel.

"You didn't get nothin' ya needle-dicked bug fucker," the blond woman screamed. "All you got was a wrinkle, all I

gave you was a goddamn wrinkle and a flap! Been fuckin'
your fist so long you don't know the goddamn difference!"

"*Chingada!*" a male voice shouted back as if it were surely
the last word. "*Chingada!*"

For Mexicans *La Chingada* is a gashing, pricking word that
diminishes those who speak it as much as those who hear it.
La Chingada is the violated Mother, *La Llorona*, the woman
who cries, she who drowned her children and must seek them
forever. *La Chingada* is Cihuacóatl, the earth mother before
male gods buried her in time. She is the Virgin of Guadelupe,
the goddess of the orphan Indians who were forced by the
Conquistadores to give up their gods of war. *La Chingada* is
anyone who is fooled, prodded, ripped open by the *chingón*,
the ripper. Every Mexican is a son of *La Chingada*. There is
no equivalent English word.

The boy ran to the door to see a blue Studebaker sedan
backing out of the lot, a cowboy hat behind the wheel.

"Get away from the door, that's none of your business,"
Josephina warned as the trailer door slammed and Vernetta's
angry voice waned.

"A man should pay for what he gets." The old man winked.

"*Viejo verde*," the old woman seethed. Dirty old man.

"Do you have to pay for wrinkles?" the boy asked.

The two old ones looked at each other.

"You and your crazy *compadres* picked this spot."

"She's your friend."

Vernetta's yellow trailer hadn't moved in three or four
years, and its wheels had long since rotted off and support
had to be provided by some pilfered railroad ties. It was the
only house trailer in Buckeye and a source of great interest
to the general population.

The trailer was almost magical in its promise of high mo-
bility combined with excellent shelter. Its hermetic, insular
form called out to sharecroppers, line shackers, and Indians
from as far away as the Four Corner reservation. Only the
brown, wooden cabooses that flashed by the Buckeye switch
boxes on their way to somewhere were held in higher esteem.

Cabooses had become the mercurial wagons of a new desert
mythology as poor children of all tribes ran to the tracks

hourly to wave at nameless men who often deigned to wave back. Their stoves smoking, their lanterns lit, they became the object of every melancholy desire to be elsewhere. Waves of greeting from an approaching tandem tractor filled the children with anticipatory joy and laughter while waves of good-bye from a disappearing caboose left them dolorous.

It was the organic Doppler effect. The red shift of the spirit.

To the sons and grandsons of slaves and to the sons and grandsons of the people who spoke in the desert with a hundred different tongues long before Spanish and longer before English, the trailer was an away thing and a stay thing that left no wooden skeleton when it was gone and did not scab the earth with concrete. To *los Negros* it was a permanent "I ain't stayin' here" house with a license plate and a trailer hitch to prove it.

To the desert Indians it was akin to a pickup truck and therefore akin to a pony. It could be tied up to graze near a stand of cottonwoods or dragged about like a travois tied to the frothing flanks of a half-ton pickup.

Taciturn Mescalero Apaches would come to Buckeye to stare at it and touch it. Once seven Piyutes who had pooled their hard-earned money came over to try to buy the trailer and after a short conference under the awning had designated a spokesman who spoke a few English words. He bravely knocked on Vernetta's door and asked, "How much?" Vernetta looked out at the Piyutes and quickly made a few calculations. She knew that Piyutes only went for straight-up missionary sex, and seven would be no sweat.

"Ten bucks apiece," she said.

The Piyutes, ecstatic and babbling over their incredible good fortune, swarmed over the outside of the trailer, inspecting every luxurious feature from the sliding window at the trailer's forelocks to the metal trim at its withers.

"It's not a gelding," one laughed as he examined the double propane tanks that straddled the trailer hitch like a pair of testicles. The spokesman had dutifully gone inside to close the deal. His thin, red face buried between two enormous chest melons, his muffled screams went unheard.

But no Yaquis or Mayos ever came. Solemn, fierce people,

they raised lintels over hand-mixed mortar and sun-baked
bricks and cursed the lifeless water that came from hoses.
They puddled and kneaded their own soil with their own
water and raised the earth up around themselves as a dwell-
ing, as an oven, as a tomb. Here, as back home in the foothills
of the Sierra Madre, they erected a living blanket ubiquitous
in time and place.

"You don't own a home, you only grace it or curse it for a
little while."

Like Seris and Tarahumaras, their aboriginal souls had been
forced to sing under the weight of colonial Spanish rule and
then of imperial Catholic. What all of the armies could not
do, the missionaries seemed to have accomplished. But their
songs persisted. In the guise of the New Testament and
masked by the sounds of Spanish, the ancient beliefs perse-
vered, moved north across the *rio de la Concepción* and into
Arizona.

The songs went underground with *los Norte Americanos'* at-
tempts to stop Yaqui gun running back to the resistance in
the Bacatete mountains during the last Yaqui wars. Then they
finally burst forth anew from their human founts in Tucson
and at the Pascua and a new river.

The trailer, to Yaqui eyes, was both a blasphemy and a
wonder. Some of the same feeling could be found in the
Yaquis' inexplicable love for the railroads that crossed their
beloved desert like a steel suture, and in their improbable
alliance with the sweating gandy dancers and the sad, singing
paddies who worked on the section gangs in starched, white
shirts.

They called the trailer "*La Cometa*," the kite. It flew but was
not free.

The old woman had retired to Vernetta's trailer for the
duration of the building process. Somehow the Yaquis had
chosen the perfect spot because the trailer that was destined
to become Josephina's second home was backed up to a stand
of red *manzanita* not forty yards away from the rising adobe.

The *viejos'* choice had surprised Josephina at first. Why would those old hermits want to build my adobe home right next to a peroxide-*gavacha*'s metal trailer house? she wondered. There was even a store and a little pink church nearby, which made her even more suspicious.

On her first trip to the building site, Josephina had spied on the trailer and she had witnessed all those shameless men coming and going. They had arrived on foot and horseback, in pickups and surplus jeeps. The Navajos and traveling salesmen all performed the same turgid arrival and torpid departure. At a distance, she had seen the huge, blond woman simultaneously greeting one customer while dismissing another.

The old woman, scandalized, had crossed herself repeatedly.

"How could you *y sus amigos locos* pick such a site for our home? What will the Good Lord think of us?"

"I found this place for you, *mujer*," he said, without explaining further. "A place for me would have been a hundred miles that way." He pointed toward the Superstition Mountains.

Josephina, after a short prayer, had then resolved to use this dilemma to reinforce her piety. Reciting the story of Mary Magdalene, she had prepared some of her famous *menudo*. She carried it in a canning jar to the fallen woman's front step. But before she could knock, the large woman had peeked out shyly, then cautiously opened the trailer door. The two strangers then stood staring at one another through a torn screen.

It was plain that Vernetta had been crying. Her mascara had smeared across her white cheeks. One of her false eyelashes had sprung loose and was standing perpendicular to her eyelid. There was lipstick on her teeth and a look of surprise on her blanched face as she stared down at the small, dark woman with the cross at her wrist and brown rosary beads in her hand.

Without taking her eyes off Vernetta, Josephina had quietly set the *menudo* down and moved straight up the steps toward the woman.

"Usted también?" she'd said suddenly, her face transmuted by recognition.

"Your people have disowned you, too?"

The whore had suddenly flung the screen door wide open at those words. She had grabbed at the old woman and hugged her with her flabby, white arms, burying Josephina in her pink robe. Then the two had cried together on the front steps.

"How could you ever know?" asked Vernetta. "Shitfire, is it so plain in my face?"

As Vernetta spoke, Josephina reached out her hand to touch the face of her new friend.

In just hours, the two women had plumbed and measured each other's soul.

Together, in just hours, two separate lives of secret, painful silence were razed to discover a mutual foundation.

"When I first saw those Indians I thought I might have to move again," she said to the old woman. "Now I am so thankful that they brought you here."

The *viejos*, in their own inscrutable way, had carefully and purposefully chosen this spot near Vernetta's trailer. Days ago, the four Yaquis had parked Manuel's old Ford truck outside of what would become Buckeye Road and had disappeared into the desert for a full night and half a day. On their return they had declared that the signposts were known and just minutes later the perfect location had been found.

Vernetta, herself, had seen the strange men coming in from the desert just days before. She had watched them as they walked the circumference of the lot near her trailer, kicking the dirt here and siting the lay of the land there. Then, in mutual agreement on the place, the Indians had driven off to the dump and returned with gunny sacks filled with tin cans.

"A place not too close to the *Negritos* and not too far from the church," the old woman had warned, secretly glad that the strange *Indios* had not chosen a place even more desolate.

First, the Yaquis pushed the cans down into the dirt to make a shining floor of tin bottoms. Then sifted mud was layered over this and pounded flat by brown feet before being rolled smooth by fifty-gallon drums filled with water. The old woman, in her black laced shoes, carefully and with great ceremony had paced off the rooms and pointed to the place where she had dreamed a *ramada* would be.

"I dreamed the stove here," came her haughty dictate. "I can smell the *masa* here; the dough rising over here." She moved to the place where sifted flour and dust would mingle beneath her feet, and with her eyes closed she inhaled slowly through her nose.

"There was trouble here, but I can handle it."

Later, while digging to level the floor, the Yaquis unearthed red bricks and tiny rosette tiles. They uncovered layers of black soot and ash where a nightly fire must have burned. One of the *viejos*, working where the bedroom would be, suddenly held up a small book that he had found, its leather cover and most of its pages charred black.

"Not too many pages left," said Josephina, trying to separate the leaves without destroying them. Despite her efforts, the pages were flaking away and falling to her feet.

"*Un milagro*," she said with a smile of satisfaction upon finding some legible pages. "It is *The Complete Poems of Andrew Marvell. Quién es?*" She shrugged, then dropped the crumbling book to the ground.

Beto, at the insistence of his grandfather, was allowed to stay outside at the work site with the men.

When not needed to carry nails or water or to mix adobe patch and carry bricks, the boy played near the trailer and could see his grandmother and Vernetta talking together over tea. Their gesturing hands and their nodding heads were clearly of no lesser significance than the men's work.

The two women waiting in the trailer had discussed the inequities of life for a full day and far into that first night. The women cemented their friendship with a running commentary regarding *la vida que da pena* and the work in progress. Their laughter, separated by a full octave, harmonized nonetheless and shortened the scorching workdays. It seemed to calm the thermals.

The house would go up in days. Each of the *viejos* had done this many, many times. The gleaming Yaquis, almost naked, carried adobe bricks and stacked them up, drenched them at

their interlaced joints and splashed mud patches at their sides.
The house was a *doble*, a double-walled adobe. This would
keep the house cool and allowed for several *nichos* to be made
in the walls. The *nichos* would become altars and shelves.

The Yaquis heaved up, then bedded down dark fir lintels
and heavy *vigas* without speaking a word. But the two young
uncles never stopped talking. Now and then the old man
would stop a moment to study his sons.

"I wish now they had gone to high school in Mexico," he
said in Yaqui to his *compadres*.

"We are antiques to them. Everything we had to give them
made them ashamed to their gringo friends. They wouldn't
even take *burritos* to school, we had to make fucking sandwiches. Can you believe that, sandwiches! Bread like air and
meat that was never alive."

"Shit," one of his friends replied, "my daughter tells her
friends that I'm dead. She says her father was Italian."

"And did you see their wives," Manuel continued, "brown
gavachas, I swear. They buy their faces from the store!"

The four laughed loud and long until a far train whistle
from up on the mesa begged piercing pardon and thirty-four
mixed cars went ceremoniously through.

Beto often heard the women's voices singing like high tension wires when they gossiped. When the Highway Comet
was silent it was because their conversation became one of
meaningful glances as they reached a point of profound, mutual, female understanding—which was often.

As the double walls of the kitchen went up, the trailer
became quieter and Vernetta grew sick and feverish. Alcohol
sick; lovesick. She slept most of the third day, mumbling in
her sleep about the theory of relativity while Josephina mixed
special teas for her and watched *novelas* on the Westinghouse,
occasionally wetting a towel for Vernetta's sweltering
forehead.

The trailer's yellow porch light stayed off for the duration,
and in the street, dusty, jaunty men were seen to walk up,
stare hopefully, then slouch away disappointed. Josephina
saw them but would never really acknowledge what her friend
did for a living. She shooed the men away like they were

coyotes near the goat pen, in eight languages, four dialects and in no uncertain terms.

Impossibly, they were kindred souls, these two women. Through some miracle of accommodation, the Catholic *curandera* had given her bleached-blond friend special dispensation. On the fourth day, as the *vigas* and *latillos* were heaved up, the two women sat together and spoke softly about important things: heaven and the Unified Theory.

The noisy Papagos had finally arrived in their green '49 Studebaker pickup, the back filled with used corrugated aluminum roofing, galvanized roofing nails, a gallon of black pitch, and two cartons of Lucky Strikes. As they unloaded the truck, the two women made a deal. They'd struck a bargain.

The white, blue-veined hand with orange nail polish and the brown one with its jewelry and fetishes clasped to form a well-used palette of colors between them.

"I will help you," Josephina had vowed. "I will help you get your boy. But you must keep your promise," she warned.

"I'll cement it shut," she swore, closing her legs for emphasis. "Only piss'll get out and not even air will get in."

Laughter was once again heard coming from the trailer as the silver roof was nailed onto the false beams. The adobe would have two roofs. An aluminum roof rose above a layer of bricks that had been laid over the *latillos*. The aluminum would soften the Arizona sun and would mean that the *canales*, the water drainage system, could be smaller.

Vernetta had insisted that Josephina keep her best possessions under the Highway Comet's awning. The precious wind-up Edison gramophone was there, its rosewood cabinet red as manzanita. The upright piano was there; the television with the round screen and the flip-down magnifier attachment shared the shade with the washing machine. Her precious 78s and 45s were in a mahogany cabinet covered with blankets and the foot-pedal Singer was under a gray Southern Pacific tarp.

Everything but the huge black stove was protected by the trailer. The stove was already standing in its chosen place; the walls would go up around it. No one wanted to move it twice or to make a special-sized door for it. All of Josephina's things waited outside next to Vernetta's empties, her towering stacks of Pabst Blue Ribbon beer and Delaware Punch bottles rinsed and awaiting exchange.

Even before the walls of the adobe house were finished, Josephina had demanded that a place be reserved where a *ramada* could be built. The spot for Josephina's new *ramada* had been roughly leveled out, then blessed by the Indians before being counterblessed by the woman. The four, on their haunches squatting behind a meat-loaf pan filled with water, sang their prayer into the east, then spilled the sacred water into the earth of the *ramada* and the home. The one, her black dress spread flat as she knelt kissing her cross, had whispered her own prayers at the place where the *ramada* would be, the white plaster statue that was either Mary or the Virgin of Guadelupe, placed with care atop an ice chest. While Vernetta watched from the Highway Comet, Josephina said ten Our Fathers for the salvation of her heathen husband's soul and five apiece for herself and for her new friend. While she prayed she had promised that once the house was finished she would name the demon that had chased the ancient family away from this spot and thus purge his evil winds.

The resolve and the hoary challenge of this vow had stiffened her and straightened the bend in her back. At a distance, such strict piety before the Holy Virgin rent Vernetta's heart. As the old woman knelt before the icon she decided to mix up a batch of saltpeter water and soak the feathers of a dead bird in it. Then she would sprinkle the liquid around the circumference of the homesite as soon as possible. That would keep those damn Africa hoodoo doctors away from her door.

Josephina's valise of medicinals was kept inside the trailer on Vernetta's ironing board near the big woman's books and her snapshots, one of the Reverend Crispus Evans, his hands laid on the forehead of a little mulatto boy. It was Vernetta's shrine and the only proper place for a bag like that one.

"The Papagos are more heathen than the Yaquis," Josephina said as she climbed the trailer's steps, waving away the smoke from Vernetta's Pall Malls as she entered.

"But not as dumb as the Pimas. The Pimas let the white

man have it all. Then the Navajos stuck it to 'em," she had
laughed, making a gesture with her index finger to palm.

"My last old man was Pima," said Vernetta, nodding in
agreement.

She reached for another Saltine, then inverted a spoonful
of Cheez Whiz over it just as black pitch was daubed onto
roofing nails by silent brown Yaquis who gave back the flesh
to a spirit home.

"This here is one of them new pasteurized spreads," she
explained.

The cracker broke in the middle and parts of it fell and
were lost in her neckline; a small cheese slick flowed almost
imperceptibly down a striation on her left breast.

"Shitfire, he bored me stiff, girl," she said, turning her
thoughts back to the Pima.

"Thought a word a month was a conversation." She
laughed and exhaled gray smoke around the words.

"A word a month." She smiled, shaking her head.

"Never told me when he was comin', never told me when
he was goin'. But I'll take an Indian over an Arizona *mayate*
any time. Coloreds out here is just too goddamn violent. They
beat their women worse than the Mexicans."

Josephina nodded an enthusiastic concurrence, a Delaware
Punch bottle at her lips and the sad voice of George Jones
dripping out of the radio behind her.

"*Los Negros* are either all the way with God or all the way
with Satan," the old woman said.

She supposed for a moment that there were some black
people in the middle but then dismissed it as non-
conversational.

"Ooo wee, Josephina," whooped Vernetta, "that George
Jones sure puts out some real fence kickers. His songs is so
sad to where my teeth hurt."

"He is good," smiled Josephina, "but he's not Lydia
Mendoza."

They listened to the music together for a moment; then
Vernetta, suddenly pensive, murmured, "A few don't."

"A few don't what?" asked Josephina.

"A few don't beat their women."

She quickly changed the subject: "You heard this new gal, Patsy Cline? I hear her singin' on the radio every day now, and it's like she's been readin' my mail."

Vernetta fell silent again. She hadn't received any mail in years. She'd even given up checking for it at the Rainbo Market, but Josephina would begin to check for her every day.

"Well," said Josephina, finding an opportunity to change the mood, "we have to decide what to feed the *viejos.*"

"*Los viejos,*" as the old woman called the Yaquis, came in from Tucson and Pascua and beyond.

They were the ones without real shoes and without good shirts. The ones that used railroad words and spoke the old language with the old man. Manuel called them his *compadres* or his *compai.* They spiced their odd Yaqui tongue with strange Celtic words and songs about Ireland, and they knew about faraway towns down the S.P. line, even as far away as Oregon. They always rose up from their work on the house to stare with reverence whenever a train passed.

In the evenings, after dinner, the old man would leave with them on foot to go sleep somewhere in the desert. Always as they walked away the boy felt left behind and wondered why they took nothing at all with them. A small tin, some water, nothing really.

The old woman, on the other hand, wondered aloud why they had taken so much. She would curse them with the evil eye and the rosary simultaneously as their forms grew smaller and smaller against the blue mountains, her right hand hoisting the rosary beads overhead and the index finger of her left hand planted squarely between her two closed eyes.

"I refused to marry in your heathen rituals and I refuse to die in them. Pray you don't die first, *viejo,*" she would cry out after them.

She swore bitterly to Vernetta, the Fuller Brush man and anyone who would listen that she would bury Manuel as a Catholic. She would mark his grave for all time with a civilized stone monument. Somehow, two divergent powers were reconciled in the expletives she sent hurtling over the sage after them.

The home inside Vernetta's yellow trailer was a wonder of movie star magazines, perfumed douches, shameless tabloids and uncounted brass and red-plaid beanbag ashtrays at least one-third of which held a smoking cigarette. Shelves and countertops were cluttered with cosmetics and hair sprays, porcelain figurines of Siamese cats and crossword puzzle books. It was crowded but it was immaculate.

On the wall above the small table at the kitchenette end hung two jigsaw puzzles Vernetta had glued to cardboard backings. One was a picture of a red gondola in a canal, two laughing lovers and a singing gondolier. The other was of two Scottie dogs, one black and one white, their heads canted in opposite directions, a tartan pillow between them.

Sticky fly strips hung everywhere, and Vernetta had stuffed cotton balls in the holes in her screen door and had only recently located a new high-wattage, yellow, insect-repelling light bulb for the lamp over her doorway. The old red bulb barely lit the front step. Her small sink and drain board displayed the new Melmac dishware of which she was duly proud. Red and yellow plates were carefully alternated in the dish rack, while matching cups hung on the side.

There was a silver-and-yellow-striped aluminum awning over the entry side of her trailer that ran its full length. In its shadow were lawn chairs and a table, a bicycle with flat, cracking tires, a Montgomery Ward washer with wringer attachment and, still in its box, a red Flexi-Flyer.

Inside, her Crosley radio on the ledge above the sink never left K-HAT, and if it happened that Vernetta was not home, more often than not she could be seen running to a pay phone. She would call the station with a request for a Porter Wagoner song, then run back to hear it played.

She was an Okie. She was actually from Arkansas, but for her own reasons she preferred Okie to Arkie. She explained that Okie was generic and had historical meaning that Arkie didn't.

"Steinbeck coulda picked Arkies. Shit, it was Arkies moved into the Joads' house after the tractors got to it. It ain't like we didn't have jalopies with mattresses roped to the top."

She had first come through Phoenix from El Paso back when she was a petite size four and had Kleenex stuffed in her brassiere; now she wore V-neck muumuus to hide her substantial girth and her bras hanging on the clothesline looked like twin feedbags.

"I reckon's to how in any bar in any shitfire town in this country, any two drunks'll tell you what Albert Einstein said about two parallel lines eventually intersecting in space . . . Well," she would say proudly, "my tits is proof."

Vernetta's cleavage was irrefutable, undeniable proof. Proof to every man and boy in Buckeye, and Vernetta knew it. The bras were for advertising purposes only. She never wore them anymore. But that cleavage of hers went from a junction just below her chin to somewhere just north of her knees, to some unspecified below. No matter how far she bent over, the two lines that would normally delineate separate breasts remained congruent.

That legendary cleavage had held ballpoint pens and pinochle cards and matchsticks, whole packs of cigarettes, had swallowed silver dollars and dimes like the seat cushions of a sofa, and held the attention of every little Papago and *Negrito* in the neighborhood, not to mention their fathers.

Vernetta herself often told the story of how once, back when she was working the Imperial Valley just outside of Brawley, an ambulance had to be called for a little Peruvian farmworker whose heart "just couldn't stand the rapture." But more credence was given to the rumors that he had suffocated.

Vernetta would never go home again, certainly not while any member of her family had a breath of life in them. Seven years before the first adobe brick was laid down for Josephina's new home, Vernetta's entire family had been shamed out of Arkadelphia by something unspeakable she had done, and by the age of twenty-eight her fates had moved the trailer to the desert outside of Phoenix where she set up shop in an empty lot that was soon to be shared by a Catholic *curandera*, Josephina Valenzuela de Castillo, her Yaqui husband, Manuel, and their mestizo grandchild.

The trip had taken years, from hooker to whorehouse to THE HIGHWAY COMET, as the decal on the side of her trailer proclaimed.

From Little Rock to Morgan City to Bakersfield to Buckeye Road, Vernetta had initiated more Indian boys than any shaman. Hers was an oral and vaginal history of the Southwest that no anthropologist could ever hope to match.

"Folks get more for their money these days," she would laugh. "I used to spread myself real thin."

The child, then the child-woman, and finally the woman had followed the currents of greed and ill fortune (otherwise known as business expedience) and had learned to live in the alluvium, those eddies and nooks where the disenfranchised and dispossessed gathered as silt at a river's bend. She had learned to locate that invisible historical juncture where irrigation contracts, union busters and corporate families made decisions that sundered real families. She had learned to follow the consequences of those decisions to places where fathers and sons would have to go to find work, find shelter, find an occasional moment for the illusion of solace.

She knew the yearly course of migratory work as a salmon knows the stream. She knew the signs and handbills that drew five hundred men for fifty jobs. She swam there, brushed aside the rocks and gravel at that spot a thousand times, and they came and came and fertilized nothing.

The same mud-caked boots and kneepads; the same mummified leather gloves; the same machetes and paring knives were left on the small shelf below the porch light time and time again.

In the early mornings after the last tired body had dragged its lonely soul to her bed to spill its blueprint into her and then sagged off for the sunrise work call, Vernetta would rise and turn out the new yellow light, telling Buckeye Road that the house was now a home.

In every moment she had alone, in every waking, sober moment alone, when the narrow window of awareness and recall that she allowed herself to open cast a thin shaft of illumination unbent by the gravity of the situation onto the face of her lost son, she would cry her tears.

Not a quiet whimper but a chest-bucking, air-gasping, drowning cry. The force of it wrenched her, sending eyeliner cascading down in rivulets. The cicadas outside and the cricket inside deferred to it. The dead still of the late night air would let the cry pass unimpeded so that custom two-piece pool cues stopped thrusting in chalked fingers to hear it and number cards and face cards froze midshuffle to hear it. Far away and down past Cady, a checker would not be kinged to hear it and the bone pile stopped its ivory slapping to listen.

Everyone knew the source of the cries, but few knew their destination. Few could follow them on the first rising wind as they circled in the morning and collected, then undulated in flashing turns like pigeons, orienting themselves by some unknown thing before heading due north.

No one in Buckeye said it, but her crying cleansed them all. Those awake might look toward her at this time in the morning and see the dull glow around the aluminum circle of her home long after the light was gone. They did say that someone or other had said that Vernetta had been loved once, long ago, for real. There had been this black guy named J. B. Woodley, way back east and way back when, who could hurt her good and she could hurt him, too. That's what it takes, they said, for it to work.

The few nights they had together in Arkadelphia so long ago were precious memories to her now: the careless, wild rides in old Mama Woodley's red Hudson Hornet, the wet trees on the back roads of Clark County raining dew on the wax job and the windshield. They always went south. She made a diving and rising airplane with her white hand in the speeding wind, and J.B. held a dollar bill out there by the teeniest corner till it ripped and flew away to the sound of their daring and their laughter.

"Was the car really moving like that," Vernetta would wonder aloud nightly, "or was it stock still in the universe, the mailboxes and porch lights flying by like fast-food orders on the carousel?"

Her white cheek and red lips crossed slowly over the car seat to kiss his black ear, the left-turn signal flashed derring-do for miles into Hempstead County and far south, deep into Louisiana, his home state.

Him down, she up, the thunderous, terminated, human flesh sine waves nodded into each other.

"I want to be a physicist, damn it!"

"Well, I'll be a cosmetologist or a beautician."

"I'll go to Howard University and do quadratics off the fuckin' blackboard and onto the goddamn walls!"

"I'll do beehives and blue rinses and perms and cook all your dinners in my pedal pushers and high heels."

The happy, clanging memory of the storage room behind the restaurant; cans of cherry and pineapple syrup falling and bottles of dill pickles and soda pop concentrate knocking together. Vernetta's panties had arched through the air toward the industrial refrigerator; a perfect pink parabola. J.B.'s pants had been around his ankles, a spatula in his right hand.

Then Vernetta's sweet, hushed screaming, "Double clutch me, motherfucker! Oh, double clutch me!"

After a time she would interrupt her cry for a smoke and a Pabst Blue Ribbon, the tall bottle. She had douched with white vinegar and distilled water before her cry so that it could be a clean, hygienic cry. She always wept with her pink towel wrapped around her head and her kneecaps pressed tightly together. She would take down the picture of her son and stare at it and begin to cry all over again. She would pull the small ironing board down to uncover the picture hanging behind it and place one picture on the other so that all four people could be on the same physical plane and three on the spiritual.

She is so thin and the little Kodak Brownie had turned the blinding red-and-yellow of her uniform into two shades of gray; her hair is surely not blond.

"Could I have been so flat-chested?"

Her thin left arm balances two Rebel Doggies and a root beer float on a tray, and her right hand is holding a hand.

Norvell Briggs, the owner of this My-T-Freeze foodstand and two others in Little Rock, stands between them, his right arm around his fry cook. The fry cook, a young black man with glasses and a part cut into his hair on the left side, is smiling, a paper chef's hat on his head and his right hand is holding a spatula in the air in frozen, mock triumph. His left hand, extending behind his boss, is holding a hand.

"God, could that man chicken-fry a minute steak," she thought aloud. "Now there's federal troops to protect the black kids from my daddy," she mused. "Just ten years too late."

Nightly penance. Without fail, she would open the box and touch the Classic Comic books she had collected.

"Danny, I bought them for you," she would repeat as if memorizing a speech. "I bought them for you. You can read these first. Then that'll get you ready for the real, bona fide books."

Physics Made Easy was there in its handmade dustcover and the letters J.B.W. written on it in pencil. It leaned against an Edgar Cayce paperback and that against the *ABC of Relativity*, about eleven years overdue from the Arkadelphia public library.

She opened the lunch box that still waited for him, the price tag hanging from the handle.

"It's Tom Corbett and the Space Cadets. It's the blue box with the new rubber stopper in the thermos bottle. The cork kind is no good," she whispered under her breath and again even softer, "the cork kind is no good."

Norvell had heard them that night ten years ago. He couldn't let them have their break in peace.

"We were on our own time!"

He had just rushed on back in spite of all the customers waiting and the four orders up and had just stood staring as the unstopped life spume spread in her green belly even as everything went cold.

The time would pass for Vernetta in this way without motion to measure it. At some point she would realize that she was dozing, that her body was cold to the touch. Then she would have breakfast alone in the cool of the morning and sleep till noon, when the heat woke her.

4

Buckeye Road

"Feed the chickens before you go! Thank the rooster that we don't need a clock. And don't let the *Chinos* cheat you."

Josephina's litany could be heard for miles.

"Ask Cheung over at the wagon for a cup of rice. Count your change, *hijo!* And stay away from the *mayates.*"

The *mayates* laughed at the mention of their name: the black beetles; *los Negros.*

Her voice rose even higher as she sent the staccato of words flying after him. It was just what Beto wanted to hear. As he ran to the dresser for the quarters and his pocketknife, he considered the route he would take to the Rainbo Market. Josephina then yelled again from the kitchen, "Stay away from the *maricones, y* those Xipe!"

As she watched him running for the dresser, she considered that the world had changed so much, too much. She was so far from home now. Long ago the thought of living in such a desolate place as this would have sent a shiver down her spine. God can find me here, she thought to herself. Her mother and father had never tried. Only Adelita had refused to shun her sister, but even word from her was rare. Were there transvestites and tramps in Lisboa?

She readied a parting salvo of words for the boy just as he

ran out of the adobe, but she was distracted at the last moment by the smell of something burning in the oven.

If the boy went to the Cadys he might see Sugar Dee or Potrice. Oh, Sugar Dee and Potrice, the thought stirred something! He thought about that alternative with strange anticipation.

They were nice, pretty ladies who did the same work as Vernetta, but they were black and thin and almost always naked in their car—sleek, wet, salamander-skinned girls. Beto had spent many an evening watching the two girls work.

They surely knew that giggling boys hid nearby every day and watched them, but they didn't seem to mind. They weren't vain women, playing up to the young boys. They just went about their business without becoming hardened by it. Buckeye Road was full of whores, but for some reason Potrice and Sugar Dee were prostitutes.

The girls always douched themselves at the passenger door after each zipping john, their shining legs spread and planted in dusty spiked heels while their waiting johns unzipped and stood in line at the driver's door. Sugar Dee was a deep coffee brown, and Potrice was like black boot polish, and their breasts were different from Vernetta's. They were small and high and a hand's span apart.

The men at the Cadys, the ones who lived in their Cadillac cars up on blocks, said that the two women loved each other.

"Lezbins," they laughed, "better than goddamn virgins. Bitches' soul ain't never felt the prod," they sneered, "but they sure wash that gash like it was gold."

"Fuckin' lezbins."

"Yeah, wash that gash like it was gold" came the response.

They were definitely a team, one douching or watching out or making change as the other worked, the smell of diluted vinegar and perfume wafting from their matching vermilion panties.

They lived and worked and slept inside that car, but each and every Tuesday morning they cleaned their cooking utensils, folded their blankets and drove away without ever letting on to anyone about where they went. They always returned on the following Friday night for their business, their clothes cleaned and their shoes shining again.

Theirs was the only car in Cady that could move, a beautiful green Pierce-Arrow sedan with electric seats and yellow courtesy lights in every door. There was a lighted ashtray for each seat, and plush velvet ropes stretched behind the front seat and above the rear doors. The two ladies would turn on their radio and send a wave of envy through the ranks of rusting tailfins. Potrice would smile wryly, then place one of her lavender pumps atop the power tune button on the carpeted fire wall; she could dial the radio with a touch of her foot.

That simple act sent the covetous, embittered harpies fluttering madly over Cady. The ruffled, toothless wastrels astride their befinned carcasses bitched and palavered endlessly at this, convertible to hardtop to brougham.

"Bitches think they shit is flowers."

"Yeah, they think they shit daisies."

Today was Saturday, and the boy knew the green car would be there with strange men milling with locals a falsely polite distance away from its doors. Sister Dora Mae would be there with her pink megaphone, painted with the same oil base paint as the church.

"Potrice, girl, you looks Senegalese or maybe Nigeria. You is from a proud peoples who done took up the Christian banner in this land long ago with pride and dignity. Now look at y'all. Jezebels. Harlots. Lettin' them filthy mens put they thang inside you."

The Cady men would certainly be there, plotting sexual revenge. Odabee Bracken, who lived in the only Lincoln Continental in Cady, would be first in line, his one good arm making every obscene gesture known to man. Odabee was a Korean War veteran, but he'd never seen action. He'd won a purple heart, but it was only a technical victory. While stationed in Seoul, he had overdosed on heroin and fallen into a stuporous sleep while lying on his left arm. When he woke up two days later, he was out of the army; his arm and his future had withered away.

His friend Onan Spillers, who lived in a '52 rear-ender, would queue up behind him every Saturday, his hand on his crotch and his shell game hidden in a pant cuff. After making various arcane manipulations with his hand, he would declare that his "one-eyed pocket snake is ready to strike."

He took great pleasure in telling everyone that a nuclear family had died in his metal home.

"There's still some blood on the floor mats," he'd say, watching closely for the revulsion he knew would follow.

But it was a lie, the boy thought. Someone had to have died in that wreck, true, but a lie about the stains, about the family. His wrecked Cady made Onan the low man on a totem pole that wasn't very high, and he needed the lie to prove that he didn't care, that he was beyond caring. Onan's car would never move. Odabee's Lincoln had a frozen engine so he was only slightly higher up.

The junkyard had been in Buckeye for only four years, and there were already thirty or forty cars in Cady. Only the most mangled were without an inhabitant or two. The cars that might run one day were the best to live in, the ones that still had a prayer of internal combustion.

"A po' blood can really sleep in a car like that. Just a few spark plugs and a new timing gear and it's the open road. A po' blood can dream in that kind of car."

They told anyone who would listen, anyone within earshot. But Beto did not believe them. No one did.

Neither Odabee nor Onan dreamt. When they retired at night into a cramped passenger seat they turned from dreaming. They poisoned their dreams. They drove dreams from their sleep with swigs of Thunderbird wine. In a pinch they swallowed cleaning fluid or pints of cough medicine. Their stagnant nights were clocked by broken odometers.

"People sometimes see an empty house and muse about the words that were spoken inside over the years," Vernetta had once said to Beto as the two stared at the wreckage across the street. "They think about the lives that were once lived in there. Empty houses, abandoned houses make people unhappy, wistful, curious. Yet empty, abandoned people never do."

As the boy thought about the two black girls, he felt a mixture of admiration and pity. They worked so hard, and

those vile-smelling men hated them so for their beauty and
for their car. They didn't just come inside them for a few
dollars; they speared those girls—in their minds those beautiful, young things were impaled and dying and less even
than themselves.

But, in fact, they didn't die. They got up sweet as you
please and washed that old, pointless moisture away. They
smiled at each other the way that lovers do, those two women,
and one of them would cry out, "Next."

Buckeye Road wasn't much of a town, just a place where
a pocked and pitted road met an invisible street. The road
ran from the highway and wound its way into the fringe
towns west of Phoenix. This town had taken the name of the
road as its own name.

The invisible street, 14th Street, was just a fanciful extension
of the real 14th Street that ended with the asphalt just outside
of Phoenix. The dirt passage that continued on into the desert
and ended at Buckeye Road just north of the market was
given the same name for lack of a better one. There was no
13th Street or 15th Street in Buckeye Road. There was only a
small desert wash in the distance that ran parallel to the main
street and cut across 14th Street just north of town. Parts of
the wash had been widened for flood relief. By 1969, the
asphalt would reach west and the fanciful street would become a paved reality. But by then, Buckeye Road, the town,
would be no more.

On the east side of Buckeye Road, in the flatland between
the shoulder of the road and the wash, were the adobe and
the Highway Comet. A long stone's throw north of the trailer
was the Mighty Clouds of Joy Church of God in Christ, and
beyond that the Rainbo Market.

On the west side, across Buckeye Road from the market,
was Cady, the sprawling Cadillac junkyard. The local water-
ing hole, the Blue Moon, was in a lot filled with dusty acacias
just northwest of Cady. Between the bar and the rusting heaps
was a small yellow bus.

A place called Tar-Paper, named for the type of homes
found there, was just across the wash and northeast of the
Rainbo Market and 14th Street. Beyond Tar-Paper were the
railroad switchboxes, a tiny bus depot and a small cemetery.
In the far distance were the highway and the horizon. If Beto
went by Tar-Paper, he might go to the Perkinses' lean-to and
maybe see Claude and Louie, his new Arkie friends. Over
there they fried their flour, not like tortillas, but it still tasted
good. They fried it in bacon fat and black pepper and fed all
the kids and the dogs with it.

The Okies and Arkies who lived there trapped pigeons
every day and ate them stuffed with rice or dried bread. They
loved Spam scrapple, too, but their specialty was deep-fried
chicken butts and potato skins. They used the skins to wrap
around the butts. Claude had shown him how to do it. It was
sort of a panhandle burrito.

On payday Old Man Perkins always bought two special
things at the Rainbo: a pair of batteries for his Emerson port-
able radio and jars of Vienna sausages for all the kids.

"Nothin' like vyeenies and beer and a little Ferlin Huskey,"
Manassus Perkins would say to Beto and to his own sons as
he stretched his long frame over an old car seat.

He'd set the Vienna sausages next to his bottle of beer, then
begin unwrapping the 67½-volt battery for the B-plus and the
3-volt for the filaments, the anticipation and pleasure smooth-
ing his face.

Tar-Paper, especially on payday, was alive and pulsing with
musicality, recorded and homemade. Mance Lipscomb singing "I Ain't Did No Hangin' Crime" could be heard in one
cluster of hovels while Spade Cooley twanged in another,
their voices booming out of disembodied dashboards and
wind-up Edisons. In the far eastern corner of Tar-Paper, Louie
Prima competed with Cuco Sanchez, Keely Smith's sweet
voice cutting through the din of trumpets while Cuco crooned
the dove's sad story. Mexican fieldhands singing their ran-
cheras practiced their complex harmonies near cloggers and
rawboned finger pickers who were giving some flat pickers
from Tennessee a lesson.

In Phoenix's unofficial trash heap, people had set up house.

In the evening, around the communal fires, the Rebel yell mingled with Howlin' Wolf. The high *gritos* of *norteños* sounded out as ragged children ran between piles of water heaters and towering stacks of used box springs.

The Arkie families had friendly and scrappy kids whose baseball games in Tar-Paper lasted till the ball was invisible in the darkness. Mexican or black or Indian kids whose first experience of the white race was the migratory Arkies could never thereafter harbor a categorical hatred of white people. Dirt seemed even dirtier on the faces of blond Arkies while scrapes from tackle football games seemed more heroic on their translucent skin. But best of all, no Arkie kid ever turned down an invitation to dinner or ever asked what he was eating. Arkie kids ate chitlins and tripe, goat brains or mountain oysters, then sat quietly hoping for more.

Claude and Louie had first shown up at Beto's house late one evening, drawn in by the scent of *albondigas* and Spanish rice. They had introduced themselves first to Manuel and Josephina and then to the boy. Both peering into the open door, one of them had asked what was cooking.

Of the grown-ups in the Perkins family, only Mrs. Perkins spoke with any regularity.

"Y'all want some vyeenies and lime Kool-Aid?" The woman had a cooing elegance about her; wisps of disheveled hair only served to emphasize the depth of her blue eyes. Her gnarled husband, Manassus, never said much, and his ancient, crippled father said even less. They both pulled at their chaw, then pulled at their jars of Vienna sausage with equal relish. She had four children by Manassus. No one who saw them together could imagine the act of love between them: a white, silk scarf caught on a rough, toppling fencepost.

The Arkies were kind of like Mexicans, the boy felt; they could suffer and do hard work and they always fed everybody's kids.

Mrs. Perkins, like his *abuela*, always seemed pleased to feed any child that came in the door. There was a true antebellum beauty in Mrs. Perkins's face as she poured lime Kool-Aid for a line of kids. Her coloring and the transparency of her skin were clearly Irish and seemed somehow exotic. There were light blue veins at her temples that made her look so fragile, and she would raise her slender fingers often to rub those temples. When she did she would invariably look away, never allowing direct eye contact with anyone, as if she knew the weariness would show. She wished to burden no one with it.

She could be seen every day, walking around the garbage that surrounded her home, gathering the children, one foot placed directly in front of the other. Then she would step delicately inside to take down her precious China bowl and use it to serve the sausages. She would wash her collection of Skippy jars for the Kool-Aid. Johnna Perkins demanded that the kids sit down properly to eat, and while hovering around them she would finger calmly through her beautiful rock maple sewing box, in the family for a hundred years and put away nightly in a corner of the tar-paper house. It had first belonged to her great-grandmother on her father's side. Her great-grandfather had broken and run at Manassas but stood fast at Gettysburg till nothing below the knees was left; his right arm loose weight in its sleeve and his debt paid.

Johnna had read the florid family letters, grim homages to faded honor, and she had long ago come to despise them. She had heard the hallowed stories told then retold, and she had seen her great-grandfather's young face in the glorious ambrotypes so many times that she often felt her own life was an anachronism. The face in the old photos always horrified her, the dignity coupled with the uselessness and the longevity of both. Her family had been poor, too poor to ever own slaves. Yet it seemed to her that her entire family had been enslaved by that war.

There had once been family land in South Carolina. Her father had seen it once and announced that he felt something special from it when he stood on it. She always felt that seeing that land might only increase her bitterness toward the rebel diaspora. Her husband's father, even to this day, wore the butternut cap on his shrinking crown.

"Couldn't they talk about nothin' else? Couldn't they just move on?"

She swore to herself that she would never, ever become

accustomed to the taste of chicory or the bitter taste of poverty.

She had once heard tell ambrotypes could photograph the spirit, that there was something about the glass plates that seemed to etch in the tragedy, settle it all in the face. In Johnna Perkins's nightmares, her two young tow-headed sons are trapped by time, are standing there in the photo with him.

The boy ran east from the kitchen and around the house. He grabbed a large handful of corn and dried bread and tossed it into the chicken coop as he ran. First he ran north, then west, passing between the house and the cesspool, then between Abuelo's caboose and the goat pen. As he ran he could hear Josephina. She must have gone over to the upright piano to take a rest from her cooking. Her voice in English was always surprising to him. Astonishing. Though she spoke English meekly and uncertainly, she sang it forcefully and perfectly. It was an Irving Berlin tune.

". . . from out of the past where forgotten things belong. You keep coming back like a song."

She loved Irving Berlin and George Gershwin for their popular songs, though she would always remind Beto that the true geniuses of American music were the Negroes and the Latins. Music, and especially black music, was Josephina's single passion outside of Catholicism, at least her only legitimate passion. No matter how often she cursed the Blue Moon and the people there, she could never deny the music or the language.

Though Beto would never be allowed into the Blue Moon bar, he somehow knew that the language spoken there would never be foreclosed to him and to the other kids. More and more black words and phrases were creeping into his sentences every day.

It was a separate tongue among many separate tongues, and it flourished and spread as always, an English of its own. It drew from audacity and revenge, and it drew from the need of an obviously separate people to have their own language.

"Whites pass," Josephina had said, her finger in the boy's face.

"Whites go into the melting pot. Polish and Hungarians shorten their names, they cut the words that bind them to their own. Germans, French forget their languages, pronounce through their noses and disappear into the Twin Cities. Not *los Negros* or *los Indios* or *la Raza*, the Mexicans," she said. *"Tenemos la insignia."* Josephina had touched her finger to her skin and then to the boy's to make her point.

"We have the badge, and if we didn't we'd make one. The Indians and the *Raza* have always had their language; the fountain of their *cultura* is right here or just across that so-called border in Mexico. The blacks, far from Africa, made theirs from the language they were forced to use, reshaped it." She moved her hands as if she were molding clay.

"They played and danced, they cried and worshiped with it. And because they were always separated from the whites, they separated themselves." She demonstrated by moving her hands apart.

"They said: 'We are always told how different we are, let's make it an act of will.' And they did. Imagine what American music would be without the blacks, the *latinos*."

It was the genealogy of Josephina's gospel.

"La verdad, it was the slaves who freed America," Abuela would say. "Now the whites are milking *los Negros* of their *música* and their language."

Josephina would pull out her 78s or her new LPs for any group of kids that would listen. Often she would bribe them with food, then play her music while they ate.

"Listen to this, *hijos*. You hear what Jimmy Dorsey is doing here, right here with the trumpet section. Shit, the black bands were doing that fifteen years earlier. Listen to this."

She would clean her records carefully with her apron, then wind the record player violently before each selection.

"This is King Oliver, a genius," she would smile as she dropped the needle into the first groove of Stingaree Blues, "a genius. He died, you know, sweeping up a pool hall in Savannah, Georgia. Can you imagine, *mijitos lindos*, the pat-

pat of his wide broom between the quiet tables after the place
was locked up? Can you imagine the volume, the explosion
of trumpets in that old man's mind?"

There would be absolute quiet for a second or two as the
stylus reached the last groove and the music stopped.

"For dessert, there is flan for all of you . . . and this is
Dinah Washington"—she would place the dessert bowls in
front of Beto and his friends, then rush to play the record—
"and a singer like her comes along just once in a lifetime."

She had lowered her voice to a level appropriate to the
dignity of the moment.

"Her real name is Ruth Jones," she began while pointing
to her picture on the album, "and she was born in 1924"—
she stopped moving for a second or two, though none of the
children had noticed, a stricken look on her face—"and she
will die very soon."

Going north Beto followed the long black extension cord
that connected Vernetta's trailer to the adobe house. His
grandmother's singing gave way to the sound of Vernetta's
radio.

"Vernetta, you need anything at the store?"

"Not right now, honey," she called back.

She was with someone. All the signs were there, the smell
of perfume trying to cover the sweet vapors of cooked black-
eyed peas, the candle glow working with the makeup to create
the illusion. A fairly new truck was in the driveway, a gringo
or a Navajo, the boy thought.

He ran around the Highway Comet, around the white
stones marking off what would never be a garden, and he
continued to run, stepping on the cord that ran to the Mighty
Clouds of Joy Church of God in Christ, Baptist. The church
building was pink, plain and windowless with a flat roof, but
it had legitimate electrical power and sold it cheaply to nearby
brothers and sisters, even fallen sisters like Vernetta. From
the back door of the church, a half-dozen extension cords
snaked off in various directions. One went off toward Tar-
Paper and one toward the Reverend Willie Drake's small
house, while another, surprisingly, went to the Blue Moon.
The black one went to Vernetta's trailer and beyond that to

the adobe. Sinners and saints alike were allowed to share in the power of the Lord.

In front of the church was a lightpole with a hand-painted sign hanging from it. On both sides was a picture of a white, puffy cloud with its bottom painted silver.

GOD BLESS ROSA PARKS, proclaimed the sign on one side.

The other side said, WE PREACH CHRIST RISEN AND COMING. Tomorrow morning the doors would be thrown wide open by the Reverend Willie Drake and his wife, Sister Dora Mae. The electric organ and the merging, soaring black voices could be heard for blocks. The jumping, brassy, tambourine joy of it would be felt by all that listened.

"All that beauty comes from suffering," Abuela would say. She would open the window every Sunday morning and again when the congregation choir practiced on Wednesday evenings. She would stop the gramophone or the piano to listen.

"Audacity, *mijo. Audacia.* The audacity to speak to God in their own way and no one else's. God can't help but listen to that. Do you hear it? He can't help but listen."

No single voice seemed to shine through in what was a beautiful fabric of separate songs. Each person seemed to be making his or her own conversation with God, held to the here and now only by the notes of the organ. Overlays of singing directly to the Almighty played on overlays of singing just away from the vision.

The bold entwined with the reticent. The cowering togetherness of the dark, crowded slave ship holds could be heard in it, as could the waxing prideful, organized anger that signaled that a dark storm of freedom would soon be visible on the horizon. The bitter, sharpened voice of the runaway was still in the fabric. The patient, enduring mammy's voice was still in the fabric. The searing, fecund, white-toothed sheleopard was in there. The indignant buck was still woven in there. The earth mother was there, her golden frock a yard wide.

Throaty on frail, old on young, the voices sailed out and up for hours, unchained, higher even than the heat.

"They once sold them on the auction block," Josephina said. "Now they can only sell their music or claim it as their own."

Then all at once a single voice would break out away from
the rest, a blasting cap voice in a round, jet aspect that lit the
others off, freed their centers, fired their singing souls in a
spiraling give-and-take ascent through the tar-and-gravel roof
and up through the universe.

Beyond the church and beyond the Reverend Drake's
house, the boy ran past the short cut to Tar-Paper and toward
the porch of the Rainbo Market. He remembered that Josephina had asked him to go to the Cheungs' wagon and borrow
a cup of rice, so he decided to do that first before he made
up his mind about which soda pop to buy.

"Beto! Beto!" a voice called.

It was Claude and Louie, fresh from a meal somewhere,
particles of it still clinging to their faces.

"Where have you been, do you got money?"

"Yeah, but I have to buy butter for Abuela and a Bubble
Up for Abuelo. But I do have six bits. I should have enough
left over for two sodas apiece."

"We have eleven cents and three empties," said Louie.
"Maybe two sodas apiece and some Necco wafers!"

"First I have to borrow a cup of rice from the Cheungs."

The three boys, like Red Ryder, circled around the northwest corner of Tar-Paper with a gunslinger's wariness in order
to avoid Johnna Perkins's eyes and her inevitable motherly
inquiries.

"The Cheungs just fed us," said Claude.

"We got some of the leftovers from the field run today; Mr.
Cheung says they only did fifty-one plates. Not too good. But
it was a hundred and fourteen degrees out there today, and
nobody eats when it's that hot."

"We eat," laughed Louie. "Mrs. Cheung says we got tape-
worms, the both of us."

The Cheungs' chuckwagon was really a converted milk
truck, the sides of which had been modified to swing up like
birds' wings. In that position it resembled a huge seagull. One
wing shaded the stacked eating utensils: the metal, blue-
porcelained plates and the surplus U.S. Navy forks and
spoons. The other side had two propane tanks that fed two
large black woks and a rice cooker.

Down the center of the truck was a walkway where the elder Cheungs stood their entire sweating workday, adjusting the heat below, pulling sesame oil from above, dipping huge spoons into soy sauce, salt and sugar. Each day the Cheung family offered food to the field-workers, hot chop suey for two bits a plate or chow fun for thirty cents.

"Mr. Cheung," said Beto, "my grandmother needs to borrow a cup of rice, please."

"No borrow," he smiled. "I owe Josephina a hundred cup."

As he poured rice into a small bag, he called out to his wife. She promptly walked over from her dish washing and stood smiling, her gold teeth gleaming over a cotton housecoat and tiny black slippers. She proudly pointed to a poultice wrapped around a huge goiter below her jaw. The boy immediately recognized his grandmother's handiwork. There was just the faintest smell of skunk fat and eucalyptus oil emanating from the area.

"Just two days and already it go down," said Mr. Cheung. "Tell Josephina thank you, okay?"

"Now for the sodas!" shouted Louie, sprinting toward the store.

The Rainbo Market was a wooden building, just a big box with a covered, elevated wooden porch in front. It had once been a Purina Checkerboard feed store, and so the elevation was necessary to match the height of the trucks and the wagons that once pulled up to load and unload. There were three front doors, the first a steel gate that opened to reveal a screen door with a picture of Little Miss Sunbeam across its waist. The final door was wooden and was the only one that swung inward, where it was held open by a kick latch that had managed to dig a deep furrow for itself over the years.

The floor was dark pine and gave a little with each step. The inside held everything that twenty races could want, from chitlins to blue corn *masa*. There were rabbit traps, .22 and .410 over-under rifles, displays of sunglasses and foot powder. There were displays of Ipana toothpaste and Pepsodent tooth powder. There were huge pictures of Daisy the Cow near the dairy cooler and one of Hopalong Cassidy next to the loaves of bread. There were stacks of Ben Davis pants and work shirts. A four-foot tower of Stetsons rose from a wooden counter. Red Wing boots with the reinforced toe and Red Goose shoes for the kids were neatly displayed near the entrance.

There were even bags of sifted dirt allegedly trucked in all the way from Mississippi for the pregnant black women to eat.

There was *masa* for the tortilla people and small bags of pine nuts for the *maricones*, the only connoisseurs in Buckeye Road.

Strategically placed next to the cash registers were two circular racks. One held comic books: Archie, Nancy and Sluggo, Captain Marvel. The other dangled ten-cent toys just at the eye level of a nine-year-old. At this particular level, these cheap cellophane packages held the Grail, the Shroud of Turin; pieces of the true cross hung there, made of plastic. The racks were meant to be spun on their axis by urchins, but over time both had frozen up solid.

Metal can be subjected to only so much concentrated longing before it fatigues and seizes up. While the men across the street in Cady hoped beyond hope that the opposite would be true of their cars, the two racks in Rainbo were daily reminders of the futility of such hopes.

To the left of the cash registers was the candy counter, the second most wondrous sight at the Rainbo. There were only two types of candy then, penny and nickel, the penny candy display by far the more interesting and diverse. There were wax tubes and little wax bottles filled with sweet, colored liquid. Next to the long straws of Lik-M-Aid were red boxes of Cherry Chan, Flav-R-Straws sold singly, chicken bones, malted milk balls, jawbreakers, Tootsie Roll juniors and Walnetto cubes.

Above it all, there was a new display of Raleigh cigarettes with the blue coupons on the pack that had eclipsed an Old Gold display and a small, dusty rack of Fizzies.

But outside, on the face of the Rainbo, was the real show, the true wonder: the blazing, prismatic, multi-hued altars where tiny slack-jawed, awe-stricken pilgrims from the burning summer heat came into the shade, their tokens of fealty palmed and sweaty. They would arrive, stepping solemnly up the stairs and walking past the pretenders and false ones, to stand at last before their chosen. After a moment of quiet devotion, reassured again of the rightness of the path, and reminded graphically of the oppressive heat, the pilgrim child would enter the store to re-emerge transformed, vindicated and renewed, bottle in hand.

There were so many tin thermometers and signs that only the small windows of the Rainbo and its doors remained exposed.

ANY TIME, ANY WEATHER, read the red-white-and-green Delaware Punch thermometer.

COME IN, GET KIST, proclaimed the long white Kist thermometer with the red lipstick kisses on its face.

BE ALIVE, DRINK BUBBLE UP, stated a yellow sign.

A huge blue-and-yellow bottle cap seemed to sing, BIRELEY'S. IT HAPPIES THIRST!

CHEERO-COLA, THERE'S NONE SO GOOD.

DOUBLE MEASURE, DOUBLE PLEASURE! a silver-and-red Double Cola sign promised.

A Big Giant Cola tin showing a cola bottle lifting weights: FOR A REAL LIFT! MORE FOR YOUR MONEY!

There was a huge red sign with the smiling Coca-Cola boy wearing his bottle cap hat.

Another monstrous, purple sign exclaimed, ENJOY GRAPETTE! next to a Barq's thermometer: IT'S GOOD.

There were Nesbitt's, Masons, Royal Crown, B-1, Mission, Nu-Grape, Frosty, Kramer's, Norka, Dybala, Crush, PAL, Hires, Legra, Moxie, Squirt, Nichol, Piff's, Ma's, Crescent, Vernor's, Old Colony, Hrobeck's, Nehi, Par-T-Pak, Fruit Bowl, Cascade, Dub-L-Valu, Hazle Club and Whistle, among many, many more signs that beckoned. A kid had a choice then, and he just had to choose; compelled by pride, loyalty and peer pressure. A choice not between bottles in a store refrigerator or between various manifestations of one company's cola drink, decaffeinated or sugarless. It was a choice between felicities, between reveries, simplistic and sometimes naive. It was a choice that determined whether years from then in some unknown place and time the long thoughts of childhood would be lightly tinged lime green or Nu-Grape purple.

There were no teams of psychologists to conjure up libido-centered advertising campaigns. No one equated this cola to a particular social stratum or that root beer with the ability to find friends. The soda companies were not run by law firms but by families, by men with sweet flavors from the old country still lingering in their memories, flavors remembered and revived. Their patient, aproned wives dreamt up the slogans and drew the labels for the marvelous bottles knowing full well that only children could be the final measure of them.

The tin signs were nailed up everywhere and were so common that their passing would go almost unnoticed as would their significance. Selective magnetic fields, a language beyond words, the signs attracted eyes that were still young; they drew on the child parts only. The colors, the thin, glass thermometers, and especially the names were an evocation of desires and of true fulfillments in a time distant and past, before the confusion, the concern and the considerations of the adult world.

DRINK ORIGINAL BW AND EAT A PENNY SNACK, BOTH FOR 5 CENTS! The BW sign had captured Louie long ago, and in his zeal he more than tithed. Every cent he got went toward accruing that precious nickel. Claude, on the other hand, went back and forth between Nesbitt's Orange and Nehi Lime.

"You can't change soda, man," his brother, Louie, had whined, his respect for his older brother clearly in jeopardy.

His apostasy had been shocking at first, but Claude rationalized it away by saying they were both citrus drinks. Beto was strictly Double Cola except when Vernetta offered him a Delaware Punch for free.

The three boys, talking excitedly, piled into the Rainbo, then exited a few minutes later with two sodas each, Necco wafers, a frozen block of butter and two extra penny candies from Louie's BW sodas. As they sat down on the benches that were bolted to the porch, preparing to imbibe, Mr. Lee came out.

"Beto," he said, "I almost forget to tell you, here a letter."

He handed the envelope to the boy and turned to walk inside.

"Mr. Lee, your penny. The postal fee."

Mr. Lee turned to look at the boy, looked at the penny that was extended to him, then continued back inside.

"*No gracias*," he said as the flapping of his slippers against his heels diminished. He was relieved just to be rid of the letter.

"*No gracias*," he repeated as he disappeared into the store.

Something was not quite right. There was something ominous about the way that Mr. Lee had handed him the letter. Beto lifted the envelope to look at it.

"To Miss Vernetta Lynn Fish," it read.

A letter for Vernetta, after two years! No . . . more than two years. It was postmarked Flagstaff, Arizona. There was no return address.

"A letter for Vernetta," he said excitedly.

The boy put the envelope into his pocket.

"Let's go to the riverbed and catch lizards," said Claude. "The bluebelly I got last week got away."

"No, Ma let it go," said Louie, opening and closing his pocketknife and chewing his candy.

"We could go see that crazy Wysteria Maybelle," Beto said. "I hear tell she's got a new dog, big as a bull."

He had gotten the "hear tell" from his two friends and felt good using it.

Suddenly, Boydeen, a black girl from Mississippi and a patron of the Blue Moon, came running down Buckeye Road from the area near what would be 14th Street if the street went that far. She was running hard, her thin ankles flashing. Sweating and holding her side, she gave a wide-eyed, wild look that told the three boys that something had gone terribly wrong.

As she drew closer they could see dark bloodstains on her blue work shirt. The shirt was sliced three times down the front, and Boydeen's left breast, cut open and bleeding, swung through one of the rips in the cloth, a brown fig spread wide open.

Boydeen ran toward them without seeing them, without answering when Louie asked what was wrong. Without a word, with sightless, guileless eyes seeing only escape, she slid quickly under the porch of the Rainbo Market. Then she frantically dashed back out into the street for a second to kick dust over a trail of blood.

More carefully now, she slid back under the porch again and lay down quietly as she could, staring back toward 14th as if waiting, her face glistening with fear and her loud breath still racking her small body.

No one came after her. Not a solitary soul. No sirens howled. No lights flashed. Hiawatha Carson's body, like the rest who died in Buckeye Road, would lie in the middle of the street day after day. In three days the captain of some precinct in Phoenix would decide to punish some underlings by sending them out to Buckeye Road to investigate. It would be bad business with that swelling corpse out there. No Navajos or Pimas would drive in to shop at the Rainbo so long as there was death on the road. All the whores' business would tail off. Even the Blue Moon would suffer as all that liquor was now contaminated by the presence of death and had to be conjured on, a two-day process involving green candles and pictures of Saint Michael.

The boys ran toward 14th to see him there. He was dead for sure. He had stab wounds on his chest and stomach, as many cuts as Boydeen had, but his ribs had parted for one of them and that was that. The hole in his chest had bubbled a little, but that soon stopped and Hiawatha lay motionless. A fluorescent green fly walked on his tongue.

In his right hand was a large, black-handled knife, dark blood on the blade.

None of the boys had ever seen a dead man before, but they knew they were seeing one now.

"Has anyone called the police?" Beto yelled out to no one in particular. The twin, crippled liquor guardians at the Blue Moon looked up but neither answered. The street was empty.

As the boys stood there, seized motionless by this spectacular gore, Sugar Dee and Potrice's green Pierce-Arrow drove slowly by, the girls staring out.

"Best get away from him, boys," Sugar Dee said. "Nigga ain't been nothin' but trouble to anybody and now he's real trouble. Go home before the cops come and arrest the first person they see."

"Have you seen Boydeen?" asked Potrice.

"She's hiding," answered Claude, still staring at Hiawatha's body, arms twisted away from the legs.

Beto thought for a foolish moment that the hard rocks under the body must be painful.

"She's . . ." began Louie slowly when he was interrupted sternly by Potrice.

"Don't tell me where she is!" She said it loudly, as if she knew that Boydeen was nearby.

"But I think the son of a bitch had it comin'. You kin only beat a woman so many times before you got it comin'. Tell Boydeen if you see her that me and Sugar didn't see nothin'. Tell her that we sure will help her if we can. Now you boys get away from that," she said, looking disparagingly at the corpse.

Sugar Dee put one finger to her lips and, after looking in both directions, handed Beto a ten-dollar bill.

"For Boydeen."

Sugar Dee and Potrice would be gone for four days. They would go wherever it was they always went. That would give the police or whoever came for the body time to come and go without bothering the two girls and their business. The boys walked back to the Rainbo as the car pulled out of sight.

They turned to look back, first Beto, then Claude, and finally Louie. Without knowing it, they had been wounded, too. They were caught and chafed by this indecent, griefless moment. They were stunned by the graphic and explicit wound that seemed to widen as muscles slumped.

They had seen rabbits and chickens die, and all three had held Claude's ancient dog as it dwindled down. All of them had seen the moment of its death, but none could say exactly when it came.

Later, on long lizard hunts in the desert washes, they believed together that something palpable had gone out of that small animal in that instant of death. It had been something lamentable, and somehow it needed a good word said to acknowledge it.

"You couldn't have been so bad as this," said Beto, looking back at the man whose huge shoulders seemed squeezed up around his neck, their power seeping out. "You couldn't have been."

"Mom says how people are treated fair and get to see Jesus in the hereafter," Claude added. "She's shown me pictures of heaven in this book of hers."

Louie crossed himself.

"You ain't Catholic," Beto chided, shoving his friend toward Claude, who shoved him right back.

There was no rising minor seventh in their ears as they stared down at Hiawatha. Somehow the sky remained the same. They wondered why as they ran away for help and they pretended not to see Boydeen down below, still clutching her bleeding chest, her black eyes huge.

5

Cruel Rust

A crowd was already gathering at the Blue Moon. The boys could see it as they ran toward the canvas top. There was shuffling and confusion down the street, and angry voices could be heard from every corner. The usual laughter and brazen music had given way to a sullen, dark uneasiness.

"We shouldn't be goin' over there," said Louie.

"It's all right," answered Claude. They're all scared, too. Maybe they'll know what to do about Hiawatha. He's one of theirs."

Claude was right about their fear. No one even noticed the boys' presence in their midst. For the very first time the boys had been allowed into the bar without being chased away. For a moment Beto and his friends forgot why they had run headlong from the Rainbo and why they were sweating and breathless. The boys stood dazed for a time, benumbed by their presence within the walls of Gomorrah.

According to the good Reverend Willie Drake and his dear wife, Sister Dora Mae, the Blue Moon was the very next place on earth that the wrath of God would strike, and the prospect of witnessing such a miracle or catastrophe, depending on your point of view, in modern times had often sent Beto, Claude and Louie scurrying to the street corner to watch it happen.

The Blue Moon was a combination drinking bar, juke joint, dance and pool hall owned by a local entrepreneur named Floyd Garman, an ex-schoolteacher and lifelong alcoholic who had managed to combine small business with great pleasure.

"Floyd," yelled Beto when he recognized the face of the owner. "Hiawatha's been killed! He's out there in the street!" he said, pointing toward the store.

"I gots to have a drink, boy," answered Floyd. "Bitch Boydeen gone git us all thrown in the pokey. I'm a wino, goddamn it! I got needs."

Floyd would tell anyone who would listen about his alcoholism, telling the story about how he had managed to turn his life around.

"Ten years ago, boss, I was a schoolteacher in Tucson with all the so-called classic symptoms of alcoholism. I drank alone, boss. I hid my bottles here and there and everywhere, behind the drinking fountain and under the desk and behind the map of the world. One bottle behind Tasmania and one behind Madagascar. I denied the problem. That's the third classic symptom, you see. And the fourth, I let everything go: my house, my family, my job, my debts.

"Now, ten years later, boss, everything's changed. I don't never drink alone, even when I want to. I live surrounded by bottles that I don't have to hide. I admit to everyone I am a wino and the problem has tripled my goddamn income."

Floyd's wife, Favorita Garman, determined and angry, had followed her estranged husband to Buckeye Road, lawyer in tow and conservatorship papers in hand. Upon first sight of his vast holdings, she had swooned theatrically, then curtly dismissed the overbearing shyster.

Favorita, her love for Floyd rekindled anew, had oozed contrition for weeks on end, but to no avail. No matter what she did or said, Floyd's heart was hardened against her.

She promised to cook for him every day. She promised to never nag him. In desperation, she had even promised oral sex, but nothing warmed her husband's heart to her. Her lamentations and the gnashing of her teeth were heard throughout Buckeye for weeks.

Desperate, she took to drinking and miraculously discovered that each synapse that shut down in her brain brought her closer and closer to an understanding with her husband. Each ganglion, each tendon sheath that went gray and insensible from the drink pulled the two Garmans closer and closer to a union that had never really existed before.

Eventually they found each other, behind the same rusting water heater in the same roadside ditch, their fingers interlocked around the same bottle neck. She became a full partner. She did the books for Blue Moon Enterprises and even opened a small kitchen offering a hot meal to Floyd's patrons. She served a steaming plate of dirty rice and smothered pork chops for a half-dollar or collard greens and black-eyed peas with ham hocks for thirty-five cents.

Her students at Phoenix Union High School soon stopped wondering what had become of her and quickly forgot her altogether. The Garman home in Tucson fell into disrepute, then disrepair, before it eventually escheated to the state.

"Bitch Boydeen's gonna bring the John Law down here and close me right on down," Floyd said to the three boys as he downed the dregs of a pint, then wiped his mouth with his sleeve.

"Topple my empire," he muttered as he tossed the empty bottle out into the dark.

"We gots to bury the fool," someone said. "There's thousands of miles of desert out here. It's so fuckin' hot out there he'll look like a leather jacket inside o' two weeks."

"Yeah, bury the fool!" another said in agreement.

"He done vanvan," someone else said in a calm and low voice.

The words were followed by an immense silence. That pronouncement had closed the subject. No one would touch him now. A little man with a horrible wig stepped forward.

"He been in contact with the juju."

The body would be left where it lay. No black person from the Blue Moon would dare touch it with all the loose magic ready to leap from it.

"We've got to help Boydeen," Beto said. "She's hurt."

"She had no choice," said the horrible wig. "We have no choice. She will make her own way. No one here know nothing," he said looking around at the black faces surrounding him.

"We don't need no white police here askin' questions. We knows they'll arrest somebody. They'll close the book on some nigga. Best not meddle. Best leave them two where they are."

He reached up to the top of his skull and rotated the wig so that the part was now on the left side of his head.

"But someone's got to say some words over him," Beto said impatiently.

"Words!" spat Toop. "You think everything on this here earth an' below an' above is spoken for in words? Shit, there's a universe between all the words we got." His wig had once again gone askew with his outburst. "The magic words sits in the spaces between the regular words." He spread the fingers of one hand and indicated the gaps between the fingers with the other. "And there's spaces between them spaces where whole lives come and go with no words attached. I tell you, boy. This here world is so crazy and bent up that all the words there is don't cover the ground good as a light rain. Now get out of here y'all. No fuckin' po' white trash and Indians allowed in the Blue Moon."

"No Messakins neither," someone else yelled out.

The boys moved out from beneath the canvas and slowly walked toward the Rainbo and the cooling body in the street.

"You boys mind you own bid-ness," a faceless voice called out.

"This here is colored bid-ness."

Only blacks were allowed in the Blue Moon and only a select class of blacks at that. If you were a black man or woman or both between the ages of seventeen and ninety-seven and you had turned your back on the Sweet Lord Jesus, the Blue Moon beckoned to you and welcomed you in. No other races need apply.

The Blue Moon sported a canvas top stretched between acacia trees and had plywood sides of sixty-by-twenty cubits that came only waist-high. It could never have looked new. There was a glaze of shabbiness about it that was more than superficial. Inside the plywood walls was the inner room, where cases of beer were stacked to the rafters and guarded night and day by trusted minions. There was no cooler or refrigerator, only a tin washtub filled with crushed ice that was continually refilled by runners carrying twenty-five-pound bags from the ice plant to the inner sanctum.

For two bits a patron could step up to the outer wall and have a Pabst Blue Ribbon, a Falstaff or a Bulldog beer. For four bits you could have a paper cup with a shot of Johnnie Walker. Whatever you drank, you could stand all day long shooting the shit or admiring Floyd's collection of miniature statuettes epoxied to the top of his cash register, each named after a sign of the zodiac. They were twelve tiny gray couples made of molten lead and forever frozen in various contorted modes of penetration, every orifice covered.

"Cain't come by these no mo', boss," he would say proudly. "No boss, cain't come by these. I'm a Libra," he would grin. "I ain't no rumprider like them Gemini."

Right next door to the bar were the pool table and assorted benches where patrons played board games or just sat out the day in the shade of the canvas. The third room was dedicated to dancing and to the devil's own work. This was Lucifer's personal spot, or so the reverend said, where the hopeless and the unredeemed came to debauch.

"This is the false ark and the false temple! Jeroboam get thee gone! This is where the new life's blood of Negro youth marches down to be corrupted with sensuality, intemperance, and graven images," railed Willie Drake, "among the Aaronites and the blasphemers."

Above the floor two small horn speakers were nailed up to the acacias and their rotting wires ran down to a turntable and an Eico tube amplifier. Some care had been taken in the decor of this particular room that had not been taken elsewhere on the premises. There were romantic appointments: two light bulbs, one painted red with fingernail polish and the other blue; their confluence was a muddy gray-green light. Together, they barely lit the room.

There was a galvanized bucket full of water in one corner for cigarette butts, and the only chair in the room was nailed to the floorboards and could be tilted back to uncover a convenient hiding place for heroin, marijuana, guns and knives should the police make a visit. Sometimes kids would yell, "Police!" just to see the scramble of do-rags to the tilting chair. Young bloods, in a panicked frenzy, would dump their stashes and weapons left and right, a frantic flurry of guilty activity followed immediately by unnatural postures of innocence.

Beto and Claude had tried it once but had been discovered. They had to run for their lives out to the bus depot and then, in desperation, out to the Mexican graveyard. No black person would ever go there. No black person would dare.

But the real fun always started when the coast was clear and the innocents tried to reclaim their property. Sometimes it took hours to do and sometimes somebody died.

The crack of gunshots from the Blue Moon was not an unusual sound. The romantic and narcotic intrigues within those plywood walls invariably led to knifings or shootings. Nor was it unusual for a body to lie in the street in front of the Blue Moon for two or three days, ripe and bloating and bad for business. Someone would rush to the Rainbo Market and place a frenzied call to the police, and the ambulance and one or the other would roll up two or three days later with sirens blaring, one gringo driving and another yawning, a clipboard covering his mouth in a vestigial act of courtesy.

On normal Friday and Saturday nights the Blue Moon boiled with black people writhing together to the sounds of James Brown or Champion Jack Dupree or Arthur "Big Boy" Crudup. These were the blue people: the hypes, mainliners, parolees, pushers, Lotharios, pimps, prostitutes and gamblers.

Beto as well as kids from Tar-Paper and the Papago reservation came almost every Saturday night to watch the revelry. But they were careful to stay back out of the light; their brown and black faces mirrored their fascination and their disgust. Inevitably, inexorably, Sister Dora Mae would walk from Goshen to Nod to stand between the children and the sons of Cain, berating first one side, then the other.

Facing the Blue Moon square on and clutching the Bible, she would scream out at them, "Y'all be transgressors, temp-

ters, harlots, satanizers," and on seeing the swaying transvestites, "abominations."

Abruptly, she would turn about to face the children and
quietly plead for them to go to their homes just before she
would launch into a holy tirade against their backsliding parents. But the children stayed, transfixed by the sights.

There were hoodoo people to look at under the canvas. The
best hoodoo was Toop, the old man with the world's most
obvious wig hat. A horrible, polyester thing. Black folks said
Toop was genuine juju hand. Others called him hoodoo from
the Louisiana bayou. Toop claimed he had the true John the
Conqueror Root, but other times he would call it the joint of
a kangaroo. No one was really sure what he had, but no one
would ever challenge his powers. He always carried his juju
bag with him wherever he went, along with a year's supply
of Preparation-H for his "ham-rods."

Toop worked out of the Blue Moon with his wife, Em-Em,
who must've been ninety years old and wore a blond wig hat
over a face as black as polished ebony. Em-Em carried an
electric fan with her at all times and would stand over it at
the drop of a hat. She fancied herself the black Marilyn
Monroe.

Not too many days went by at the Blue Moon without Em-
Em squealing "Fireballs o' the Eucharist" over her fan, her
ragged skirt flying up to her face, her spread legs looking like
a split topographical map of the Pyrenees.

"Fireballs o' the Eucharist!"

It was all she ever said, and nobody in Buckeye Road knew
what she meant by it.

She said it again as Beto, Claude and Louie walked out of
the lights of the bar and into the dark street.

"Fireballs o' the Eucharist!"

The boys turned back to see the sea of black faces staring
out at them as they left. None of the three knew it at the
time, but something had changed. Their fascination with the
people under the canvas had taken a subtle turn on this night
and had begun to die.

Wop-head and Spindley, the ice runners and liquor guards

at the Blue Moon, were standing together, staring at the boys.
They were a pair of ancient, clumsy cripples who'd found
each other in the same line years ago waiting to be fitted with
identical prosthetic appliances. Between them, they had two
good arms and ten good fingers.

Men and women with the "chemical" faces stared out. They
always garnered the most curiosity and pity. Beto found that
he could not help himself when he saw a chemical face. He
stared beyond all politeness . . . past the spotted and blotched
skin, right into the person's self-conscious eyes. It was as
though they represented walking, living despair. Their skin
was blotched black and pink where lye compounds or sulfuric
acid mixtures had been applied to whiten the skin.

Osiris Williams was the worst of these, and even he seemed
to be staring. His skin treatments had caused total blindness
in both eyes, or so he said. Some said that he had blinded
himself so that he would never again have to see the proof
and the folly of his desperation. Tonight, even Osiris had fear
in his dead eyes, fear of Toop, fear of the white police.

There were "sissy mans" watching the boys leave and
straining to see the lonely body in the distance. Normally they
would be prancing there under the canvas of the Blue Moon,
transvestites and homosexuals who were only marginally tol-
erated and were constantly ridiculed by other customers. They
were called "sissy mans" or "queers" by the patrons. "Maricones" or "pisaverdes" by the Mexicans, and "Bardache" by
Mister Andre, who said he got the word in Louisiana.

Beto thought that the sissy mans were the toughest people
in Buckeye Road. They had been hardened by their constantly
frustrated quest to be gentle. But on this night they were as
weak as their tormentors.

Manuel called the chemical people and the sissy mans the
Xipe after the ancient Toltec and Aztec god of the flayed and
god of the new corn.

"They worshiped Xipe by dancing in the stretched skin of
a sacrificial victim," he had once explained. "I think their
dances were not very well attended. But the god lives on.
There are Xipe worshippers everywhere these days, people
who want to wear a lighter skin or a younger one."

"No one here is going to help us," said Beto, turning away from the faces in the Blue Moon.

"We just can't leave him out here to rot," said Louie, swerving to the far side of the street to avoid the body.

As the boys walked slowly back toward the light of the Rainbo Market, where a single porch light had attracted a thousand moths, a voice behind them began to sing. It was the words of the Hiawatha Blues being composed even as they walked, the notes being picked out on a homemade git-box. Beto smiled now, his disgust with *los Negros* gone with the realization that they were indeed saying words over Hia-watha's body. Custom-made words about Hiawatha's life and death. He had seen the blues at the source. He turned back to watch the ashen fingers forcing sweat into the frets, a black face uplifted to moan an elegy.

Mr. Lee was standing below the light, the insects making a living halo above his head.

"I already call police, boys," said Mr. Lee, who scratched his butt as he said it, then realized that his father had done exactly the same thing when he worried.

"This bad, this bad. I try to sell this place now."

He shuffled to the back of the store shaking his head, know-ing he could not sell the Rainbo Market. He couldn't sell for years to come. First, the rest of the family had to be gotten out of China, then brought to America through British Co-lumbia. Immigration would require that they all have jobs. They would work in the Rainbo for him until they could afford to buy it. It's what he had done. It was what had been done to him. It was the only way.

Mr. Lee, who had almost forgotten his own true Chinese name and who had certainly forgotten it in its anglicized form, sat on a crate in the back of his store and watched his two small children on their elbows and their bellies, filling in their coloring books.

In Canton they would both be working now. His daughter, Maria, looked up and smiled, then silently returned to her coloring. His little son, Newton, was both left-handed and near-sighted, and it sorely worried his parents. They are even farther from their true names than I am, he thought. Named after the mother of the Christian God and a box of cookies with a fig filling.

The real Simon Lee was a child and would always be a child. He had died at the age of two, and the grieving family, somehow, on a wet Seattle day had given up that birth certificate so that another might come. He silently and selfishly prayed that his children would live forever and that no one would ever use their names.

Mr. Lee would watch from the steps of his store as Phoenix began to swallow up Buckeye Road. He would still be there at the Rainbo Market when the asphalt and sidewalks were laid down by the city and a sparkling new Circle-K convenience mart went up where the Blue Moon now stood.

"I have to tell Abuela about this," said Beto. "You guys can come over and eat if you want."

"No, that's okay, Beto," Louie said, smiling at his brother. "Tonight we got ham hocks."

As the boys walked down the steps to the bottom, they looked at each other, then turned and left two bottles of soda behind the trellis that hid the foundation work and the old basement underneath. They left a BW and a Bubble Up. Claude, without protest, left one of Louie's candies. As they separated to go home, Louie pointed and yelled out, "Look, the knife's gone."

Everyone in Buckeye knew about Boydeen and Hiawatha. It was a shame, they said, how he treated her, and didn't she have no more sense than to cleave unto a fool like that? Hiawatha was pure no 'count. Some in Buckeye blamed her for what happened. Little home wrecker. After all, she was better raised than he was, had a trade and all.

Boydeen had appeared alone and without baggage in Buckeye Road one day about two years before and shyly stepped into the Blue Moon one evening for a drink. She had come from Rankin County, Mississippi, a small town named Piney Woods. Her father was a Baptist minister who kept a small business to help sustain the ministry. He sold clear plastic covers for sofas and easy chairs and even lampshades. Her father was the sole southern representative for a small Ohio plastics company that was owned by Methodists.

The plastic covers guaranteed that no stains would ever soil a piece of soft furniture again. They also guaranteed that no one would ever want to lay eyes on it, much less sit on it.

The business did not prosper, nor did it perish. Either one would have been better. If the reverend had done his business in East Los Angeles, the Mexican families there would have made him rich. The plastic was a perfect complement for orange, crushed velvet lampshades and sprayed ceilings. If he had done his business in San Jose, the Filipino households there would have given him wealth beyond Midas. The product would have given that final touch to floral upholstery with matching wallpaper and plastic French provincial sconces. But he was in Mississippi, and once he had exhausted his small congregation as customers he was forced to pin his hopes each week on the wicker basket passed at Sunday services.

His hopes were seldom disappointed, and he believed his small congregation to be both loyal and generous. In reality they were a guilt-ridden lot, the plastic covers stuffed into closets, hidden in cupboards and only pulled out for an occasional visit by the Reverend himself.

His wife, Loretta, worked at a specialty bakery in Jackson. She did the frosting on custom-made birthday cakes, following designs and hand-drawn pictures brought in by white mothers from all over Hinds County. It was this vocation that caused her to covet a special name for their only daughter.

"How many white children can be named Brittany and Tiffany?" she asked herself incredulously after doing her third "Tiffany" cake of the day.

A standard new name, as standard as the pink lard and sugar rosettes she placed so carefully on the perimeter of the cakes. On the other hand she was not overly fond of the new urban black predilection for naming the child after the first thing the new mother sees in her hospital room after delivering the child. "Visine Robinson" did nothing for her, nor did "Aspirina," "Chlorina" or "Sylvania."

She thought of the boy in Piney Woods named General E. Williams (the E stood for electric). She shook her head at the thought and asked God to bless that poor child.

In the big cities black mothers were going for the "eeshas"

in a big way. Lateesha, Kaneesha, Vaneesha, Syeesha. She imagined an endless line of little black Shirley Temples.

It must be a black Baptist impulse, she mused. There's no need for a priest between us and a personal God, no need for convention to stand between us and a personalized name.

She had heard the name Boydeen in a restaurant in Harlem, where she had gone with her parents as a child. Boydeen was a waitress, a beautiful Liberian girl named after her great-grandfathers, both former slaves who had returned home, their Bassa and Vai tongues seeded with English.

The girl had waited on the family as though they were royalty. So the name waited twenty years from that table of food.

Twenty years for her only daughter.

Beto rushed into the house and dropped the bag of rice on the table. He had lost the butter somewhere in all the excitement. There was candlelight as usual in every room. Both *abuelitos* preferred them to light bulbs. Abuela was busy cleaning the small tapestry of the Last Supper that usually hung on the wall over the kitchen table.

"Abuela," the boy said breathlessly, "Boydeen, *la Negrita,* is hurt badly. She's hiding under the Rainbo right now and she's bleeding!"

"Was it that *chingon* Hiawatha?" asked Josephina, already knowing the answer. She put the tapestry down.

"He's dead. *Muerto.* He's still there in the street, and he had a bloody knife in his hand, but it's gone now."

"Was there anything in his hand? Did you see something in his hand?" she asked, the wrinkles on her forehead mirroring the concern beneath.

"Yes, he had an egg in his hand. It's still there."

"*Madre de Dios,*" she said, making the sign of the cross. "Now Boydeen will linger in pain unless something is done quickly. Were the police called, *hijo?*" Without waiting for an answer she said hurriedly, "That gives us two, maybe three days. Why didn't I see this? You wait here."

She got her black medicinal bag down from the shelf and hurriedly threw her mantilla over her hair and shoulders.

"Tell *su abuelo* . . ." but she was interrupted by his voice from the next room.

"Don't let no one see you over there, *mujer*."

She disappeared through the door facing east, then turned west and was gone.

"She runs away like the day."

The boy knew his grandfather had been drinking again. He stood there in the kitchen for a moment thinking about this long day that would never be forgotten and seemingly would not end. When he had first come to this part of Buckeye Road, he had seen a knife fight between a barefoot man and a small barefoot woman. They were both black and both stood by the roadside oblivious of the staring traffic going by or the people trying cautiously to intervene. They were intent only upon themselves. Both were cut and bleeding profusely. The hate he had seen that day in their eyes was unmitigated, unquenchable hate.

That man had been Hiawatha.

The other, a little, dark woman with a thin face, had two children by him and had been cut deeper by his infidelities and his words than by his knife. After numberless public humiliations, as everything in Buckeye was public when you lived on the street, she had had enough.

"She just a chile and you fuckin' around on me with her, and right in front of my face and in front of my friends. I gave you two babies and you fuck around on me with her! You ain't shit, old man. Both babies is mens, too. You don't care if it rains on your sons. You don't care if they eat good or starve. You let your friends stick they funky hands in my panties! Don't think I can't smell the vanvan oil you put on to drive me out. Conjure this!"

She lunged at him and caught him. The little woman survived that heart-sinking day. She took the kids and caught the Continental Trailways bus back to somewhere in Alabama, leaving Hiawatha's cuts to be tended by his new woman, Boydeen.

"Dem chilluns ain't the first I had and they sho' won't be

the last," he had said as she dropped her knife and walked away from him.

It was a mindless, nimble, cutting idiom, words he had heard spoken by his laughing, salacious friends at the Blue Moon and now found himself repeating. He never knew it as he said it; they were killing words. She had heard them before and had winced at them, but now for the first time they were aimed at her.

Neither the speaker nor the listener understood the chill it brought on or ever knew why the tongue and the ear, spitting and receiving this exact phrase, changed something in the atmosphere, excited some hideous harmonic and started dark sympathetic resonations below that would spread unchecked from them both.

They had come from families with mean, absent fathers and embittered mothers. Now, they had passed the bitter gift on with this blood-letting ceremony, more ironclad than any Last Will and Testament done by a clean, white lawyer.

Hiawatha's small sons, waiting at the depot in Fort Worth to transfer to the Fort Worth-Montgomery bus, sitting together on a wooden pew and splitting a Charleston Chew, would always remember those words. The words were stuck in their supple, green muscles, tearing like a fishhook, a rusted barb left behind from an old accident. Cruel rust, heading for the heart. Their mama had to cut the romance from her own breast just to live on, after those cutting words. Frostbite words.

"Abuelo, I gave your soda to Boydeen, your Bubble Up."

As he said it his hand brushed across the bulge that was the ten-dollar bill and the letter stuffed into his pocket, Vernetta's letter.

"Vernetta got a letter today. I'm going to take it to her."

"No," Manuel responded, his face now suddenly sober.

"Let your grandmother take it to her. Let her take it. Besides, I wanted a Mission Orange. But, come on now," he said, rising from his chair and walking over to the boy, "let's eat. No one's going to serve dinner to us tonight. We *hombres* have to fend for ourselves."

They walked together to the wooden table in the kitchen

and sat down in the candlelight. Both turned their own tortillas on the *comal*, then spread *refritos* on them.

"*Un poquito queso, un poquito chorizo, y cebolla,*" the old man whispered and exhaled his words as he tossed the condiments on with his fingers. "A little atomic energy," he grinned as he grabbed a *jalapeño* and ate it whole.

He woke to the sound. It was a low, quavering moan and the boy, frightened to the end of his wits, opened only one eye and that one only the smallest slit. Now he was sorry that he had fallen asleep with his back to the doorway and knew that it would take all of his courage to turn over.

What if it was the man with the white bulldog? The man who had been killed on the railroad tracks many years ago while walking his dog. People around here still saw them both. People still saw them entering and leaving this very adobe house. Beto wondered why he had never seen the small white man with the black Irish linen cap and red scarf walking his old dog. Strangers would talk to the man and pet the dog only to find out later that they both had been dead for years. Abuela said she often saw them.

"The man moves his mouth but can't speak. He's lonely," she would say, "and he wants to send one last message to his wife."

The low moan came again, but this time he heard his grandmother's voice along with it. Mustering all his courage, he turned his head as fast as he could and, to his great relief, saw no one in the doorway. He got out of his bed and walked toward the blanket that was hung in the archway, giving him some privacy.

There was a yellow light burning on the other side. He could see through the blanket that his *abuela* was on her knees, and someone, not Manuel, was sitting in the rocker. When he pushed the blanket aside, he saw Boydeen—her soiled shirt was completely off of her body and heaped on the floor near her feet. Rags soaked with blood and hydrogen peroxide were piled in a pan to the side of the chair. She had a dazed, innocent and distant look in her eyes.

She looked strangely young to the boy. He thought she no longer looked like an adult. She looked like a child. Josephina was carefully sewing her breast closed. Stitches climbed from the lower heft of her breast up past her sooty-colored nipple, each perforation a dot of claret against ebony skin.

"This is not for boys to see," Josephina hissed, another needle between her teeth.

Manuel, who was holding Boydeen's head in one hand and a glass of whiskey near her drooling mouth with the other, motioned with his head and eyes for the boy to return to bed.

Instead, the boy stepped toward his *abuela*. He reached into his pocket and dropped the envelope and some money on her black dress where it had fanned out behind her knees. There was Sugar Dee's ten-dollar bill and seven dollars of his own saved from selling *café con canela*.

"The money is for her," he said, then walked slowly back to bed.

6

History You Can Eat

If you gaze out into the desert even now, in the present day, the hawk still harries its prey and the falcon turns with rippling wings on planes of rising air. Even now the coyote runs alone and the chuckawalla and the silica hide in the sand. It seems timeless. It's as though the desert itself can bring time to a stop.

But there are, in truth, three kinds of time. There is the collision of moments that we all know, the sequential measurement of our actions and our days. The time that is warped by mass.

There is mythological time; the time of gardens; of Eden and Aztlán. It is a time when all times, past, present and future, may coexist.

Then there is Mexican time.

The Aztecs believed that Quetzalcóatl, the plumed serpent, was the inventor of time. They believed that he mixed life and death with the sun and the moon to fabricate the hours. The Aztec priests bundled time into parcels of years; reeds were pulled from the lake, then cut and carefully tied together. The largest reed bundles represented spans of fifty-two years. When Quetzalcóatl left his people to sail into the sun, he promised them he would return at the end of one bundle and

the beginning of the next. Instead, it was Cortés who came
in the year 1 Reed, at the start of a bundle of time.

Yet Mexican time is older even than the Aztecs, who probably learned their long count from the Maya or the Olmec.
Mexican time is a *mestizo* time, a mixture of the mythological
and the sequential, but even beyond this mixture there is
something else. There is a time machine. Mexicans have a
time machine. It is a mechanism that re-creates all times at
once and allows all who participate to breathe the past; to
touch every bundle of time; to taste the ages. It is called a
fiesta.

Three weeks after the adobe was completed, on a warm
Sunday after church, the hugging, chatting people began to
trickle in for the housewarming fiesta. All who had been to
church were still dressed in their best clothing and glowing
with the piety of the morning's sermon. Others did the best
they could. There were spit-shined cowboy boots and newly
dyed high heels everywhere. In the yard there were bare feet
and shoes made of tape. They had been taped up so often
that no one knew if there was any leather left.

The week before, when she was satisfied with the location
of her furniture, Josephina had asked her grandson to go
out and invite the people that he wanted to come to the
fiesta.

"Anyone that I choose, Abuelita?"

The old woman had closed her eyes in mock disgust, then
nodded her head yes.

"You can bring abominations into our home," she said with
sarcasm.

"You can bring those old hobos and that *pendejo* with the
hairdo, but no *ateos*. Do you hear me? No atheists! Now, go
tell them to clean themselves before crossing my threshold."

She crossed herself as the boy ran off. She knew where he
was going. He would invite *los sinónimos y los maricones* and
that greasy hairdo with a little man underneath it.

All at once she laughed out loud. She startled herself with
the force of the laughter and wondered at its origin. For all
the desolation of this place, there was a lot of life here, she
thought. Nothing fancy. Basic life like the cactus and the

wildflowers. Twisted life like the desert plants that had learned to live on nothing but a drop of rain a year.

Behind the Blue Moon was a row of rotting, sun-bleached, connected seats that had been recklessly scavenged from a demolished movie house; the lag bolts and anchors still clung to the feet, each arm welded to the next like a line of galley slaves. This was the Blue Moon's informal convalescent home. The geriatrics sat there talking the whole day away in the shade of the canvas. When not doing a traditional "telling" to the children, an allegorical tale that required straightforward narration, the old ones followed to the letter the ancient rule that old black men sitting together must repeat everything six times.

Though Beto loved to hear the old African tales told, it was the singsong of everyday speech that lured him in to listen.

"It sure is hot," one would say, a red hanky to his brow.

"I reckon you is right about the heat," his compatriot would sing back.

"Yeah, it's hot. It's hot," said a third.

"Uh, hum, burning," from the chorus.

"Yeah, burnin' up."

"Goddamn temperature."

Convention required the introduction of at least one new subject before returning to any previous subject. Having applied the rule of six to any new subject, any previous subject is once again subject to said rule.

"That Em-Em sho' be ugly."

"Uh, huh, bitch face stop a clock."

"Shit, stop a goddamn train."

"Yeah, her tears come out, get a load o' dat mug and go right back where dey come from."

"Left leg look like the Sandia Mountains."

"And that goddamol' fan. You think that's hair down there or flies."

"Big leg bitch."

"Do us all a favor and put on some panties."

"And what the shit is a Fireball o' the Eucharist?"

The factorials were endless, exponential; a googolplex. One

would call out the new subject and the rest would respond. Four *viejitos negros* could talk all day, each one having only five decent things to say. Any lull was taken up by a discussion of the weather. It was a song in the fields where they once sat a century ago pulling seeds from cotton bolls. It was a work song for the killing times on the savannah; for the skinning of gazelle on the veldt; for the work of living another day on S.S.I.

Josephina called these old, black men *"los sinónimos,"* the synonyms, for obvious reasons.

Beto had walked up to them carefully, still a little wary about being near the Blue Moon.

"We're gonna have a housewarming fiesta next Sunday afternoon, and *mi abuela* says I can invite you. Can you come?"

"Does I smell me a bowl of salsa?"

"Uh, hum, chile sauce."

"Yeah, a red pepper sauce."

"Muhfuh *picante salsa*."

"Seems I smells me a messakin condiment."

"Mo-lay poblana."

All those words meant yes.

Upon seeing Beto approaching the do-stand, Mister Andre had flashed his gold teeth at the boy and bowed gracefully at the waist.

"I sho' will be dee-lighted to attend your little function. Fo' yo' sweet grandmother I will unveil a new creation which I shall wear upon my own nappy cranium. I call it the Inquisition since everybody is goin' to ask how I did it."

He was smiling again and hoping that his teeth were catching the sun. He loved to glint. As a younger man he had considered deeper philosophical questions of being and nonbeing. There was half a diploma from Howard University in every sentence he spoke. He had dropped out of school for lack of funds and began doing hair to pay for room and board and to save for tuition, but the distance between himself and Descartes soon became insurmountable.

"I comb, therefore I is," he would smile.

Now, as an older man, he was satisfied that a gold sparkle

reflected from his teeth onto Beto's face proved his own existence.

"I will even bathe."

Thanks to Mister Andre, "Conks-jobs" were everywhere in Buckeye Road and incredibly diverse. Strutting, crowing, signifying conk-jobs. Lye and pomade mixtures were applied to the hair to straighten it and train it. Do-rags were tied around the head to preserve the shape until the time came to unveil the work.

The Blue Moon had an in-house do-parlor behind the bar and the architect in residence was a man whose only name was Mister Andre. His own do was a wonder of a cantilever job that extended half a foot in front of his face. His handwritten sign proclaimed that he had once applied hotcomb and Dixie Peach Pomade to the head of none other than Little Willie John, whose autographed picture was stapled to the sign.

"Yeah, I sho' fried Little Willie. Fried his nappy head right on up. Bonified conkified the muhfuh!"

Mister Andre claimed that he had "done" Clyde Mcphatter and Hank Ballard, and all the Midnighters, too.

"If you are interested," Mister Andre had smiled once to Beto and his friends, "I got a menu here for you."

Each of his front teeth had a gold star in it.

His menu of hairdos was typed up and sealed in a yellowed plastic sheath.

"Now le'see you can have a three-finger wave for five dollars, a quo-vadis for six dollars, a bird's nest for six-fifty and a Lord Jesus for ten dollars. The Lord Jesus is the almightiest do f'yo' head. With a Lord Jesus do you can be ace-number-one, King Shit, my man!"

A neck rub was also available for fifty cents or a two-dollar comb-out if your do just needed a tad of spiffin'. To the straight-haired children of Buckeye, the Indians and the Mexicans and Okies, the wonder of the do-parlor was something forever foreclosed to them. Many children actually resented it and some Pima kids, to the supreme dismay of their parents, wore do-rags anyway.

The *maricones'* bus was located in the field between the Blue Moon and Cady and represented the only real competition that Mister Andre's do-parlor had. *Los maricones* were the transvestites, the homosexuals that had pulled their bus into Buckeye from parts unknown. The bus was painted yellow with the words THE SECRET SHARER scrawled in large white letters on the side. The words THE RACHEL were blackened out next to it, but still visible. As he walked toward the bus, Beto knew that the five girls would love to fuss and fret over a coming social event.

They were two blacks, two whites and one Mexican, boys who met at college, the University of Texas at El Paso, and who had managed to turn their mutual misery and alienation into an odyssey.

Together, they had discarded their Jaymar Sans-a-belt slacks and Levi's with the button-down fly. They tossed out their Fruit of the Looms, their letter sweaters, their Hush Puppies and wing tips. They opened the doors to the secret closets within their closets. Together, in quiet ceremony, they renamed each other and, like Adam, gained dominion, but only over themselves and only to some degree.

Robert became Angelique. Wilson, after suffering through three failed personas, became Diablo. Roosevelt had settled on Evangeline a decade before while reading the poem to his grade-school class. Lawrence chose the name Starlet. He had been the last to choose, and the others felt that the hesitancy might go deeper than just the choice of name. But Lawrence did finally choose, and his new name was chanted over and over by the others as an act of acceptance and familiarity. The incantation sealed it; Starlet could not go back.

Francisco took the name Panocha, a Mexican brown-sugar candy, among other meanings.

Buckeye was not aware of it, but the portals of that bus gazed upon the future. When it first arrived in Buckeye, the bus created quite a stir. In the right light at the right distance with the eyes squinted just so, these were women. These were slender, lissome, well-coiffed career girls. These were spindly legged, high-heeled young things obviously lost in

Buckeye and walking helplessly across the dusty roads to coyly ask directions.

These were a Chinese silk jacket with matching clutch bag, a stunning brown skirt with a matching top of silk *peau de soie*. These were riding pants and boots, a daring little dark green blouse under a herringbone jacket. And best of all: a riding crop. These were black toreadors above gold slippers and below the naughtiest little waistcoat.

The local sissy mans were just sad cartoons of these. Stunned at this new sight, the catty locals first turned on their own, biting and scratching and calling each other tired old queens. In a frenzy of jealous self-hate they tore at one another, littering 14th Street with foam pads and sprawling, lifeless wig hats.

Then, the catharsis complete, feeling humiliated and displaced by the audacity and color of these newcomers, a platoon of sissy mans gathered in the dusty heat of Buckeye Road. There, the day after the arrival of the bus, they conspired. Those that wore wigs donned and rearranged them. Then, together they undulated ambiguously over to the bus and pelted it with plates of corned beef hash with side orders of green beans, the plat du jour at Favorita's concession.

Instead of the anticipated anger, spiteful threats and retribution, the five *maricones* descended their carriage in dignified array, weapons in hand, and did six complete facial makeovers on the spot. Sneers were softened a bit and lip-penciled away. The five who had turned the other cheek highlighted the cheekbones of their would-be tormentors with shades of red, crimson and carnelian and reviled them softly with simple and quick beauty tips. Teasing combs and eyelash curlers, their armament, had carried the field. Raised hackles were rinsed, teased down and sprayed into place.

The *maricones'* bus soon became a mecca, a magnet for those who wanted an alternative to Mister Andre and his electric irons, his gallon cans of Dixie Peach and his clammy dollops of Butch Wax.

Though preached against mightily by the Reverend Willie Drake as abominations in the sight of God, the five girls

quickly became the social and cultural center of secular Buckeye Road. The boy had become good friends with all five.
The anomalies of their gender and their dress were only cu-
riosities and wholly secondary to their conversation, their
language. Aside from the good reverend, they were the only
formally educated people in Buckeye, and Beto found them
to be the most interesting.

Their bus was filled to the luggage racks with clothing and
cosmetics, books and cooking utensils. Their record machine
played only Italian opera and Mozart, the sound of the castrati
different from any other voice, they said. Their presence created a minor renaissance in Buckeye. The incumbent transvestites were soon coming every day to the ochre bus for
fashion and sewing hints and to read up on the latest Swedish
sex-change techniques.

"The men around here look better 'n the fuckin' women,"
growled Odabee, reaching across his body with his right hand
and into his left pants pocket.

"That pretend pussy look better 'n the real thang."

He felt the key to his Lincoln was still there. He needed to
squeeze it a bit to separate it from the nickels and dimes, but
that done he was reassured. He could save money in that
pocket seeing as how he couldn't reach it. He reached over
the opposite way to see if his friend Dismas Skully was conscious. Finding that he wasn't, he stole his wine.

Sugar Dee and Potrice were seen at the bus every day now.
They did specialty shopping in Phoenix for the girls and in
exchange were allowed to use the kitchen inside the bus to
prepare their own meals. To Sugar Dee and Potrice these were
sisters, or men who wanted nothing of them but friendship.
It didn't matter which.

Though he was often invited, Beto seldom ate meals at the
bus. His friends Claude and Louie ate there every chance they
got and would then run off to eat somewhere else, their thank-
yous still in their throats. Beto thought the food was tasty,
but there was never very much of it. It just wasn't the Mexican
way to serve such sparse plates. Mexicans embrace one another with their meals, sumptuous, ample embraces.

These girls could serve twenty people with one sliced-up

piece of meat. They called them medallions. They had been sauteed in clarified butter and whole black peppercorns. They would put the medallion on a plate, then finger two stalks of steamed asparagus around a slice of tomato until some semblance of symmetry was accomplished. A dollop of curried mayonnaise would be centered on the tomato.

No one knew it at the time, but this dusty desert lot with a small bus at one corner was the Kitty Hawk of the West Coast gay restaurant industry. Angelique, her hand on a thesaurus, wondered if a string of adjectives in front of every noun on the menu wouldn't make the entrées sound more seductive.

"East Indies veal medallions *au poivre* with French Camp asparagus spears."

She sat there pondering, on the fringe of destiny, as Beto ran up to the bus to invite them to a soiree, the social event of the entire Buckeye season. Of course they would come!

"*Mon Dieu*, the sewing that has to be done, the perms, the facials!" cried Angelique.

"All I own are rags," sighed Panocha as Beto ran off to find Potrice and Sugar Dee.

Like all things Mexican, the *fiesta* began with the separation of the women from the men, all tensions in Mexican life being a variable of the distance and duration of that separation and the splendor and anger of moments when it lapsed. It is an inverse square relationship.

"The *vaqueros* wait outside, *mijo*," Manuel explained.

The boy saw their chromed horses gleaming and parked every which way; all the radios were tuned to the same Spanish station and would stay on until the live music arrived.

The hunters, the Apaches and Mayos, were squatting in circles and smoking. They bantered together in different areas outside.

Anxious suitors, having followed their loved ones from the church, paced quietly just outside the front entrance, overtures in abeyance. Their stylized, silent serenade could only be sung from without to someone within. The agony of expectation hovered there outside, while coyness and patience moved demurely within.

All the women, irrespective of age, gathered inside to organize the kitchen work while the men stayed out in the sun or in the small shade of the lean-to or the *ramada*. They went to the kitchen but only after first placing their hats, gloves and purses on Josephina's bed, a figurative paean to an ancient source of power.

In the kitchen they joined in the noisy gossip and the peaceable making of a meal that would soon be rapaciously devoured.

The distance and duration was at its greatest now, the fence about the enclosed garden at its highest.

The beans and rice had already been prepared and were being kept warm on the oven. The women would subdivide into two groups, one to make the *enchiladas de pollo y queso* and one to make the tamales. Little girls in white, flowered dresses were sent out with trays of *antojitos* for the men; red and green salsa and stacks of chips. There were plates of fry bread *y papas* for *los Indios*.

Some girls were put to work rinsing the buckets of corn husks that had soaked all night or set to whipping the small vat of white *manteca*. Thirty pounds of *masa* was hand-mixed into eight pounds of *manteca*, three quarts of red chili sauce and enough beef broth to facilitate the mix without softening it. Sixty pounds of boneless, lean beef and pork had been simmering since dark morning.

Josephina had risen before Vernetta's light was extinguished for the evening. While Vernetta cried, Josephina was slicing the meat and piling it into the vat. That done she had walked out into the dawn for more mesquite branches to burn when she saw the flock of pigeons circling overhead.

"Vernetta's dreams," she said to herself and walked back inside to stoke the fire. It had been Beto's job to keep the embers in the stove glowing while Josephina went to church. As this was such an important day, she had eschewed her usual Catholic services in downtown Phoenix for a short walk to the Mighty Clouds of Joy, where she was welcomed in as a member.

The beef and pork had simmered all morning. Since before dawn, it had been swimming with fifty cloves of garlic, ten chopped onions, cups of crushed *comino* and a handful of *cilantro*. Then it had been brought out of the broth to cool so that it could be shredded. Beto and Manuel had gladly done the shredding. They would be the first to taste the meat.

The salsa had been made days before, and a huge pot of it sat waiting on the stove above the embers. Señora Vasquez had come two days early, her skinny son, Edmundo, lugging a paper sack filled with dark, carmine chiles bought for her especially from a certain *mercado* in *Ciudad Juarez*, a little store in her old neighborhood in the old country.

She and Josephina had turned the red chiles on the embers till the skins pulled away easily. Then the red flesh had been ground by hand on the stone *metate* along with the potent seeds. Garlic cloves followed the chile into the *metate*. To the garlic and chile were added a bit of broth from the meat pot, some sifted Gold Medal flour, and a handful of oregano. The chile sauce, according to Virginia Vasquez, could only be simmered in one of her old, battered pots. She had brought a trunkload of the pots with her and made sure that everyone used them.

"It takes no effort to be loyal to something that serves you so well and so long. These pots have freed me from always wanting new things in my kitchen."

Her duty as keeper of the chiles done, Virginia had gone home with her son in tow to return on Sunday, the appointed day. The broth from the meat would be added to her salsa with more garlic cloves, then reduced down in one of her pots before some of the shredded meat was poured back in. Then all would be simmered together until Buckeye Road itself was rendered, permeated, saturated with the glorious scent of it.

The selfish heat always gave in to this fragrance and kept it down to the earth, where it wafted through Cady, waking even that ashy, reptilian crew, their lashing tongues tasting the air. It floated to the bus, where the five girls nervously made ready for their debut appearance at a Buckeye function. It wound its way to Tar-Paper, where Manassus and Johnna Perkins took their Sunday sponge baths in preparation for the event.

Just across the lot the yellow light would not come on at all today, and Vernetta, her face under green mud, made ready. She had smelled the aromas now for two days and realized that as much as she had loved her own mother's cooking, there were no smells like these in Arkansas.

They reminded her of that ride so long ago when J.B. and she had crossed into Bossier Parish, Louisiana, and headed straight for the Gulf. Black faces at their destination had welcomed him inside noisily but had only stared coolly at her.

Inside an unpainted wooden house there had been an enormous bowl of hoppin' John, and on the fire, creole okra was sauteed with shallots, cayenne and tomatoes. There had been lace cookies and *pain patate* alongside square pans of pecan pie. Her tongue had been resurrected from its Ozarkian torpor that night. She considered then that food was another translation of life.

A recipe is history, she thought as the piquant memory of her lover flooded up into her nose.

The aromas outside her trailer were like those had been. Around her trailer and around the folds of her blanched knees, the tomillo and oregano, once dead and dried, came back to life, rose up with the *comino* and the *cilantro* to fill the air, to resurrect the butcher's work.

"V equals the speed of the moving frame," she said aloud to herself, just as the scents made her swoon.

It calmed her. She repeated the laws of physics to compose herself.

"T-1 is the time between clicks on the moving frame, and T-2 is the time on the stationary frame."

She sat breathing steadily. Her voice began to break as she spoke the familiar words.

"C is the speed of light."

Across the lot from the Highway Comet, a long line of women would be forming to make tamales. Hands only, they bent husk around corn, then passed it on. Then cornmeal was formed around meat.

"You think it's just food, boy," one of the old *Indios* suddenly addressed himself to Beto.

"Shit, it's history you can eat. The *tamal* is history you can eat."

He made an eating motion with his right hand toward his mouth, then smiled.

"You see, we were once, long ago, hunters for meat. Then we learned to raise our own animals. So the meat is there at the center of things. Then we were given the gift of the corn. So the corn is second, on the outside," he said, while making a cupping motion with his hands.

"It is the generations, boy. The farmer enclosing the hunter, then the herdsman. In Mexican kitchens"—he smiled again —"Cain lets Abel live."

The enchilada group, led by Virginia, worked in relative seclusion in a corner of the kitchen. The enchiladas would use the same red chile salsa for their sauce, but with a difference. Sage and basil would be added. Virginia, after making sure that no one was spying on her, had surreptitiously dumped the spices in.

Twelve dozen corn tortillas were fried in hot oil for no more than thirty seconds each, then set to drain on paper. The next group took the softened tortillas and drowned them in a flat pan of Virginia's chile sauce. Each anointed tortilla was then stuffed with spiced and shredded chicken and onions, rolled and placed in a shallow pan with others of its kind. Cheese was spread over a filled pan and chile poured over that. These were set aside for later, when they would make a short trip to the oven just before the offerings were laid to table.

Virginia's husband, Arnulfo, had gone straight to the *ramada*, where the men were busy drinking in the shade. He squatted down in his tight new Dickie jeans after greeting his old friends and meeting some new ones. Then he ceremoniously rolled up his sleeves for some serious drinking among men. His small son, Edmundo, had run off to set up a game of marbles with some Pima kids.

The house swelled with people, with words and with the scent of lighted candles. The old Yaquis had appeared from the south, from somewhere in the desert, and waited patiently with Manuel for their food.

Johnna Perkins and Manassus brought over a pan of Spam scrapple that Josephina rushed to take off Johnna's hands. As she did so she said in Spanish for everyone in the house to hear, "You have to eat this." It was an order.

The Mayos and the Papagos came, all loaded into a single straining pickup.

The gaggle of *sinónimos* and Mr. Andre walked over from the Blue Moon together. The old men were going on and on about Mr. Andre's incredible hairdo that looked for all the world like someone had dumped a plate of black spaghetti on his head.

Even Wysteria Maybelle, the local *loca*, showed up with her dogs. Old Wysteria Maybelle was an ancient white woman who lived in a cardboard cabin in the small wash behind Tar-Paper. It was said that her late husband had been a railroad man. She was a deft and mobile pile of life wrapped in four layers of sweaters under the sweltering Phoenix sun. She was too obscure for age.

She was a wraith, a harmless collection of seeming expletives that defied eye contact. Words burst from the old woman's mouth like cherry pits, though none were ever for her own kind and none of her own kind ever heard.

Whenever Beto caught sight of her, he imagined that her words spun around her soft center like shells of electrons.

She was the kind of woman you talked to only through her dogs. Six dogs in all, some lunging and humping while others pranced and romped in a dusty whirl around her crusty skirt and taped-up lumberjack shoes.

She was a hunched, flea-ridden enigma of wrinkles under rags. Somehow, impossibly, she loved Andrew Marvell. She'd named every animal she owned after the poet. She had for a decade. Somehow all those crazy outbursts to her dogs, taken as a whole, were always in perfect meter.

The five girls from the Secret Sharer arrived, causing an immediate sensation with their clothing.

"A hunting motif," Angelique explained before gliding into the kitchen with the rest of the women.

Starlet lingered outside for a moment, drinking in the stares from the men, pretending they meant something other than disdain.

The Reverend Willie Drake and Sister Dora Mae arrived
after a short stopover at the church. The reverend was thin
as a rail, the pants of his black suit no wider than the sleeves
of his coat. His wife, however, was four times his size, and
the tiny new pumps she had tortured her feet into that morning were already spreading at the seams.

The Cheungs brought their wagon with them; they could
never have left it unattended across the street from Cady.
Mrs. Cheung was wearing a beautiful silk dress, deep red
with yellow-and-green butterflies. Her tiny slippers were
hand-embroidered and had not touched the dust in years.

Vernetta ambled over just after six o'clock with a pot of
tapioca pudding under one arm and a bottle of maraschino
cherries on the other. She'd wow 'em with this dessert.

"That time at the My-T-Freeze wasn't a total waste."

Claude and Louie followed behind her, carrying a case of
Delaware Punch for the kids and two cases of Pabst Blue
Ribbon for the men. Vernetta, her ample rear end swaying
like the pendulum of a grandfather clock, advertised her
bleach blond way past the dark men at the *ramada* and into
the crowd of women.

As with all such *Mexicano* events, someone fought with
someone else. Someone's ex showed up drunk. An *Indio*
pulled a knife. Someone tore an antenna from a car and bran-
dished it before passing out. A suitor left, angrily tossing some
flowers and spinning the wheels of his Hudson Hornet in the
soft gravel.

A young woman in a white dress with red flowers and
surrounded by a throng of sympathizers cried inconsolably
out of jealousy.

Tía Lencha fell down.

A trio sang songs that became more and more maudlin as
the evening wore on. Some who can recall say that "Caminos
de Guanaguato" was played fifteen times. Arnulfo and Tío
Jorge cried together during the last three renditions.

"*La vida no vale nada.*"

At dusk an Indian child needed the cactus needles removed
from his back. Some *borrachones* demanded a fashion show of
the five *maricones*, but the women in the kitchen had rushed

outside to defend them and ushered Angelique and the girls
safely indoors.

All the food was gone by two in the morning. Tamales *y*
enchiladas had been dispatched to every corner of Buckeye
Road, and sleeping children lay everywhere.

At the very end of the evening, the jumper cables were
pulled out and passed around between good-byes. Jumper
cables held aloft are the traditional sign that a Mexican social
event has ended.

When Wysteria Maybelle finally rose from her first hot meal
in years, she began the task of rounding up her six dogs for
the trip back to her cabin. The *perritos* had gorged themselves
all night on scraps and had gone looking for more. One of
them, a huge German shepherd, had wandered around the
back of the *adobe* and found the heaping garbage can near the
kitchen door. When Josephina saw the dog, she'd let out a
terrible scream. Then she fell sobbing to the floor.

"*Soy una viuda!*" she'd cried softly.

"I'm a widow!" she whispered tearfully until one of the old
Yaquis assured her that the dog was certainly not Apache.
Beto had never seen her so desolated. Her elation in the very
next moment was even more confusing to him.

"Why is she crying?" Beto asked Tío Jorge. A barely conscious Arnulfo responded for his comatose *compadre*.

"If you could see *el futuro*, you might not want to go there
either."

Arnulfo could barely keep his eyes open. It was clear that
he would sleep deep into the afternoon.

"No matter how far away you go," he managed, "no matter
where in this world, from El Paso to Salinas"—he swept one
limp arm to demonstrate enormous distance—"the food you
had tonight and the *música Mexicana* that you heard . . . there
will never be better."

Arnulfo's arm dropped and he slept.

The old Yaquis stayed outside all night, and at dawn they
formally blessed the house. Not this house, specifically, but
the one that had always been there.

7

Whatever Descends into Flesh

Josephina knocked on the trailer door, even though she knew that Vernetta was watching and waiting for her. She had watched her walking all the way from the adobe and across the lot to the trailer.

Vernetta had sensed something, and the fact that Josephina had knocked had only reinforced the feeling. Josephina never, ever knocked. When the yellow porch light was out, this was her home, too. There had been a formality in the old woman's walk on that morning, in her knock. There was a charge in the air, a rift in the space that had couched Vernetta's life. Then there had been nothing, no light, no sound as everything that was Vernetta's world collapsed into a small white, paper rectangle that Josephina had held in her right hand. Vernetta had fainted for an instant, her head hitting the small pane of glass on her front door.

As she received the letter she had seen that Josephina's smile was wistful, distant. That was two weeks ago. She had been preparing herself for the trip, even then, thought Vernetta. The trip to Flagstaff. Would it be a pilgrimage or a heresy? Vernetta felt the precious letter in her hand and realized that for the moment she did not care.

Now, disheveled and drawn, she watched as Josephina packed her small, cracking leather suitcase. The old woman

smiled confidently, but her stiff movements betrayed her true
feelings to her friend.

"I can't talk now," she said softly. "I think I should pray.
Maybe it's too late for that now."

Vernetta began to respond, but Josephina cut her off with
a look.

"We'll talk more in the morning. God's will can be a confusing thing. Right now I have to pack my bag."

It was on Josephina's bed splayed open. One side held two
Bibles, one Spanish and one English in matching brown cardboard bindings. The same side held a rosary, a small picture
of Jesus Christ, three O Henry candy bars, some Sen-Sens
and some of the well-used jars from her medicinal bag.

"I have to leave early in the morning," Josephina explained
to her grandson, who was standing next to Vernetta.

The other side held soap and lotions, underwear and a dress
and mantilla that were almost identical to the ones she wore.
There were two crosses, and a pocket of the suitcase held her
old brown cloth.

"I'm only going for a few days, *mijo*. You have to mind the
house and give Manuel his coffee in the morning. I will have
some other things for you to do."

"I can make my own damn coffee, *mujer*," his voice had
come from outside.

"You never have, and when you do it's like mud and not
fit for Christians," she retorted. "Anyway, there's a pot of
beans and I have some tortillas made and there are cans of
soups and Pet milk and a box of Shredded Wheat over there.
There's some *queso* in the icebox if you want a *quesadilla*.
There's also a box of Quaker Puffed Rice. You can have some
chicharones, but not too many. There's money where it always
is, but don't go crazy with it, Beto."

"Where are you going, Abuela?"

She looked down at him thoughtfully, then said, "I'm going
to Flagstaff on an errand."

Her eyes met Vernetta's as she spoke.

"It's for Vernetta, isn't it?"

She didn't answer the question at first. She snapped the
suitcase shut and tested the brass locks. Then she lifted the

suitcase and tested its weight in her right hand. Satisfied that
she could carry it easily, she set it near the front door, where
it would wait till the early morning.

"Her son is up in Flagstaff," she said, letting the words out
one at a time.

Vernetta nodded her permission.

"You know she lost him a long time ago."

The words came from behind her teeth like reluctantly released prisoners. She didn't want to lie to him; he was getting
too old for that. Besides, she thought, lying to children ages
you; each lie to a child is one more wrinkle. But he was still
too young for these kinds of truths, she thought. She was
glad that Vernetta was there.

"My son is up in Flagstaff," Vernetta said. "He's just a little
older than you are. His name is Danny and he lives with his
relatives."

"Are they your family?" asked the boy.

"No" was all she said.

She knew. On that night over ten years ago, she knew that
her father and her two brothers had been told. She just knew
they had.

Just like she knew that the phone call to Wakely would cap
off Norvell's night real fine, what with the new sign breaking
and having to shut down the restaurant early. But Norvell
didn't have to hit J.B. so hard, she thought. It was harder
than just a white man hittin' a nigga who'd just had a white
woman; it was evil hard, hateful.

Jesus, he went and hit him across the mouth twice, then
dragged him to the front door right in front of all those staring
customers. J.B. never even put his hands up. He just dropped
the spatula from his hand, then pulled up his pants. He just
stood there and took it.

"Here's your mulatto Einstein," he'd screamed over and
over again as he'd kicked J.B. in the side. "Goddamn nigga
Einstein. Got above his place."

Norvell, in his fervor, had even knocked over that precious

new sign of his, the My-T-Freeze clown with all the neon hair and the red light bulb nose you were supposed to see all the way from the highway, and that had made him even madder. Sweating and bellowing, he ran to the storage room and came back out with J.B.'s books. He walked to the front door and heaved them out, notes flying everywhere.

"This ain't your business, Norvell," Vernetta had screamed, pulling on Norvell's jacket, her panties in her pocket and the proof of the thing, chalky and dripping slowly down her leg.

"Wakely's got to know," Norvell had sneered as J.B. pulled away and pushed the door open before looking back dolefully at them.

"Wakely's got to know his daughter's givin' pussy to a nigga boy."

They had waited up for her. She could see the three of them sitting together at the kitchen table like always, three sets of overalls and three sets of bad teeth. The two younger ones, both duplicates of the elder, were drinking coffee with hot milk and chicory and dunking their sugared *beignets*. All three burst out laughing at one point, and one of them suddenly ran to the sink, the coffee running from his nose. If they think it's funny, she thought, somebody or something musta gotten hurt. Probably some poor doe taken out of season.

For a moment she imagined a beautiful female deer slung obscenely to a fender. She took a moment to really stare hard at them and realized that she would not miss any of the three men when she left this house. Wakely was never much of a father to Vernetta, and now that such thoughts crossed her mind, she suspected that he wasn't much of a husband to her mother either. Not like J.B. would be. She had never seen Wakely hold her mother's hand, not like J.B. held hers. She had never even seen them kiss in all those years together.

Wakely was hard and silent, and tonight she knew he would be both and probably crazy mad. It was always his way, nothin' or too much. He hadn't beat her in a couple of years now. Not since that time she'd gone into the pin money. She knew she could take it if he did.

Vernetta's shift ended at eleven o'clock, and she had spent

the whole time after J.B. had gone trying to talk Norvell out
of calling her father. The My-T-Freeze was almost empty, and
the cook was someplace out in the dark, bleeding, so Norvell
chased out his few remaining customers and closed down the
restaurant. Just the two of them were left, sitting in different
booths lit only by the light of the marquee. There was glass
at their feet from the multicolored neon tubes that had
splashed all over his linoleum floor.

"Fuckin' exploded my sign," he said at last.

"Imploded," said Vernetta sternly.

Then, after more silence, he'd started by lecturing on the
evils of mixing the races, stuff about how raccoons and 'pos-
sum don't mix, but before long the counterfeit words gave
way.

"You coulda had all of this, Verny"—his arm swept across
the room—"and I got two more restaurants just like it, you
know that. Shit, didn't you know that? I had Wakely's bless-
ing. Don't you remember back when he told you to come
down here and fill out an application? It cost me a new shot-
gun to get you in here. And I paid you twice as much as the
other help, too."

His face dropped into his open hands.

"You're just filth now. Just spoilt filth. If it'd been a white
man . . ."

Norvell was sobbing now.

"We coulda sent you away or somethin'. But a fuckin'
nigga!"

She implored him not to call her father, but he would listen
only to his own self-pity.

"Shit, Verny, I had dreams for you," he sobbed, "season
tickets to the Razorbacks."

Norvell pulled his wallet from his back pocket and opened
it halfheartedly. The tickets were somewhere in there.

"Imploded?" he said suddenly. The crying stopped instantly as he finally heard the word said minutes ago.

"Imploded? Shit, that's not even a goddamn word! Where
did you get that goddamn word, from him? That's not even
a goddamn word."

Vernetta had gone first to a friend's house to wait up until she could be sure her own household would be sleeping. She wanted to get her things and, especially, to get out of Norvell's damn My-T-Freeze uniform; it was a strangling thing. She felt as though the cloth was suffocating her skin and pores. It was four in the morning, but when she arrived the light and the men in the front rooms told her that too early and too late had merged. Her brothers' pickups were outside, and their radiators were as cold as she knew their hearts would be. The men had been there waiting for some time now. Vernetta imagined them on their haunches in the kitchen, huddling over a plan drawn on the floor with a stick. She'd seen them act like that before a hunt, especially out of season.

She felt sure now that she would get the strop for this. Wakely would take it from its resting place in the bathroom closet and greet it like an old friend. She'd have to pull her panties down, as if those tiny cotton things offered any protection. And the boys would watch. That would be the worst part, their snickering and nasty comments. As she imagined the pain in her butt, she suddenly realized that she had no panties on and found a place behind one of the trucks to pull them out of her jacket pocket and slip them on. She was still very wet, a swamp.

She thought back to the storage room and to herself on her back looking at her own two feet poking into the air and oscillating one complete cycle for every thrust by J.B. She tried to recall the exact feeling of it but couldn't do it. Just hours later and she couldn't recreate the feeling in her loins. She decided that God wanted it that way, to make folks do it until it takes ahold, until something irreversible happens.

She smiled at the image of two red circles circling, the polish on her toenails contrasted against the white ceiling. She let the circles circle in her mind and hoped it had taken. It had cost so much for them to make love, she hoped the seed had taken.

Poor J.B. had been fired on the spot, and Norvell had refused to give him his back pay or to let him use the phone to call for a ride. Then he had commenced the beating. The last time she saw J.B. he was pulling himself out of the front door of the My-T-Freeze and heading toward the bus depot.

He had stooped outside to collect his books and notes and push them all up under his arm.

Their eyes met above the stares in the restaurant as he left, and J.B. said the single word "tomorrow" out loud. It had been said, in English, out loud, for all to hear. The weight of the word had garnered every thought and every object from that instant and place and had pulled it all into itself so that she saw and heard nothing else. They had never done anything out loud before.

They would meet again in the morning at their special place, at their usual time. They would be twin vectors convergent. Their special place was a truck stop out on Interstate 30, where J.B.'s uncle Flynn cooked breakfast every morning starting promptly at four o'clock and afterward did the prep work for the lunch crowd. They usually had breakfast at seven: buttery grits, pigs in a blanket, and whatever else they wanted in the kitchen there with big old Flynn.

Vernetta's mind's eye squinted at the shining metal tables in his kitchen that were always as warm as his drawl. It was so hot there: the steam tables, the yellow heat lamps, the gas burners licking upward blue and orange around black-bottomed pans. She and J.B. had gone there just two days ago after riding all night from the Gulf.

Flynn, his Alabama roots sounding in every word, had just studied about Marcus Garvey and gave a kind of talk about the man to the kitchen help and the folks in the colored section.

"Way ahead of his time," he grinned, "far ahead of the time, even now. Or maybe he was jes way behind and the rest of us is even furtha back. They was two thousand Africans surrendered with Cornwallis, you know. The British promised them they freedom and they fought for it. They didn't fight to belong here or to fit in over here. They wanted more than that. They fought to be free on they own terms. The lucky ones went to Liberia. You'd think we'd a done better by now. Shit, here it is the end of the forties and the beginning of the fifties and I cain't even eat the food I cook when and where I want. Cain't ride to work but in the back of the bus. Bank won't give me no loan to buy a car cause I ain't got no account.

Then they won't give me no account. Joseph there gots to study on his own cause we'uns ain't got no classes fo' him out here."

Afterward, J.B went on and on about the speed of light; something about two trains and some flashlights; what looks different isn't, so it must be happening in a different time. Tomorrow morning, Vernetta knew, they would sit together again. But this time they would sit out in the red, white, and blue booths—American Leatherette. They would sit in the white section, goddamn it. The white section. Each one with its own lava lamp and menus shaped like diesel tractors, Kenworths and Whites.

The fountain drinks were printed on one wheel and desserts on the other. Out with the regular customers, out loud. Vernetta smiled as she imagined the scene, J.B. poring carefully over the plastic menu card, all the time knowing exactly what he was going to order. And that Easter Day McCarthy or Delvina Mae Griggs or whoever was on shift then would have to stand at their table and ask them what they were havin', nice as you please.

Vernetta could almost smell their small thoughts burnin' their little minds yellow just like their tobacco-stained fingers.

The three men were in the kitchen, talking quietly now when she inhaled deeply, sucked some courage from out of the air and carefully turned the lock to the front door. Their talking stopped, and she knew they'd heard. There was nothing now to camouflage her footfalls. She walked through the living room and toward her own room without the need to see her way. She had walked it so many times. But then, in the hallway, she decided to get it over with; so she walked straight into the light. As she stood there, none of the three looked up at her, even toward her.

"Pa," she said.

Still no one looked up at her. All three looked downward as if focusing on a spot below the table surface, the faux-granite, six-piece dinette table surface. They piled on the way they did at their so-called touch football games. They piled on the silence, heaped it on her.

"Git to bed," her father finally said coldly, moving his head toward her bedroom but without meeting her imploring gaze.

"We got a far piece to travel tomorrow."

Puzzled a little and numbed by his coldness when she was sure he would be raving mad, Vernetta turned her body slowly away while keeping her eyes on the men. She had expected a lot of screaming and a real whipping.

"Then pack up your shit," her older brother said slowly, "all your nigger fuckin' shit."

Suddenly the father rose up and slapped the son savagely, leaned over the table and lashed out with a blow that nearly knocked the younger man from his matching green Naugahyde chair. Then the two men sat staring at each other strangely before slowly resuming their former postures, the younger one rubbing his jaw.

"Pack ever fuckin' stitch. We is ruint in this town for you. But we goin' out proud for us," her other brother added, a gloating smile on his lips.

These men were in a family separate from Vernetta and her mother. They had always been in a family separate. As she turned away she told herself that she would never again sleep in the little house she had been raised in. She walked silently past her parents' bedroom door and could just make out the form of her mother lying on her back. Her mother always slept on her side, facing away from Wakely. She must be awake.

"Vernetta, you shamed your pa."

The voice barely made it to the bedroom door where Vernetta stood, but the frailty of it somehow carried the weary sight of her with the sound waves. The voice told Vernetta that her mother had been sounding her own weariness there in the dark, finding its depth.

"You shamed us all and now the men says I gotta move outta my house and I gotta leave my friends and my church on account a you and some nigra boy."

"But Ma," Vernetta whispered plaintively.

"Hush up," her mother spat back the words.

"Malvern ain't far enough way to suit your pa, but we got some o' his kin up there and they'll put us up. I don't want to move again, Vernetta. I made this house what it is. You and I made it a home for us; the menfolk don't seem to need one. You don't remember Terrebonne Parish and Du Lac, do you? I guess not, you was too young. The bayou weren't much to some, to most I guess. But I swear I'd give all I have for this here house to pitch and roll a little like it was floatin' on one."

Vernetta barely remembered the bayou. She knew more about it from conversations with J.B. than she did from memory. Joseph loved the bayou, too. The mother and daughter stared upward together at the black ceiling toward their uncertain future as muffled voices filtered in from the direction of the kitchen. They sounded far away.

"They's planning to take you somewheres tomorrow. I promised Wakely that I wouldn't tell you where to. But I know you're not staying here no more."

From somewhere in the darkness a twig of a hand reached up and held Vernetta's hand. For a moment Vernetta resented the fingers and the cold palm. She could feel how small her mother was; it was the first time she had ever measured her, had ever known her size. She had been big all of Vernetta's childhood and small all of her adulthood, but she had never really had a size in Vernetta's mind. Vernetta resented the empirical reality of it; she could feel her mother's humanity. She touched her small shoulders and her back, and there it was again, her spine barely beneath her skin.

At that moment, with J.B. waiting out there for her in the dark somewhere, she did not want the reality of her mother's mortality infringing. She pushed the selfish thought away and drew the hand near.

"I cain't forgive you today, baby, right this here minute. But I know I will forgive you someday soon. I'll be up in Malvern, honey, when you need to find me. I hear tell there's a particle of water up there, lakes and such, so I won't get too unbalanced."

Now she sat up in the bed, another concern played out on her face.

"I pray to God you ain't pregnant. I pray to God."

She let Vernetta's hand go and dropped her voice down to

almost no voice at all, just breaths of ideas, a small, cold breeze of ideas from inside her out to her daughter.

"Just yesterday you started bleedin'. Remember that? You was just eleven and you walked straight to the dinner table with them red spotted panties. God, did you and your mama cry. The curse ain't the bleeding, child. The curse is when you don't bleed. The curse is when the thought takes form and the fears take substance, and it happens in you. Inside you. Lies, seductions, promises. Words take shape inside women."

Her mother spread her fingers over her abdomen as she spoke.

"We got to live with whatever descends into flesh, Vernetta. If it's love that descends, it's good. If it's not . . . we got to try to make it good. Either way it takes from us, food even as we is just eatin' it; from out our nipples, even if we could use the strength our own selves. It takes from us and we give to it because it's ours. But these menfolk don't seem to be connected; they ain't attached. Maybe that's why they can be so mean, why they can shoot does out of season and hit tiny armadillo babies with they trucks. God, I've heard the lost fawns bleating out there. Maybe that's why they can . . ." She stopped herself short and sat in the dark, alone with herself.

Vernetta could hear her mother sighing, exhaling; the breath seemed to be going out of her.

"We are women, Vernetta, you and me."

She said it with such bottomless sadness that her only daughter would not fathom it for years to come. Even with the chilling words, Vernetta felt a warmth down in her belly and prayed opposite things to herself.

"God sakes, Vernetta, a nigra boy!"

She sounded tired there in the darkness.

"I married a white man, and there ain't hardly been no happiness in that! What did you think you could expect with a black boy? I don't know. Maybe the nigras is stronger than us. They seem to live on sorrow. Who knows? Maybe they's just closer to God."

Vernetta bent down and hugged her mother for the last time.

"What did you talk about with him?" she asked softly in the darkness, barely hugging back. "Wakely don't never say nothin'."

"We still do talk, Ma. About everything, Ma," Vernetta whispered, "even about wave theory and about Manilamen. He's part Filipino, you know."

"Part what?" her mother asked, then groaned with the weight of the secret pressing down on her thin body.

She knew exactly why the men were laughing the way they were in the kitchen. She could almost hear Vernetta's bleating. The woman embraced the dark outline that was her daughter and decided that she could not tell her.

"Wave theory is like the river?"

"Yes, Ma, something like that."

"Sometimes I lay here and I can feel the house rockin' and I swear I can hear the slap of a wake agin us. When we moved here, you was real small, but you always liked to swim. Yeah, you sure took to the water. You sure took to the water. Whatever happens, darlin', promise me you will never despair. Talk to God a while before you do anything crazy."

Her daughter's unseen nod was somehow communicated.

"I've been a mother to you, haven't I? I've been a mother to you?"

Another nod. In that black room, for a second or two their souls orbited around the same memories; then Vernetta, her heart split and her mind on so many tangents, spun off and away, down the hall to her room.

Slowly and without turning on the lights, Vernetta changed out of her work clothes into her blue jeans and a sweater. Her room felt like a death had happened there; it felt as though her toys and mementos were mourning. As she stood there, she found she already missed her matching yellow-and-white furniture and the special "water scenes of Venice" wallpaper she and her mother had picked out of the catalogue and saved a slap year for.

She grabbed the My-T-Freeze outfit from atop her bed and threw it down to the floor with disgust and relief, the look

on Norvell's face as he stood in the storage room coming back
to her again and again. That look would someday be her
living. But right now the thought of it thoroughly chilled her
inside and out. She whispered good-bye to her room and the
thousands of childhood nights stored up in there. She touched
her pillows. Her finger smoothed along a stretch of wain-
scoting, then lightly touched the wallpaper that had started
every one of her dreams and soaked up every wish.

Then she slid silently out of the window. She stood in the
soft dirt below her bedroom and said good-bye to her little
Scottie dog buried beneath her feet, then started walking back
toward town and toward the interstate. She took care to keep
off the sidewalks just in case her father or one of her brothers
came looking for her. With about two hours to get to the truck
stop, she had more than enough time to walk there and enjoy
her fantasies about a life together with J.B. They would eat
together today and make plans together and everything would
be all right.

Now that their secret had finally been wrenched out into
the light of day, Vernetta felt exhilarated. The painful family
meeting she had imagined so fearfully over and over again
had passed with a minimum of rage from her father and her
two brothers. She had fully expected to be beaten, but that,
surprisingly, had not happened.

She came over the rise, finally. She had never had to walk
to the truck stop before, and she was surprised how far it
was. Once she had taken a bus, but the driver made J.B. sit
in the back so she swore off the bus lines. She had expected
to see the sky lit up for miles by all the neon and running
lights. She realized for the first time as she descended the
crest that the restaurant had no name, only descriptions of
itself and a command. OPEN ALL NITE. EAT HERE. But the
descriptions were nowhere to be seen this morning. The building was dark. The truck stop was empty, deserted. The WE
NEVER CLOSE, open twenty-four-hours-a-day on the interstate,
was empty.

The dining room lights were out, and all of the waitresses
were sitting together smoking in a station wagon. The oil in
each lava lamp had settled to the bottom, the senseless ooze

resting for the first time in years. Hungry and half-fed truckers
were grinding gears and lumbering out toward the asphalt.

There were two sheriff's cars in the back of the restaurant,
behind the white dumpster and the loading dock where the
black dishwashers were milling around and wondering whose
time they were on. That wasn't unusual, but these cars had
their red lights going. Their doors had been left wide open
and their engines were running. Even at this distance Vernetta
could hear the blare and scratch of radio transmissions.

As she walked down the rise toward the truck stop, she
saw what she thought was a black man sitting alone at the
end of one of the old telephone poles that had been brought
in and laid down to mark the edges of the parking lot. Was
it Flynn? Then she knew it had to be Flynn from the white
apron and the tall, white chef's hat on his head. Flynn was
crying? Was Flynn crying?

Vernetta ran now, her hair flying loose behind her. But for
her narrow heels digging into the grass of the rise, she flew.

"Get away from me, goddamn it," cried Flynn when it
became clear to him just who was flying down the rise.

"Get away from me, you white bitch! I tole J.B. you was
poison. I tole him you was nothin' but poison. Now he's gone
and died. Now he's dead."

Flynn slumped back down. The words had gone up the
rise and ripped at Vernetta, cut her legs from under her. They
sliced right through her will as though it were a fleshy tendon,
and Vernetta, helpless, fell to her knees in front of him.

"What do you mean?" she screamed. "What do you mean?"

Her quickening, red face was right in his. "Please God,
make him tell me! What do you mean!"

Flynn could not answer, any more than Vernetta could
understand anything beyond what he'd already said. The
words had been all too real, and the tearing she felt inside
was like her soul was being ripped out. It seemed to her,
looking back on it over years, that it was like God had reversed
the breath of life.

"The suck of life," she would call it, sarcastically.

"The *sustos*," her friend Josephina would someday say.

She hung on to Flynn while she buckled and the air sifted

through her clenched teeth, but he hated her right then and right through the embrace. He hated the tears he saw on her white face as much as she hated his, the message his tears had sent her. The two cried at each other. There at the end of the pole, they sobbed at each other like they were both swinging clubs of sorrowful sound.

Then hugging him, stupid and vacant, she vaguely thought that her brothers had seemed so smug. They were so fucking smug.

Thirty yards to their right were two observers moving at a constant speed in their own undisturbed direction, a direction they had inherited from their fathers and grandfathers. Yes, Velton and Earl-Joe were two good arguments for absolute determinism, men who moved in a universe that was both constant and unchanging. They were two of Clark County's finest. Two living cartoons, they leaned against their patrol vehicles, their red necks flashing even redder each time the lights on top of their twin cruisers rotated their way.

Their lives were the exact sum of their parts, no mental gymnastics, no leaps of lyricism, no sacrifices of any nature. There were no existential risks or unaccounted-for assertions of will. Just two cartoons with badges and Smokey hats posturing in their field jackets.

Velton and Earl-Joe pounded their red cigarette packages on their car fenders without really knowing why. Both had recently considered switching to Raleigh cigarettes for the valuable coupons. Both hid Archie comics in their patrol cars, and both were crazy about any girl with an overbite.

Velton and Earl-Joe lit up their Marlboros with identical custom Zippos and laughed at the scene before them.

"You reckon Wakely's gonna do us right?"

"Fuckin-A, we is the law," the other laughed.

"The fucker sure tore up that kitchen. Some fuckin' emergency, huh? A buzzerk nigga fry cook and a skinny white bitch with black fever."

The rope was still there around his neck. The once smooth brown skin under his jaws was stretched and swollen blue, the striations deep. The neck hadn't broken; he had suffocated, his lungs burning inside for air.

There were still memory embers in him when the pickups drove off and still a faint flickering scene from childhood when they cut him down. The scene expanded downward as he fell, from the linear to the cellular as tiny, long-dormant memories flared, then switched off. The last to go was an ancient fear of lions. The eyes, catfish gray, saw the sidewalk coming up just as he felt nothing.

Joseph Bonifacio Woodley lay twisted on a metal table just like the ones at the truck stop, only these were very, very cold. In a lime green vault lit only by long fluorescent fixtures, the chief under-assistant mortician was across the room on the telephone, his wig line turned up in a circle around his tiny skull.

As he spoke, he shamelessly scratched his narrow, porcelain asshole through his nightshirt. The mortician had no flesh on his bones, no vitality and no patience with the living. He cleaned his teeth with the edge of a matchbook and swallowed the dislodged pieces of corn and pepper pie as the conversation continued. He was accustomed only to the dead as company; the living were a goddamn nuisance. They came in here day after day grieving first about the death, then about the price of the burial. They came in here covered with ten-cent aftershave and cheap makeup and demanded that the loved one look lifelike.

This time they just brought the body in without notice, without calling him first, and he hadn't even had enough time to comb his hairpiece out properly to meet the beloved. Someday he would be the boss, and someday some other lackey would have to sleep in the add-on behind the Repose Rooms.

They had stuck his physics books and notes inside his pants, then tied his hands behind his back. They had pulled his shoes off to throw at him while he hung up there and his knees rattled. They had groaned in disappointment when he didn't shit in his pants. They stood there as the charge that lit his eyes blinked out; then they set out searching for his daughter and their sister, the source of all this trouble.

Vernetta, the cause of it all, the one who would soon lovingly ravage the dead man's peace, probe his clothing and prod the skin with such tender viciousness, hoping for some sign of something transcendent in the material, some spark, some tremor in the flesh.

"Answer me a little, J.B., please answer me a little here."

She placed her pallid, pleading fingers across his at right angles; she would have settled for palsy, spasms like the ones the scary old man in front of the post office had would have been acceptable. But only one set had the priceless quiver; the other did not.

"Cut his hands aloose," Vernetta had sobbed, "y'all cut his hands aloose, it's cutting into his skin."

"Can't hurt him now," the chief under-assistant mortician said, smiling his most waxen smile.

The evidence had to be preserved for an investigation that would lead nowhere and an arrest that would never be made. There were bruises on his face where he had been beaten again on top of Norvell's beating.

"Animals," the assistant mortician said after slamming the phone onto its cradle. "Less than animals. Don't they know, by law, I don't even have to work on niggers. They don't even want him embalmed. Don't want his mouth glued shut. Don't want a box. Not that I'm in no goddamn hurry to cut open a colored, or a mulatto, or whatever this is. Let 'im grin."

One day later, a small crowd of black and brown faces led by Mama Concepcion Woodley came to cut him loose and take him home amid their circling antiphonies of grief. Her beautiful red car became the hurry-up wagon and led a procession of headlights back down south and into the bayou. J.B.'s dog, Mister Marvel, would be there waiting for him at the door and turn to follow as he came in.

The pine table that held the hoppin' John and *adobo* would be his cooling board, and the folks from 'round would bring sweet yams and *bibinka*, sweet rice candy, and their best white swatches for his winding cloth.

His uncles, Vicente, Willie, and Tino, would come over from Morgan City, still green from the cane with coins in their pockets for his eyes and one for his work hand.

There would be a strange procession in the sulking Louisiana bayou. A large paper figure of the Virgin Mary would lead the way and black people with Asian eyes would carry him. Mestizos, some in *barong tagalogs*, would hoist him down to his own wet soils near his own waters and his own blood would then sing him home.

She had ripped the books out of his pants, held them to her breast, and she ran nonstop to the hoary oak tree in front of the lending library. She had already shinnied halfway up its noble side when Flynn caught up to her and heaved his guts out onto the lawn. He had been to the mortuary, too.

"Jesus, they jes' twisted the life outta him." Flynn could barely get the words out.

"I wish to God I ain't seen it. I wish to God."

She crawled across all those initials and hearts carved into the crusty bark and out onto the brown, mottled limb that pushed out over the walkway. Then, cut and bleeding, she held on with her fingers and let her legs swing out into space. She hung in just the place—she could see where the sisal rope had newly cut the bark.

As she swung slowly she felt alternating cold and warmth till she came to rest in the center where the air still held his heat. Sobbing beyond her ken, she took his warmth into her, then let go limp her skinny, white limbs and surrendered, eyes closed, to gravity. She was alone there in space, a singularity, the tensile limb free of her, swinging upward. She let go, released herself to forces, and after a timeless time she woke up suddenly in a pickup truck on her way to Louisiana, her caked knees bleeding.

"Believe me, darling, it was for the best. We all done it for you. We considered what had to be done and done it."

She looked up to see her father staring intently through the windshield, his bony hands gripping the steering wheel of his precious Jimmy half-ton.

"Why did you have me?" she asked, without looking at him, turning away farther.

"Why did you have me?"

"The boys and me got a little carried away, I'll give, but that's all over and done now, and after we get you cleaned up we can start over again up in Malvern. Your ma's happy about moving up 'ere, and we got folks." He reached out to touch her shoulder, but she pulled away from the lie, and his right hand fell to the seat before resuming its place on the wheel.

He considered that the girl was just like her mother, who wouldn't let him touch her either. She never wanted him to touch her.

"I know I wasn't born from love, none of us was. Why did you have me?"

"Shit," he said aloud; both hands lifted from the steering wheel, then slammed back down.

He looked down at her sobbing there, knees bleeding through her pants, and knew that he cared more about his upholstery than he did his daughter, his tiny, flat-chested daughter. It was a revelation. He thought to himself that all those years of guilt over shunning his daughter for the boys, leaving her home when all three went hunting or making sure the boys had what they needed while the women made do, all those years of guilt were a waste.

Vernetta was supposed to be a Vern, shoulda been a goddamn Vern! A fuckin' waste! She deserved to be shunned, and especially now, after what she done. He felt relieved, vindicated by the thought, and drove on with a smile on his lips. There was something about the situation that brought the taste of venison to his mouth.

"Till you leave my house and my sight, girl, you are mine. Your pussy is mine and I decide who you gone give it to. I decide!" He was screaming now. "Some decent white boy of my choosin'! My choosin'." He pounded his right hand against his chest and realized that he was enjoying himself.

"Somebody just like me." Wakely grinned at the third revelation.

"Now let's see, you give what's yours to yourself," said Vernetta sarcastically. "Sounds like you is busy diddlin' yourself."

Vernetta did not see the blow coming. But it didn't surprise her. It was a relentless, unchecked blow that sent spit and blood arcing across the metal dash. It was the first honest communication between father and daughter that either of them could recall. They stared straight ahead into the night after that, refreshed by the clarity and the finality of the thing.

That blow would suffice just fine in lieu of phone calls, letters and family get-togethers until death, and it would surely suffice for now. Wakely, his boot heel spearing the flank of his Jimmy six, could make out every detail by the roadside as the truck crawled to their destination. It seemed like half an hour between road 38 and road 39. To Vernetta, the damn truck flew.

She saw the state line go by and knew they were in Louisiana, in Webster Parish. She had crossed this very state line with J.B. only weeks before. A few days could mean all the difference in the world, a few seconds even.

Just days ago she crossed this same invisible line singing "Long Tall Sally" at the top of her lungs along with the radio, her pants and panties down at her knees and J.B.'s index finger flailing at her clit like it was a Jew's harp. God, she'd wailed like a banshee, three octaves above Little Richard.

She moaned now as she realized for certain she was going to get cleaned out in Shongaloo. She visualized spongy inner tunnels being scraped and scrubbed raw; a twinge of pain shot through her. She had never gone anywhere with her father that she could remember, much less back down to Louisiana. She had heard for years of a juju woman there, a black woman who helped girls who were in trouble, for a fee. Everybody knew about her. A couple of the girls from her high school had gone there after bein' knocked up. None of them girls was ever the same. It was like more had gone out of them than just an unfinished child. Shongaloo, she thought fearfully. A thousand babies must be curdled in the murk and mossy froth of that slow-moving water.

Vernetta imagined every rumor she'd ever heard, a funnel stuck up her, her legs splayed out like a wishbone. She imagined the coat hanger with the tape balled up at the end, some old lady plumbing her like it was a dipstick. She felt herself diving off the couch onto the floor, an ugly belly flop onto a hand-knotted rug. She could almost hear Wakely laughing.

Generations had gone to the old woman with the one white eye, and now it would be her turn. They were going to kill J.B. again, she said to herself. Twice in one night. These men were taking everything she had, she thought, and the confused feelings that she had held for the men in her household now resolved themselves into hatred, just like a disturbed puddle settling down. Simple hatred.

Somewhere between Springhill and Cullen, on a dark one-lane back road Vernetta lost her family. She let Wakely and the others slip away like that dollar in the wind. It had torn loose from its little corner along with her childhood and the romance that was surely due any young girl. Some pipe was severed between her spirit and the fecund notch in her legs and all of her soft sentiment drained out there on Wakely's upholstery. Vernetta envisioned herself, at that moment, slung obscenely over the fender.

"Time'll heal these here wounds too," said Wakely, feigning concern. "Time always does."

"Time is not a constant," Vernetta answered coldly.

Then somewhere in the dark between Cullen and Shongaloo she opened the passenger door of the red primered Jimmy flathead and rolled out of the speeding truck.

Vernetta had spent a year on the bayou before she realized that she had to leave, that the family did not want her there. She had appeared one evening with her tight jeans and white heels, just walked into the Woodley house like they were family, and told the old woman a grandson was coming.

What she had seen in those faces was not joy at the sight of her. She had assumed that it was the grief that still lingered after the burial; after all, it still lingered in her. She assumed that they blamed her some for what had happened, and, after all, she blamed herself. Nevertheless, she considered herself part of the family by dint of her grief and the blood inside her. So she moved in and helped to clean up. She even learned to cook their strange food.

Then one sweaty morning in a house on stilts, she had an enema, broke her water, then had her light brown child.

"We'll call him Danelo. Sure, I know, it's the mother's place to name him, and he has his own name, but we'll call him Danelo. Look at those eyes. Filipino eyes without a doubt, just like his father's." Mama Woodley's face beamed as she spoke. "Vernetta, did you think we was just strange-looking black folks? Good Lord, our people been here longer than yours. They brought the slaves in 1619 and then the Manila men jump off the Spanish ships here in 1775. This water here must look like Manila Bay; they must've seen Luzon right here."

She glanced around her with a look of familiarity and affection on her brown face.

"Banana trees and banyan all around, just like home. Pinoys been here almost two hundred years now. Did you know they got a float every year at the Mardi Gras since nineteen thirty-five. Taught them white folks how to weave flowers around chicken wire and they had the first motorized float, too." She nodded proudly.

"They stayed together for almost twenty years way back then, without mixing. But there wasn't no Filipino women here back then, so they mix with the Indians and the Negroes and some even with the whites. Ain't nobody within twenty miles of this bayou that don't got some Filipino blood.

"You know, all those people out there think these seafood and fritters and rice dishes was invented by the whites? Ay, Jesus Maria, not on your life! Oh, look at him."

Mama Woodley lifted the baby boy, held him at arm's length in front of her eyes.

"He so puts me in mind of my boy. Skinny as a goddamn

rail. Show me where the Cajuns brought hot chiles down
from Nova Scotia. Negroes and Pinoys was eatin' okra when
the whites wouldn't touch it. No ma'am. The flame we burn
in this corner of the world so far from Africa and the Philippines may be small, but it ain't never gone out in two
hundred years.

"I hear tell there was Pinoy settlements in Peru and Ar-
gentina and even Guatemala, everywhere they could jump
ship from them Spanish press-gangs. You know, they built
stilt houses down here a way back when everybody else had
tiny houseboats; now you see the stilts damn near everywhere. There are whole villages here up on stilts."

She stopped a moment to look out over the porch toward
the small settlement down near the gray pier.

"The Pinoy ain't solitary like them Cajuns, and the Negro
sure ain't a solitary creature. We got to do things together;
eat, dance, sing. We's the only Catholics there are in the world
what raises spirituals, I betcha. Lord, none of that Latin Mass
for us. We raise our hymns up and the black part of us soars
right on out.

"We got Indian Pinoys out here and even some Cajun Pinoys. Long about nineteen forty or thereabouts we got some
women from the islands in here and even some Manong come
in after the war. Now we got Pinoys running around here
look like guaranteed Pinoys.

"Even got groceries; bean thread and *longonisa* and *Patis*.
Used to be real hard to get. Real hard to get. But you know,
the shrimp paste we make here is better than the stuff they
send over in the bottles. I swear it's better, lawd have mercy!

"Danelo's grandfather, Joseph's father, was a *mestizo*, too,
just like me. I swear that man sure loved his dirty rice and
adobo. But you know the blacks and the *mestizos* got pushed
out of the shrimp business down here. Men were killed 'round
that. Weren't nobody at all to protect us back then. Police
was even more crooked than they are now. It got so bad I
thought we might have to move away from this bayou. Thank
God there was work in the cane field. No white man wants
that work. I don't know if I could stand bein' away from the
water."

She lifted her grandson and shook him playfully. The little boy laughed.

"He's gonna need a balanced diet, Vernetta. You got to learn to cook *adobo* and *lechon* and *pancit* to go along with the red beans and chitlins. Otherwise, his soul will be starving and you won't even know it. You feed him that white food and you take the red out of his marrow, kill his spirit. That other food will stick in his gullet."

She lifted the baby boy again, the affection heating her face.

"Then he'll probably be lost like all them disconnected white folk eatin' all that processed food."

"I can cook cajun food for him, too," said Vernetta.

"Yes, I guess you can," answered Mama Woodley, "but first you got to do some bonding with this chile. All you do, Vernetta, is pine. You are ignoring the life for the memory. Damn it, girl, I had eighteen years with the boy and you ain't had but a coupla months. All that's left of Joseph is here in my arms, and you ain't hardly been a mother to it. Joseph wouldn't cotton to how you ain't been a mother to it.

"I know we got our ways here, but you are the mother, and where this chile is concerned you are the boss, not me. But, I swear, you ain't hardly ever here. Lord knows, the things I hear about where you are. I hope it's not true, Vernetta."

She looked up at Vernetta for some sort of response but got nothing.

"I swear, you better wake up soon or I will decide what's best for the boy. My grandson."

She rocked the little thing from side to side and made faces and noises. Around them, Joseph's sisters and brothers looked nervously up from their tasks, eyes glancing at their mother and then to Vernetta and back again. They had heard what Vernetta hadn't. They had heard her youth end, her laughter wither.

Just days later she had reappeared at the truck stop outside of Arkadelphia. She walked up to the service entrance and through the swinging doors of the kitchen. Flynn was there. Old Flynn was there cooking, as usual. But his smile was gone, his omelettes never again so lofty. He'd obviously given up on the part that he had tried to cut into his hair.

She had come back up from Louisiana with a question for him, oblivious to Easter Day McCarthy's stare and the lava lamps. She had come with the only question she had.

"Flynn, how can I live now? How can I live now? I gotta know. I gotta know. I had to come back and ask you. There's no one else. There ain't no one else no more."

"Ain't shit to it," he responded, his round face expressionless now, and staring up at the carousel of orders.

"Jes' when you can smell yourself fallin' apart you lose yo' sense of smell."

He laughed aloud as he said it. The question had been his too.

"God sees to it. When you cain't walk no mo, yo' old, decrepit mind wonders why anybody would ever want to. Ever seen the old men jes' sit an' sit? It's easy. Everbody does it. People sleepwalk through they lives and into they graves by the thousands ever fuckin' day. It cain't be all that hard."

The whisk in his hand stopped spinning for a moment that betrayed his calm.

"Ever time you buy a bigger pair of pants"—his thumbs pulled at his full waistline—"you keep the old ones and promise yourself you'll get back into 'em. We treat our lost time the same way, only you cain't keep the time. You bumps into folks and talk about the weather or politics and walks away forgettin' you had this same conversation thirty minutes ago or thirty years ago, but so do the person you jes' talk to. The point becomes that you talk, not what you is said.

"When you is young you would rather die than wear a green sweater vest, and when you is old you cain't bring yo'self to wear nothin' elst. You becomes each chapter in the book, and where you stand always seems to look okay. Even the last chapter. You look around and see, yeah, they is people with me on this page. Maybe even the last page. By the time you gets there, you cain't see to read it or you is tired of readin' altogether. An' the folks around you is just as old and messed up as you is."

He poured the whipped eggs out onto the griddle and spooned chopped ham and bell peppers onto the spreading omelette.

"You don't see no idiots hanging out at the lendin' library; they's all the time hangs out with other idiots. That way they's all right. They's okay. Together the idiots can poke fun at the bookworms. That's how you live it, Vernetta. Probly when you stand at your own graveside it looks okay. It probly looks real good if you can't do shit but fall into it. I think God makes it so when you cain't do nothin', it's time to do nothin'.

"Hell if I know a goddamn thing, Vernetta. Why you ax me a question like this? I ain't got time to meditate on things like this. That's all. Do it look to you like I'm livin' the American dream? If you ask me how to make mushroom gravy, now I can answer that."

He lifted the paper hat from his head, then ran his fingers through his thinning hair.

"You look at yourself in the mirror and what you see in there don't look bad because you don't want it to. That's why Easter Day McCarthy out there is wearing the same uniform she put on fifteen years ago. It's two pounds o' sugar in a one-pound sack. None of us can see ourselves, none of us can see our own lives."

He turned back to the carousel. There was a "C" scrawled on the order so that the cook would know that the customer was black. Flynn shook on some cayenne and Crystal hot sauce. He sprinkled pepper cheese and oregano over the omelette, spooned on a side of grits and set it in the pickup window for the colored section. If the order had a "W" on it, he would shake on some dill weed, bust a sprig of parsley over the thing and slap on a piece of white toast.

"You jes' fuckin' live. That's all, you jes' fuckin' live."

He rolled the omelettes over and cradled them on the long edge of the spatula before easing them onto a plate.

"Life is a self-inflicted wound for people like us," he said as he hit the bell for a pickup. "I never know what to think, Vernetta. Sometimes you got the weight of the world on yo' mind. Other times you lucky if you can cross the room without spillin' yo' coffee."

"Flynn, I done had J.B.'s baby."

She spread her ten fingers over her abdomen as she said it. Flynn stopped moving and gave her a sort of desolate look.

"But at that moment, that coffee teasin' at the rim of the cup is the most important thing they is."

8

El Demonio Verde

It was still dark outside. He heard his grandmother shuffling around in the kitchen. She was humming softly, so Beto knew that the coast was clear, that he could roll from his bed without first having to peek through the folds of his blankets to check for the ghost or his ghost dog. He had trained himself to wake without stirring and to survey the room carefully through the slit of one squinting eye before moving. The thought of seeing a ghost was not very frightening to him; he had long since come to accept the existence of ghosts as a reality. His *abuelita* saw at least one almost every day. It was this particular ghost that bothered him. His *abuela* had seen the man and the dog in the kitchen and once again out by the cesspool. She had explained to Beto that the man and his dog were still roaming the earth for one purpose only. She had seen it in his face. It was the prospect of seeing purpose in the ghost's face that scared the boy. He knew that such singularity of purpose distilled from the body and soul then decanted into a dead face was more than he wished to see.

As Beto threw off his covers, he knew his grandfather would be outside, probably hundreds of yards into the desert behind the house collecting and breaking gray mesquite branches for the stove.

Beto walked toward the warmth of the kitchen and startled

the old woman, who was measuring coffee grounds into her battered percolator.

"Ay, *Madre de Dios*, I thought you were a ghost, *mijo*," she said with breathless surprise and a little fear.

"I saw one here just yesterday, but it wasn't for me, wrong adobe. I told the little *pendejo* he had the wrong century, too, but he wouldn't believe me. How is your earache this morning?"

He sat at the table, reached behind him for a can of Pet milk and punched two holes in the top with his pocketknife.

"It's gone."

He realized that the pain he had gone to sleep with had disappeared with the morning. Before her evening prayers, Josephina had knelt by the boy's bedside with her bag. She ground a small, green *ruda* plant in a mortar along with a dab of olive oil. She then rubbed the pungent mixture inside the boy's hurting ear. Finally, she took out a pouch containing what she laughingly called "*yerba buena*" and poured a small amount of it into a cigarette paper. She licked an edge and rolled it into a small brown tube. She then lit the cigarette and inhaled deeply, but she exhaled the smoke into Beto's ear, her lips not an inch away. The last thing the boy remembered from the night before was his grandfather's voice calling out, "*Vieja*, my ear hurts too."

"How did you get rid of him?" Beto asked.

"Who?"

"The ghost who had the wrong century."

"Oh, him. I had to go over his head." She nodded, a little bored with shoptalk.

"Are you afraid of ghosts, Abuela?" he asked.

"It depends on which ghost, when you see them and why you are seeing them. It depends on whether or not you see the ghost because it wants to be seen or you have just worked a vision and invaded its privacy. You see that I have no fear of that Refugio, your grandfather's father, even with his cocoon rattles and his songs. I just refuse to acknowledge him when he barges in here at all hours and I refuse to acknowledge his ways.

"Ghosts are like tumbleweed. No one pays attention to the

plant when it's green. No one even knows what it's called.
But when it's dead it receives a name and people who see
the weeds rolling across open fields are suddenly stricken
with loneliness. People who see the weeds hanging from
barbed wire are suddenly overcome with a desire to free the
weed. Have you seen them hanging out there, *mijo*? Can a
dead thing be trapped? If so, then it can be freed. Some ghosts
just brood around; some are single people and some are whole
tribes in one spirit. This whole country, *por ejemplo*, is haunted
by slavery.

"With some, to contact them is like stepping in a place
where a perfumed woman has just stood. You can smell it."

She sniffed the air as she spoke.

"With others it's like jumping into the last thoughts of a
drowning man. It is a swirling of unrecognizable and painful
things that exist and move in the air all alone. Sometimes
there is such pain."

She winced visibly as something shot through her, a
thought fast as the flash of a minnow.

"The ghosts are not complete spirits; they don't always
know why they remain behind. Most are only moments lived
over and over like a phonograph needle stuck at a point in
time. None of them can hold a decent conversation because
they could just as well exist before the question is asked as
after. Believe me, I've tried to talk to enough of them.

"You see, they don't have to wait for time to pass. They
can just be in this time or that one. A spirit can look at you
and one of his eyes will be seeing the child and the other eye
will be seeing the bent old man. If he decides to speak to
you, does he speak to the *niño* or the *viejo*? If you were a
ghost, God forbid, would you tell a little girl that all of her
children will stick inside of her and she will die childless?
Would you tell her that her husband will be a thief? When
you can see as they can, it's probably best to say nothing.
When you can move back and forth in time like they can, the
potential for ironies is enormous."

This last statement seemed to give her pause. She remained
deathly still for a minute or so. It began to frighten the boy.

"They are kind of rude that way," she began, at last, "but

it's only because they're impatient with us. We can only talk
in one direction. I like the moments better than the conversations. In one of my favorite *momentos* I can see my own
hands carving glyphs at Chichén Itzá. I especially like the
momentos of this young *señora's* wedding night," she smiled.
"She is from Guadalajara and she is as pure as a girl can be.
Ay, the anticipation and the fear are *si delicado! Qué desflora-
ción!*" she laughed out loud.

"I contact that one a lot. Over and over, that one! Well, to
tell the truth, not so much anymore. Ghosts are not cruel,
they are only sad."

She was silent for a moment, her back to her grandson.
When she spoke again there was a darkness in her voice. It
seemed to descend as though a mourning veil had been pulled
over her face, its sunless shadow dimming even her words.

"Most I do not fear. But once . . . once I saw Satan in a
cantina in Denver, Colorado. I was afraid then."

Now she spoke softly and carefully chose each word to
convey the import of this to the boy.

"I saw the prince of darkness himself, and I spoke with
him, face-to-face. I was so young; I had just come to this
country and I was very pretty, too."

She smiled at this last assertion, and both of them held the
same image of her in their minds, an image preserved nowhere but in the photo on the dresser and in the mind of
Manuel.

"My uncle's small company in *España* sold leather goods in
this country; you know, wallets and belts. So I had the chance
to work at both places, in Madrid and in Denver. You see, I
could type and take dictation and balance books and even
compose letters for business purposes. I could have been a
professional woman, *mijo.*" She smiled with a glint of pride
in her eyes.

"I kept telling *mi tío*: shoes, *zapatos.* The money's in shoes.
But he wouldn't listen. So the *Italianos* kicked his ass. *Qué
desmadre*, they kicked his *culito* real good."

She shrugged.

"But I brought the bag with me, too." She nodded toward
her medicinal bag resting in its customary place.

"My mother gave that bag to me when I left *España*. She knew . . ." Josephina turned away now, the tears welling up. "She knew we would never see each other again. *Qué dolor,* I wish I had known that would be it. It was not by my choice!"

Josephina's face glazed over for a minute, and she bowed her head to have that minute to herself. When she spoke again, it was of her mother.

"The bag belonged to her mother and to her mother's mother and back who knows how long. It carries a grave responsibility with it, one that I most assuredly did not understand when I first brought it here to this country. I was told that some of the things in this bag were gathered by gypsies and some by Moors. See the purple lining? That's the gypsy's color.

"My dear mother instructed me that I must never let any bottle of medicine become empty. So I fill each one when it is half gone. That way some of the oldest, most ancient herbs and powders will still be present and will give their power to the new herbs. It's like God does with children." She touched her grandson's cheek, "There's some of me and Manuel in you. When your life is half done, you will refill the bottle and we will still be in there, and in your son, too."

She walked over to the bag, lifted it and carried it back to the table. When she opened it and spread the top, a hundred tiny bottles of herbs and powders were revealed; small sacks and envelopes of admixtures, blends, compounds and amalgams. Mustard, eucalyptus, raspberry and rosemary leaves. From these leaves came oils to reduce swelling. *Camomila, menta, capulla de rosa y manzanita.* Marijuana buds, *mota* leaves, y dried cactus tunas. Lamb fats, skunk fats, and animal tallows. She had jars of fish gall for blindness and for the treatment of cataracts, and cans of flaxseed for urinary problems. All those individual scents, and yet surprisingly, the bag had no odor.

The boy had seen these things many times before. He had seen her preparing her bag late into the evenings. He had once felt a twinge of embarrassment on seeing his grandmother rummaging through the body of a flattened skunk on the highway looking for special parts.

He had often carried the bag for his grandmother on her emergency visits to the Nueva Pascua in Tucson and into Buckeye and as far out as the Papago or Apache reservations, sometimes in the middle of the night with Manuel bumping the old Ford along from one bad road to another, the two arguing over directions.

Also in the bag was a brown leather book, a Bible, and four or five small binders kept shut with rubber bands. There was a sparkling set of needles and spools of suture. There was a horrific enema kit, a pair of thermometers, one for each end. There were rubbing alcohol, razors, a sewing kit, candles tied together and small branches covered neatly with Saran Wrap. She had organized squares of gauze, vials of *pastillas* and tubes of salve. There were tracheotomy tubes, tweezers and a cauterizing iron.

At the very bottom of the bag was a strange bottle. It was an old glass bottle filled with clear fluid and the bodies of dead scorpions of every size and color. The boy loved to take the heavy, prismatic bottle out of the bag when Abuela was not home. He had learned to breathe deeply whenever he reached for it and to hold his breath when he lifted the bottle from its resting place. Once, out of curiosity, he had sniffed at the edge of the rotting cork where a faint odor lingered— a petrified vapor that turned his daydreams into stone images, his wishes into inscriptions overgrown by jungle. It had taken all of his energy to break the spell, to chisel his imagination free, and the experience left him resolved never to repeat it. Yet, he was drawn to the strange bottle.

Carefully, he would hold the bottle next to a burning candle to see the five dying suns of the Aztec people. And when held up to the night sky, the scorpions would swarm over five moons.

In a pocket by itself was an old piece of brown cloth, its ends wearing thin.

"The moment I accepted this bag from *mi madre*, I accepted the power to be one of two ways, travel one of two paths. It was this power that Satan saw in me that night so long ago. It is the power that he sees in me now, today. It was this power that he wished to turn to his own ends when I was a mere girl in a strange land. You see, *mijo, brujas y curanderas* must choose to work for the ways of Christ and his holy mother or for Lucifer and his horde. You must choose whether to heal people or to hurt people—to bring life into this world or to bring misery to it."

"But Abuela, I see you deliver babies in the middle of the night and cure people's sickness all the time. Did you really have to choose to do good?"

"Good people care about things like *la familia* and children and neighbors; about buying chorizo without too much fat. *Cosas* like that. All they need is enough to go around. Evil people, on the other hand, only care about having more. *Más, más, más.*"

"More what?" the boy asked.

"More whatever, but mostly money. So if you deliver babies you probably won't be around people with much money. You know these *Mexicanos Católicos*, they keep having kids. They even have a saying that each child is born with a taco in its armpit. *Dios mío,* they got a million sayings like that. Another child just means another cup of water in the beans."

"What do the evil people want from a *bruja?*" Beto asked.

"They want a spell so somebody will get sick and die so they can take his job or his wife. They want a love spell so a wife will leave her husband and children. They want a finding so they can know where an old man has buried his life's savings. Men who stick their things in every hole they can find, even knotholes and ewes, want to know if señorita so and so is a virgin. *Idiotas.*"

She stopped for a moment and wondered if the boy knew what a virgin was. Has anyone told him how babies are made? She certainly had not. Manuel, that goddamn Indian? She decided to herself that he was still too young and that she would tell him next year.

"There is hoodoo medicine here from Africa, too. There is old magic from everywhere, and some of it is not good. Remember the egg in Hiawatha's hand?"

The boy nodded.

"That's to keep the killer nearby. They want her to suffer. *Pobrecita,* I had to make her step backward over the corpse

and say, 'Please release me Lord Jesus,' just to try to counter
the spell. But I think we were too late. Too late. *Pobrecita*,
even with me and Manuel dragging her together, she could
barely do it. She struggled with us like we were hurting her
or something. I don't really believe in their spells," she cau-
tioned, "but I think she's spoken for herself for the last time.
I dreamed she was buried alive."

Abuela pulled a kerchief from her sleeve and dabbed her
eyes before continuing.

"A man even came to me once and asked me to make his
older brother sick so that he would die and the land would
go to this man. I threw the *pendejo* out into the street."

She gestured with both hands as if tossing out garbage.

"Satan knew who I was; he saw the bag below my chair
and the pure heart above it."

She placed both of her hands on her left breast.

"There was power in both. There still is."

She pulled out a chair and sat at the table next to the boy,
obviously enthralled by her own story.

"And there I sat in a new dress in a strange new city,
suspecting nothing, drinking a sarsaparilla with a brave girl-
friend of mine who only wanted to go sit in a *cantina*, and he
just walked right over to me. You see, *en España*, we couldn't
sit in the *cantinas*, couldn't even look in the front door to see
what was happening inside. Anyway, he walked over to me
exactly like a prospective suitor would. He did not take his
eyes off me from the moment I sat down. He bowed regally
and sat down right next to me; he smiled at me with a face
that I had only dreamed of. He seemed so handsome and
dashing, and he spoke only to me and to no one else.

"It seemed there was no one else in the world at that
moment but the two of us. It was like we were living by our
own clock, altogether. Everyone else by theirs. He spoke to
me and in the most marvelous, educated Spanish. Not *Mexicano* Spanish or *Español de Nueva Mexico* or that *pocho* stuff
from over in California, but *Español de Granada, de Seville*. It
was perfect Spanish, a gentleman's Spanish.

"But as we were talking"—she placed her hand to her
forehead with a look of deep distress—"I slowly began to

realize that he was using phrases that my papa used and no one else. Phrases I have not heard since I left Spain. I realized that he used phrases that only my mama used and no one else. You see, my mother, God bless her, always said, 'as God wishes,' after every sentence, but in the old way, with the archaic subjunctive that her ancestors used.

"And my father, God please forgive him, used to always say, 'I shit in the mouths of ten saints.' It was his favorite saying, you know. He and all the old men would say it as they drank their anise. But my father economized the phrase and made it his own. When he said, 'I shit,' we all knew what the rest of the sentence was."

"*Me cago*," she said, smiling.

" '*Me cago*,' to him it was like saying 'you don't say' or 'can you believe it?' *Qué scandaloso! Me cago en las bocas de diez santos! Ay, qué lástima*, how that phrase scandalized my poor mother! He had no love for the Catholic church, to say the least. He hated it. His father was a Basque separatist, you see." She rolled her dark eyes and smiled at the thought of her dear father. "They say a blasphemy is a prayer reversed.

"Satan said both my mother's and my father's phrases to me after he had softened me with wit and poetry and news from the old country. It was then that I knew he was using Spanish from my own memories. Pulling them from inside my very skull."

She made a motion as if picking something from beneath her brow. Josephina seemed distracted for a moment as a thought struck her seemingly for the first time.

"It was the ultimate seduction, *qué no*? The greatest perfume to the human race is a whiff of their own smell, and Satan knows it. He had to be reading my mind. He was able to know my thoughts even when I was not thinking them. It was at this moment that I happened to look down at his feet. What do you think I saw?" she asked, her eyes widened and her lips pressed hard together.

"Down there"—she pointed to the boy's feet—"down there where an ordinary man has boots or sandals or moccasins, I saw two cloven hooves, *pezuñas*, just like the feet of a goat or a bull."

She looked around the room to make sure that no one else was present.

"And he had fur above those hooves, fur that was as green as moss. It was then that I knew who he was. I knew who he was!"

She snapped her fingers with enthusiasm.

"So I pulled out this very cross." She put her hand into the bag and retrieved a wooden cross with a small, rusted Christ figure nailed to it.

"I pulled this sacred thing out and stuck it not two whole inches from his face and I spat on him. That's right. I spat and said the name of the Christ almighty at the same moment. My spit burned his cheek where it landed and ran down. I could see it steaming on his face, my spit. When I looked around the bar, I could see that time had frozen for everyone but me and the beast. All the people in the *cantina* were like mannequins. It was then I knew that spirits live in different time and to reach them you must be able to move in time.

"Anyway, my spit opened his skin like a glowing blister and millions of flies emerged when the blister broke. Then the beast screamed my name with a breath that smelled like ten cesspools, and I ran out of there without ever looking back. It has been war ever since. I have fought Satan every day of my life since the day he let me see his pretty face and his ugly feet. I fight him when I fight against the *sustos, como pobre* Vernetta."

She realized that she had said too much and hoped that he hadn't been listening too closely. The coffee on the iron stove began to percolate, its wondrous fragrance filling the adobe house. The story did seem to frighten the boy, and the old woman, gratified, rubbed his head to reassure him a bit.

"Don't worry, *mijo*," she said. "I can kick the devil's green ass."

She made a sweeping fist and smiled.

"He's a real *cabrón*. He picks on good people, on poor people. He leaves the rich alone because they're already his." Then she reached up for a piece of chorizo, chopped it up and began to fry it without ever taking her eyes off the boy.

"You mustn't swear like your *abuela*, okay?" she said hopefully. "I guess it's in my blood, and I hope it's not in yours."

The boy reached into the bag and pulled out a second cross, one made of rough wood and held in a crucifix form by a rusting nail. Glued onto its arms were a tiny plastic baby figure, a little trailer like Vernetta's, some toy metal bananas, a little tin bus and the postmark from an envelope. The postmark said Flagstaff, Arizona, on it. Below the postmark was a small vial of oil, sealed with wax.

"Why are the two crosses so different?" the boy countered quickly, feeling a bit guilty about all the bad words he had already learned from Claude and from the Blue Moon.

"One is Catholic and the other is only for curing, for special purposes," she answered, hoping he would be satisfied with that.

He seemed to be. The second brown cross was barely Christian. It was Indian with a thin Christian veneer, like Manuel. It had ancient pre-Spanish origins and little to do with Christ, and Josephina knew it. It had been a gift from another *curandera*, a Mayo. A gift from a withered, powerful old mystery woman named Ana Martinez, who, like Satan, had long ago recognized Josephina for what she was.

Josephina had met the woman years ago while on a mission of mercy near the Nueva Pascua. She had never before gone to a Mayo *familia* because they had their own *curanderas*. She was surprised when the call came to her, but she had gone anyway. She had endured that harrowing ride in a horse-drawn wagon. The driver had been a leering old Mayo who had filled the gaps in his diseased gums with wads of chewing tobacco.

"You'll never get that baby out," she said.

The voice seemed to come from nowhere. Josephina had not noticed her before, the small room had been filled with women who surrounded the expectant and suffering mother and were speaking quietly among themselves.

"You'll never get him out without turning him. He's in there crooked."

It was true, both things had been true: it was a boy and he was in there crowded and crooked. It would have been a breech birth, long and painful. The voice came forward, and the group of women quietly and respectfully parted for her. Ana Martinez, seamstress and *curandera*, came forward and knelt beside Josephina, then patiently showed her the ritual for the straightening of babies. She brought out a strange and childish-looking cross, with curious, naive, little things hanging on it, the same cross that now lay in her bag. She had carefully laid out her cloth of significance and set up her handmade candles.

Then she lit dried herbs afire in a tin bottle lid, wafted the pungent smoke toward the mother, then began to sing a prayer in a language nowadays so lonely for mouths. Within two hours, the baby began to turn.

"Why did they call me?" Josephina had asked at last, staring at the baby draped purple and glistening across his mother's breast. Both women had taken a seat on a bench in the birthing room.

"They did not call you," said the old Mayo woman. "I called you. This cloth"—she held it up near her face, her hands hidden beneath it—"never washed and never to be washed, will make its meaning known to you. It is yours now." She handed the old brown cloth to Josephina, who placed it upon her lap.

Then Ana Martinez held up a square, handmade bottle with a dark cork in its neck. Josephina had stared intently at the sediment of whole scorpions suspended in a clear, viscous fluid.

"*Esta botella?*" asked the old Mayo woman.

"I've heard of it," said Josephina, deeply shaken by the sight of the thing. "*El agua de alacrán*. Scorpion water. I thought it was just a story," she said, taking the heavy bottle in her hands. "The stories say there is a final choice . . ."

"May it never, ever be used," interrupted the old Mayo.

"*Ojalá que 'sí*," responded Josephina, crossing herself with severe and rigid motions from forehead to breast.

She had stared into the thick, translucent elixir where hundreds of angular, segmented insects had drowned while flailing and stinging at one another, their crescent hands pinching.

"They call the fluid '*lágrimas*,' tears. Some of my tears are in there, but I think it's mostly *mescal*," said Ana Martinez.

"Have you ever tried to kill a scorpion? When there is nothing left, they still claw at life. You must place the scorpions into the *agua* while they still live. That way the potion will have both the venom and the desperation of scorpions."

"Is your husband dead?" Josephina had asked.

The old woman would not answer. She only turned quietly away as if to hide an answer that would be all too clear in her eyes.

"A sniff of the cork is good for epilepsy," she said.

"That insulin stuff will kill you. It's no good. And just a tiny drop in a glass of water makes a good eyewash for cataracts."

"Which did you choose?" persisted Josephina, still thinking about the stories she had heard.

The old woman would never answer. It was as though the question had never been asked.

"This cross came north with my great-great-grandmother," she said finally. Her voice broke as she spoke. She had been visibly moved by the questions. "Its power could not possibly be said in Christian words. It is older than churches, older than missions; it is a key to doors that others cannot even see." She put the cloth down carefully, then lifted the old cross up to her eyes with both hands.

"It is a key that can be changed by the things placed on it to open doors that others cannot enter. As we *Indios* have hidden ourselves beneath their religions, so this old wood takes this form, the cross. The cross is only a translation of the wood as the singing prayer is a translation of the spirit. I called you here to give these things to you."

She handed the cross to Josephina. The word PHOENIX from a newspaper article was glued to the right side and next to it was a small Spanish *peseta*. Josephina recognized her own handwriting on a scrap of paper glued to the crux next to the small toy trailer exactly like Vernetta's. There were white hairs glued in a clump on the other arm of the cross. Both the Mayos and the Yaquis used the hair in their rituals, and Josephina recognized them as such.

"You see there," the old Mayo said, pointing to the objects

glued to the cross, "I ran a check on you. I have already
investigated you. It's like a screening; don't worry, it's standard procedure. I have to be certain." She smiled.

"In many years your own time to do this will come. You
will be the ear and the mouth for these old powers; then you
will turn them over to the next."

The old woman dusted one hand with the other.

"Then maybe you will have to answer the questions." She
gave Josephina a tired smile.

The old woman turned to leave the birthing room, then
stopped and turned back.

"Adelita, your dear little sister, she is well," she said.

"Can I walk to the bus depot with you, Abuela?"

"*Sí, pero* you have a job to do for me this morning. Why
don't you put on some *música* so I can finish the dishes with
a song."

Then her voice took on a very serious tone. She wagged
her finger at her grandson, who was leafing through her 78s,
her LPs and her 45s.

"Satan is everywhere these days, *mijo*. He seems to have
gained ground in this country, but he hasn't won yet and,
God help us, he never will. He hides, but I look for him
everywhere, every day."

She looked around the room as if to demonstrate.

"I thought at first that he hid out in fears or even that he
hid out in lust. I thought he would reveal himself most often
in those two things. But in Denver I was neither afraid nor
lustful."

She placed both hands on her heart.

"After considering the matter over these last thirty years,
and after meeting him on so many battlegrounds, I think I
have found out where he hides mostly."

She walked over and lifted his chin and made their eyes
meet.

"He hides in *satisfacción*. What is the English word, complacency? Yes, *mijo*, complacency. This crazy country here has

a morality vacuum, and they keep trying to fill the hole with laws and more laws. Here they throw their children out of the house and the children grow up and throw out the old ones and then everybody wonders why they're all so lonely."

"Listen to me, Beto," she leaned close to him.

"There are stangers in the house. The people who now have dominion over this land that is sacred to your grandfather and his forefathers have no respect for it. When you grow up in this place, in this strange country, you may not always have me or your *abuelo* to teach you what is right. Lord knows your mother doesn't have any sense. You must hear us and listen to what we teach you while we are still here on earth. Okay?"

She paused to gather her thoughts into a single sentence that the boy would understand and remember. The boy chose an Alberta Hunter record, but she shook her head in disagreement.

"Doesn't this feel like a Hank Williams morning to you?" she asked, both eyebrows raised.

As he cranked up the machine, she inhaled then exhaled slowly, wondering if he would really remember what she was about to say. She walked over to her grandson, bent down to take his face into her hands.

"You must distrust any idea that the majority of people believe in. *Entiendes?* Do you hear me? Do you hear your old grandmother?"

The boy nodded.

Outside, Manuel started the old Ford and gunned the engine and played the radio for a while, until the thermostat popped open, sucking down the water beneath the radiator cap and until the filaments in the tubes glowed red, before turning both off.

He was pleased that they, like he, still worked. He ran his fingers over the oil-bath air filter, and he checked the battery level and the oil and topped it off with a quarter-pint of Eagle re-refined, paraffin-based econo-oil. Then he dropped down to all fours and gazed beneath the oil pan at the spreading dark spot in the sand. The only spot in Arizona without ants, he laughed. The rear seal, he thought; the sphincter is weak.

Manuel picked himself up, dusted his hands off, then walked down to the highway to the strains of "Cold, Cold Heart," ready to hitch a ride to work. The old Ford had gone to pasture before its owner and was only used in emergencies or for trips out into the desert with his compadres. Manuel would stroke its flanks every morning and touch its smooth, rustless hide. The desert air had been good to it. He would walk backward ten or twenty steps as he left for work, affording himself a last lingering view of his old metal friend.

As he walked the two miles to the main road, Manuel passed the small covered depot where his wife would be sitting in about an hour. He saw her there, fussing over the handle of her old suitcase and wondering whether to return home for a needle and heavy thread to repair it. One end of the leather handle had torn free of its metal ring.

Ahead of him he saw a familiar Studebaker truck coming into Buckeye with a load of adobe bricks, the dust rising behind it. He waved the truck over, leaned in to speak to the driver for a moment, then he continued his long walk to work.

Tension would soon rise up in his skinny body as he neared the overpass at the Black Canyon Highway, his personal perigee. Standing in the wrong place, his eyes saw a wood and rope bridge swaying where there was static, poured cement. Anxiety mounting as he stood over the concrete canal and the *rio* Yaqui both, the Ironies would seize him, tear at him for a moment; then with a mind toward a more heightened state, they would release him to go work his construction job. With savage delight, the Ironies, spirits of the *desplazada*, the displaced, made the deer dancer, the *peyotero* soul, go to some job site, some address on West McDowell, to worry and fuss over re-bar and drill bits.

At the adobe, Josephina scrambled *huevos con chorizo* and poured the boy a cup of hot coffee. She dropped a cinnamon stick into the coffee and smiled at his obvious pleasure.

"*Canela, gracias*. Don't the majority believe in democracy, Abuela?"

"They do," she said quietly, "but only if you agree with them."

He pulled the paper label off the Pet milk can after he laced his coffee with the thick white liquid and began to read the recipes on the back when a shadow fell over the morning sun in the doorway. They both saw the old Papago standing there, his black felt hat in his red hands.

"Manuel sent me, woman," he said. "You must fix the handle on the suitcase before you leave today. It has already broken in *el futuro. Y otra cosa más,* I saw *su perrito* Apache about ten miles outside of town."

Then he was gone. He had not looked at the food. If he had glanced at it, the quickest glance, it would have been graciously offered and accepted. Since he did not, it meant he was not hungry and was spared the dishonor of declining. It was a custom that worked well.

Without questioning, a shaken Josephina walked over to the suitcase and carefully inspected the handle. She got an awl from the old man's lean-to along with a roll of silver crab line and with sadness resident in her face began to reinforce the leather handle at both ends just to be sure.

Now something different will happen than would have happened, she thought to herself, trying to ignore the *Indio's* statement about the dog. The future would not be the same as the one where she walks to the depot and the handle breaks. But she knew that worry would be foolish. Neither future had been revealed to her in this matter, and anyhow, either might have been the one she would've seen. Perhaps in this future the dog is hit by a truck before he gets here. Then all at once she became furious and disgusted with herself and these heathen considerations. She slapped her thighs and stood defiantly, remembering the sacred heart in the kitchen alcove and the votive candles burning, remembering *España,* her Catholic country.

"*En el nombre de Dios,*" she said, "I must remember who I am."

Relieved and satisfied with her own analysis of the situation, she broke her silence.

"*Mijo,* I have to go over and talk to Vernetta on the way to the depot. You have to wait outside. This is woman talk. I know you're not going to the depot with me because your *abuelo* would not have sent the Papago if I could've sent you back home for the needle and thread."

"Maybe you did send me and he saw you afterward, waiting for me to come back," answered the boy.

The old woman thought about it and realized that it was possible, though she did not feel it to be the case. If it were the case, Manuel would have passed the boy on the road.

"Well, you can't go with me," she answered. "I have an important mission for you."

The boy picked up the suitcase for her and followed her out the door and across the lot toward Vernetta's trailer. The yellow porch light had been out now for over a week. Out since the day that the letter had arrived, the day that Hiawatha had been killed and Boydeen had taken her place below ground as an independent observer. Before this, only flash floods, Christmas Day, Easter and sometimes Vernetta's period had extinguished that light.

The Vernetta that greeted Josephina this morning was not the same woman the boy had known for most of his life in the desert. She seemed thinner, milder. This Vernetta had no makeup on, the brown roots were inching upward above her forehead, and she seemed almost solemn in the way she opened the door for Abuela and sat her down to tea served in her precious Melmac. Her voice was not the raucous, bawdy voice he knew, and she was wearing an opaque blouse buttoned to her neck.

"I swore that I would never do this kind of thing again," said Josephina's trembling voice. "Things are crazy. Someone has spotted the dog and what am I doing? I'm going to Flagstaff because of spells and prayers that no priest would say. I don't know what this trip will do to me, but I am afraid. *Madre de Dios*, what am I doing?"

"Is it that different from midwifery for the Indians?" said Vernetta, her voice starting to crack. "You use spells to turn the children. You use your power to make the barren women fertile."

"This was different," said Josephina. "We found out their names. We probed in the air for their address. We used words

against them. We changed their minds. We took a child away
from them."

"But a child that wasn't theirs," sobbed Vernetta.

"I know who we called upon that night, Vernetta, at least
I think I know. But I don't know which power answered,
which power complied. I don't know. I tried to include the
Lord in this, but He just might be ready to punish me for all
my sins."

She thought with dread about Apache, his tongue hanging, his haunches bouncing as he bounded ever closer and
closer. She could almost see his cold eyes, eyes she had once
loved.

"I might end up being beholden to a bad thing. When the
new letter came from those people, I knew. We have cracked
the flow of things right in two."

Josephina's voice sounded strained and uncharacteristically
weak. "I have no problem at all with the first time; I know
the *sustos*. I've seen them many times. Getting them out of
you was no problem, any God-fearing *bruja* can do it. But the
second time, Vernetta. We changed people's minds from the
inside. We put a stick in their ears and stirred up their brains
so those two people woke up the next day ready to give up
the child."

"You did it for me, Josephina. You did both for me, how
can that be a bad thing? Maybe they just realized that the boy
needs his real mother, or maybe they didn't love him as much
as they did their own kids."

Vernetta was crying again.

"Shitfire," she sobbed, her shoulders quaking. "Shitfire. I'll
be beholden, not you, Josephina. Jesus, if God can forgive
these last ten years, maybe he'll see his way clear to cut me
a little more slack, just a little more. What about the sparrow?
You said that meant something."

Josephina did not seem to be listening, the look on her face
plain with worry. "I'll be back in a few days, as fast as I can.
Pray for us." She lifted her bag and turned to descend the
Comet. "My dreams are out of my control these last few days.
It seems my entire night is filled with Cantonese and no prayer
can tell me what it means. Then I began to dream another

dream, even more frightening than the first. Huge green dragonflies. I saw them again and again last night. I hope to God we have done the right thing."

Beto stood up when he heard the creak of the screen door opening. His *abuela* stood on the step for a moment before letting the rusted spring pull the door shut behind her. She adjusted her mantilla and comb, buttoned her black velvet vest and brushed lint and dust from the dark green dress. She felt for the silver chain on her wrist and stood with her brown, leather lace-ups side by side to inspect the shine. There was none.

"You must go find out where Hiawatha and Boydeen were living. Go there, but be careful. Understand me? I would do a finding, but, these days, so many things are on my mind, *mijo*. I'd ask your grandfather to do a finding for me if he didn't enjoy it so goddamn much. Sometimes I think he's got a drug problem."

She wagged a finger at the boy, then continued.

"Look for a small black valise; it's a shiny, hard case about this big." She demonstrated the dimensions to him using her hands.

"There is also a *tripode*—how do you say it in English?"

"Tripod?"

"*Sí, sí,* a tripod."

She had difficulty accentuating the first syllable rather than the second, and she found it equally as difficult pronouncing it as a two-syllable word rather than a three.

"A three-legged metal thing that goes under the valise. Get both of these *cosas*. If someone has already taken them, you have to track these things down. Offer the people a dollar for both. Here's three dollars, but you shouldn't have to pay that much for them. No one in Buckeye knows how to use these tools, and there's no one else to sell them to."

She handed the boy three one-dollar bills.

"Bring the two things to Boydeen. *Entiendes?*"

"*Sí,* Abuela."

"*Pobrecita, la llorona negra,* the curse is set too deep in her flesh. Now she will cry for all of us. She will give us all an epitaph."

She inhaled deeply, then exhaled to calm herself for her journey.

"And watch my medicinal bag. It's on the kitchen table. I know you like to look at the *alacrán*, the scorpions. But you must never open the bottle, *entiendes. Una cosa muy peligrosa.*"

At that the old woman looked through Vernetta's screen door at the woman standing there, then turned to walk to the bus depot, her destined-to-break suitcase handle now secure. As she walked away she decided that it was a good sign.

"Oh yes." She stopped momentarily and turned to her grandson. "If you find a paper or anything with Boydeen's name written on it, backward or forward, burn it or throw it to the west and bury it where it falls. Keep the candles in the altar burning, *mijo.*"

Vernetta, in the distance, stepped from her trailer, then walked slowly to the road to watch Josephina disappear on the horizon. Vernetta's pink skin was flushed red around her eyes, her body trembling.

The letter was clutched in her hand, the handwriting near the folds disappearing from wear. Read over and over, hundreds of times, today and yesterday and each day since Josephina had handed it to her. Over the years she had written so many letters to the Woodleys. None had ever been answered until the first letter came from Flagstaff two years ago, the one that called her an unfit mother and a whore. Flynn had written once, too, years ago. Her only photograph of Danny had come from him. She had managed to take some comfort from his assurances that they were good people, that they lived on a tree-lined street in the northeast part of a small town. It was all he knew.

Yes, Vernetta was a changed woman. She had become an invalid in just the last few days and accepted the fact; memories and dreams of the future were crippling her now. Where once she had been paralyzed from the neck up, now she existed only in her resurrected recollections and her revitalized hopes.

The letter had come to her almost as a miracle, almost an accident, a good accident that breaks crooked bones and resets

them all at once. An accident that Josephina had foreseen
when a while back a little brown sparrow had flown into her
trailer.

"God has chosen you for something," Josephina had said
as she helped to nurse the little thing back to health.

After gaining strength, the sparrow had flown into a glass
pane trying to escape and just about killed itself all over again.
Vernetta felt the sparrow had chosen her. It hadn't wanted
her tits or to slough off a piece of life into her crotch; it wanted
just to sit on the sill for eleven whole days, then simultaneously break her heart and please her as it flew away. Vernetta
recalled how she sank as it soared.

It was this omen that all at once set Josephina about her
mysterious work.

"Eleven days for eleven years," Josephina had said. "Now
is the time. It could have been so many other kinds of bird.
But a sparrow is God's favorite."

"There are two things to be done, one before the other,"
Josephina had explained that night.

"The first is to return the breath to you that was stolen that
night almost eleven years ago. The *susto* is the loss of the
soul, like a wind out of yourself. It is a terror from magical,
evil power. The worst part is that you don't die even though
you don't really live. It's a common disease nowadays." She'd
shrugged.

"It was your father's evil and the evil in that town that
stole your soul. No wonder you couldn't care for the kid. *Dios
mío*, you've been hurting yourself over that guilt for so long.
First, we must restore your soul and your breath to you."

Josephina had seemed so uneasy as she said these things,
but when Vernetta tried to comfort her, she would not
have it.

"I must include Christ in these things," she'd said finally,
"I must include Christ even if he doesn't belong. God forgive
me for even saying it. But you must promise me that you will
never tell my husband, Manuel. I call him a heathen all the
damn time, and then I find myself turning to his ways. I don't
understand the power. I know it's not Christian, but I'm not
sure it's not what God wants. *La verdad*, I don't even know

what the Mayo words mean, but I'm sure they're not the Lord's Prayer."

"Maybe they are," said Vernetta. "After all, God is older than Christianity. J.B. used to say that mathematics is closer to God than King James English."

Josephina had removed the old brown cloth from her bag and reached for the cross with the toys glued to it. Then she had explained the second step.

"Then we will do the most dangerous thing I've ever done. We will compel an act at a distance. In all truth there will be no distance. We will just jump from one furrow to the next. It's good that your friend from Arkansas told us where to aim. Flagstaff is a big target."

"Flynn," said Vernetta.

"Maybe we should've done this two years ago," continued Josephina. "None of us was ready back then, I guess. That first letter from those people was so hateful. But now that we've received a sign, I think it's now or never. And last night, just as sleep came to me, I saw the house. What we will do is we will make a good spell, a good prayer. We will open the doors of that white bungalow."

Vernetta recalled that Josephina had cut the old postmark from the letter. She had glued the small scrap of paper to the old cross. Vernetta could smell the old cloth as her friend unfolded it and spread it out.

"It smells like deep dirt, like when they dig a well," she'd remarked, "or a grave."

"Press it to your brow," responded Josephina, who shivered with Vernetta's words.

"It will draw in your distress, too. There are a million people in the weave and the smell is soil all right. It's like an adding machine of the *espíritu*. I suppose everything, in the end, smells like dirt. I once made the mistake of falling asleep with my head on this cloth." Josephina had crossed herself as she recalled the incident. "I was dreaming the dreams of an ancient Bolivian woman one moment and the next moment I was in a whorehouse in Juarez. Jesus, there's power in that cloth."

Vernetta watched silently now as Josephina disappeared up

the dusty road, her small body and luggage bending with the heat waves. The letter that Vernetta clutched in her hand had arrived within days of Josephina's prayers, her good spell.

There were vehicles going in both directions today on Buckeye Road, and the dust soon obscured the old woman with the suitcase. Vernetta lost sight of her much sooner than she wished.

Slowly, an old dog took her place in the hot, quavering distance.

9

La Maravilla

Beto zigzagged across the dry lot, kicking a red Prince Albert tin twice, three times, before losing interest. He wondered as he wandered in the lot if the thing his *abuela* wanted him to get was valuable. Did it contain all of Boydeen's worldly possessions, the key to her past life, Hiawatha's legacy? He waited at the weedy ditch, squinting right then looking left before attempting to cross the road.

"*Cuidado, cuidado!*"

A mottled deuce and a half carrying a heavy load of *mojados* to the fields rattled by, the men in back silent. It was the driver who had called out the warning. The boy recognized him by his silver teeth and the baseball hat he always wore.

"Hi Judas," the boy yelled out, waving good-bye at the same time.

That name brought a smile to the *mojados'* faces, though the boy didn't know why. Abuela said he was Judas and that he sold his own people cheap to the white man. Every time Abuelo saw him he always said the same thing: "The ax handle and the trees are the same wood." So now the boy repeated the phrase to himself.

"The ax handle and the trees are the same wood."

The boy waited for a crippled pickup to stagger by. It limped along in the dust of the deuce and a half, its flat tire flapping and grinding noisily between the rim and the road while the two round-faced Pimas within grinned as they passed. They were drunk. There was a distance in their eyes that only Indians got when they drank. Their land wasn't vacant anymore, just their eyes.

He waited until crazy Miss Wysteria Maybelle and her platoon of dogs whirled by, re-stirring the settling dust, before walking across the road into Cady, where the red-eyed, slurring denizens were engaged in a leisurely game of seven-card no-peeky.

World enough and time? the boy thought. Is that what the old woman just said?

"World enough and time."

The morning was clear and crisp; sounds carried. The boy loved mornings like this one, when the desert moved back in to reclaim Buckeye. The Blue Moon was silent. Floyd and his wife were curled up on the dance floor and sleeping placidly. The bar was closed, allowing Buckeye to listen to the crisp snapping of a cloth jump rope, the songs of skinny-legged black girls in sack dresses and white socks.

> *Not last night but the night before,*
> *Twenty-four robbers came a knockin'*
> *At the door.*
> *I asked them what they wanted and*
> *This is what they said: Spanish dancers*
> *Do the splits,*
> *The kicks.*
> *The turn around, touch the ground,*
> *Get out of town.*

Alert to any possible craziness, he walked watchfully, looking for any clue that would tell him what form the men in the bestiary were taking today. One of them, Dismas Skully, was spinning out frayed playing cards to the four corners of a detached Cadillac trunk.

The boy tried to size them up from a closer distance and, feeling safer, walked still nearer. Were they cantankerous today, were they hopeless? It soon became clear from their laughter that they had abandoned their usual misanthropic faithlessness this sharp morning for a communal day in the summer heat. Each one sat right next to his own stash of tobacco and fortified wine, the bottle pressed hard against the ankle bone for security. They called their wine "Sonny slap Mammy" or "Must can't tell" or simply "short dog." It was the precious salve that eased their slide to the grave.

"Naw, man, we is a legitimate automotive club as you well know. The world moves and we jes go with it. We ain't got no use for none o' them down to the Blue Moon."

"Nope. No use."

There was general, mumbling, repetitious agreement all around. One of them decided to toast the accord with a swig.

"All that beautiful liquor over there and they got to have that ol' hayron, too. All that beautiful liquor. If God wanted mens to use hayron he'd a put a hole right here in the vein."

Odabee Bracken pointed to the crook in his withered left arm while the others joined him in his righteous dismay, heads nodding and smiles vanished.

"On the other hand," observed another, "that ol' Floyd is sho as shit gettin' rich. Got his old lady workin' for him, too."

All four turned over the first card.

"Jack o' hearts bets," said Dismas.

"Uh-huhmm, plenty money."

"Plenteee."

"No, uh-uh, Hiawatha didn't have no use for none o' us. Never had no use for none o' us. Guess he didn't like no elegant means of bein' transported round this here universe. And that Boydeen filly never even stopped over here. Not even a howdy do."

"No, not even so much," said another.

"A stuck-up little bitch, I guess. She got above her raisin' and look where she is now. Tied down by a spell. Someone done paid the juju man. It sho do smell jes like it. Now the bitch be plumb out her brain. Why don't you try over there to the fifty-fifties, yonder."

He turned to point limp-wristed toward the bus.

"Boydeen used to visit them fools all the time. Shit, for the life of me I cain't hardly see why. And don't be bringin' none o' them abomolations over here, boy. I everday hears 'em blasphemin' over there, hootin' and hollerin' like biblical Sodomites. Lord knows that kinda shit near my sweet '52 Cady like to rust out every quarter-panel."

They all laughed while a lucky winner raked in a handful of washers and fuses, his nervous fingers clawing at his earnest gains. There was only one dime shining in the pile, a token to an ever-diminishing ante.

"Dicks in dresses."

"Peckers in pedal pushers."

Their laughter rose up around them.

"Balls in baby-dolls."

"Sissy mans'll rust out yo' radiator."

"Shit dey totes'll corrode yo' chrome."

"We is iron over here. All iron. Mens is hard."

"Boy, if you spot a gallon o' gas, carry it on over. I might take a notion to jes might start my ride on up today and drive on outta here."

"In yo' dreams, muhfuh," scoffed another, "in yo' dreams."

"Where the fuck would you go?" scoffed Dismas.

"Yeah, mens is iron."

The boy knocked on the door of the bus, and it swung open with a flourish, releasing a sudden flood of smells and sounds that splashed down the three black "watch your steps" out onto the boy's face and the red soil beneath him. Red pepper soup scents wafted out, carried by the strains of "Che Gelida Manina." The steaming soup was simmering over blue propane flames. The boy had seen the girls the day before, braising off the pepper skins in the coals of the outdoor fire, and now the scent of it was everywhere in Buckeye Road.

"You can't be afraid to use cumin," one of the girls had been saying. "It's certainly worth the risk of an aftertaste, and just the tiniest drop of lemon juice, smack in the pot, will fix that."

Diablo, in leather pants and a brief, frilly little blouse knotted above the belly button, had pulled on the silver lever that swings the door open.

"Exact change, no bills please," she said, smiling just hard enough to let the boy know that she wasn't serious.

Even though her face was only a few feet away, she had to speak loudly to be heard over the towering voice of Enrico Caruso.

"Move to the back, please, move to the back."

The other girls were gathered in the back of the bus, lounging or sewing and talking among themselves as the soup slowly evolved. Each one was in a different stage of cosmetic readiness. Panocha was spreading Nair on her legs while Starlet was brushing Dippidy-Do on her white curlers.

On the shelves around them, in niches one for each, the girls kept their folded clothing and their toiletries. Above each niche each girl kept a montage of photos of a past life. Mothers and fathers smiled ironically down, their happy assumptions still intact. Sisters and brothers embracing. They were analogues of an unsustainable instant, its shadow frozen on paper.

"Those drapes just have to go," said Evangeline, nodding toward the faded blue drapes hanging from the pullstops and covering the starboard windows.

"They're just so . . . they're just so . . . Velveeta!" She laughed happily at locating the perfect word.

They all smiled at Beto, and Angelique got up to offer him a cold soda pop, fresh from the drip pan in their Koolerator.

"It's a Nu-Grape," she said. "Not one drop of grape juice in it." She smiled proudly. "It's all totally artificial. The Rainbo finally got some in after I don't care to count the number of requests I've made."

She dried her hands with a towel, as the drip pan had been full.

"My little hands are cold." She smiled.

"You wish," said Panocha, feigning cruelty.

"Not even hormones will shrink those knuckles."

"Would you like a bite to eat?" asked Angelique, refusing to acknowledge the jibe.

No thank you," said Beto. "I just had some breakfast."

Angelique reached over to pull the needle out of the groove, and Caruso's voice evaporated.

"Yes, well, first we saw your grandfather leave; then we

saw the Papago fellow come by. Then we saw your dear grandmother walking by with her suitcase and wearing her best little outfit and we noticed poor Vernetta trailing after her, shaking like a rag doll. It all looks kind of important," she said, hoping to beguile some gossip out of the boy.

"*Pobre Llorona, la gringa*," chimed in Panocha.

"We all noticed that it wasn't her medicinal bag that she was carrying. It's certainly unusual, if not obviously important."

"Yes, it's important," Beto said, putting the Nu-Grape bottle to his lips.

They were right. It sure didn't taste like grape juice. It tasted better than grape juice. It tasted incredibly purple, and the little sweating bottle was shaped like one of Popeye's arms.

"I wish you wouldn't walk through that Cady place," said Starlet, who had begun dyeing a pair of white heels a bright yellow.

"Those old snakes can't be trusted. Whenever they pull themselves out of those rusting shells, my skin just crawls. How on earth can Potrice and Sugar Dee allow scaly things like that to touch them?"

"Do any of you girls know where Boydeen and Hiawatha lived?" interrupted Beto.

He no longer felt awkward at the use of the word "girls."

"You're changing the subject, Beto," cooed Evangeline. "We girls have surmised some things, you know. We know it has to do with Vernetta's child. Your grandmother must've located him somehow?"

Beto did not respond. There was impatience on his face.

"That poor Boydeen," began Starlet, obviously disappointed that the boy wasn't talking, "living like an animal down under there and that Hiawatha was such a pig. She wore that same shift every day, did you notice that? That little flowered thing with the tacky collar, heaven forbid. And those shoes. I'm sorry, but I think he got what he deserved."

There was the sound of agreement all around the bus. The yellow spike heels were placed on a shelf near a window to dry.

"*Otra Llorona, verdad?* Men can be so cruel and insensitive," said Panocha, breaking into an ironic laughter that the others soon joined.

"I'm not sure where they lived, but it had to be close by, because we saw poor Boydeen almost every day."

"She always came from that direction," said Diablo, pointing west to a spot somewhere beyond the tar-paper shacks.

"Come to think of it," she said, "she always walked back that way too when she couldn't get you-know-who to leave the Blue Moon."

"What in heaven's name did she see in that fool?" Evangeline wondered out loud. "Here she's got a trade and all."

"She said he was once a poet," said Angelique almost apologetically.

Angelique knew that this revelation meant that she had been holding out, contrary to the most important rule of the Secret Sharer. "She said he wrote poetry in prison. You know how Boydeen likes words."

"He must have said something pretty powerful to bewitch that poor girl like that," sighed Panocha. "Nothing penetrates like words," she added wistfully. "She ate with us almost every evening. She'd follow him like a puppy till the Blue Moon was in sight, then she'd turn around and walk straight over here. *Hay puras Malinches allí,*" she spat.

"She always needed to talk, poor thing," said Starlet. "She seemed to enjoy the civility here. She had such a way with words, herself. Sometimes she'd eat over with Potrice and Sugar Dee if they weren't already here. You might ask them where she lived."

"Thanks for the soda water," said the boy, already running down the aisle of the bus for the door.

"Come back later for dinner, Beto," Diablo yelled after him. "We're having red pepper soup with soft slivers of avocado, braised summer squash and yours truly has laid her hands upon the utmost, absolutely, most delectable capons."

As the boy ran westward, he heard the laughter from an unintended joke and he wondered what a capon was.

Potrice and Sugar Dee were stretched out, lounging in their

long, green car. As Beto approached he could just see the tops of their heads in the backseat of the huge Pierce-Arrow. One small black foot connected to a slender ankle fell lazily through a slightly opened door and rested lightly on the running board.

Their morning fire was still going strong and a red coffeepot hung from its iron hook. Two Sears and Roebuck sleeping bags, both green, were draped over the windshield and one door, airing out for the day. The trunk lid was up; douche bags, plates, eating utensils and food packages were arrayed neatly within. The radio was low: Charlie Parker. In the early morning, there wouldn't be any customers, so the boy felt it would be all right to just drop in.

"Hello ladies, do you know . . ." He stopped short as he reached the door of the car. The two women stopped kissing to look up at him, but neither removed her submerged hand from the crotch of the other; their hands were both still mired there, and Sugar Dee's left breast was out and shiny with spit. The places where their dusky skins touched still shimmered like a distant fire line. Now he knew why the sleeping bags were on the windshield.

"Do you know where Boydeen lived?" he stammered, feeling too awkward to look away.

"Don't tell the men, Beto, please," Sugar Dee placed her index finger to her lips and whispered, pulling cloth up over her breast.

"It wouldn't be good for business," said Potrice, "though lately I'm beginning to think they'd like it if they knew."

"I think they already know, Potrice," said the boy. "I've heard them say it."

"Heard them say what?" asked Sugar Dee.

"That you are *lesbianas*," answered the boy, a little awkwardly.

"Shit, I wouldn't be surprised," said Sugar Dee, a little incredulously. "They probably like the idea that we're lesbians."

"Every one of those damn fools thinks he's gonna be the man to set us straight," laughed Potrice. "What were you asking about poor Boydeen?"

Each woman had managed to ease her hand from the crotch of the other during the conversation.

"Do you know where she lived with Hiawatha? *Mi abuela* wants me to go there and get something for Boydeen."

"Somewhere out near the levee," said Potrice, "out past the old Mexican graveyard. I do know that much because she was always afraid when she had to walk by it. Hiawatha never let us near their place so we never learned where it was. He used to get real pissed when Boydeen would come by just to pass the time of day. Guess he thought we were gonna turn her little head away from liking men. Shit, he did that himself," spat Potrice.

"Here she is a child, good parents and such, and she had a real trade. Lord, a woman who can support herself without having to marry or drop her linen and she's jealous of those hippo-women at the Blue Moon. Shit! What's the name of the bitch yonder with the big ass, Back-Porch?"

"Back-Porch Threadgill," answered Sugar Dee. "Ass like a backhoe."

"And that other bitch, the milk cow with them African old-lady titties?"

"D-cup Devoreaux."

"Yeah, D-cup. Them bitches is almighty proud of being so damn unbalanced. The fool man used to hanky-pank with them bitches right in front of poor Boydeen."

"She was the only clean woman that nigga would ever see and he's everyday down there playing stink finger with those blimps. And those stupid bitches, always gonna steal him away from her, always teasing with that black cat bone and those scraps of paper. They paid that Toop fella to make him up and leave her. It just killed her."

"No," said Sugar Dee, shaking her head, "it killed him."

West of Tar-Paper was all desert. The road passed Wysteria Maybelle's shack and eventually reached the bus depot, a small bench covered by a canopy and surrounded by a vast garden of cactus teeming with blue-belly lizards and huge black ants. It was a straight line out of Buckeye to the depot, the kind of straight line that can exist only in a desert or in the air.

To the left of the road was a wash where an old levee had been built against the flash floods that tormented Phoenix in three- or four-year cycles. The dry levee guaranteed that Phoenix would be saved in the event of another flash flood and Buckeye Road would be wiped from the face of the earth.

To the right was the Mexican cemetery and more desert, vast patches of scrub and manzanita, mesquite and ant mounds. As he passed by, the boy tried to avoid seeing any of the crosses and headstones that were enclosed by a small iron fence. To catch even a glimpse of the crosses would be to eavesdrop, to intrude upon the conversations going on beneath them.

But one cross managed to catch his eye, a small one with a bouquet of plastic flowers in front of it. A child's grave. Though he was almost past the iron fence, he felt a dolorous twinge, a tugging in his sideward glances. There seemed to be traces of thought rising up everywhere, piercing his skull with strings of words, skeins of sensation. With photons of memory. As he began to run, he thought he heard soft whispering in Spanish.

"*Buenos días. Con permiso,*" he said before hurrying away, "Abuelita is right."

Still farther out were the Papago and the Apache reservations. Sometimes those people wandered over as far as Buckeye Road, staggering drunk or just moving to move. The train whistle lured them over, pulled them in.

"Brown cabooses stoke their stoves with Indian dreams," Manuel would say.

Some Indians came to see Vernetta or Potrice and Sugar Dee. Others moved just to fight the claustrophobia. They wandered, crisscross, looking for something, these dark-skinned, laconic people. Out here was nowhere to live if you were not red or brown.

The boy walked to the edge of the levee but stood looking downward for a moment before descending. He had often played in the levee with his friends, sliding down the sides on flattened cardboard boxes. Something about this day was different. Something that he did not understand held him at the top of the escarpment for a solemn moment and a deep

breath at the earthen edge before going down. He carefully
slid down the side to the bottom of the wash. The dry gravel
and loose dirt followed him downward in small landslides.
Some fanned out at the base and some found its way into his
shoes.

He remembered that there were old iron conduits stored
down there by the city. They were huge pipes in stacks of
five, pyramids that all the kids had played in at one time or
another. Just as he arrived down at the rusty stacks, he was
startled by a sudden, loud rustling, and then he was immediately put on guard when he saw a black man in rags pull
himself violently from inside one of the five-foot-wide pipes
and stand menacingly ten paces in front of the boy.

It was Onan Spillers, Odabee Bracken's pal, drunk and
mean-looking. His huge chest heaved with the sudden exertion. All of his hair and clothing was the color of the rust
that attacked the pipes.

"What you want down here, boy?"

Beto stared back at him from a safe distance and readied
himself to run should the need arise.

"I said, what you doin' here, boy? You got any money,
boy?"

He took one off-balance step toward the boy, who ran a
few easy steps backward. Onan was a big, muscular man who
had been a mule some time long in the past, a laborer's
laborer, a two-slide mule. It was said he could drag a double
blade through the mud with his own shoulders and his own
neck if it came right down to it. That's how the other old
black men described him: a two-slide mule.

He could lift this here and put that over there like no other
man alive. If you said, "Gee" he would, without thinking,
spin to the right.

"I'm looking for Hiawatha and Boydeen's place. Do you
know where they stayed? I have to get some of Boydeen's
possessions."

"Her shit is mine now," said Onan, almost losing his balance from the effort of speech; his hands in their fingerless
gloves clawed the air in front of him for balance.

"He's stone dead cold and she's gone off somewheres, and besides, possession is mine tents o' da law."

He seemed very proud of that last bit of wisdom and smiled; his last remaining tooth stuck up from black gums like a cypress stump. But he was quickly brought back to the here and now by the realization that the boy was circling around him toward the pipes.

"So you movin' gee, huh?" Onan grinned. "Well, I kin jus' move haw, too."

Onan dragged himself slowly to his left only to have the boy break to his right.

"Movin' haw!" cried Onan, whose move to the right caused him to fall to his knees.

"Why did you leave Cady, Onan?" asked the boy in hopes of distracting him long enough for a look into the pipes. "I just saw all your old friends there playing cards and having a good time."

"Shit, my car was jes' as good as dey'n. It was good as dey'n. None of dey muhfuh cars run no how. How come dey better 'n me all a sudden, one time?"

He was stumbling without direction now, unmindful of the boy.

"An' the gummint, dey cuts my muhfuh disability chit in haft. In haft, goddamn! What I know 'bout malingering?"

Onan was crying now. Sitting flat on the ground and crying, any hopes of catching the boy gone. The reason for catching the boy forgotten.

"I'se in here," he screamed, holding his hands in front of his eyes, his fingers and purple nails shooting out of the remnants of his gloves.

"I'se in here! You knows the trouble?" he asked the boy without really asking.

"You knows the trouble? Niggas cain't commit no suicidal! That's right, we cain't commit no suicidal. Who else could take livin' like this? That goddamn right's done been taking away along with everthane elst. We endures, that's our fuckin' curse.

"White boy gets pimples and he turn aroun' an' slit his

wrist." Onan made a motion with his right hand over his left.

"White boy think he a queer and he go on ahead an' slit his other wrist. Niggas been sold, niggas been worked like mules, nigga been used up since the first day on this land and he keep on livin' and he keep hopin'. Shit, I don't even know what it is I'm hopin' for. It's like it's in the blood, jes like the sickle cell. I cain't relieve it. So I keeps on keepin' on."

Onan rolled over slowly and carefully got to his feet.

"Paper in my shoes ain't nothin'. Teeth comin' out ain't nothin'. I jus' keeps on. I'se in here. Paper in my shoes ain't nothin'. Indians belongs here"—he swept his right hand across a far horizon—"and they ain't got jackshit. I seen 'em out here, like they was wanderin' through a house they used to live in."

Onan walked to his left a little, sat down on a battered, rusted mop bucket, and seemed to be inspecting his hands and gloves. As Onan sat trying to recognize himself, the boy walked through the pipe and emerged from the other side carrying the black case and the tripod. He left the three dollars behind, dropped it into the pile of rags and rubble that must've been Onan's home.

"We's got to kill this way o' doin' things. We jes' has to be. We has to be, without no reference to them. Why they transplant us, then call us a weed?"

He made no effort to rise to his feet now or to finish what must have been a cherished thought.

"Stay a while, boy. Keep ol' Onan comp'ny. Stay on a while, boy. I got nobody out here. You know that Sigmund Freud fella was fulla shit? We ain't scramblin' to screw. We's scramblin' not to die! That's all. Not to die! These here used to be high-grade pants," he said quietly, looking down at his torn clothing.

"Hiawatha prized 'em. Nobody out here but me and every once in a while that crazy Irish woman and her dogs. Nobody, 'cept me and that weird little white fella with the bulldog."

The boy, who had been walking away, stopped dead in his tracks when he heard the last sentence.

"Onan," he said, "does the guy have a vest and a little bow tie and a black Irish linen cap?"

"That's the fella, jes' smile at me and go on his way. Never say a goddamn thing, though, and that dog of his don't never bark. Cain't trus' a dog don't bark."

"Onan," warned the boy, "if he doesn't have a shadow, him or his dog, if neither one of them's got a shadow, move out of here. If he smiles at you and nods at you exactly the same way every time, like he was a needle stuck in a groove, move away from here. There's room back at Cady, I was just there. They can't make you leave."

"A haint?" said Onan, suddenly stock still. There was a terrified look on his face.

"A goddamn haint without no shadow out here wit me? Oh, mebbe I done seen the rock o' ages now! Mebbe I'm comin' into that great room. Mebbe it's the debble come fo' me. Wait! He come by here dis mo'nin', right over here, walk by jes as nice."

Onan rose and scrambled over to the small path between two stacks of pipes and began to scour the ground.

"Dey ain't no feetprints!" he yelled. "Man nor dog. Shit!" he yelled as he ran back into the pipe that had been his home.

His voice could be heard reverberating down the length of pipe and up the gulley as the boy walked back toward Buckeye Road.

"Dey is a nice little Nash Rambler I'se had my eye on over there. Thrown a rod; sticks outta the block like a hard-on outta my high-grade pants." He smiled. "But the headliner's damn good, and the hood's still got the ornament. It's a two-barrel flathead six. Talking 'bout two-barrels, I sho could use another glimpse or two of that sweet Sugar Dee."

Onan seemed happier now. He smiled and ran his tongue nervously around his tooth.

"Sweet Sugar Dee! And that Potrice . . . dem titties flap like bird's wings!"

The ghost meant things weren't all set, things couldn't always be foretold, not even the inexorable rush of a wasted life toward a predictable end.

"We ain't the white man's shadow, is that what you say, boy? We ain't the white man's shadow."

There was a hard, metallic click, a reassuring sound. A sharp snap, like quality, milled parts holding, then releasing dutifully. It was a hard click, clean as a working equation. Boydeen rubbed the dark case with her soft fingers, then opened it gingerly, tenderly, slowly. She looked up at Beto and smiled as she did so, a smile that bypassed adulthood completely and went straight around grown-up to a forgotten moment of childhood contentment, a pure, depth-plumbing smile. The boy returned the smile with ease, a perfect reception, translation and re-transmission of it.

For the first time since the stabbing, Beto felt that Boydeen was really aware of the presence of another person.

Unblinking, she looked back down at her prize. Her first smile since that terrible day was a radiance. She had carefully set the thing on its legs and then quickly dashed to the other side of her room and back to grab a box to sit on. For a minute she sat there as inert as the shining machine. She squared her narrow shoulders and placed her fingers on its keys and was instantly transformed and transported.

"What is it, Boydeen?"

Her fingers moved for a second only, just a few flashing movements.

"What is it, Boydeen? Is it a kind of typewriter, Boydeen?"

Her fingers danced again, and a thin sliver of paper pushed through and folded down quietly into a receptacle.

"Wait here," the boy said, knowing good and well she was going nowhere. He crawled to the front of the Rainbo and called out to Claude, who happened to be talking with a friend on the front porch of the store, his voice clearly audible.

"Who's that?" said Claude, looking up the street and down.

"It's me, Beto, down here."

Claude stuck his head under the porch, and when his eyes had adjusted to the dark, he smiled, then scrambled down and stopped cold at the sight of Boydeen smiling behind her machine, her fingers moving slowly and steadily whenever a word was spoken.

"What is it?" he said, rubbing his shock of blond hair, a gesture he'd taken from his father.

"I'm not sure. I think it's some kind of record-keeping thing or word keeper."

Her dark fingers danced.

"It's a court thing!" exclaimed Claude. "I seen one when my uncle was in custody court in Little Rock. He was a alcoholic drunk so he lost all the kids."

Boydeen smiled to herself as they talked.

"There was this pretty lady in front of the judge that took down ever word my uncle said, even the dirty ones. She took down ever word even when six people were talking at the same time. God, my uncle cussed! My auntie cried and the judge was pronouncing stuff, but she took it all down, ever word, and her face never moved. Her face was like one of them pictures in the illustrated Bible."

The boys looked closely at the ribbon of paper that had collected.

"She must really know words," said Claude. "Look how she's busted them up. The pieces don't look nothing like when they was said together."

"Maybe it's like a microscope," said Beto. "You've seen those pictures in the magazines. That one picture that looks like a jungle is really the body of a housefly. Maybe, up real close, words ain't the same either."

The faster they talked the more Boydeen smiled, till an hour passed and the narrow paper ran out and through and no one even noticed. The two boys sang "Dixie" and "Hello Walls" till Mr. Lee, up above, stomped on the floor and yelled out for some quiet. Boydeen got each and every word, broke them all up into their fundamental parts, and set them down in order.

Boydeen had moved into the abandoned storage space below the Rainbo Market, the old grain and feed basement. She had used her last words to a living person to refuse Josephina's invitation to stay in the adobe. She had also ignored the old woman's careful warnings about the police. She got

up from the rocker and walked directly to the Rainbo bottom
and set up house almost as soon as the last stitch was tied
off and cut and Josephina and Manuel had finished dragging
her tiny, resisting body backward over poor Hiawatha's body
in an effort to reverse Toop's curse.

With her hands, she'd scooped up old, rotting grain sacks
and stale dirt 'til she reached the cement floor. She chased
away the mustiness and the silverfish with pomatum-scented
candles. She tried shooing the rats away with sign language.
She made a mattress of gunnysacks and fashioned shelves
with milk crates taken from Mr. Lee's store above. She silently
decorated the walls with cardboard advertising discarded from
the walls above, and when Mr. Lee chanced to see the glow
of candles coming from the basement of his store, he had
kindly consented to one extension cord and a sixty-watt bulb
in the interest of safety.

Potrice and Sugar Dee had donated matched sets of sheets
and blankets, some soap and towels, a little sterno stove and
a water bottle. The reverend Drake came by with a tiny kitten,
just weaned.

"She's named Rosa after Rosa Parks," shouted the reverend
from the porch as the kitten made its way down to Boydeen.

"She'll make sure those damnable rats is kept at bay."

Josephina had arranged with the Cheungs to leave Boydeen
a plate of food every day when they returned from the fields.

Boydeen had stayed hidden under there while the sun
baked Hiawatha for another full day, and she had been down
there when the city truck came for Hiawatha's stiff body. She
had spoken to him from down there. She had used her words
to try to move him from that position the way she had used
words to try to pry him away from the Blue Moon and away
from those other women. Words like those that Hiawatha had
metered and rhymed to woo her.

She sent her pleading words, like tiny Asian kites, across
to him from under the market. *"Hiawatha, please come over here.
You can hit me for what I've done. You can beat me good for what
I've done."* They crossed the street obediently and struck his
swelling chest softly. *"Hiawatha, say a poem to me. I'm not jealous*

now." Then one after another, the words all dropped away, rebuffed by ears groping only to hear the grave.

The vowels had almost no power in themselves; they depended on the consonants to carry them across, the unpuckering of lips or the slap of the tongue on the upper teeth. Then weak, unheard and disheartened, the words refused to go out there anymore. No more forays for these phrases. No more sorties.

The police had come as expected, blustering and bluffing, three days late. They asked their questions, threatened weaklings, wrote down names and had gotten nothing. It was clear that they wanted nothing. After all, it had been a public service killing. Buckeye Road had long since decided that justice was already served, and all that was left was a pine box for Hiawatha at county expense. After all, stabbing was the prerogative of romance. It was pithy and poignant. It was penetration and personal. It was forgiven when shooting was not. Buckeye Road understood the slash in the heat of passion. Stabbing was the intercourse of rage.

A real inquiry into the death would have called the existence of Buckeye Road itself into question. There would be the inevitable questions about property lines, squatters, sanitation and sewage, and so on. The inevitable survey would be proposed. No one wanted that, especially not the big farmers in Glendale. So Boydeen remained everyone's open secret.

Wordless weeks later and the stitches on her breast were almost ready to come out. The scar, the blemish, the cicatrix would be small. But her mind wasn't quite so lucky. Her soul had suffered a great slapping around.

Josephina, cutting the stitches off, thought the good spirit breath had been sucked away by evil, the *sustos*. Josephina had begged to cure the evil wind, but Boydeen would not delay her destiny.

The reverend, praying for her as he knelt under the Rainbo's porch, announced that the chile seen Satan's vile work.

Potrice, watching her lover being speared softly by a hairless, young white boy, conjectured that a door had been opened that should have been left shut.

"Toop should've let things be," she said.

"He should've left off that vanvan and them black candles."

Sister Dora Mae, her megaphone in hand, had shouted her own thoughts down to Boydeen.

"I am the word. I am the way."

The diagnoses ran rampant over Buckeye after the stabbings. It was said by Vernetta that Boydeen had stepped over to the wayside and only chronicled the days, took them down word for word, without being a party to the action.

"She's a true independent observer."

Unanswered by her lover, Boydeen defaulted in everything but the stream of words around her, none of which belonged to her.

Boydeen got everything down.

She got the Pima kids dividing the Cherry Chans they'd stolen from the store above. She got Mr. Cheung calling to her, saying that the food would be right here waiting for her when she was ready.

Mr. Lee always watched the Cheungs' wagon as it rolled out every morning just before the sun left its grip on the horizon. Every morning when he drove in from Phoenix, he would marvel at their unabashed sponge baths at dawn and the silent, bending children busily slicing bok choy. His only Chinese acquaintances in this hellhole and he had no use for them at all.

Laundries and restaurants, he thought, the American-Chinese curse. A mom and pop store was barely a step up, especially way out here in this nowhere. The first China man to buy this place must've been very desperate. He spat his bitterness out past the porch onto the dust as he peeled back by rote the security doors of the store.

Not long now, he said to himself hopefully, not long now. I've done my share here, he thought. Some other young family fresh from Vancouver can have all of this. He looked around himself at Buckeye Road and recalled the first time he and his wife had seen this place. It might as well have been the moon. They had explained to him that the store was small and a bit isolated, but there was certainly no competition and he would have a captured clientele.

"They can't buy anywhere else," the man had said as he handed over the keys, "and besides they're all aboriginals. You can charge whatever you want."

His thoughts were interrupted by the sound of Boydeen below his feet as she pulled her breakfast, a plate of chop suey, back down into the basement. Her presence below his store seemed to ingratiate him with the locals just when tensions had arisen because of his recent price increases.

So Mr. Lee walked outside to the pay phone one morning and ordered paper and ink for the mute girl, then took delivery the next day, upstairs at the store. No one ever bothered to explain it to the bewildered man from the stationery supply house when he delivered his court reporter supplies to a Chinese store in the middle of an eyesore. The nearest courtroom was fifteen miles away.

Sugar Dee and Potrice volunteered to pay for the deliveries. The five fashion plate *maricones* decided that the bus needed redoing and so contributed a substantial amount of furniture and utensils as did Josephina, Vernetta and the Cheungs.

But Boydeen paid her keep on more than one occasion. If bets were made or deals were closed, they were made on the porch of the Rainbo, where Boydeen the listener would take down every syllable.

"I said thirty quarts of whole milk," Mr. Lee had once complained to the Borden delivery man.

"No sir," he'd responded. "It says right here, fifty quarts of whole milk for the Rainbo Market and ten buttermilk." And as he held out an invoice in his own handwriting.

"Boydeen!" Mr. Lee had yelled out. "You got August 16th, the dairy delivery?"

"Yes, sir," came the soft answer from below the floorboards. The confused Borden man looked downward, between his feet.

"Can we have readback, please?"

The only words she ever spoke were on readback. Mr. Lee had discovered the fact while joking with his silent tenant. Then the soft voice below began to read.

"Mr. Lee: 'I can't seem to get rid of fifty quarts of whole in a week.'"

"Mr. Borden's man: 'Well, we got eighteen returns so what say we try thirty-five and move up again if you need to.'

"Mr. Lee: 'Okay, that sounds fine, how about ten of buttermilk and ten orange drink?'

"Mr. Borden's man: 'Okay, you got it. Jesus, hot enough for you?' Do you need more, Mr. Lee?"

"No, Boydeen, that will do. The only time she speak is when she read back." He smiled.

If ever read, her notes would show that "Fireballs o' the Eucharist," Em-Em's singular exclamation, really meant she had fibroids of the uterus. Only Boydeen knew that Em-Em was like a small hen filled with painful, unlayable eggs.

If ever read, they would show that asphalt would eventually come to Buckeye Road, that the Blue Moon would burn down under suspicious circumstances. She would record Mr. Lee's eventual loss of the Rainbo to an eminent domain action. She would type that he cried quietly on the porch, and the record would reflect that he spat on Gold Mountain.

Her final notes would record the moment, years later, when rough, disrespectful men climbed down to get her.

Boydeen, below, got it all down.

In the middle of the night, desperate mothers would come to the porch to pray and have it written. Young black nobodies from nowhere would walk together, hand in hand to the porch and say words to marry each other in writing, on this fringe of life.

People with so little to have and so little time to have it would come to the porch and say their words to someone: "I leave what I got to my little child. I'm sorry to have to go like this, but the child's mother is makin' life impossible fo' me. I fought in Korea. I was born in Raleigh and I'm headin' back this mornin'. Please say this to her if she should ever ask to know about me."

Nothing within earshot of the Rainbo Market would go unchronicled. Anyone who wished to say a thing and have it kept could come to the porch and speak into the depths.

Nothing went unrecorded.

She even recorded that particular morning when the porch of the Rainbo was buzzing with Indians and field-workers, the morning when they all spoke excitedly that Josephina's dog had been sighted. When Apache arrived in Buckeye Road, dark-eyed, alert and with his tongue hanging from the left side of his muzzle, Boydeen peeked out from below the porch and wrote down that he seemed gaunt but friendly. She wrote that he loped past the Rainbo sometime during the early morning hours, the day after Josephina had left for Flagstaff, and that he was waiting there in the adobe when Beto woke.

He was there at the foot of the bed, staring at Beto when the boy cautiously opened his eyes. Apache was a mongrel, a German shepherd and collie mix who was Josephina's dog and had been so for almost ten years. But just over three years ago he had disappeared, running off into the desert with several wild dogs and some coyote mixes. *Indios* hunting in the desert reported seeing him once or twice out near *Palo Verde*, but the sightings stopped when the red handkerchief that he wore fell off near the old mines.

"Apache, Apache!" the boy cried on seeing his old friend, then tossed the covers aside to embrace him.

His grandfather rushed inside on hearing the boy's voice in an empty house and froze in his tracks at the sight of the dog.

"Your *abuela* will not be happy to see him," he said as he bent down to pet the dog.

"She will act all crazy and my life will be made miserable," he shook his head. "Shit, the woman's gonna make my life miserable."

"Doesn't she love Apache, Abuelo?"

"Yes, but you see, a lot of *Mexicanos y Indios de Mexico* believe that a dog is something more than just a dog. There are wolves, dogs, coyotes and *tigres* in Mexico, *hijo*. All these things are what they seem to be and then much, much more.

"Remember how I once told you about the *tigre* dance in Guerrero y Tabasco, where the yellow *tigre* and the *verde*, the green one, fight to determine which crop will be successful in the next year?"

The boy nodded.

"Well, the dance is different from people to people among the *Indios*, but one thing is always the same. It is the dog that leads the people to the *tigres* every year. Even for those *Indios* where there is no *tigre* dance, it is the dog that keeps them safe from the wolf and coyote, even when the dog is really the wolf and the coyote in his deepest heart. You see, men should learn to see forms. Unfortunately, most men only fear forms. They cover them.

"*Por ejemplo*, the form behind the Virgin Mary *aquí en Aztlán* is the *Virgen de Guadelupe* and behind her is *Tonantzin*, the nurse-goddess of the *Aztecas*. An Indian may kneel before the first two, but he prays to the third.

"Long, long ago, before the gift of corn, the dog led the people of the many tribes to the deer. He helped them reach the deer before the wolf could come take the deer from us. You see, we hunted with and against the wolf. It seems to mean that we love and fear the same thing. At the far end of things, right and wrong and human concerns such as that disappear. There are only shapes and forms out there, you see, all powerful yet nothing to be afraid of.

"When the deer left, he gave us the wolf in another form. When the wolf left this plane, he gave us the deer, but in another form. It sounds confusing but someday you'll see."

The old man nodded at the boy and smiled. He scratched the old wolf-dog behind his ears.

"In the end, whether you have wrestled with the forms, seen behind their backs or merely spent your life living for your own belly, it is always the dog that comes to lead its master to *Mictlan*, the land of the dead, or to the other worlds there. But the dog cannot come for this last purpose unless he has first gone away. You see, only the dog is allowed to go to the underworld and return.

"To the Aztecs he was a clown dog, fickle and unpredictable. He was always named *Maravilla*. He goes sometimes in a lightning flash and returns by the same means. He has other ways of going, but only he knows the way in and out. For men, it is a one-way trip. When *Maravilla* comes for us, we must follow."

The boy thought for a moment, then forcing himself, he asked, "Who has he come for, Abuelo?"

"Your *abuela* will believe he has come to lead me away, *mijo*. She has prayed hard against his return. You've seen her at the *ramada*. You've seen her spreading black pepper everywhere. Hell, every dog she sees these days scares her to death. But look at him, he's just a tired old wolf-dog. Tired of running with *perros mestizos y coyotes*. He just wants some good chorizo and some leftovers. He is no *Maravilla*."

He patted the old dog lovingly.

"He just wants to come home and lie around all day and be fed from the table. You miss the *carnitas, viejo?*"

The old man rubbed the dog under his jaw, then rose up from his haunches and walked to the kitchen. He returned with two chunks of *carnitas* that he dropped in front of the old dog's muzzle. The dog inhaled the meat in two gulps, then walked over to a spot in the corner of the bedroom and began to lie down as though he had never left.

Apache turned and spun in the corner, like a twister in the Superstition Mountains, like a coyote bitch playing coy. He turned and turned again, and things came dimly to him: Josephina's spoon stirring his meat and bean leftovers, the taste of rabbit blood.

"He belongs in two worlds, *también*," the old man said. "He is like me. Josephina will be crazy."

He started slowly for the door, deep in thought, then remembered the boy.

"I will be gone for half of a day, *mijo*, but I will be back."

The boy heard his grandfather rummaging through his lean-to *nichos*, the cans and bottles ringing and scraping as they were shoved around, lifted up, inspected and rearranged. He heard him pick up the battered pot and the canvas water bag and toss them both into the pickup bed.

"If you drink some coffee with Pet milk, let some cool off and give to it to Apache. Do you remember, Beto, how much that old dog loves coffee?"

"*Abuelo, qué quiere decir la palabra Maravilla?*"

He heard no answer.

"What does *Maravilla* mean?"

He heard the old Ford pickup spit once through the air cleaner, cough, then gun to life and drive away.

"Don't fear *los gritos de los lobos*, the howls of the wolf, Beto," he heard Manuel call out from the pickup.

"All sounds are a *ventriloquia de Dios*."

The pickup had gone away from Buckeye Road, in the opposite direction from Vernetta's trailer.

Out to the open desert.

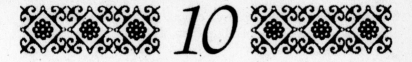
Spilt Children

You could see it in her walk, that sassy, spindly, in-heat walk that was whore and high school all at the same time. She sidled down the aisle, hips brushing the seats as the bus rolled, tossing her hair and scent like chum on the water.

Some women spend the best part of their lives being attractive, no . . . existing as something attractive. There is a difference, smiled Josephina. This one's entire life could be seen in a compact mirror. Eyes, two tiny pinhole nostrils and bright red lips; the *gringo Americano* code requirements dictated that there could be no distinguishing facial features, no pores, no hairs on the upper lip. The nose itself simply must not exist.

Josephina saw it in every advertisement in the magazine she had on her lap, and now she saw it coming down the aisle of the bus as it drew away from a stop at Black Canyon City. This girl had wiped out every evidence of pink flesh on the surface of her face by troweling on some sort of cosmetic compound on which was painted a set of lips. She looked like a beautiful ghost.

The white on her face stopped just under the chin and made her neck look like it was in eternal shadow. Every male face that looked up seemed to buoy her as she came toward the back of the bus. The sailor looked up from the letter he was writing, pulling his tired tongue in from the exertion of spelling. The *bracero* looked up from his papers. For a moment he rested from memorizing his new name. Every male gaze that did not linger seemed to weaken her. Josephina felt sure that a woman such as this would surely not sit down next to her.

How is it she looks so familiar? There were just too many men sitting alone. She would certainly find an empty row to sit in and wait for someone, some man, to come sit next to her.

The woman, the girl, without meeting her gaze, passed up row after row of empty seats, then sat down right next to Josephina. She sat down without a solitary word and exhaled breath slowly as if the trip down the aisle of the bus had been a long, wearying voyage. Perhaps the voyage happened before she ever got on this bus, thought Josephina, or maybe long after she will leave it.

"It was strange walking back here. I could swear I was going forward, but as far as the rest of the world is concerned I'm going backward, I guess. Please," she said, without turning her incredibly white face toward the old woman in black. "Please, would you remove this *chintete* from my neck."

Josephina, without a change of expression, turned in her seat, reached out her hand and gently pulled at the small gray lizard clutching to the soft, white expanse of skin just below the woman's left ear. The little lizard's claws held on for a moment, then released under Josephina's careful insistence. Its tiny claws were covered with the white cream.

Near Arcosanti, a window slid upward on the left side of the bus and the tiny animal went flying into the weeds by the roadside, where it lay limp for a second or two before darting off.

"Now the men, they won't look at you," said the old woman while staring out the window.

"It's been so damn long," said the girl, breathing now as though a huge weight had been lifted from her, "so damn long."

"You can't live in everyone else's eyes, *mija*. You can't take your value from your own reflection in everyone else's eyes."

Josephina bent forward to open her suitcase. She carefully pulled the old brown cloth from its pocket in the side.

"Here, take your makeup off. I want to see your own skin."

The girl took the cloth, stared at it a second or two, frowned, then began to remove the compound from her face.

"Is it over?" asked the girl.

"Not for years it's not over," answered Josephina, looking downward and away from the girl's imploring gaze.

"But the lizard . . ."

"That's now. Don't you see, that's my now. But it will happen to you. I promise you it has already happened, but not for you. Not yet."

Josephina, seeing the confusion in the young girl's eyes, softened her voice.

"We can change some things, only some. Other things can only be lived through."

"Are you going to get my baby, now?"

"Yes, I am. The people have changed their minds," she answered, but there was a tinge of guilt in her voice as she wondered if those people even had a choice.

At that the girl rose in her seat, her eyes imploring and expectant.

"You can't get off the bus with me. I don't know why I know it's true, *pero es la verdad* and you know it too."

"I won't even be able to see him, will I?" said the girl. "The baby, I mean?" Her efforts to keep from crying were distorting her face even more than the makeup had.

"The baby is a big boy now, a big strong boy. No, you can't see him."

"How big is he, please tell me! Does he look like his father?"

"No, *hija*, it would only cause you to suffer if you knew how long you've waited . . . will have to wait. *Entonces*, where are you going from here, *mija?*"

"To the Imperial Valley out in California. I heard he was there. I got some news from a trucker that he was out there. I've looked so many places now, but I'll never give up. It means so much to me, maybe not to no one else but to me."

"Kinda like crossing the floor without spilling your coffee?" smiled Josephina.

"Yeah, just like that. Like my personal universe focused down to that," the girl said excitedly, "crossing that floor. Am I paying now for leaving the child? Why am I talking to you like this—it's not like I know you? I don't know you?"

It was more of a question than a statement. She brought her small hand up to her cheek as if struggling to recall.

"Am I paying for leaving my child with those people?"

"You just weren't ready, *mija*, just like my daughter, Lola, isn't ready. Now, I don't really know if you are being judged by God. I do know that God gave me the power to change some people's minds, that He gave me the power to help you. I only know that it will be some time before you understand what I'm saying and that you have a very long way to go before we see each other again."

"I went to Little Rock and I tried to work, even found a job as a secretary for a while; then I worked at a skating rink and as an usher in a movie house. But somethin' was always wrong; men was always reaching out for me and telling me I didn't need to work and all. Not at all. It was like they was making it too easy for me.

"Pretty soon I almost forgot how to get to Mrs. Woodley's place. After J.B. there didn't seem to be nothin' I cared about, much less goin' home. It seemed like the way down to Terrebonne was wiped out of my memory like streaks from a water glass. I confess I liked the money well enough. I liked payin' the beauticians big tips and havin' myself all done up all the time."

"*Mentirosa, mentirosa!*"

Josephina waved her finger in front of the girl's face.

"You would sit here under these crazy circumstances and lie to me like that," screamed Josephina, who was then suddenly aware of her own outburst and the heads turned back to see the source of the disturbance.

"Don't you know that you really do believe in your heart that you are nothing, a *puta*? That's what you believe and that's how you act and what you will keep right on doing. You will do it for years! You take their money and you give them nothing because that's what you feel about men now and that's what you feel about *su* vagina"—Josephina pointed to her own crotch—"down there. You think it's dead. You think you're not connected to it anymore. The more money you take and the more men you have, the less you think it's worth. You mock the single act of love that brought your child to you and took your husband from you. You mock the single act with a multitude. Now you mock your own betrayal of your son."

The old woman turned once again to face forward. Her entire face was trembling.

"*Válgame Dios*, girl, getting back at this world like that will only hurt you more. Your own fire will only burn you up. I know. I've seen you. Your own fire will change you."

Suddenly thoughtful, Josephina laughed and blurted out, "Things never really change where you can see it. Change is an atomic thing, a *corazón* thing."

"It wasn't long before I longed for my little son with all of my heart," said the Vernetta girl, never having stopped to listen to Josephina.

"You became a mother in that moment."

"I began to search for my child, but the Woodleys wouldn't tell me where Danny was. Oh God, how I begged those people."

"Filipino and black is not an auspicious mix," said Josephina, obviously having studied the matter.

She looked out of the window again at the crimson sky and quickly pulled the girl toward her so that the window framed their two faces.

"See those pigeons there?" She pointed to a small, dark flock passing above the bus, going in the same direction. "Those are your tears."

After the flock disappeared over the horizon, the girl turned mechanically in her seat, opened her purse and methodically began reapplying her makeup. Her voice took on a dark, robotic monotone.

"Why should I go look in Imperial Valley if you already know where he is? Why should I?"

She spread a foundation to her hairline and under her eyes and began rubbing it in.

"Other people are stupid, and they don't have to suffer.

Isn't stupidity a constitutional right? I only use Richard Hudnutt shampoo with egg, you know. I just don't believe that God gives us suffering so we can share Christ's passion. I just don't believe that. I only put Alberto VO-5 on my hair, nothing else, except for maybe peroxide. Who would want to share that? Who in his right mind wants pain? Can you see me, are you looking at me now? Why are so many fat men stepping on my feet? God, I love my boy."

She snapped open her small purse and pulled out her lipstick.

"It's so close, what I feel. It's spinal."

Josephina knew that Vernetta was fading, going back to her own place and time, but there was one more moment for her to have before she left.

"Why don't you go talk with him?" she asked politely.

Vernetta's crying turned into a strange anger.

"I know it. Shit, I know it. I know he's here. I been knowin' that for some time. Why are you pushing me?" she answered sharply, then almost instantly changed her demeanor again.

"How are these?" she cooed as she held a pair of earrings up to her lobes for Josephina's approval.

"They are God's will. Copper is soft; copper is woman," said Josephina, turning her face and eyes away from the miniature copper lizards that now swung below Vernetta's soft ears.

"I can't talk to him now, I just can't. Aren't these earrings just darling! Look, he's still got the damn rope on his neck. Don't he have better sense?"

She sobbed now.

"Don't he have better sense than that?"

At the front of the bus, in the seat just behind the driver, sat J. B. Woodley, his canted head astride a creased neck. There was grim ashiness to his coloration and a sisal rope around his neck. He looked listless and tentative; his burial clothes were mud-caked, his lips wooden. Even so, he seemed to be having a fairly animated conversation with the driver, but every few minutes he would turn his head slowly toward the back of the bus and work his dead muscles into a smile at Vernetta. The first time he looked back she was working her blue eye shadow straight up to the brow. The second time he looked she was busy ladling on the rouge.

"They caught me about a mile from the food stand," he began to yell from the front of the bus. "I was feeling so good. I'd just lost my job and had my ribs kicked in by the boss, but I was feeling good about us, me and Vernetta. I had the bus stop in my sights when the pickups skidded up and surrounded me. A pendulum! A black, bleeding pendulum. You know that's what I was."

He reached a stiff arm up and pulled at the rope end, tightening the noose around his own neck.

"For Chrissake, here I'm hanging, I'm strung up and kicking like a mule and I'm thinking about Galileo! Don't that beat all? You know what, I really saw myself being cut down."

The third time he looked back she was crossing her arms in front of her and readjusting her falsies.

"These damn falsies are surely an everlasting bitch."

"You won't need those for long," laughed the old woman. "The faster you live the bigger you get."

"Do you mean I'll gain mass with velocity?"

"No, *mija*, I mean you'll live fast and you'll gain weight. Aren't you even going to look at him? He wants you to look at him. He lived almost two minutes after he was cut down, you know. He spent most of that time on you."

"Oh God," sobbed Vernetta, "I'm gonna be without love for such a long, long time. Couldn't I stay on this bus? I wouldn't mind just stayin' on this bus. I could ride to the end, then back to the beginning, and then make the whole trip again."

"Of course, his very last thoughts were of Mindanao and Africa. Imagine those last screaming cells, a lion roaring in his *cabeza*."

Josephina reached out and hugged the oblivious young white girl while the conversation between J.B. and the driver grew louder and louder.

"I shoulda been more worried about her relatives and less about relativity," J.B. bellowed. "I shoulda slapped that Norvell silly and stayed right there at my job. Now look at me!" He jerked once more at the rope, then let it fall. "That swamp back home is pushin' me back up to the surface. It's that poor nigga cemetery. It never works to bury folks in wet ground, you know. Just look where the armadillos got to my leg." He lifted a pant leg to show an ankle gnawed to the bone.

"Do you know what it's like, risin' between the cypress trunks, laughin' at the mushrooms and that crooked worm? It's like insomnia. It's like . . . amnesia. Bayou clay burns you like green fire; it keeps you awake by pryin' at your eyelids. Did you know that flesh that is half earth is so damn forgetful? Why, the dirt above me is just littered with names that I've forgotten. They're like brown leaves. If I could only remember, then they'd be green and wet. Jesus, now I gotta see the order of things from way out here beyond chaos." He let the pant leg fall. "Now I gotta bend time around just to look after my own blood and see my woman buried in makeup. It's all that I remember. Nothing else. I am the shadow that my son casts."

His gaze moved from the bus driver to Vernetta, who turned her face toward Josephina.

"You're seein' more than just me, aren't you?" asked Vernetta, her eyes wide. "More than just here and now?"

"When you look at me, can you see the young girl there?" answered Josephina.

"They're both talkin' somethin' strange now, like Chinese, Josephina," whispered Vernetta, looking toward the front of the bus.

"J.B. don't know Chinese. How could I know your name?"

The conversation at the front of the bus swelled till it covered the engine noise and bested the sound of the wind at the windows; it swelled and spun and filled the bus.

"Look," Vernetta screamed over the wind of words, extending her thin right arm against the raging gusts to point, "J.B.'s got dragonflies on his face!"

The twin jade green dragonflies with shimmering wings simultaneously released their hold on J.B.'s catfish-colored eyes and flew directly toward Josephina's seat. As they flew toward the back of the bus, they began to grow in size so that by the time they reached the old woman, their wings brushed both walls of the bus, fluttered against the glass.

The dragonflies settled near her seat and began to suffocate Josephina with newly beaten wind, louder than J. B. Woodley's complaint. Their huge, gray eyes spun above her face, inscrutable, alien and inhuman.

In the next instant, Josephina, her arms up protecting her face, found herself deep inside one of the insects. In the soundless moments that followed, she was unable to tell if she was within the dragonfly or had become the dragonfly itself. In one moment she was being carried far from her secure, beloved soil, and in the next, the land below was of no concern, was beneath consideration. All at once she understood how it was to live dominated by air, to assume the third dimension.

Maybe the old man isn't so crazy, she thought, as she lifted above the bus, banked and spun. Maybe the gift from his strange gods was really a gift after all. Altitude. She felt the pure exhilaration of altitude, the effortless, mercurial counterpoise of translucent, veined wings.

The bus was a toy now, lumbering far below as she climbed. She could see Mormon Lake off to her right and the city of Flagstaff just ahead on the horizon. She saw poor Vernetta step off the bus at the Sedona exit, then accept a ride from a passing red convertible. The man reached out immediately and grabbed Vernetta's knee. Josephina looked right down through the man's white Stetson, down the spine into the driver's heart, and saw shallow, craven chambers pumping the thinnest broth. She sensed that Vernetta saw the same thing.

Vernetta saw, but smiled. She shook from a chill as the man's hand moved under her dress.

Then all of a sudden, from a tree line on Josephina's right, she saw fireflies in formation arching up toward her, then another martial line of fireflies, glowing red, arching down to meet them.

She saw blurred forms like nascent children, taking shape within her body; she felt them shifting in her womb. In a sudden, single motion the arching fireflies flew up anew, but this time dumbly struck her side, and she shook with surprise and staggering hurt.

Flight was painful now, labored. The desert below was no

more. There were plants, more plants than she had ever seen. The forms, now green like herself, huddled closer inside of her for safety. They clung to her spine for safety. She felt them all shifting again, turning away from her sides as if prayed over by Ana Martinez.

From below, the fierce fireflies continued coming up toward her by the thousands. She shuddered with the impact of hundreds. She canted and raked in the dark with the blows. There were electronic voices screaming inside her. Within her, one of the shadow forms, a young green shape with a black human face, was chewing Juicy Fruit gum faster than humanly possible while the mouth of the face next to his was heaving its words into a metal bowl: "Oh God, oh God, oh God."

A weak light turned green within her, and she spilled her children out feet first; she gave birth without giving light. Some staggered. Others could run with their very first steps from her womb. They fell, then ran again, scattering in the dark and heading for a distant tree line. Some spilt children who hit the skids were stillborn.

The bus swerved momentarily, then jolted suddenly as the driver braked to make a wide turn. Josephina's face bumped lightly against the hot window glass, and she blinked her startled eyes and woke abruptly from her sleep.

"A hot landing zone," she mumbled without hearing her own words.

The bus and the people around her were as quiet as a tomb compared to the noises that had just evacuated her skull. Her brain still rang with the clamor of it, and she found herself wondering why no one else had heard it.

"They must've heard it."

It surely must have leaked out of her ears and annoyed everyone near her. It had been so horribly loud. But as her mind cleared she knew that she had been alone with it and that only she would feel the pain, the responsibility of it.

They were here.

They had both been here. They had come to see her and each other. They had both come through impossible portals to send her off on her mission to collect their child. Together.

"But, *Madre de Dios*, what was the rest of it?"

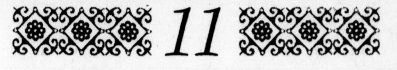

The Death Letter

"Christmas'll be coming in just a few weeks. It's very strange that here in America we think it's unfortunate to have Christmas without snow. I lived in Palestine for years and I never once saw snow. Maybe once, in the far distance. As a matter of fact, it was more like this at Christmas, a lot of sand and dust. Only pilgrims celebrated Christmas in Palestine. The Christians. The latecomers, my father called them." As he spoke, he reached his hand out to touch the piece of cardboard that had been nailed to the *adobe* wall in the living room. It was cut into the jagged shape of a pine tree and painted green. Josephina had used crayons and ribbons to decorate the tree.

"I don't really celebrate the holiday. But I'll admit that I do exchange gifts with the wife and the boy. He likes the gifts, and I haven't the heart to deprive him. The tea is very good, quite good. Raspberry, isn't it? My wife would love this.

"The snow is really Germanic, you know. So are the green trees and the decorations, the wreaths and such. Holdovers from ancient pagan, animistic traditions. Do please stop me if I become too didactic. No one will ever give me a classroom again, but I guess I'll always be a teacher at heart. This is one of the few places I go on my route where I can have intelligent conversation. In fact, this is the only place other than the schoolteacher in Gallup. Mrs. Beery, you really should meet her sometime. She's such a gentlewoman and so incredibly well read.

"Did you know that the Catholic church did not even recognize the Christ Mass until the fourteenth century? I think their emphasis on the Mother of Christ is particularly appealing to Mexicans. It dovetails so well with their attitudes toward women. You do know that there's this whole tradition in Northern Spain, Greece and parts of the southernmost regions of Mexico that Mary was impregnated through the ear? It's supposed to be why women are such good listeners," he laughed. "Actually, this is a roundabout way of asking you why you're so quiet."

"Because I'm cooking," answered Josephina. "Besides, my fertility days are over. I only listen out of curiosity now." She smiled.

"Your grandson did well this morning, Josephina. Not the slightest wince or even a quiver in his eyes. Remember that first time, what, three years ago? I came by here while you were still putting the roof on this adobe. You were staying in Vernetta's trailer. Bless him, he tried so hard. You warned him about me, I know you did, and he marched out here determined not to run away or to stare at me, my face. He really tried.

"Oh, speaking of Beto, I brought some more bottles of McNess drink mixes for him, raspberry, orange and lime."

He pulled the bottles from one of the large pockets of his coat.

"I have a pocket comb for him too, even has a clip on it just like a ballpoint."

He knelt on the floor to open the large gray trunk that dominated the center of the living room. The two sides of it folded down, then folded down again to reveal four neatly stuffed compartments.

"You know, your husband, Manuel, is the only human being I have ever met who seemed to have no reaction to me."

"Was he smiling when he first met you?"

"Yes, as a matter of fact he was."

"Well, he was smiling at yesterday and days gone by. He's got his head buried back there or up in the sky, and he probably didn't even see you," grinned Josephina.

"No, he saw me. He shook my hand and looked me right in the eye. No, he saw me all right. Here's the hairbrush you ordered, the wire suede brush and the feather duster. As you can see, my hairbrush days are over. I just sort of whisk the hairs over the crown now. It's getting to the point where I can almost count each one of them.

"Oh, the matching towels you wanted came in, and your back order of fly strips and pine wicks for the outhouse came in, too."

He took each item from the case as he described it. Josephina took each in turn and placed it on a spot she had cleared on the kitchen table.

"And since you're a very preferred customer"—he managed a wink—"I'm authorized to offer you a choice of gifts, compliments of Fuller Brush."

He held out the choices: a toilet plunger and window squeegie. They both laughed out loud.

"Well, Harold, *por favor*, give me the plunger and maybe someday I'll have a toilet. I know I'll never get windows."

Harold was a Jew. Somehow it meant more to him than saying that he was Jewish. "I am a Jew."

Harold had a number on his arm that was not meant to be seen and a face that had been horribly burned in a manner he never cared to explain, though he relived that moment every day. The scars lay across his eyes and cheeks like cooled waxen waves. He had to look sideways, around himself, to look out at all.

Harold made his monthly rounds in a small two-tone, turquoise-and-white Nash-Metropolitan. The gray trunk of merchandise samples and orders was strapped to the small trunk rack and was almost as large as the car.

He and his wife, Mariam, lived in Phoenix with their young son, somewhere out on McDowell Road in a two-bedroom ranch-style stucco house.

The recent past had all seemed like a dream to him. A sterile man and his barren wife who had been blessed so late

in life. It all seemed a dream, now. Stored in the small bank
in his soul where the most profound moments are kept, he
is burned then re-created anew and flawless. Yes, Phoenix
was appropriate. They had never used birth control. They
thought it impossible at their ages. Unheard of at their ages.
Yet, there he was crawling on the floor, dragging them both
back into life.

He only saw them for one week a month as his lonely route
carried him across two states and took three weeks to complete. Sometimes he cheated. He would reroute his trip so
that he could surprise his small family, have dinner and talk
about the one-horse towns that still waited for his visit.

Not the large towns and cities, but places like Buckeye Road
and Gallup, Palo Verde and Liberty. Places where his little
tube radio received nothing 'til the late evening when the AM
beams bounced off the ionosphere and somehow caught him
on the road between Deming and Lordsburg.

"Please don't be frightened, ma'am. I'm your Fuller Brush
man. *Por favor, no tienes miedo, señora.*"

The floor of his little car was usually littered with deviled
ham tins and Sunbeam bread wrappers. He saved money by
making his own sandwiches and by stopping at truck stops
only for gasoline fillups and coffee for his thermos bottle. He
slept where he could.

Two thousand miles a month, and it seemed to him that
most of them were done in first gear. Each day the little tires
crunched onto invisible turnoffs and into unseen defiles for
two brushes and a jar of hair creme.

Some of the Fuller Brush sales reps never drove more than
two miles, and they needed accountants to do their receipt
books. Some had the better neighborhoods in Phoenix and
Albuquerque and had even managed to buy into homes there.
He had been given this particular route the very first day on
the job. That was over twelve years ago. He still had the old,
bruised clipboard given to him that day.

When the others had gotten a slice of the cities, he had
been given a road atlas, a small fan that plugged into the
cigarette lighter, and a wave good-bye. He'd been told that

advancement would come once he proved himself. Harold knew better.

But this route did have its benefits. On that long dry stretch of Interstate 25 between Socorro and Truth or Consequences, that long straight-edge stretch without a town or a pueblo, in the late afternoon, Harold's dreams came to him. They bounced off the ionosphere from Riga and caught him again. But, mercifully, they left his nights alone, and he was thankful for that.

"Remember, Harold, when you tried to sell me a vacuum cleaner? You said it would get all the dirt off the floor, and I told you the dirt is the floor. When you finish up at the reservations today, Harold, come back for dinner and you can use the same cot as always right here in the kitchen."

"You sure it's no trouble, Josephina?"

"If you don't stay, Beto will never forgive you. He's up to M, you know. He's out with the little Arkie kids playing baseball. The ball will be completely invisible pretty soon, and he'll be hungry."

"Has he gone to school yet?" asked Harold.

"No," said Josephina curtly, a little guilt showing through despite her efforts to disguise it. "Not yet, but he's up to M."

"You know, Manuel is very surprised that you let me talk to the boy about things the way you do."

"You can speak Spanish?" she asked.

"No, he speaks some English."

"I've never heard an English sentence come out of his Yaqui mouth in all these years. Some railroad words and some Irish. Well, what do you know?"

Josephina seemed to enjoy being surprised by her husband after so many years.

"I know that I get too mad at Manuel for teaching Beto that Yaqui stuff. It's just because I want to be a good Catholic. But there are other things, too."

Her voice trailed off, as she thought of the old Mayo woman and of her bag beneath the table.

"They all come from the same power, Josephina."

Harold pronounced the "J" in the English fashion.

"We're the ones who put names on everything; things that should be together, we've managed to separate. When Adam was done naming the animals, he just kept right on going, and he passed the habit right on to us.

"We all say that He surpasseth understanding; then we go right ahead and make Him look just like us, whatever color we are and whatever gender is in control at the time. The power behind it all is beyond concerns like gender and nationality. God forgive me, I must not be much of a Zionist, but I think that the power that started all this is beyond our local wars and tribalisms. He's beyond being beyond it all. What is it that the physicists call unmeasurable, ununderstandable things? Things that become less measurable with each attempt to measure? Singularities? Well, I think God is a singularity. That's the best I can do after all these years."

"Einstein believed in God," said Josephina from the kitchen.

"Yes, but not a God that lets us win the lottery or gets us the job we want. Not a God that saves us from deformities. Not a God that rescues people from torture. Not even from torture," said Harold, his face scarlet with a painful memory.

"Not even with such a small request as a peaceable death. An anonymous, peaceable death."

The old woman stopped chopping onions to turn about and look at her dear friend kneeling on the dirt floor in his worn herringbone jacket and black slacks. His huge trunk was open next to him, its center compartments lit up by the dusty light from the window.

"God has sent me a message," she said. "He has told me that my husband is dying."

She walked over after wiping her hands on her apron.

"He seems to be sending me a lot of messages lately. Most of them I can't seem to make out. But that one came through loud and clear."

With some effort she knelt beside him in the amber light, the Holy Ghost and the Virgin Mother within the walls of a Mexican mission.

"Beto is asking questions now about *tiempo y espacio*, time and space. He talks a lot with Vernetta, and he reads those books of hers. Did you see the model that Vernetta and he built? Can you explain it to me?"

Harold carefully sketched out on the dirt floor the mirror placements of the Michelson-Morley experiment; side by side they sought God in the dusky aether, then cast their secret ballots together.

"Who was His messenger? Did the Virgin Mother tell you that Manuel is dying?" whispered Harold.

"No," said Josephina, "the dog did."

"I thought your grandmother said you were up to M, and here I see you've brought the P volume to the dinner table," said Harold.

The boy opened the beat-up volume of the *New World Book Encyclopedia* and began leafing through the pages until he reached the one that concerned him.

"Who was Lily Pons?" asked the boy. "Here's her picture. She looks so beautiful. Is she really dead?"

"How platonic, boy. You find it incredible that beauty dies? It doesn't. You see, facial beauty just visited her for a couple of years, then went on to other things and other people. The vocal beauty stayed to the end. But I guess you can see all beauty has skipped me altogether," he laughed, wondering secretly if death really is sadder for the beautiful.

"So, Beto, it's been a whole month now. What did you like best about M?"

"I liked Mars and marsupials," answered the boy.

"It talked all about the Roman god and about the discovery of the planet. It talked all about the canals and the possibility of life. Could there be life on Mars, Harold? It looks so dry."

"Those photographs are taken from millions of miles away, Beto. If you photographed Buckeye Road from just ten miles up, do you think you'd see signs of human life?"

"Quiz him," called Josephina from the kitchen.

Across from Harold, Manuel smiled and chewed his food with anticipation as all awaited the month's question.

"*Pregúntale*," urged Josephina.

Harold considered for a moment, a steaming hunk of beef enchilada poised on the fork tines in front of his lips, the cheese stretching all the way back to his plate.

"Andrew Marvell," he said, finally.

The category chosen, three adults passed the remainder of the dinner in pleasant conversation, Josephina translating suspiciously for her husband and Harold laughing at her. All three were keenly aware of the quiet boy, who was barely aware of the food going into his mouth. When the coffee arrived at the table, so had the long-awaited moment.

"Are you ready, Beto?"

"Yes, sir," he answered.

"For a nickel," said Harold, looking as serious as he could, "the average television watcher's answer."

"I don't know," responded the boy with confidence.

"Right!" proclaimed Harold, while simultaneously placing a five-cent piece on the table in front of the boy's plate.

"Now, the ten-cent question for the almost extinct, semi-learned opinion."

"He was an English poet."

"Right again!" yelled Harold, slamming the dime down next to the nickel.

Josephina and Manuel beamed at the scene before them, exulting at each response.

"Two bits now. Two bits for just a small bit of modern light shining on a long-buried fossil: the learned, the educated opinion."

" 'To His Coy Mistress,' " said the boy. "Wysteria Maybelle knows every line by heart, and I heard her reciting 'The Nymph Complaining for the Death of Her Fawn.' She says that one when one of her dogs gets run over. All this time I thought she was saying crazy nonsense, then I read that part of the book again after seeing her the other day. Harold, I don't think I know enough to understand that old woman."

"A banner night!" yelled Harold, clapping his hands. "A banner night. Anything else?"

"It said that he defended Oliver Cromwell, remember him from volume C? That poor king with the stutter."

"He raped Ireland," muttered Manuel in a pure Irishman's English sentence that brought a look of shock to his wife's face.

Harold rolled the new fifty-cent piece across the table where it clinked against the side of the boy's plate, then fell over onto the quarter, dime and nickel.

"Don't ever have a cheap opinion, boy. Go for the four-bit opinion every time."

Four red Mexican bowls appeared on the table. Each had a shiny mound of shivering flan in its center. Josephina poured caramelized brown sugar over all four puddings and placed a hammered metal spoon beside each bowl.

"You can talk with that old woman Wysteria Maybelle," she warned, "but don't get too close to that crowd of hers. You can get sucked in to that crowd."

"But they're just dogs, Abuela," responded Beto.

"They are spirits," warned Josephina. "They carry their own powers with them, and those that get too close must follow them."

Harold noticed that Manuel had turned away from this discussion and seemed quite uncomfortable. He understood that something he could never understand had been communicated between Josephina and Manuel, but for the boy's sake he decided to change the subject.

"Next month will be N–O month, Beto. I'm thinking about mathematicians or famous women, okay?"

When the boy and his grandfather had finished their dessert and gone outside to see the full moon, Harold and Josephina moved from the kitchen table to the living room area. Neither sat in Manuel's chair.

On the other side of the lot, the choir at the Mighty Clouds of Joy began working on "Children, Go Where I Lead." It seemed their voices were in the same room with Josephina and her friend.

"I almost died when I saw him," she said, nodding toward the sleeping Apache, remnants of enchilada still on his muzzle.

"I walked over from *La Cometa* after being away from home for three days. I had just left the little boy with Vernetta, and

I headed directly for my own doorway when he came out to speak to me."

She nodded toward Apache.

"The joy that was filling my heart at that moment just vanished, just evaporated. I see what you think, Harold, but he didn't wag his tail or come up to me for petting. He just came out and stood before the door, grinning like *La Maravilla* and staring at my eyes to tell me. I knew. I knew."

Tears were forming in her eyes now. Harold reached out his hand and touched her shoulder.

The dog's eyes opened just as though he knew he was the subject of their conversation and scrutiny. Harold looked into them, into those brown eyes, and saw neither malevolence nor beneficence. But the longer he looked, the more uneasy he grew. Perhaps what he saw there was a singularity, a glimpse at the edge of one. It was how he felt about Josephina herself. Catholicism was the most inadequate of descriptions where she was concerned, the least of her faculties.

"Forgive my ignorance," said Harold, "but what is *La Maravilla?*"

Josephina dried her eyes.

"It means a marvel," she said softly, "or a marigold."

She had a power that was somehow tied into the real powers that gripped this land. Familiar, hearth and field powers; horizon energies not on paper. Josephina kept trying to name the nameless, and somehow Catholic wasn't exactly it, though she desperately wanted it to be.

Manuel, on the other hand, did not suffer the same conflict that his wife did. He hated the Catholics. He hated the Spanish part of Mexicans while loving the Indian part. He especially despised the word *Hispanic*.

"Would the Irish like to be called English just because the language was forced on them and because they were subjugated by the English?" he would snarl whenever that offensive word was used: *Hispanic*.

"Find me a black man from Johannesburg who would like to be called Afrikaans. Just one. Find me a black man from the Congo who wants to be called Belgian."

It was precisely this that drew Harold to this house over

and over again. Here it stood, like a wormhole in recognizable
space where dimensions met and contorted with each other
behind foreheads. It was his own conflict. He recognized it.
He had bound himself to rationalism as a response to the
primacy of the unrelenting pain he'd suffered. Yet it was the
mysticism that drew him, the same mysticism that he had
forsaken so vehemently for so long. It was the sense of connection that drew him.

He listened to the music coming from the small pink church.
The walls of the building across the lot seemed to pulsate
with his temples.

"Harold, you will have a son, a niño."

She'd said it over two years ago in the same way that a
friend would tell you that a mosquito was on your arm. Manuel had laughed at the statement, not in derision, but as
though it were already true and congratulations were in order.
Then Manuel had actually taken his hand to shake it. Harold
remembered that trip, the drive home had been his first leap
of faith in a decade and a half.

Somehow, faith had penetrated through his covering of
scars and cynicism. His wife was smiling when he drove up,
fundamentally different. She was filled with joy. Her hips
were swelling with it.

Somehow Harold knew that his next visit to this house
would be a sad one, a terrible one. But he would come nevertheless and some elemental, unknowable thing would again
be verified.

"I thought for a while that it might be for Adelita, but it
was for Manuel. Apache has come back for my husband. Mi
Manuelito. Did you see the lightning the last few nights? Did
you see it? And look at him." She pointed at the dog.

"He's not the same dog that left me so long ago. He's been
there, to the other side. See where his fur is burned here and
singed there. I am a widow," she sighed. "And now that
Wysteria Maybelle with all her dogs is starting to hang
around. She is a widow."

"How long?" asked Harold, surprised at his own easy acceptance of all of this.

"Months, weeks," she said with resignation. "This Christmas will be a sad one, our last one together." She used her apron to dry her eyes.

"Manuel will take the boy now."

She turned away from Harold and spoke to herself now. She pointed to some vague, far-off place.

"He'll take him out there. I can't stop him and I really shouldn't. *Dios, ayúdame*, I won't. It's the Yaqui way. It's the least I can do even though it will surely hurt my heart.

"I have to tell the boy to watch out for the wolf. Remind me, *el lobo*. Remind me to tell him. God forgive me, I've been a stubborn and selfish wife. I've tried to be better lately, ever since he got sick that time."

She crossed herself, then kissed the small cross on her wrist. She squeezed the tiny vial for a moment, as if drawing comfort from the liquid inside.

"More coffee, Harold?"

She brought her favorite percolator over to the table.

She offered Harold an opened can of Pet milk.

"Cream? Make sure you leave the new Fuller Brush catalogue. Do you know how many times I've baptized that boy?"

As she poured the coffee Vernetta and her son walked into the adobe. Harold had been struck dumb by what he had seen earlier in the day when he knocked on her door to make a delivery. The woman who greeted him was half her former size and still shrinking. She wore no makeup and no longer smelled of alcohol and cigarettes.

Dumbfounded, Harold had dropped the bag of cosmetics that he'd intended to deliver.

"Come in, Harold," said a strangely calm voice.

"I won't need those things," she nodded toward the cosmetics, "but I'll pay for them. They're mine."

Her cotton blouse had been safety-pinned on both sides, and her pants required at least one hand to hold them up when she moved. As she had searched through her purse for dollar bills, she leaned against the sink to keep her sagging pants up. As she handed him the money, a nail file and a small Duncan yo-yo had fallen from beneath her blouse and rattled across the floor.

"*Buenas tardes*, Danny," said Josephina.

"*Quieres* chocolate *Mexicana?*"

The boy nodded.

"Coffee for me," said Vernetta.

Vernetta had not eaten a bite since the second letter from Flagstaff had arrived at her door. Somehow, she could not bear to eat; nothing solid stayed down. She could only drink the *atole* that Josephina made especially for her. Today would be her first coffee in weeks.

"Here's that butter knife you loaned me," Vernetta said sheepishly. "It fell out on the way over here."

In the days since the second letter, things she thought she had lost years ago, her eyelash curlers and driver's license, began to reappear as her breasts grew apart.

"Danny had been in Flagstaff for almost seven years," explained Josephina. The older woman looked at the younger, who nodded. Harold knew the story. He was family. "One of Mrs. Woodley's sisters took him there from New Iberia when her husband got a better job. She told me that Vernetta had gone running off again for two weeks or so, and the family decided that it was best for the child to go with these people. They said he's had the slow eye from birth. Do you remember it?"

Vernetta only shook her head, not wanting to say the word. Her mind went back to the instant just weeks ago when Josephina had squeaked open the screen door and pushed a hesitant, shy child into the trailer. She had peeked through her windows, and she had seen her friend coming, her suitcase in one hand and a little boy's hand in the other. Vernetta had scrambled from one corner of the Highway Comet to the other trying to find the place she wanted to be when her son saw her for the first time.

In the end she gave up and just stood there in the aisle, long-lost beads from a cheap necklace falling like hail from beneath her blouse.

Then J.B.'s flesh, her own blood, stood there staring at her. For the first time in memory, for the first time in years, she felt naked.

"Remember what we talked about," Josephina had reminded the nervous little boy.

The boy had walked forward to hug his mother. But Vernetta had fallen to her knees and had engulfed the boy in her
arms. Crying, she had pulled at him as if to pull him inside
of her and start all over again.

"That's why they had him at the Reverend Crispus Evans's
traveling tent revival all those years ago, to see if he could
cure the slow eye. When I got to Flagstaff, the reverend was
up there again on his coast-to-coast tour. The handbills were
everywhere up there."

"I've seen them," said Harold, whose route included
Flagstaff.

"They said it was a triumphant tour," continued Josephina,
"but I sure couldn't tell you why. I saw his tent put up over
near the train depot. I don't think Danny wanted to go see
him this time."

The three adults looked toward the boy, who only smiled
and shook his head in the negative.

"I sure don't blame him either," said Josephina. "That Crispus fellow looks like an oil slick, and he smells like a talcum
powder factory. Everything is 'praise be this and praise be
that.' Why would a man of God need to wear all that gold
like that? How many masters does he have? So"—she lifted
her shoulders in a mischievous shrug—"I just fixed the eye
myself."

She smiled at the boy as she thought of the cozy Bide-a-
Wee, the little motel on the south side of town where she
and Danny had stayed and of the happy ride back from Flagstaff. It had been so much more pleasurable than the long
bus trip north. They had eaten Baby Ruth and Butternut candy
bars and guzzled down a whole six-pack of Five-O chocolate
soda. She had recounted for him her childhood in Spain. She
told him of Adelita and the beautiful Alhambra, of the parlor
in her home where the family once gathered to read aloud
and to sing.

"His eye was slow because it was always hanging up
on . . ." She looked at Danny, then leaned toward Harold
and Vernetta and began to whisper.

"This eye was always seeing the shadow of something, like
catching just a glimpse of someone's back before he disap-

pears into a doorway. He was seeing something like that. His slow eye was hanging on to every second that passed, lingering on it while the other was already moving on. You see, the slow eye was seeing treachery and devotion in the exact same moments that the other eye was only seeing events, only the surface of the water.

"*Pobrecito*, he inherited such a lot of pain. So much pain! The day he was conceived there were so many evil misconceptions acted upon."

The two women stared at each other for a time; then the older one began again while absentmindedly pulling at her hair and drinking her coffee.

"Don't worry, Vernetta, being born with such a *susto* will make him an artist. Anyway, the *susto* is gone for now. A little prayer and some *hikuli* oil did the trick. *Pero*, it will be back, you know. Someday he'll need to see into the shadows. Someday you're gonna have to tell him everything. Between now and then feed him a lot of *lumpia* and okra. Make him listen to Clifton Chenier. Then when you have to tell him, the ability to understand will already be there inside."

"Can I pet the dog?" asked Danny upon catching sight of Apache.

"*Sí*," said Josephina, "but don't listen to a word he says."

Manuel and Beto sat on the cot outside listening to the music emanating from the Blue Moon. The practice at the Mighty Clouds of Joy had ended, and the choir had given way to the voice of Son House singing the Death Letter blues.

It was blues from the time when blues were sung alone in boxcars or jail cells, black prayers from the underground. It was blues from a time before anyone wondered if it would sell, if it could be watered down so white folks would buy it, if lawyers would purvey it. It was ashen as knuckles, deep as whip cuts, and blues hard-driven as a hurry-up wagon in wet Montgomery.

Sad flesh makes this sound.

"This Saturday, Beto, I'm going to take you out into the desert, okay?"

The boy nodded, excitement building within him.

"We will need food for the two days, *agua* for us y *los viejos*.

We'll need the big thermos jug with coffee and some condensed milk. Bring those dark glasses we got at the Rainbo last week. Wear the Pima shirt and the pants *su abuela* sewed for you. No store-bought clothing."

"Abuelo," said the boy, "I was going with you *y los viejos* this Saturday, even if you didn't ask me."

The Death Letter blues ended, and Buckeye was silent for the moment it took for some anonymous sufferer to turn the record over, then reset the needle in the groove.

The sound was of metal and bone. The strident, lilting opening riffs of John the Revelator.

12

The Whisper of the Lizard

"That one there," Manuel pointed toward his friend, "the one with the stubble face, the only stubble face I've ever seen on an Indian, that one is Huichol. His name is Epiphanio. His people come from the blue mountains below Durango. Near them the Cora and the Tepecano nations live. The others over there are Yaqui. Well, that's not exactly true. Pascual, he is Yaqui-Tarahumara mestizo."

Pascual did not look up. He did not acknowledge the fact that his name had been spoken though he had certainly heard it. He would not speak to the boy until the morning, not even hello. There were pieces of Pascual that were just too bitter for this night. More so than any other man, an Indian can go insane in a prison cell. He would refuse to speak with bitterness on his breath.

"Salvador, the old *yoeme* over there, has a good twenty-five years on me."

He had used the Yaqui word for a Yaqui person: *yoeme*.

"Shit, he looks good, huh? Still slicks his hair back with that stinky Tres Flores Brilliantine. He's never eaten in a restaurant. He has never spoken on a telephone. He has never flipped the switch on an electric light. His narrow ass has never once sat on a porcelain flush toilet."

"Neither has yours," retorted Epiphanio, smiling at his old friend.

"Hell, you still prefer them religious tracts over toilet paper?"

"Shit," said Salvador, "he still uses corn husks."

Manuel laughed with the Huichol, then winked at the old man, who smiled back somehow without using his face.

"He's worked the oil derricks down in the Gulf and over in Oklahoma, and he was a *minero con los Mexicanos* over in Morenci. He used to be a real one for the ladies in his time."

"Shit, Manuel," the old one grinned, "all them wells ain't gone dry."

"He is the only one of us who knew the *rio* Yaqui before the occupation, when the people were still together, in the great days before Porfirio Diaz *y los otros*. Shit, I think he was already old when the revolution started."

"*Hewi*, he was farting dust in 1928."

That brought smiles to every face.

"Since that day," one of the silent ones began, "he has taken out his vengeance on all the Mexicans by seducing their women."

"Shit," added another, "he's married three of them."

"*Hewi*, it's true," said the old one, smiling, "but at least I've never been divorced. Divorce is a sacrilege, you know."

"*El tiene dos casas chicas en Casa Grande*," laughed Epiphanio.

"I've seen the *rio* Yaqui myself," continued Manuel, "but not when the people were all together. I've seen it all from Esqueda to the Gulf of California and back up. Even though I can vision the eight *pueblos* at almost any time, I wish in my soul that I could have lived my life when the nation was whole. No, no, that is not quite what I mean to say, Beto. I can't say this. Spanish can't say this," he said looking at the faces of his old *compadres* as they nodded in agreement.

Manuel switched to the Yaqui tongue. Salvador, who had spent the longest time in America, translated into English while Epiphanio translated simultaneously into Spanish. The three languages interleaved and beat frequencies; only the summed, third upper harmonic excited a vestigial bandpass in the boy's mind.

"I do live my life then."

The voice of his grandfather seemed clearer than he'd ever heard it.

"My spirit life, my vision life is in Cokoim, what the Yoris call Cocorit. Right now, even in this very moment and each time I am with the spirit, I can skirt time and space to be where I belong. But my wrong place life, the one that gets up and goes to work in Phoenix, that life I wish was back home in Cocorit. I am made of that soil."

The three tongues stopped at exactly the same instant, leaving a blanket of quiet over them all.

The men drank steaming hot coffee in the setting sun. Each washed a breath down while staring at the crimson-streaked sky. They drank the light down while squatting in a small circle at the end of the wash. None but the boy wore shoes.

"There were eight Yaqui cities along the river. Salvador there is from Potam, and you, Beto, are from Cocorit; your blood, *tu sangre*, is from Cocorit. You will always feel better when you are near the water.

"Something in you will remember a place and time when the smallest, driest seed seemed to grow right when you pressed it into the silt of the Yaqui. It remembers how *sewam*, the numberless flowers, clogged the banks. Each turn of the river is right here." He placed his index finger to the boy's forehead. "Each white rapid and each petaled inlet. It was a flowered world, a *seeya-aniya* like the world of forms.

"I will never tell you, boy, that there is only one way to believe. I will never tell you that there is only one way to know about things. But tonight, I will tell you that our way is better. Shit, I'm not ashamed to say it. I'm proud to say it. I can show you much of who you are. I will give you a sight of your own blood so that someday years from now you will not be made anxious by wrong questions and you will not look for answers in the wrong place. You don't need to see no psychiatrist, Beto. Never. *Nunca.* You just need to look into yourself and beyond, past yourself. Let them have the psychiatrists.

"Remember, you are not white, and if someday you find yourself asking a white man's questions, the answer will not be there for you. Those questions are not yours to ask. There are other questions for you."

"Or the same kind of questions but asked in a completely different way," added Salvador.

Manuel pushed his finger playfully into the boy's chest and smiled.

"Tonight you will see when and where you have been since time started out on these sands. You might become other things. Perhaps you can see and hear what those things have to say to you. To become one life form or another is just a change in perspective, a new place to sit and look."

"You can only turn into what you already are," interjected the old *yoeme*, Salvador, his almost black hands still wrapped around a blue enamel cup.

"We will have the *wakabaki* and rest before the *partillo*. Then we will have a telling, an *etehoi*. Don't treat the boy like he is a child, Manuel. Shit, he's gonna have to live with those people, not us."

The *wakabaki* on this night was a *menudo* soup that Josephina had prepared for the occasion. She'd poured it into a large gallon jug secured with a cork stopper. She'd chosen *menudo* because of its incredible flavorings and spicings. Hers was the most distinctive *menudo* in Arizona, and she meant to be remembered by all involved in this *etehoi*. In this telling of things, she would have her say.

To the bottle neck, she'd carefully taped a brown paper bag that contained four orange Melmac bowls and one green, along with some navy surplus soupspoons. Josephina had inherited Vernetta's old Melmac, and she knew very well how much Manuel hated to eat anything from it.

"Melmac has never lived," he would say.

"Did you know," said Manuel, "that the Huichol believe that Joseph won the Virgin Mary for his bride in a contest? Yeah, he won her in a fiddling contest," he laughed.

Near the jug, but in the shade, were five or six large canteens, a dented pot and a small pan. In the pot was a round yellow gourd, dried, then hollowed out. Next to the pan was one of Manuel's tins from the lean-to. There was aluminum foil pressed over the rim, secured by a large rubber band.

On the horizon above the gravel wash, silhouetted against the distant lights of Phoenix, were the pickup trucks.

"Forgive me if I am too strong on you, Beto. I have seen you as though you were a piece of my flesh going on, my arms, my eyes. *Pobrecito*, you have my fingers, Indian fingers; my feet too, I think."

Both looked down at his gnarled feet.

"Not meant for shoes," he smiled.

"Some people let go small toy boats in a stream and feel very sad about it. I let you, my flesh and blood, go in the stream of time. Parts of me are identical in you, and at the same time nothing of me is the same in you. I know I am probably not making any sense to you."

He reached out and rubbed the boy's head.

"I have next to no time at all to be with you, but if you learn what we have to tell you, in a way, I will have all the time there is."

Manuel turned his head away from his grandson and toward the old *yoeme*.

"Am I a fool, Salvador?" he asked, turning back toward his grandson.

"Have the strength, Manuel, to be judgmental."

Salvador lit a Chesterfield, then exhaled slowly.

"Shit, our way is best."

The plant was stubby and gray and undistinguished save for its white hairs and the nine lines that segmented it. It was kept in the small tin that Manuel had brought to the wash, the same tin that he always took with him whenever he and the *yoeme* left for the desert. The boy had often seen the tin in the lean-to and had always understood that its contents were beyond his ken and beyond his right to ask. His *abuela's* extreme feelings about the contents of the tin had made that very clear.

Now, the boy thought, he would finally see why Josephina cursed Manuel so hatefully every time he left with these men for the open desert.

He had also seen the stubble-face Huichol many times before. Each time he visited Manuel at the adobe, Josephina would become instantly morose and detached and strangely

hostile to their visitor. It was he who came once each year
with the *hikuli* for Manuel the *hitebi*, the curer and son of the
old shaman. It was the Huichol who now prepared the tea
using the old pot, the water from the water bags and shreds
of the grayish-green plant.

Salvador, who had disappeared into the dark for a time in
the direction of the pickups, suddenly reappeared in the circle,
but now he wore a skin belt with hooves hanging from it and
leggings covered with hundreds of dried cocoons. He made
an eerie sound as he walked back toward the group. It
sounded as if the first fall of rain was pelting dry dust, a
torrent with each step. Over his head he wore a mask, the
skin and horns of a deer. Only his mouth could be seen in
the open neck stitching that had torn loose over the years.

Appearing out of the same darkness was Pascual wearing
a strange shirt without a front or a back. He had leather
pantalones held up by a belt of yellow-white cocoons, and he
was placing upon his head a black mask with blood-red cheeks
and white goat's hair that sprang from the eyebrows and
below the mouth. He wore the mask near the back of his
head, as though looking in two directions. He had gourd
rattles in each hand.

"You know how Harold talks about the god of the gaps?"
said Manuel, pouring tea for himself and his grandson. "You
know, people putting God in the cracks where science can't
see, where science hasn't been . . . yet? These people believe
that every scientific discovery makes God weaker, less important. And people keep thinking the gaps are getting
smaller and smaller and science is getting larger. They think
their world of modern kitchen appliances is outgrowing God."

"We are only informed clay," Epiphanio interposed. "Those
who seek information reaffirm this. Men were not created to
just eat and own things."

Manuel lifted his cup, then indicated that the boy do the
same.

"There are not many *peyoteros* left these days."

As he swallowed the tea, the boy began to realize that his
grandfather's voice was becoming more and more clear to
him.

"We are people of the gaps, *mijo*. Only we know that the gaps are where life really is. We know that science doesn't make God smaller, it makes God bigger."

He drank his drink down, and the boy, without hesitation, followed suit.

"Can you think in all of your *World Books* A through Z of one big leap of humanity that was ever accomplished by the majority, by all those people out there rushing like mad to be the same? Can you think of one great jump of art or thought that was ever accomplished by the mainstream?

"Rosa Parks," Manuel continued, "got up from her seat all alone and became a black magnet in the gaps. Now, thousands of black people are following her in. Every shaman, every conjure man who buries the world-wonder root, every artist, every scientist or schoolteacher that goes to the edge of the usual and acceptable world and risks looking over, risks the sight of real principles, sees right into the gaps.

"If you follow what is true you will find yourself paying more for every breath, but it's sweeter air. Stay in the gaps, *mijo*. Love for the land is here. Resistance is here. The company's better in here."

Salvador and Pascual, without communicating in any visible way, began their dance at precisely the same instant: the deer, the *pascola*.

"The fountains are in the gaps, Beto."

Manuel was whispering to the boy now. The Huichol, who had taken such pain in preparing the tea, did not drink it. Instead he had torn his own peyote buttons into shreds and touched them to his forehead, his eyes, his throat, before he placed the shreds into his mouth.

"Every people, the Huichols, the Coros, the Apache, the Creoles, have their fountain in the gaps, in here, *como el rio Yaqui*. Harold, the Jew, has his fountain.

"The water tastes best here, near its source. It is the water in the mainstream that is tasteless. Just look at what the white man has done to the black man's music!"

The *Indios* laughed out loud together before again raising their cups to their lips.

"The human heart is like steam," said the Huichol. "You can't cover it. If you do, it only becomes stronger. You push people into the cracks and their voice becomes more beautiful, their thoughts more potent."

"Is Albert Einstein in the gaps, Abuelo?" asked the boy.

"Shit," laughed the old *yoeme*, Salvador, "he's probably the goddamn doorman."

The boy, taking his cue from the old *Indios*, drank the gray tea to the dregs.

"The Huichol believe that the *hikuli* is God, not just a way to see him. The *hikuli*, the peyote itself, is God. They believe that the deer and the corn and the peyote are one and the same, that the gift of corn and peyote sprang from the head of a deer."

"Some believe that way," Epiphanio explained. "Some say that when the deer left, our ancestors found the gifts of corn and *hikuli* in his footprints. Do you see? It was the command, the *manda*, to live and to follow. The *hikuli* is the gift of life. My father and my father's father told me what really happens when you chew the gift with reverence. God lends you his heart."

"The old Yaqui do not believe that peyote is God. You know the word *genius*, Beto?"

Manuel turned to face the boy.

"Remember in your books how in old times and even before then, it was believed that each person had a familiar spirit and that these familiar spirits were always trying to communicate with the great spirit? The genius was an in-between spirit that could make that communication possible. There are other words for that genius, *naguales y tonales*, though these words now have many more meanings.

"It is the tonal that *su abuela* located with her power, then returned to Vernetta after so many years and so much heartache. The old Yaqui *peyoteros* believe that peyote is like the genius. It is a dream that connects."

"The Tarahumara, on the other hand," laughed Salvador, "think *peyote* is recreational."

Pascual, now squatting on his slender hams, was silent. A term in prison for possessing the tender genius had hushed

all his subsequent years with a sorrow learned far from his
fountain.

"*Entonces*, peyote is our gift to our brothers. We gave it to
the Kiowa and the Lipan Apache, the Cheyenne and even to
the Delaware, who are far, far from here."

The boy was beginning to feel sick. The ends of his fingers
were becoming numbed and claylike. With effort he managed
to rub his two hands together but still felt nothing below his
elbows. It seemed to him that the clay was rising up from the
ground beneath him and was somehow claiming him before
his time. Frightened now, he clapped his hands together only
to see his senseless wrists flailing oddly against each other.

The voices of the *Indios* around him sounded far away,
though all were close by, clearly within the light cast by the
fire. In one moment he felt himself to be among the men,
while in the next, he felt as though he was watching them,
as well as himself, from somewhere high above. The cold
numbness began to spread up his sides and chest, and with
growing fear he imagined it racing toward his frenzied heart.

"*Calmate, hijo, calmate*. This stuff is much better than alcohol,
because the hangover comes first and it never lasts too long,
I promise. If you want to get sick, that would be okay, but
what a terrible waste of Josephina's good *menudo*."

The old man rubbed his grandson's forehead as the *viejos*
began the *una va-ti*, the night song. The boy began to speak
to his grandfather as the song began; he tried to say that he
was going to vomit, but the words never came.

"You have nothing to say, boy?" the old man said, smiling.
"It's just as well. Perhaps, in the end, there is only counting.
In this we are the *chintete* and the deer."

The boy could not respond. As his grandfather was speaking, the clay had begun draining from his body and was being
replaced by a completely different sensation. There was an
agile, anxious anticipation spreading from his darting eyes
downward. All at once the secure, cloying earth seemed but
a trap. He felt hooded and jessed by his contact with it. With
great effort at first, the boy felt himself rising in discord with
the ground, his wimpled wings straining for the leisure of a
thermal.

He climbed, tacking in the darkness, enraptured by his own swiftness and the perfect clarity of his vision. He saw the small fire flash by somewhere far below, to his right. At the height of his climb he banked left and flew back through a thin, ragged thermal filled with what seemed to be gnats. A billion gray gnats buzzing upward. He wondered what they were. "The prayers of fools," the voice of Salvador echoed from somewhere, "prayers for the advancement of commerce. Prayers uttered in fear of old age. Invocations to God from both sides of a war. Prayers written on money. Cheap prayers."

The lift within the thermal had been minimal, so no compensation at his wing tips was required. He knew it without thinking. All at once he found himself above himself, the tremulous retchings of his small human body below completely immaterial, yet vaguely important. He caught his own form rooted far below but then lost it again almost immediately among all the other forms.

Banking once more, he hurtled upward because it was a thing that hawks do, what they added up to. The slender thread could be stretched out endlessly between the shaking, shivering boy in the black desert and the hawk that now followed numberless geometrical grids, flowed in them, running parallel then not, banking again across perpendicular grids, then skirting them all for an angle common to both.

The thread could be stretched endlessly, forever, as the grid shifted beneath the bird whose talons touched nothing but the void. Each one of the old men in the distance, at the end of the thread, had acquired a glow about him, a growing light that seemed to emanate from a point behind each of them. Yet, when each moved or turned, the blazing light followed. Slowly, the glow engulfed the form before it. It began at the feet and moved up toward the face. Each man was now a blinding torch.

The boy saw the brown Huichol's flame rising from the desert floor, a stick in what must have been his hand. A stick protruding from his fire. The same gourd Beto had seen earlier had been inverted and placed in the pan, and water had been

poured in around it. The Huichol fire struck the gourd with
the stick. He struck it slowly, with almost imperceptible motion. The hollow sound that flowed forth was eerie, as if
hunger had a definite sound, a note. It was haunting and
hallowed. It was longing.

The boy could see the sound; he could smell it. It was a
sound to match his sickness, his yearning. It was howling.
Then it was joined by the soft rattle of dead butterfly children
as their small, clear coffins bounced against the pellucid legs
of the dancers in the glow.

"The sound of fertility and death is the sound of eternity
to us. There were once wolves in this land, and there were
once *tigres* and deer. They were one and the same sound."

"And when they left," another distant voice joined in, "they
left us the corn that we might eat and the *hikuli* that we might
see."

"Life unmasked is death. This life is the cocoon," said Salvador, his voice now disembodied.

"The next is the *mariposa*. The butterfly. We will see beyond
violet.

"The tiny lights below is where they dance," rang the same
distant voice over the rattling sound of eternity. "The small
men and women move between the timorous and the terrible.
The tiny lights below is where the *chintete* whispers to the
fecund girls, a sentence that takes forever to say. Oh, can he
hiss the antique song! It is a lizard's smooth palaver that gains
access, his murmurs open all their legs, the legs of their rip-
ened mothers, the legs of their blossomed daughters, the legs
within legs yet unborn. It was the whisper of the lizard into
the ear of La Malinche that led her astray. It wasn't Cortés
who made her betray her people."

Without warning, there appeared enormous, dark figures
moving just outside the tiny lights below.

"*Xolótl*, the wolf, moves out there on the fringes."

The boy could sense each thing as it was being described.
He could circle above as each thing came into view.

"He skulks as he always has. He is a murmur in back of
the church. He is a rumor behind the altar. He moves just

beneath sensibilities, the lord of wolves. His is the form before the Aztecs first called his name, before Columbus, before Cortés.

"Look there, at her! Look, she flees him. She beckons him. She is the lord of the deer, the feeder and the nourisher."

Beto now truly felt the presence of enormities; their titan footsteps rumbled at a frequency far below hearing, something heard in the stomach of a dream.

"They run beneath the *Pascua*, beneath the *pascola* dances, beneath our numbers and our consciousness."

" 'Hear how the lizard calls to the people to multiply,' the deer says coyly from her place in the shadows."

" 'Understand that the lizard's words are aimed with equal power at the flowers and at the weeds,' the wolf scowls as he stalks her nearby."

"The poets and storytellers have told us such things just as they always have. But beyond even their vision, beyond the vision of man, even past the gift of *hikuli*, the forms come together, the rivers and waves converge. We live in an eddy. Beyond knowing, beyond language. Things that must always be apart come together. Things that long to go go backward."

The dancers in the middle of the void, stepping neither forward nor back, facing each way and going all ways simultaneously, sang of the forms behind their forms.

"The wolf wipes away the Spanish and the Catholic and the distance between us and our sacred river," sang one.

"Can you see it, Beto? Can you see yourself leaving the *rio Yaqui, Cocorit*?"

"Abuelo," answered the boy in a high, screeching voice, "I can't see you. I am flying high above and I can't speak to you."

The boy made a sweeping turn in the darkness at the deepest edge of the wolf's maw; then instantaneously the profound darkness was shattered by the blinding, searing light of Sonora.

"Ah, so you are my great-grandson," said a voice cradled in the sudden silence. The gaunt, shirtless Indian lowered himself to one knee to be at eye level with the boy. He placed his right hand upon the boy's shoulder. He was a tall man for an Indio, very dark and with *pelo chino*, curly hair. His eyes were a striking green. Slung across his back was a battered Remington lever action and a cloth bag for carrying bullets. There was a deep, red gash across his stomach and another on his thigh.

"*Bayoneta*," he said, answering the boy's questioning glance.

There was a large group of black-haired people behind him who seemed to welcome the rest—almost all were Indians. One thousand Indians along with their goats and their bags of corn. Some held repeating rifles and water bags. Many of the men were wounded. Some held babies swaddled against the heat and dust, while others held a long line of brooding Yori hostages still dressed in their *Federale* uniforms.

"There is your grandfather there, the one with the *pelo chino y pantalones azules*."

The Indian gestured to the young boy to come forward.

"Come here, boy," he said. "Don't be afraid to meet your grandson."

Many of the Indians nearby laughed as the boys moved forward toward each other. The *Federales* could not laugh. Theirs was the pained look of rope-fettered goats before slaughter.

"If I look forward," the young Manuel began, "and you look backward, we can always meet right here."

The young Manuel lifted both arms slowly to gesture. His eyes were as green as his father's. "It's as if the same head will be looking in two directions. Did you come here at my request?" he asked.

"Yes," said the boy, "you are with me, waiting for me to come back. Apache has come back home and Abuela says it means you are going to die. Please, Abuelo, tell me she is wrong."

"She's not wrong. You should know that. She's not wrong in that way. When the singing tree spoke to us so long ago, it told us that death is the gift we must give in thanks for the bounty the world gives to us."

A grave look came over his face; then he lowered himself to his haunches, pulling his grandson down with him. They whispered together for a time.

"Don't forget the mask, Beto," he said.

"The *chapayeka* must be placed with me. It is our old way. Don't forget the mask. Promise me."

"I promise."

Manuel stood when his father came for him. In silence, the two ancestors backed away from the boy. The long line of Yaquis began to move on. Each person stared intently at the boy as they passed him. Each woman, each baby, each warrior sent something of themselves to him with just a look. The staggering line of *Federales* walked by the boy, and each pleaded with him with his eyes. Some were barefoot and had bleeding feet.

"You won't die," said the boy, suddenly hating the line of Federal soldiers. "You'll just lose your soles."

"What do you see, Beto?"

The question seemed to pierce the measureless moment of timeless black.

"Keep your eyes closed and tell me what it is you are seeing."

The boy's eyes shot open reflexively, and the fierce light of the fire thrilled him, overpowered him. As if by habit, he closed his trigger eye until the flash passed.

"How much time has passed?" he asked.

There was no answer.

"I see," he began after closing both eyes again, "I see a piano out in the rain, or at least it's getting wet. I can follow the drops of water falling down between the keys."

"Move, move around, *mijo*. Force yourself around. Are there things near the piano, around the piano. Do you recognize it?"

"No, it's just old and beat-up, not new like Abuelita's. There's a pile of clothes nearby. A pile of woman's clothes. They seem unused now, just waiting outside for the St. Vincent de Paul truck to come by and pick them up. That's all I can see . . . no, there's something else. A small wooden house. Is it on fire?

"Two white people are sitting together in a small living room. There is dark, fat furniture and white antimacassars. They're having tea. They are kind of young, but I feel that I know her. I feel like I know her! He is reading to her. He reads to her a lot, every night for hours, for years. I can almost see her face."

The boy opened his eyes to see that he was back on the ground and back in his own body. Morning had come. Pascual was busy piling wood on the fire, but the night chill was still very evident at the boy's back. The mestizo was singing the *vako tia-way* as he worked, the song for dawn. The bitterness was gone.

The circle of men drank coffee in the early morning light. Beto and his grandfather, squatting near the old pickup, sat apart from the group.

"Most of us found jobs with the Southern Pacific railroad," Manuel began. "My father worked on the gangs that laid down the first iron in many places. The army and the sheriff were coming around back then, arresting any Yaquis who had rifles or who didn't have a job, so he hooked on with the railroad gangs. He went as far up the line as Seattle.

"I met *su abuelita* when I was working the rails up in Denver, Colorado. Jesus, what did she see in me?" He shook his head at the old, answerless question. "I touched her like she was glass."

As he spoke Manuel stared off at a scene projected up in the aether.

"They would always have the Yaqui road gangs carry the dynamite that they used to blast through the hillsides. Shit, we used to walk barefoot with blasting caps loose in our pockets and cradling crates of black powder in our arms. That was how I carried her, like dynamite."

After a moment of quiet the spitting fire called him back.

"Her parents practically disowned her for marrying me. Your *bisabuela*, your great-grandmother, was what they called a *blanca*. There must've been a Moor in the woodpile," he smiled.

"She was a *curandera, también*. And she was a Catholic, too. That kind of shit will make you *loco*. I will never forget my first sight of *su abuela*. She was beautiful. There she was at the piano playing Fats Waller. Did you know he died not far from here in a pullman car, a Santa Fe sleeper?

"When the railroad work slowed down, a lot of us got construction work in Phoenix. I left S.P. with a couple of Irish friends and we hooked on real quick. When I first started swinging the hammer, Phoenix was not much more than a pueblo. But all the old gringos who fucked up the air in other places needed a place to come breathe their last breaths, I guess.

"I started out as a plater and framer on those balloon houses the *gavachos* live in. I could never understand it. Shit, what a waste of wood! They need air conditioners in the summer and heaters in the winter. The adobe house kicks the shit out of those houses."

The boy had never heard his grandfather talk this much. He had always considered his grandfather to be more of a listener. But now Beto seemed to understand the urgency of it, and he became the listener.

"Don't misunderstand me. I don't hate the white people. Taken individually, they are as good a people as anybody else. But together they have a great many problems. They let things happen around them, even bad things. They just let it happen. You see, they have no tribe, so if a person across town is hurt or hungry, they feel nothing. Soon they will have no communities at all. Plus, everything in their world is for sale. Everything. Even religion.

"Pretty soon they'll be chopping up this country and selling it overseas. I sure wouldn't put it past them. There are some exceptions, though. Your Arkie friends have a sad but enduring tribe. They still live that war of theirs over and over. Your *abuela* sure loves their music, though. It has an Irish heart."

The old man smiled at the thought of his wife in the kitchen, singing along to the hillbilly music.

"Harold has a tribe, an ancient tribe like yours. Ay,"—he shook his head—"those other Fuller Brush people are *pendejos*, *idiotas*. The Irish have a tribe; *los Negros*, too, even if they don't know it yet. I think that Reverend Drake knows it. Many of the rest have no tribe, no headman. They have no heroes, just celebrities." He shook his head with sadness and resignation. "The white man has all the rights in this country, but we have the rites, the rituals. Their children see a world without mysteries."

He paused for a moment.

"It's a shame. I don't know how much of last night and this morning you will remember, Alberto, but you must promise me one thing. If nothing else, promise me this one thing."

The boy looked up at the sound of his full, given name. Alberto. The recognition that his name had changed caused him to smile broadly. He thought again about the *chapayeka* mask of the dream and realized that this would be his second promise. He nodded in agreement.

"You must promise me you will never ever cross a picket line."

The boy was asleep in his bed when Josephina woke the next morning. It had been a fitful night's sleep for her. The green dragonflies had returned to her sometime in the earliest morning. Again, the red fireflies had bombarded her starboard side. She had awakened sweating and startled and had torn off her nightshirt to inspect her right side for the wounds she knew must be there. Nothing. No wounds, only a shivering fear and a premonition of another land war in Asia.

"Not again," she spoke aloud.

It was then that she remembered that the Yaquis had taken her grandson out to the desert. There was no resentment now. She was simply glad that it was over. She had feared it for so long. Turning in the bed, Josephina felt next to her for her husband. She could tell from the sheets that Manuel had never made it to the bedroom.

She rose, pulled on her robe, then walked slowly through

her terra cotta home to the doorway where the blanket hung. She crossed herself tentatively, then pushed the woolen blanket carefully to one side.

The boy had gone to sleep with his back to the doorway again. He would be frightened of the ghost when he woke. She imagined him trembling and turning under the sheltering covers to position himself for a stealthy glimpse at the doorway. The thought brought a smile of relief to her lips.

"Abuela," his voice cut through her reverie and startled her. "Abuela," said the boy, now sitting bolt upright in the bed, his covers tossed off. "Wysteria Maybelle," he began in an earnest and excited voice, "Wysteria Maybelle had a husband. She had an Irish husband who worked for the railroads. They lived here, right where our house is, but a long time ago. He read to her every night. Poems. Poems by Andrew Marvell. He's the ghost with the white dog that people still see on this road."

The boy was standing now. Behind him, Apache stretched and yawned before trotting out to the kitchen for his food.

"You were wrong about grandpa, Abuela. *Yoaniya* is not bad, it's just real old. It's a place where time doesn't work. He is with *seataka*, the flower way, and he says that you are, too. He says it is a divine gift to see into hearts."

Josephina's own heart sank and soared all in one confused instant.

"I don't need to be baptized anymore."

He kissed her cheek as he passed her on his way to the kitchen.

"Alberto," she whispered. She fell against the archway, losing her balance.

"*Pinche lobo,*" she muttered.

Fucking wolf.

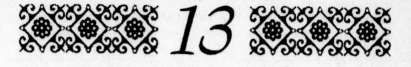

13

Scorpion Water

Manuel was sitting in his beloved rocking chair, his muscular leg pushing him back and gravity pushing him forth. Apache was asleep on the floor, curled up next to him. There was the familiar scent of *frijoles y queso* wafting in from the stove. Outside, Buckeye's usual noises were dulled by a sense of contentment.

Then there was singing when something like vinegar rose in his nostrils. Josephina's soft singing as she brushed her hair in the kitchen. He caught the smell of vinegar when something cut swiftly into his well-being like saw blades. Something that vandalized his thoughts and sent his recollections reeling into *una retrograda*. The life poem read backward.

Then there was an infinite moment of suspension, the dark twin of the womb.

There was the hundredth stroke of a hairbrush when whole blocks of memory flickered golden, then were extinguished.

There was familiar humming while he died.

The dying man was wrenched to the side by a heart muscle that seized up, driving his right foot, his rocking-chair engine, an inch deep into the hard-packed floor.

Half in the grave the dying man was seeing through soil. Submerged to his eyes, he was seeing in that moment into

the dark kitchen, into cobwebbed switch boxes in cold Portland; he seemed to be seeing from everywhere at once.

Submerged to his eyes, he could see his dog, Apache . . .
gone again *a toda madre*, gone at full speed. He could hear his
howl, and some part of him followed close on his tail toward
Tlalocan, land of those who die by water. There was whiskey
still on his lips and a river roared in his ears.

Each rock forward in his chair pushed his eyesight deeper
into the earth below the adobe and brought visions from
farther and farther away.

Each rock backward into the amber light of life found him
straining to call to his wife, who was so happily singing and
brushing her hair in the hot kitchen.

He rocked downward into an undying hatred of Porfirio
Díaz, instigator of the Yaqui diaspora, the builder of grand
latifundios. De repente, all at once *El Presidente, El General* himself
stood before Manuel, summoned up by the sheer power of
the old man's hatred. The toothless and transparent general
strode through the adobe in his Austrian epaulettes and
French boots to stand before Manuel.

The woman in the kitchen stopped brushing her hair for a
moment. A look of concern flashed over her face.

"Two spirits?" she whispered without thinking. Then she
shook her head and continued to brush.

The old man struggled in vain to rise, to kill the arrogant
politician before he could live out his royal life in exile, carrying filtered remembrances to the tree-filled parks of Paris.
The pungent smell of hemp swirled up around Manuel as he
struggled, his chest imploding. Every Yaqui spirit would re-
joice if only he could reach the monster's neck and carve it
into a tenon, the earth of Mexico the mortise. Suddenly the
general's ghost was gone. Manuel could see that into his
vacuum flowed *los pelados,* millions of trampled peons like
noisy bits of light. They were generated from nothing and
were bent upon hounding *El Presidente* until the world's end;
sursum corda with the breath of corn and venison.

He rocked upward to the swirl of notes, Fats Waller below
the flickering face of a male actor wearing white makeup.
There were men in a circle arguing that narrow gauge has no

future. There were men laying cog track in Colorado, speaking in words of steel and wood. Words of weather.

Abajo, he saw the shining sillion mound centered in the trough of her legs, the flora of eight children sliding sleek and purple and rooting at her breast. The cracked, autumnal evenings of four stillborn, their corn silk hair embrittled by the light, their sad, wrinkled husks already ancient. Four lovingly chosen names, unattached, vaporous, lost in time.

Arriba, the brown *vigas* above are his arms, the *latillos* his fingers, the wet *canales* his ears.

His thoughts piled out of a closing soul.

My narrow gauge woman sings, her skin cracked with my seed.

I cannot speak.

I must have the old *chapayeka*. I cannot send my heart out to her, it's not mine anymore. *Yo puedo,* I can.

We are elemental. We are entwined, dark and light like a peon's world.

I have been lying this way forever. I am bound here by dimming ligaments. I am cleared for takeoff. I am pinned here breathless by the light of candles . . . and I hear a needless apology trickling into my soul. No need.

No need. It is just flight *mi querida*; it is just clay, a lazy meander down to silt.

He had pulled at his neck to squeeze out a sound that would not come. He had struggled with the air inside of him to carry words over to her before the chair rocked forward. Now he could taste the *pura tierra mojada*, the pure moist earth of his home, stronger than whiskey.

Back or forth? Thoughts like fibrillations.

He had wondered which way to go just as it all stopped, the decision made without a memory to keep it in. His bottle had spilled as his arm dropped.

His strong hands went too.

Josephina removed every piece of jewelry from her body, every adornment but her wedding ring.

She sighed softly as she slowly removed her *mantilla* and beautiful white comb for the last time. She had been brushing her long hair in that grievous instant. All at once single strands stood away from the rest of her hair and clothing clung to her body. She had turned just in time to see the wolf-dog run out of the house. Then she slammed all the doors shut and put blankets in the windows.

Before the death could be announced to all of Buckeye Road, there was still one final act to perform. Shattered, the old woman rushed from room to room in the adobe house sealing the two of them in just moments after her own screams had died away with her husband.

Her grandson had heard her cries and knocked loudly at the locked door. The old woman called out sternly to him to go stay with the Perkins or in Vernetta's trailer.

"Please go away!" she cried out from the darkened adobe. "We're having a discussion," she explained. "We need to talk." It was her euphemism for a fight.

Alberto circled the adobe, listening for some clue to the subject of their discussion. There was something in his *abuela*'s voice that he had never heard before. He found that she had taken her beloved wedding quilt from her bed and moved it outside to her husband's cot, where it was forced to lie down with Indian blankets. Something had changed. Something was going on.

Inside the living room, lit by a single candle, Josephina cinched her belt tight to the point of pain and pressed her brown thighs together hard as if to seal shut forever that part of it all. No evil force would enter her that way; no flesh would defile the purity of her intentions, even if her methods were strange and unknown to the Pope. She blew out the candles in her kitchen altar and asked God's forgiveness for her dark blasphemies.

"God forgive me. God forgive me."

Alberto heard the same solemn words over and over again as he tried to listen through the front door. The sound of her cracking voice scared him.

"God forgive me," he heard once again as he turned and walked slowly toward the Highway Comet.

She would tell no one outside the adobe of Manuel's death; not even her grandson would know until the next morning, the day after the day of the dead.

She rushed to her medicinal bag and plunged her hand to the very bottom where the square bottle lay. On its way downward the hand bypassed the crucifixes and the precious cloth. A finger brushed against the brow of Christ. There were tears of shame and agony rushing down the forearm to wet the grasp.

"May it never, ever be used," Josephina repeated the words of the old Mayo woman.

"*Ojalá que sí*," she had answered so long ago. Even then she had used words that were not Christian words, words from a Moorish past. Finally, her shaking hand had lifted the bottle from its resting place.

"*El agua de alacrán*," she said as she gazed wearily around herself at her precious home. After what she was about to do that evening, she could never allow herself to sleep another night in the adobe. Her trembling grasp had agitated the horrid contents of the bottle, and the mottled, dead scorpions within were swirling and bobbing. She wondered if a pincer had suddenly moved. She thought perhaps the scorpions revived when the unthinkable became a thought. Do they arise to sting at death and for a moment drive it away? Can a poison to life kill death for a few precious seconds?

She rushed to the rocker where her beloved husband still sat, the sounds of Buckeye Road now as meaningless to her as they were to him. The passing trucks meant nothing. Vernetta's radio meant nothing. The sound of the choir at the Mighty Clouds of Joy singing "Mary, don't you weep, Martha, don't you moan," meant nothing even while the song dimly mirrored all.

"*Si Dios quiera!* Please, let this be God's work!" she cried as she was hit by the full impact of her actions. In the somber dusk she bartered ten thousand Our Fathers for this, and rosaries enough to wear her fingers away.

The amber light around Manuel was following other rules at that moment. There was shadow where light struck him full and a bright glow in the crevices of his face where darkness should have been.

"God help me choose," she whispered quietly as she pulled the rotting cork from the thick neck of the bottle. A sharp, acrid odor filled the room. Her fingers quivered.

"A drop in the mouth of the dead and you will hear his last words," Ana Martinez, the Mayo, had explained solemnly.

"And a drop in the ears and the dead will hear your apologies. But it must be done quickly. The spirit must still be within, gathering itself to ease away from all its tiny, wet connections."

Josephina knelt beside her slumped husband to pray, checking behind her back for the presence of the green beast. He must be laughing, she thought.

"Virgin of Guadelupe, please forgive this last vanity." She repeated the prayer in Spanish as she tilted the bottle. As she poured, her eyes were swirling as when they had first danced together in Denver. Her pores were exploding as on that first day when he carried her to bed.

His head canted, her tears filled his eyes as the fluid filled his ear.

"*Cielo, mi cielo. Alma de mi corazón.* More than Rudolph Valentino," she said among many other things.

"If we are lucky, it is joy that assassinates us; it is contentment. Listen, *escúchame*. I know we will embrace there, *viejo*. You by the Yaqui and I by the Tagus or by the desert wash, ages beyond the flood. Forgive me my lifelong *intolerancia, mi amor*.

"I now see that all waters are confluent and all graves are congruent. *Espérame*, wait for me, I am only moments behind you. And please don't drink too much of the shadow or swallow too much of the dark before I get there to take care of you. You know, I am the only one who can feed you properly. I have no regrets, *mi viejo*. No regrets at all.

"If I had died as a child, like one of my poor stillborn, I could say to God . . . I had no life.

"If I had lived a thousand years and not known you, I could say to God . . . I had no love.

"I tell God now, while you listen . . . God, *Dios mío*, I had both.

"Our life together was perfect."

The fluid, in a small rivulet, dripped down from his lobe as she cradled his heavy head to her breast. They sat that way for hours; then she rose in silence to cook his breakfast.

"Before we begin our own service, I want to tell you all that there will be another service at the graveside, a Catholic service according to the wishes of our dear friend, Josephina."

He nodded respectfully toward her. There was no response from beneath her veil.

"I wish to thank her for allowing our little church to have him here with us and for allowing us to do the service for the Buckeye Road community." He gestured with his Bible hand toward the coffin. "When I have finished my meager say, Sister Dora Mae will lead our magnificent choir in song; then those of you that wish may follow the Cadillac hearse out to the burying ground."

Reverend Willie Drake glanced toward the organist, who raised the volume a bit to give the reverend a moment to gather his thoughts.

"Don't you know, there's been a landslide in here, in my heart, and I don't have words for it. The dust won't settle for years and I don't have the words for it.

"There's been a natural catastrophe, but God ain't gave me articulate words to describe it to you, to say to you that a soul has torn loose and broke free in here, and though heaven is much the better for it, such a severance is always measured in terms of human sorrow. I am measuring now with my sadness. We are all measuring now.

"It seems that our lot as children of the Lord is to tape-measure up on things, to speculate on distances, to comment in our hearts on things that come to pass. Maybe the clock-work of the universe would go on without us, but then who would wait up till all hours of the night to see a dim comet? Who would make a wish on a falling star? Who but a maiden-fly would call a day an eternity?

"But it is not just the stars and faraway things that thrill

us and hurt us. The grass we step on will cut us deeper and
finer than any knife or fine-stropped razor. The tiny insects
and creatures we trample underfoot everyday will have their
way with us finally. But you see, praise be, it's God's way of
cutting our moorings loose and letting us drift free from care,
from always measuring up to see where we are. Oh God, to
drift free! To slip our bindings at last and be released to sail
on ancient seas!

"Now you all know that Manuel weren't no Christian, and
he sure never went to church. But you and I know of some
mighty loud-mouthed, Sunday only, fairweather Christians
that backslides the whole rest of the week, but there they are
on Sunday, spiffed up to beat the band, sitting right there in
the first or second pew and acting like God is a fool and blind
to boot."

Reverend Drake waited till the murmuring agreement died
down.

"The first time I ever saw the man I noticed that he slept
outside, over there across the lot. I'd see his small oil lamp
burning. I'd see other Indian fellas come by to sit and talk
with him 'til all hours. I'd see his grandson and him squeezing
into that little cot, settling in for the night. Here he's got a
fine new adobe home with a shiny tin roof and the man sleeps
outside. Being curious, I asked myself why is that?

"So one night after sweeping the church I walk on over
there. I perambulated over there. Do you have the picture?
Do you have the picture? Here I was a Negro minister who
had heard the call in a colored diner in Atlanta and I was
walking over to ask an Indian why he slept outside.

"Now I didn't know a thing about Indians at the time. You
see, to me America was white and to a lot of us America was
white and I was kinda white and the Indians, well, they were
just invisible. I say I was kinda white because I measured my
life against theirs. I saw their wealth, I hated my poverty."

Heads nodded.

"I saw their clothing and Lord, I despised my rags."

"Yes, yes," people said.

"I heard their English and I deplored my gulla-speak. I saw
their meat and potatoes and I shamefully hid my poor neck-

bones and grease. Yes, I was kinda white when I crossed that lot."

The congregation's assent was ascending.

"I'd gone to college, you see."

The reverend smirked, mocking himself to the great pleasure of the congregation.

"I'd cut a part right here in my head, and when I looked in my mirror I saw a reflection of the white man there, a sort of little brother to the white man. Well, I'm here to tell you that it was no reflection that I saw, it was a shadow. A shadow. The white man standing between me and the sun.

"Good Lord, I laugh at myself now. I didn't know that to see the world you have to be able to see yourself; you need the power to see yourself. I walked across that lot out there out of curiosity, and I must admit before God that I felt that I was condescending to speak to one of the invisible people. God could look down from his throne on high and see me, his servant, doing his work among the heathen. I felt good about myself stooping to converse with this obviously uneducated man.

"As God is my witness, I musta been seeing with white eyes too, 'cause I'd never seen the nations that live in this desert. I couldn't see them any more than I could see the true image of myself. Just like white eyes staring at the nations of the Cameroons or the Gold Coast and seeing only chattels, only property.

"Well, maybe two hours later we, Manuel and I, had finished off his bottle of good Irish whiskey and we were a workin' on his *tequila*. We were hugging each other right out there, arms around one another. We were hugging each other like a pair of wasted prizefighters.

"When I sobered up I found that I had never been so sober. When Manuel was through grappling with me, I walked back here to my little church later that evening an African-American man of God. Not a Negro minister no more."

The congregation roared. A huge woman swooned with God's vapors.

"God in your corner," they shouted out. "God is the greatest cut man!"

"An African-American man of God. I'se be swearin' the man sermonized me! Can you believe it, he lectured me. I'se be swearin' he didn't say thirty English words, but when he was done I marched my black self right back here, found my best bristle brush and painted GOD BLESS ROSA PARKS on our beautiful sign.

"Now, he weren't no philosopher in the book sense."

The congregation shook their heads.

"But the man knew who he was and wanted to keep himself."

The reverend wrapped his arms around himself as if to demonstrate.

"He told me that black folks are not the same."

A loud accord filled the room.

"You see, he was a tool of God on that day and probably on so many other days. He said to you and to me that we are naturally different."

The congregation could barely keep from jumping to its feet.

"And . . . we are different. He's saying it to us right now. He said to me that day that we are no one's shadow, no one's reflection, a separate element altogether, a different atomic weight. Like coal, like common coal, you hurt it; you squeeze it; you put it under immense pressure and you get . . . the blues, the mother tongue of our enslavement; you get jazz, the American classical music; you get a joyful sound that God must hear; you get diamonds."

The congregation began to jitter and swell with energy. Black behinds could barely be kept in pews; voices were no longer restrained.

"To free ourselves, be ourselves!"

As each soul gained speed the pressure on the pink walls grew. The reverend smiled at his folk. "We'uns gots to sing now; we have to sing."

The line of cars behind the long hearse stretched from the church grounds out past Cady and beyond the Rainbo Market.

Alberto waited in Potrice and Sugar Dee's beautiful car though
he was blind to its magnificence on this day. He was deaf to
the fifty voices and the organ notes that piled out of the
Mighty Clouds of Joy. He was deaf to the reverend's chain
of words.

Behind the Pierce-Arrow were flatbed trucks and pickups
loaded with dogged, leathery people. Pimas, Huichols,
Mayos, Apaches and Yaquis waiting for one of their own.

The five *maricones* had placed themselves on the back of
one of the trucks and looked for all the world like a window
display at Macy's.

The Cheungs' food wagon waited in line, its small kitchen
dark with cool, resting metal. There were white cloths tied to
its door handles and fenders.

At the end was Harold's tiny Nash-Metropolitan. He had
arrived early in the morning without his Fuller Brush case but
with his wife and son. The three of them were somewhere
inside the church, singing.

Old Ana Martinez had come. Tía Cecelia, Lola, Lencha and
Tía Mona had arrived with their families. Virginia Vasquez
had driven in with her husband and children. Beside the
entryway to the church, Wysteria Maybelle sat calmly with
her sleeping dogs. She was deathly silent, and her face was
visible to the naked eye for the first time in years.

In the rest of Buckeye Road there was not one sober soul.
The day that Manuel was buried some diesel engines had
whined like women, their cries coming in low from the northeast. How could they know? Even the Buckeye switch boxes
had been dolorous and cumbersome that day and very slow
to close, so slow that two lumbering Cushion-Aire boxcars
ran headlong off the track and into the wash where some of
the grieving denizens of Buckeye were quick to shake off their
grief. They ran to eviscerate the beached, haughty leviathans
that had always rhythmically clicked their cold-shouldered
distance from all those pinned by poverty to the same spot
on the map.

"Distance. Distance. Distance."

They had always rolled the word through their iron voice boxes out to the unmoving folk who stared longingly after them. But on that day the boxcars went nowhere; their living innards had been carried away into the four blocks of Buckeye Road, their thin wheels spinning in the hot air. On that day it was the mired who moved as a train was sacrificed in honor of the dead.

One car had been filled with shock absorbers, leaf springs, and ball joints that would soon find their way into every battered motor vehicle from Yuma to the Four Corners Reservation. But it was the other car that would be talked about for years.

"*Qué milagro! Ay, qué milagro!*"

Men would forever shake their drunken heads about the other car.

"It was like Miss America went blind and thought I was her husband," said Dismas Skully.

"Blond bitch on her skinny knees in front of my black ass," he grinned. "Jes' like that." He made a motion as if pulling at two ears toward his crotch.

Children would wait through old age for another such car. They would defer schooling and day trips for the merest possibility of another such car careening into their lives. From that time forward each death in Buckeye would send a shiver of expectation up each living spine.

Thousands of bottles of good, bonded whiskey had spilled out for a hundred yards both north and south of the wreck. Buckeye Road had drowned its sorrows in honor of Manuel.

With swollen eyes, Josephina had finally thrown the house open and let Alberto in to see his *abuelo*. The boy had gone over to him and touched his leaden face and looked deeply into eyes beyond blind. An untouched plate of *huevos con chorizo* was on his lap.

"*Te prometo, Abuelo. Te prometo!*" he'd cried as he ran outside and into the desert.

Alberto had searched everywhere for the mask. He had
searched the adobe and the goat pens and even the *ramada*.
Every inch of Manuel's *fogón* had been searched: his bed, his
blankets, his tin cans and bottles. Josephina, bent by her grief,
would answer none of her grandson's frantic questions and
pretended to know absolutely nothing about any *chapayeka*
mask.

No matter how the boy had persisted, she chose to sink
deeper into her grief and reply only that her own life was
over in the instant that her husband's rocking chair had
stopped moving. After a day she had refused to answer any
more of her grandson's questions or to speak to him or anyone
at all.

Not even Vernetta could pry a word from her. She'd come
over with Danny and the two had spoken to her while she
put on a black mourning dress, quietly removed from a
dresser drawer as though saved for the occasion. It was the
same dress that she would wear every day for the remainder
of her life. She would be wearing the dark dress when she
herself fell at last.

The boy had continued his feverish search for the *chapayeka*
mask. It was his first promise. It had not been in the outhouse
or in the goat pens or the chicken coop. It was not among
Manuel's tools or hidden somewhere in the old pickup truck.
Alberto had angrily torn Manuel's bed apart and left the
ground under the lean-to strewn with tins and bottles.

With Claude and Louie, the boy had searched in the desert
for a mile around the adobe to no avail. In desperation he
had hitched a ride with some Papagos out to the desert south
of Tucson, where he searched wildly for Salvador, the old
yoeme, the one who stood now, waiting with the others on
the back of the flatbed.

He had located the old *Indio* out near the abandoned mines.
The two spent the night around his cooking fire.

"The *chapayeka* mask is not lost."

Salvador sat stirring the embers after a long morning of
finding.

"I feel its presence nearby, but its exact whereabouts are
being blocked. *Su abuela* is a resourceful woman."

"What can I do, Salvador? I know what she wants: a Catholic priest, flowers and a big headstone. He will be trapped in there," he said, fuming. "*Qué desmadre!* He never wanted a funeral or even a coffin. But she wouldn't listen to him, and now she won't listen to me. She just won't listen to me! Now I won't keep my promise, my dream promise."

"You will keep your promise," said Salvador calmly. "I have seen it. Don't be too mad at her."

He rose and began kicking sand onto the still smoking coals.

"Josephina was always headstrong," he laughed, musing on his first sight of her, years ago at a theater in Denver, then at Manuel's wedding.

He remembered vividly the young woman so frightened and so enthralled by the savages. Manuel had asked Salvador to perform a dance at the wedding, but in the end Josephina had refused to allow it.

"Did you know that you are blood of unthinkable blood? The *Español* brought their *pinche* caste system to Mexico after the Conquest. There were over twenty levels of human beings starting with the European at the top and ending with *los Negros*. No *mestizo* could own land and no European ever paid taxes. You know, there was no category for a Spanish woman mating with an *Indio*. It was unthinkable!" he laughed.

"Xipe," said Alberto.

"Oh, Manuel told you about the god of the flayed? The Spanish were so fucking shocked when they first saw an Aztec priest wearing another man's skin, now they have the whole country doing it. You can't get nowhere in Mexico if you are *Indio* or *morenito*. It's the same up here.

"No one from her side of the family came to the wedding. *Nadie.*"

As he spoke to Alberto, he could almost hear Josephina's curses striking his back as the *viejos*, the Yaquis, walked out into the desert together as they always had. He shrugged. He knew Josephina would do as she promised. It was her strength and her weakness. There would be a Catholic funeral. But he also knew that it was not the right thing to do. Manuel was washed in the blood all right, but not of the lamb.

"Did you see Manuel?" Salvador asked.

"Yes, we met at almost the same place, but I think it was before I met him last time."

"Ah, you keep going to see him and you'll end up in Cocorit. When you get there, you'll see that time is longer then. Have you noticed that Phoenix has no benches for people to sit on? Miles of sidewalk and no benches. It is a bad sign. Time is short there. Did you see anything else?"

Alberto had not wanted to answer the question, but the old *yoeme* persisted.

"I saw your wives mourning you. Three Mexican wives. They mourn you like crazy. They've lit a thousand candles to prove it."

To Alberto's surprise, the old man only smiled proudly at the news.

"One of them, the saddest one, keeps seeing the face of the Virgin of Guadelupe on burned tortillas. *Mucha gente* line up every Sunday after church to stare at her tortillas."

"How did it happen?" asked Salvador, obviously amused by the revelations.

"In a hogan on the Salt River, a Maricopa widow and her toothless mother-in-law double-teamed you to death under woolen blankets."

"Shit," laughed Salvador, "that's not death!"

He rose and stretched slowly. He retrieved his battered aluminum pot and his hunting knife.

"Now," he grinned broadly, "I know a truck stop where the chorizo is as orange as Florida *y* the waitresses there got *tétas como melones*."

It was a long ride to the cemetery. Too long. Far from the adobe and into distant, cement-bound Phoenix. Only the driver of the hearse knew the way and he got lost twice. The whole caravan had to stop each time and wait while the driver got out to ask directions—once at a Mohawk gas station, and once at a place called Frank's Footers, a hot dog stand with an enormous papier-mâché hot dog on its roof.

Vernetta and Danny rode in the Pierce-Arrow with Alberto, Potrice and Sugar Dee. Ahead of them, on the highway, they could see Josephina in the back of the hearse, with her trembling arms draped over the coffin, her flowing black hair filling the rear window. At first, Alberto had mistaken her hair for a curtain.

He watched her up ahead on the highway and knew for certain she was dreaming behind her swaying hair. During the service by the Catholic priest he knew that she was dreaming hard, that things raged loudly under her veil. He had felt it as if on his own skin, secrets beading up on her scalp like sweat.

When they finally turned into the cemetery grounds, Alberto felt sickened by the sight he saw.

"Goddamn," exclaimed Sugar Dee, pointing at the manicured lawns and San Jose junipers, "the white man even wants obedience from his plants!"

Josephina had stood staring intently at the plot next to Manuel's even as the coffin was being lowered into place. It was her own plot; she'd bought a place in eternity right next to her beloved husband. They would solve the mystery hand in hand.

The contract and the receipt were right there in her pocket, signed and sealed.

When the service was over, Alberto followed her to the green edge to throw flowers down to him.

And he stood by her when all the others had pulled back respectfully and gone over to wait by the cars.

Together, with a hollow world at their backs, they stood on the ledge of turf and loose soil and watched small landslides fall and strike the coffin. The smell of newly cut earth and grass rose in their nostrils.

The old woman quivered there on the edge, a powerless breeze through her veil making her sway.

"Only you," she said.

"Only you."

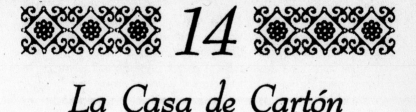

14

La Casa de Cartón

There was silence, only senseless, staring silence. The old woman passed seamless days after the sepulture wrapped in distance and interred in silence. Though she no longer slept within the adobe, she would go inside during the day to prepare her food or to pack her things. The thick walls of the adobe lent a profound quiet to these days. The flapping of the butcher paper in the windows was unbearable to her now. As she packed her belongings into boxes, painful light glinted mercilessly in her eyes reflected off different objects in the adobe rooms as the sun moved across the sky.

Even the raunchy, raucous Blue Moon laid low. Dominoes rested in their tiny casket; pool cues huddled upright in a corner. Business at the Blue Moon had plummeted with the mood of Buckeye Road after the funeral. All that whiskey from the wrecked boxcars had paralyzed Floyd's business. Every drunk in Buckeye Road was busy guarding a hoard of bottles.

In Cady, Onan, Odabee and Dismas were strangely silent. There had not been a card game in days.

Potrice and Sugar Dee's glistening green car stayed away a full week out of respect.

In Tar-Paper no one sang, not even the heat-loving cicadas.

Josephina went through the rituals of mourning as though

she had always known them. On inconsolable evenings she
would sit stoically by herself watching while her grandson
disappeared alone into the desert time and time again.

Since Manuel's death she had not once gone to church in
downtown Phoenix. Three huge women from the Mighty
Clouds of Joy brought over a basket of fried chicken and their
condolences. They had forgiven her absence at church.

Her prayers at the small altar to the Virgin Mary were not
the same as before. Her prayers were modulated now by
shame and by supreme loss.

"*No puedo esperar*. Send out his heart to me," she pleaded.
"Send out *mi Manuelito*'s heart to me." The old woman wept
as she knelt alone in the *ramada*.

"I need to see a sign of his forgiveness right here in these
craven hands. I apologized to him. God help me, I did."

She stared down into her own palms for a moment, then
suddenly spat into them with disgust. After a pensive minute
or two, she rose from her knees to brush the sand and the
desperation from her dark dress. She dried her eyes, then
stiffened her back and her resolve.

"I swear in God's name I shall wait for the Resurrection."
She spoke with detachment now. By rote.

"Then the grave will give up its masses; the coals will suck
in the flame, then swell into wet, living wood. I swear that I
can wait," she whispered while looking skyward through her
lowered veil.

She shuffled to the left of the small altar for a better view
of the open desert. She shuffled now. It was an affectation
she had taken upon herself as an act of contrition. In Spain
she had seen widows of the civil war shuffling in just this
fashion, young women in huddling groups already cackling
about their husbands' meager pensions.

Once past the *ramada* she saw in the distance a large group
of hawks circling high beyond the shimmering cottonwoods,
slow, easy circles. Did one of them see her? She tried to push
the absurd thought from her mind, then strained visibly as
she reined in her anxious, restless spirit.

"To hope is to wait, *esperar*," she thought out loud, "or is
it so only in Spanish?"

But her gaze was suddenly drawn again to one of the high redtails as it abruptly broke away to chase a loud, complaining raven for a few miles, and she watched it turn toward her as if guided by her concern. She stifled a cry as it streaked ahead, straight for the *ramada*.

"Send out his heart to me," repeated Josephina as he came streaking on.

She clutched her tattered brown cloth of significance beneath her veil but brought it out now to signify, to hold up to the sky as he came.

"*La Santísima Virgen de Guadelupe*, forgive me," she cried.

The redtail turned its aquiline eyes downward, screeched directly above her, banked then braked in the air to calmly settle there on the *fogón* not ten feet from the slumping woman in the black dress.

"Josephina, Josephina!"

It was Vernetta who had dashed from the door of the Comet to lift up her limp, swooning friend where she had fallen.

"*Pobrecita*," she said as she carried the old woman into her trailer.

"*Pobrecita*."

A small wave of shame washed over her at the twinge of gratification she felt, as for the first time, she spoke the word rather than had it spoken to her. She hoped as she walked into her trailer that Josephina would not look into her heart tonight. This worried Vernetta as she laid her friend on the bedspread. Now that she had lost so much weight, her heart was so much closer to the surface of her skin, so much more visible.

"Josephina will see into it for sure."

She walked to the sink to wet a towel for her friend's burning forehead.

"Danny told me about your stay in Flagstaff. Neither one of you had ever been in a motel before. He says you flushed that indoor toilet about a hundred times."

She noticed that Josephina's eyes had opened.

"Was that really your first hamburger?" said Vernetta, awkward in the role of nurse.

Josephina looked around without answering. She had not

really heard the question. She lifted herself onto her elbows, then wondered how her dress and veil had come to be on a hanger in the doorway of the Comet. She looked down at herself and realized that she was wearing only her faded underclothes and baggy knee stockings. Even her shoes had been removed, and she noticed Danny sitting on the bed shining them up, a smile on his face.

"Would you like some raspberry tea?"

Vernetta walked over and placed the folded towel on her friend's forehead.

"Sí Dios quiera," she answered.

Now it was Vernetta's turn to cool the brow and serve the tea, thought Josephina.

"I'm moving away from here, Vernetta."

The other woman seemed to quake a moment, and it was with some visible effort that she regained her composure, but not before a cigarette lighter dropped from beneath her blouse and clattered across the trailer floor.

"I'm leaving here, too," she said weakly. "But I didn't want to go down to Terrebonne just yet. I need to be a mother before I can be a daughter again. Backward, huh? You have to teach me. You can move in here with Danny and me, Josephina. Alberto will move in too. You will always be welcome in my house. Shitfire, Josephina, if it wasn't for you I wouldn't even have a family. You are my family! Hell, I can buy a bigger trailer. I can buy a double-wide with a real living room and curtains. I'll park it as far from here as you want. The Papagos can have this one."

She looked around her small trailer and knew she would never sell it.

"They've been wanting it forever. Lord knows I been saving money for ten years, and I ain't bought hardly nothing if it weren't in a bottle. And on them I get a refund. I got lots of money, Josephina," pleaded Vernetta to a friend whose mind was obviously elsewhere.

"The demon's name is Soberbia," said Josephina in a distant and distracted voice.

In the lot between the adobe and the trailer, she watched the whirling Irishwoman and her dusty dogs moving in aimless circles. For an instant, she thought she saw the woman's eyes, but dismissed the possibility as madness.

"His name is pride. Pride caused that tormented Irish man to linger in his old homesite so long after his time, and my own pride drove a spike between me and my dear Manuel. Now we are separated by a chasm."

She crossed herself at the mention of his name.

"Now that woman out there circles here to be near her husband's restless spirit. *Y horita*, even my husband is circling here this morning. Did you see him? *El halcón*, the hawk?"

Vernetta nodded.

"He's back already. He landed right there on those antlers! *Qué raro*, he's eyeballing his own chickens!"

She pointed to a four-point rack nailed to the top of the *fogón*.

"But is he accessible to me? He's back already. He's supposed to wait for the conversion of the Jews."

"I know the Yaquis, Josephina. He doesn't think the Jews should be converted. If he's flying around out there, he's happy."

Vernetta placed a Melmac teacup in front of her friend, and the two women moved from the bed to sit in the small breakfast nook between the bed and the stove.

"I suppose you're right," sighed Josephina, "but it's not how the Resurrection is supposed to work. Do you think a hawk could be God's favorite?"

On the table was a large bowl filled with cereal of some sort. Next to it was an empty box.

"I told Danny he could empty the box of Rusket's Flakes," smiled Vernetta. "He couldn't wait to get the prize."

On the bed Danny smiled, then pulled the string on his tiny, whirring gyroscope.

"I just can't stay in that house anymore. I can't sleep in the *fogón* anymore. I find comfort just being near his things, and I have a penance to pay. Until I am truly together again with *mi viejo*, I have a penance. Oh, Vernetta, that last night I should have let him speak!"

She was crying now.

"I should have chosen his lips."

Vernetta looked out across the lot to the abandoned adobe. Its windows were shut up with plywood squares held in place by metal spikes driven hard into its sides, into the flanks of the adobe wall. It had once seemed so formidable. Now its thick sides seemed pinned up like limp curtains to the huge lintel beams. She thought the house looked wounded and brooding.

"So sad such a beautiful house has to be sacrificed."

There was something always unmistakably empty about an abandoned house. She felt strange, as though she were suddenly privy to a contrary world of houses where the people burned down instead. She wondered what the lonely house in Arkadelphia must look like now, sad and grieving over a family charred to rubble. Only the east-facing door of the adobe remained uncovered. The Navajos did this sort of thing, she thought. Do the Catholics?

The boy walked from the bed over to the women and handed the shining shoes to "Abuela." It was what Josephina had asked Danny to call her.

"Abuela, where is Alberto?"

She smiled down at the boy, at the little high-yellow boy with the Asian eyes.

"He is with his Tío Eugene. They will build me a new house so I can live out my new life. You can help them if your mother says it's okay."

She turned and pointed out into the desert.

"They will build me a new house out there."

The deep gravel wash she had chosen was about a block behind the adobe that Manuel had so lovingly built for her. From down inside the low wash, neither Buckeye Road nor Phoenix could be seen. The old woman had walked out there with her son and her grandson, and she had ceremoniously chosen the spot herself.

"There must be no shade. The elements may be heartless with me. There must be a flat, wooden floor. Each splinter will ease my penance."

Her sad treatment of Manuel did not deserve shade. No adobe. No cast-iron stove. No luxuries at all.

"I will own no more than Christ himself owned."

This house would be made of cardboard.

"*Una casa de cartón!*" she had demanded as she stood, feet planted in the wash, enshrouded by a profound deafness of the heart. She stood pointing to the spot—indignant, petulant, frozen in her pious determination. With a stick she carefully outlined the dimensions of her home. She would listen to no one.

Her new home was exactly ten feet by ten feet, barely large enough for her double bed and a few furnishings. It had been built on eight concrete nailing piers that had been placed on small stacks of foundation block. The house was raised three and a half feet off the desert floor because there were clear signs that a flash flood had run through this small sidewash of the main levee in the last decade or so.

The floor of the penitentiary was made of redwood slats over fir joists, and the frame that rose above it was construction-grade two-by-four tacked together with sixteen-penny common nails. It was precisely the kind of construction that Manuel hated. Eugene had purchased a small stack of sheetrock and exterior plywood to cover the framing, but the old woman remained adamant, cursing the sheetrock and pounding on it with a crooked manzanita branch. Both stacks had to be returned.

So Eugene and Alberto went back into Phoenix and located a kitchen appliance warehouse that didn't care if they carted off every piece of scrap cardboard they had. Two thicknesses of overlapping, flattened boxes were nailed up to the studs from the outside; each fire-stop became a shelf.

The boxes had been used to ship Philco washers and gas stoves. Both inside and out the word PHILCO was repeated over and over again. So the paper house got its name: *La Casita Philco*.

In sleep, in dreams, the paper dome of heaven was fragile and demanded to be handled with care. In this sidewash, the universe, whether negatively or positively curved, was oriented correctly: this end up.

Josephina had placed the television and her record players in front of the only Kelvinator panel in the house, right at the foot of the bed. To the right of the bed was the hot plate

and a small shelf for spices and for necessities of life like
frijoles, masa, manteca and white flour. She kept all of her dishes
and cooking utensils outside on her old pine table, dragged
from the adobe and placed under the cardboard awning. Her
precious upright piano was out there too, but its weight required that it be placed at the base of the steps, right on the
gravel.

Despite Josephina's heartfelt protestations, Vernetta had
purchased industrial-sized extension cords and with Danny's
help had joined them together and dragged them the entire
block out into the desert.

"What's the use of a hot plate and a television if you got
no electricity?"

When the move was completed and the adobe was left to
the desert, Josephina blessed the cardboard and the extension
cord in her usual pious fashion. But this time, she did it side
by side with old Salvador. The old *yoeme* squatted down next
to her, his eyes hard and red with last night's debauchery in
Tucson. His breath was heavy with nicotine, and his spirit
was soaring again, eighty-nine-years old and still with moisture. Not ready for the Salt River yet.

"May God bless and keep this poor house. Alberto sees the
pinche wolf on his own now?"

"Yeah," said Salvador.

"He doesn't even come to get me like he did at first. You
should give him the *chapayeka*, Josephina. Manuel searches
everywhere for it. He's *loco* and flying real low. He scratches
around in the desert south of here and out in the fan of washes
to the east. I know you're hiding it with a spell or a prayer.
You should give it to Alberto or to Manuel."

She had spent the first mornings at her new home walking
out into the desert alone, where she gathered herbs and barks
into a small woven basket. She found herself almost enjoying
the image of herself as a pastoral widow. She smiled at the
ridiculous conceit. Some of her time was spent reconstructing
her altar to the Sacred Heart, but this time it was placed
outside on a small shelf above the dishes.

In the desert evenings after dinner, Josephina would sit

behind her upright piano in the wash and play Fats Waller
or George Gershwin tunes for the two boys and Vernetta, the
Indians and the owls. Sometimes the Perkinses or the *maricones* would come by after dinner for the concert.

The upper registers, the plinking of the right-hand keys,
always carried so much farther in the night air than her voice,
that is, until she reached a song that clearly plumbed her.
These songs she belted. These songs her audience waited for
and sat up for.

Manassus would shove an extra plug of dark tobacco into
his gums, punch his sons playfully, then yell out for a Hank
Williams tune, any Hank Williams tune.

For these songs wood fires were built against the night sky,
and her singing Spanish shadow stretched for three fathoms
or more.

"*Escúchame bien.* Ella Fitzgerald, now there's a genius."

Her black shoes danced from one pedal to the next and
back again. The bottle on her wrist slapped against the dark
wood edging of the keyboard as words flew from beneath her
veil.

"This is called stride," she said as she stretched her small
hand from D to F sharp.

When she sang the Lydia Mendoza songs, even the moon
stopped moving.

In the mornings the old woman no longer had to get out
of bed to cook for her grandson. She would dangle her short
legs over the right side of the bed and fry *huevos con queso* or
con chorizo on the single hot plate. The two would eat in bed,
their ceramic and tin plates laid out on the wedding quilt,
while Josephina's new kittens were busy wrestling and stalk-
ing one another nearby.

"Your memories of me will taste this way."

Since Apache had disappeared again, she had talked of
getting cats. She reached over to pick up the tiny black-and-
white female she had named Mamacita.

"Cats all live in three dimensions," she explained. "They
are always climbing on things; they live upward almost like
birds. Mamacita here never does a thing I tell her"—she

smiled—"and Benny there will eat anything, even brussels
sprouts. He even eats salsa, a real *Mexicano*. I named him
after Benito Juárez, you know."

"Tezcatlipoca."

"What did you say?" asked the old woman, incredulously.

"The cat of the Aztecs was named Tezcatlipoca," responded
Alberto.

"He was a Toltec god first. He is called the smoked mirror,
the god of the moon, of *tigres*. He is the other side of things.
He is a symbol in Mexico of early resistance to the Spanish."

Josephina's spoonful of food paused just in front of her lips
as she considered the ramifications of what she was hearing.
All those baptisms and her grandson was still becoming an
aboriginal.

"The Catholic church outlawed *tigre* dances in 1631 as an
offense against the Catholic faith."

Josephina realized that instead of anger she felt only loneliness as she heard Manuel's words from her grandson's lips.

"The *tigre* became the symbol of resistance again, but this
time against the church."

In the weeks since her husband was buried, she seldom
left the cardboard house or the area around it and had not
gone out on any medical calls. Her heart just didn't seem to
be in it. Her medicinal bag lay under the bed patiently waiting.
Whenever she reached for the bag, she would recall the scorpion water at the bottom and her hand would recoil. The bag
could wait a while for its new owner, but a certain question
she had for Alberto could not. It was a question she had held
for her grandson and finally asked.

"Do you ever think about heaven?" she asked as the two
sat on the porch on a particularly crisp morning.

It was clear that she did not expect an answer.

"People always talk about heaven, but I don't think anyone
ever really thinks very hard about it. You see, people always
think about heaven as their now, as the age they are right
now. They do that until they are as old as me; then they
begin to think about which age they would like to be in
heaven. Who wants to be decrepit in heaven?

"*Por ejemplo*, what if you were to choose an age like nine-

teen? What if you were to be nineteen again? Would you want
to keep your old mind and all those memories? If so, you're
not really nineteen. How can you be nineteen without fool-
ishness? Nineteen is the age for mistakes and for heartbreaks.
An old soul would avoid all that.

"On the other hand, if you lost all that recollection you
would also lose any memory that you'd ever chosen an age
at all. If that were the case, then you would already have had
heaven back when you were nineteen and heaven has gone
right past you. But that's not the only problem.

"Can you pick in heaven the ages of your loved ones? If
you can, what if your loved ones pick different ages? What
if your child doesn't want to remain an infant the way you
want him to? *Es demasiado*, no? Can everyone have what they
want?

"There can be only one or two conclusions: either heaven
is completely in the mind or in heaven what people want is
immaterial."

She turned to the boy to see if he was thinking about what
she had said.

"I know its *un poco* confusing, but since Manuel has gone
I've begun to reflect a lot about heaven. Some have said that
there will be no wolves or bears, only birds and shepherds.
Whose heaven is that? It sure isn't your grandfather's. Nowadays my reflections are not clear at all. Will he be in my
heaven or will I be in his? What would I choose?"

She smiled sheepishly now at her grandson, as if the answer
to the question had always been at hand.

"I just might choose a front table at the Cotton Club, right
near Duke's piano. But an eternity of even that might be too
much."

She closed her eyes for a moment, imagining her Yaqui
husband in a tux, grinning around a cigarette holder and
suavely giving the cigarette girl a tip. No, that wasn't Manuel.

"Now I think that heaven is the very edge, the point-edge
of time itself."

She pointed a finger through the doorway, out into the
purple desert, as if to demonstrate.

"It's like a veil made of particles or maybe not, something

thinner than measurement. *Entiendes?* A sheer margin, a tension. Now. It's now, Alberto. The thing we always have and can never own. You see, the last word to leave my mouth is already irretrievable."

She looked at the boy, and her tone became even more serious than before.

"Don't make my mistake, *mijo*. Me, I had these images, you know. All my life. From the books, I guess. Someone else's images of lions lying down with lambs, a home in the clouds. Images of endless days without concern. What would I do in the clouds? What would I do with no concerns to consider? You know, an eternity without gossip doesn't really interest me."

She shook her head at the thought of it; her gray-black mane and veil flew around her shoulders as a unit.

"I thought so much of heaven. I wanted it so much that I may have lived right through it. May God forgive me, but I've begun to wonder if the Resurrection only means that someday things will turn around and go backward. Will the ocean push its drowned back up to the surface? Will *mujeres y hombres* shrink back to the womb? *Madre de Dios*, these questions are driving me *loco*. I wish Harold would come by soon. He's due here anyday now."

She stood on the porch now, her hands in her pockets.

"I could use a new hairbrush."

She knew as she said it that she was drawing farther and farther away from such needs. She sighed the widow's sigh.

"I miss my *viejo, mijo*. His death makes me so sad. I wish I could mourn for him like those crazy *Mexicanos*. They bake death and eat it. They roll it in sugar and put it on sticks for the children to lick at. They deride it and mock it. It's like death is just another *Mexicano* dialect. The rest of us can only mumble our desolation."

She smiled then at her grandson to reassure him.

"I know you have the *hikuli*, the peyote. No, no, don't worry. I won't take it away from you. You see, I've learned something too. I used to think the Indians out here were all powerless, but they're not, far from it. They just refuse to join up, that's all, and that is a very great strength. They have the power to remain themselves.

"They're the only ones who seem to see that so much of the white man's work is not progress. How can it be progress? How can it be going forward when everything on the land is going cold? Vernetta says the Yaquis and all the Nahua nations have always known about the second law of thermodynamics or something like that. Maybe it isn't a law at all. Maybe it's a Yaqui prayer.

"But even so it still hurts me that this land doesn't seem to need the Pope."

She spoke the last sentence with a distracted, somber air as if now she were recalling her personal battles with Manuel, the war between peyote and the sacraments, the war for the child's soul.

"But I still want you to go to church. I guess I'm just too old to change. I worry. Tell me, *mijo*, do you dream now? Have you seen your *abuelo*? What do you dream?"

The boy looked at his grandmother, then smiled broadly.

"I've seen him, Abuela. He says you have nothing to be sorry for, but I've already told you that so many times. Sometime last evening we met in Cocorit, and he told me of the Aztecs swinging from tall poles, pretending they could fly. Then I could see them. I guess they could never take the secret away from the Yaquis or the Huichols, so they swung 'round and 'round, forever stuck to the ground."

The boy laughed but then stopped short on seeing his grandmother's face behind the veil. Her question had been in earnest.

"I dream of Potam and Cocorit. There is the river to the sea. I wake to roosters. There is protection of the young and loyalty to the old. I dream, Abuelita, that I am on the porch of a windowless, cardboard house in the middle of a desert wash and I am talking to my grandmother."

The last week of summer of the year that Billie Holiday died was a work week when nobody worked, nobody at all.

The buses came back to Buckeye Road long before noon on Monday and quickly disgorged their torpid passengers. The company flatbeds bounced in on aching leaf springs and sun-hardened tires and set mute, lethargic workers down in front of the Rainbo Market, where they shuffled wearily off without good-byes.

Judas in his deuce-and-a-half left a listless group of *mojados* at the Rainbo, where they moved as a unit to buy *cerveza fría* from the *Chino*.

On the north side of the Rainbo, the Cheungs fanned themselves beneath the single raised wing of their truck; no hot food would be sold today.

The soda pop thermometers on the front of the Rainbo all agreed that it was 116 degrees in the shade. Mr. Lee had placed a large tin tub in the shade of the porch. It was filled with ice and soda pop bottles, and a small handwritten sign read, TWO FOR THE PRICE OF ONE. Inside his store the candy counters oozed melting chocolate and wax lips down onto the pine floor. Beneath his store Boydeen typed the words of a sweating Pueblo Indian who stood on the porch telling three Mexicans that there had been thunderheads in his dreams.

Across the road in Cady every car was abandoned for the scant shade of the Blue Moon's canvas. Odabee, Onan, Floyd and his wife, Osiris, Toop and Em-Em were all lying on the Blue Moon dance floor. They were melted together into a fetid, perspiring morass of alcoholic sloth. Em-Em's fan droned pathetically nearby, its paltry breeze wilting down-ward to join with the rising heat of a dying electric motor.

Across the lot, Potrice and Sugar Dee were commiserating with the five girls inside the Secret Sharer. They would be drinking icy Nu-Grape and complaining about the effect of the sweltering heat on their hairdos and clothing.

"Well," said Angelique, "this is certainly a test for those new Five-Day deodorant pads. Dear Panocha isn't convinced, I know." She smiled. "She swears by that Daisy Deodorant Creme, but it's gone and yellowed all her blouses. By the way, does anyone want some chilled Pacific salmon bisque with cucumber squares?"

Everyone, everywhere, from mean hovel to poor hutch, hid

from Huitzilipochtli, the sun, and waited patiently for the
precious surcease that would be evening.

Burdened by the seething heat, no one dared look up to
the cruel skies. No one noticed that the piling thermals were
empty of life, that the startled bats and birds had gone
elsewhere.

On the far, far north horizon, between the Pagago and
Apache reservations, and barely discernible even at blessed
sunset, were dark, hulking thunderheads moving at the be-
hest of the northwest wind, monolithic and enormous.

The old woman had her back turned toward Alberto. She
took a single steaming pinto bean from the wooden spoon
and tested it delicately between her teeth. It was *perfecto*. She
took the pot and a battered colander outside to the edge of
the porch and poured the contents of the pot into the colander;
the water disappeared onto the sand below, where it ran off
without ever breaking the surface tension. Before going back
inside, she looked out into the beauty that is the desert at
sunset—vermilion ridges and lavender defiles. Manuel is resting, she thought.

She mashed the beans into a thick paste, then added some
grated cheese and ground Mexican chile. She spread the
steaming *frijoles* across a hot *tortilla de harina*, folded it, then
handed it to Alberto, who devoured it, then waited eagerly
for another.

"I don't know for sure, but I think I dreamed about you
again last night."

She handed Alberto his second burrito, then turned off the
hot plate.

"Since *su abuelo* left us, I can't seem to direct my dreams
as well as I used to, and at times I don't know what they're
trying to say to me at all. I guess I'm a little bit unbalanced
still."

She walked first to the old gramophone, then over to the
electric phonograph.

She put the Ink Spots record on the newer machine but
then suddenly pulled the stylus from the first groove of
"Whispering Grass" and stood craning her neck to hear, listening intently.

Alberto saw her standing frozen, motionless, with the tone arm jerked straight up into the air and knew something was wrong. He strained to hear what she listened for and got up to go outside, hoping to hear better.

"Come back inside!" she screamed. "It's too late! It's here already! It's too late!"

She was right. There had been a low roar, like the sea, calming at first. Beneath notice at first. All at once the boy saw the dark, frothing water streaming from under the house, rushing around the piers and leaping through the redwood steps, and he saw the piano being carried away down the sluice.

If there had been time enough to contemplate a flood, the boy would certainly have been more frightened. But it seemed to have come upon them instantly, with no warning. He could barely make out large pieces of tar-paper and wood swirling by, battered and spun by the banks, and he knew that Tar-Paper was suffering, too. He thought about Claude and Louie and hoped they were all safe.

"Let's get on the roof, Abuela," he screamed over the cries of the shuddering piers.

He pulled at her, but she would not move.

"I can't climb up there, *mijo*. You go. Maybe this is part of my penance."

Both of them stood where they were, hand in hand, as the water rose ominously, growled and billowed beneath their feet. The carboard house shook on its underpinnings.

"I've dreamed you beyond this day," she yelled over the rising din, "but I certainly overlooked all of this."

The overhead bulb went out suddenly, making the darkness complete. Any one of a dozen patchwork extension cords would have shorted out, blowing the fuses at the Mighty Clouds of Joy. Much of Buckeye Road would be black. Hundreds of families would be huddling together now in the darkness, waiting for the waters to subside.

The platter on the record player slowly spun to a stop; the dropped tone arm had fallen and bounced onto the third cut; the stylus was twisted into a microscopic analogue of a single syllable sung long ago by Bill Kenny. In the darkness Jose-

phina felt her grandson's hand tear away from her own. He
was gone before she could pull him back. She was barely
aware of him going toward the door. Then she heard his voice
coming from the porch.

> *How high's the water mama?*
> *Five feet high and rising.*
> *How high's the water papa?*
> *He said it's five feet high and rising.*

It was his favorite Johnny Cash song. Despite her fears,
Josephina stood in the dark room smiling. Then all at once
she dashed out to the porch, where she grabbed a butcher
knife and began to cut at the rain. She swung the blade as
though swinging at the ligaments of a giant.

In twenty minutes it was all over, and the roar had become
little more than a soft trickle. The water would be miles away
spreading out into countless small canyons and defiles. The
boy and his grandmother spent some moments first thoroughly stunned then relieved by the almost tactile profundity
of the silence.

"I think I've lost a step or two, *mijo*," the old women said
dejectedly. "Five years ago I would have cut the water short."

Beneath the Casita Philco the floor joists had hardly been
moistened by the heedless floodwaters. Somehow the cement
blocks had held. Tío Eugene's careful inspection of the side-
walls of the wash had paid off. The house had been built just
high enough above the gravel bed. She'd ridden it out.

"I dreamed this, Abuela," said Alberto. "I saw this in a
dream! Abuelo told me to move around in the vision. The
piano will be down there about fifty yards or so and there
will be a pile of women's clothing near it. *Me cago, Abuelita,*
I dreamed this!"

During the night, two of Wysteria Maybelle's dear dogs had
been killed, washed away by the flash flood. With her remaining pets she had systematically scoured the wash for

miles till both tiny and unnaturally bent bodies were located:
a brown spaniel named Thyrsis and a toy collie named Do-
rinda. One had gotten tangled up with manzanita branches
and old electrical wire, while the other was found hardening
beneath some roofing paper and flashing that had washed
down from the Okies' camp. Vernetta noticed her first, in the
distance on her knees and digging frantically in the sand.

"She lost her home last night in the flood. All her possessions scattered for miles. Most people were pretty lucky. A
couple of the Mexican families had their houses collapse on
them, but no one was hurt. The levee held up real good, but
there's still a foot of water in the lot across from Rainbo. Them
old fools is living on top of their useless cars now. Shit, for
some of them this is the first bath in years. A couple of them
colored fellows over there even turned out to be white!"

She laughed heartily, a bathroom key from a Texaco station
in El Centro dropped from beneath her blouse to the ground
at her feet.

"Things is pretty much dried up already, what with this
heat. Sure looks like another scorcher."

She set a case of Delaware Punch on the porch, then walked
up the steps to sit with her friend. Down the wash a bit,
Claude, Louie and Alberto were busy pulling the piano back
up toward the Casita Philco. The piano was wet, but it seemed
to work fine. Louie plinked away at the wet keys, pretending
to be Jerry Lee Lewis.

"When you're done with that," shouted Josephina to Alberto from the doorway, shading her eyes with her hand, "go
out there where the dog woman is and tell her."

She reached into her medicinal bag for the first time since
the funeral and pulled out a small, dark object.

"Put this around her neck."

She handed Alberto a small pouch hanging from two leather
thongs.

"*Una asafétida*," she said. "Say to her exactly what I told
you."

She pointed to the distance, where Wysteria Maybelle was
about to bury her two dogs.

It's strange, thought Alberto. It's strange seeing her this

way, actually being able to focus on her this way. It alarmed him not to see her dancing in the center of a dust devil, syllables swirling around her like leaves and litter.

When the three boys walked up on her she barely moved, and for the very first time Alberto could see that her eyes were blue, striking blue, and the skin beneath all that dirt was white as rice paper. The three boys moved carefully around her pack of dogs and stood a respectful distance away from the shallow hole she had carved into the sandy soil.

Up close, Wysteria quivered over her entire body. She shivered the way the tail of a squirrel shivers when seen up close. She reminded Alberto of the doe that he and Claude had saved from the highway the year before. She looked just like that slender little doe. It had been stunned by a collision with some sort of vehicle, but *la pobrecita* had been lucky—nothing was broken, and there was only a little blood in the corner of her mouth.

No amount of stroking or petting or worry would ever communicate to the doe that the boys meant her no harm. She almost died of fear, but with Vernetta and Manuel's help the doe regained its health and was released not far from where Maybelle's services were being held today. The little thing had to be chased away.

Up close, Wysteria's thin-boned, dirt-dappled body trembled constantly while her eyes darted between instants, back then and right now, alighting nowhere. The grave would be simple. There would be no small, wooden boxes, no markers. Poverty and pathos always meet at necessity.

Wysteria Maybelle sighed aloud, then wearily pushed the soil over her poor, stiff children and began in a low voice to recite the poem that Alberto had first heard over a year before at another similar service. On that occasion a well-loved German shepherd, rigid and mange-ridden, had been laid to rest out beyond the bus depot and the Mexican graveyard.

On that solemn occasion, he had hidden himself behind a stand of cactus to hear it. Now he stood near her and spoke the words aloud with her.

"There at my feet shalt thou be laid, of purest alabaster made . . ."

She looked up at the boy, then suddenly stopped short, leaving his voice to carry on alone to the end. He had practiced the poem for some unforeseen reason, perhaps this reason. He had begun memorizing it after that first small funeral.

When the poem was done, Alberto, Claude and Louie began to push the remaining dirt into the hole; then they flattened it with their feet while Wysteria Maybelle stood quietly by, the nervous fingers of one tiny hand clutching at the wrist of the other.

"My *abuela* says to you," Alberto said finally, "that you should come to the wash to live near us."

Wysteria gave no sign that she heard, but Alberto continued.

"My *abuela* has talked to your husband, and through her he has spoken to you. There is something important he has wanted to say to you for years now."

He approached her carefully, then tied the thongs behind her neck, letting the pouch hang at her breast. She did not move.

The very next morning the two small, grieving women met in the center of the drying stream. They approached one another slowly at first, tentatively. They stepped as though shared grief had exposed a specific path between them, circuitous but inexorable. They orbited one another in the dust and gravel in circles of diminishing radiuses. They paced off a hidden gridwork until only an arm's length separated them.

"How much time has passed?"

"I think almost ten years," answered Josephina, "but I can't be sure. My dreams are obscured, mixed up *como huevos revueltos.*"

"Ten years before the flood? Are we near the end?" Wysteria asked, looking around herself for a sign.

"Are you Catholic, like me?"

Josephina crossed herself in response, and the other quickly followed suit as if in an effort to end the signs simultaneously.

"He wasn't Catholic, but he was educated, mind you." She spoke in a tiny, wispy voice. She had lost the faculty of speaking in prose to a fellow human being years before. She had grown accustomed to addressing the past with couplets, swirling her poems protectively about herself or wailing the verses in arpeggios of undecipherable woe to her animals alone.

"Oh, he was born Catholic sure enough," she whispered, "but he gave it up for America. He was a gandy dancer sure and a drinker, a fair one with the whiskey."

Her voice seemed to be gaining strength as she spoke.

"I swear, sometimes at night he'd waltz in sweet as you please and lift me like I was no more'n a cross tie. Faith, you'd think when he was smoothin' the bed it was rock gravel strewn there. And sometimes, mind you, when he went to touchin' my skin you'd think he'd rather 'twas creosote. But he had a way. He had a way. That he did."

She looked up at Josephina from under the cape she wore. With each sentence, more and more of her ice blue eyes became visible.

"I know what you're thinkin'," she smiled.

"Why is it I burned the house down. It was a fine balloon house, finer than any they gives to families along the lines and in the turnaround towns. Finer than any you'll find in them water-tank towns. Lord, I burned my dear house! Tiles on the floorin' of the kitchen, small tiles with tiny blue rosettes.

"It was the image of my mother's house in Castlerea, County Roscommon. She ran a railroad inn, you know. Named me after flowers that climbed the walls there. His folk was from Galway near Glennamaddy. Had the railroad in 'im then, too. His father was a fireman and his father before 'im.

"What is my name?"

Josephina was caught off guard by the question.

"Wysteria Maybelle," she answered.

"No, my new name."

Josephina considered it for a minute.

"Silvia," said Josephina. "I will secretly call you Silvia."

"Things can accelerate just by changing direction, can't they?" asked the Irishwoman.

"Silvia. Yes, my name in my new life is Silvia now. My own private name between ourselves."

There was a moment when nothing needed to be said. The

two women only stared at each other and the desert sky that
framed the other.

"He's sorry, you know. He apologizes to everyone he meets
when he appears, but most can't hear him and for some
reason he couldn't speak to you."

"And what could I hear?" answered Silvia. "Wasn't I busy
now praying madly? Wasn't I berserk with prayer? I couldn't
even hear time at my back. I couldn't even feel it pulling at
my temples."

She reached up to feel the deep crow's-feet that pulled at
each eye.

"Praying?" asked Josephina. "You were praying?"

"Now shouldn't sermons be poems? Wouldn't the very best
prayers be poetry?"

"He's sorry he didn't stay home and read to you over tea.
Forgive him. He asks you to forgive him."

Josephina relayed the cry for forgiveness with the sincerity
of one who asks it for herself.

"He left me alone. He left me all alone here not ten months
after he'd retired from the railroad. Jobs dried up around here
for firemen. Union says only one per train now, no matter
how many tractors. Took a Pullman porter job on an interstate
run just to be movin' again.

"Too proud he was to budget the rest of his life on that
puny retirement pay. Too proud to sit with me anymore
whenever the diesel tractors come pullin' through the switch
boxes. Too proud to work in the garden I had over there.

"He left me here for his first love, he did. He went and got
drunk on a layover in Portland, fell asleep on a sidetrack with
that poor dog. It was months later when someone told me
they'd found his body. Sure, I'll bet he was proud it was a
steam engine that did it."

"Do you remember the years after that?" asked Josephina.

"No, I have just the endless dreams interspersed with hunger and dark. Dreams about a mad spinning prayer and my
precious dogs. I prayed to go nowhere, you see. I prayed to
go nowhere, to be nowhere without him, to be stuck in time.
Mind you, I harbored no desire to travel through the phases
of grief, to age on while my memory of him never does.

"I saw it in my mother. I saw her grieve. I saw her skin fold and her thick hair given up to the dust and elements. I saw sadness suck at the sweet oils of her face."

She looked down at her four remaining mongrels.

"My precious dogs. You know I never had dogs before he died. Perhaps it was madness for true. Then one morning, it couldn't have been by accident, I saw the funeral for your husband at that little pink church over there. I heard the black man's sermon and the singing, and I thought for certain that you were me. I thought I saw my own grief passing before me. I believed you were me.

"I thought maybe they'd had the kindness to send his body home and that was his funeral. But I looked hard and I saw that my dear little house had changed so much, and so had I."

She looked down at her ragged, dusty clothing.

"What a shock to see these lines on my hands and feel this stiffness in my knees. My dire instant of lunacy had vanished, evaporated and left me to myself. Then it all began to come back to me. Faith, I remembered setting those darling curtains on fire. Lace they were, from my mother's hand. I thought maybe that's why there were no windows. I'd burned them out."

She faced Josephina with a full gaze now.

" 'Twas then I knew that time had passed on despite my prayers. I'd failed to stop it."

She reached up with both hands to pull down the hood that covered her long, straight hair. She motioned toward the adobe house.

"You lived your own life there now, didn't you? I mean, after us in the time that I was mad."

Josephina nodded.

"Why didn't you go mad like me? Was it your faith that kept you sane?"

She placed her fingers to her temples. She stood in front of Josephina, a simple face with a small soul resolved to know.

"Go get all of your things, Silvia. We can build you a new house right next to mine, but we don't allow flower gardens.

Josephina turned her new friend, faced her in the direction

of the bus depot. Silvia took the leather pouch into her hands, pressing it to her nose.

"You know the Yaquis believe that God first reveals himself as a scent?"

"It smells like Castlerea," said Silvia.

"Don't forget to bring your books along. We'll need to dry them out quickly. You'll like my friend, Vernetta. She'll put a braid in your hair for you. She'll clean you up and put nice lotions on you. You'll see your own beauty."

"You won't leave me, will you?"

Josephina shook her head.

Wysteria Maybelle, now Silvia, walked slowly toward Buckeye Road and out toward the bus stop and beyond where her flattened home lay. No one who saw her recognized her as she walked on while repeating her new name.

"Silvia."

Not even Potrice, who saw her upside down, recognized her, though Silvia passed by not ten feet from the open car door where a deathly thin Hindu farmworker weakly suckled Potrice's breast and pumped pathetically at her crotch. Potrice could not bear to look up at the man. The Ganges flowed in his eyes and ash was already collecting on his dark skin.

"Silvia. Silvia."

Boydeen typed this strange woman's repeated incantation over and over, as she walked past the Rainbo.

"Is it my church that keeps me sane?"

Josephina had answered the question almost as an afterthought.

"I am told that for me to join my dear husband again the world must be severely altered . . . to a changeless state. Now I think it can't be. We must be altered."

Above Silvia the burning thermals moved in a swelling, raging flood to dwarf any flood on earth's surface.

"How can we begin to think of alterations in the inconceivable?"

They ascended sweltering to join a seething half-eternity of things that lose heat to the other half.

"*Jesus Santo* . . . He dreamed," she called out. "It's written that He dreamed. I should have remembered that all along.

I should have remembered. He had to dream because His disciples couldn't. The church can't."

Josephina ran down the steps now to yell in a straight line to Silvia. The shuffle was gone.

"Like the fisherman, He had to pull them all the way out of their lives!"

She jerked both arms upward as if pulling on an invisible net.

"They pulled Him out of His life! They kill the dreamers!"

She was shouting now just to shout.

"The wilderness. Manuel tried to tell me. Only now can I see the wilderness."

Josephina kissed the cross at her wrist, then whirled to stare into the open desert, her back to the wilderness.

The sound of the tires caused every head to turn. Heavy, slow-moving tires. Someone was curious or stunned by the sight or completely lost among the dirt roads and alleys. Whoever it was, Buckeye Road was not their home.

It was an Oldsmobile, long and black with a metal continental kit, whitewall tires and a red outboard sun visor over the windshield. There were fender skirts over the rear tires, and both sides of the car sported curb feelers. Here was someone who was rich or someone whose entire life was that car.

Those who watched carefully saw the driver attempting to avoid each piece of visible glass in the road, skirting every larger-than-average rock. He was not rich. A rich man would've driven straight through, ignoring the tires and raising clouds of dust to settle on clotheslines and drift into open windows that he would never notice. This man avoided deep ruts, keeping his passenger side tires up on the shoulder. A rich man wouldn't even know there was an oil pan to worry about.

Certainly no one of means would turn his car into the lot between the adobe house and the Highway Comet.

Lola stepped from the car, then stood in high heels staring at the empty adobe house, her two white gloves in her right hand and her purse strap over her left shoulder. She had not bothered to close the door. She wore a light turquoise suit with a small stewardess's cap and two-tone high heels.

"Joe," she ordered curtly, "go over to the trailer and ask Vernetta where my mother has gone. Just like her not to tell me a goddamn thing. And hurry," she ordered.

It was the kind of order and response that testified to her undeniable beauty, just as it spoke to the fact that the man behind the wheel was only temporarily in her graces and clearly in over his head.

The man, Jose Pescado, leaped from the driver's side obediently, then marched briskly to the trailer. He was short and squat and wore black slacks and a white T-shirt that was stretched beyond belief over a belt buckle that read SEMPER FI. He had tattoos on both forearms, a mermaid and an Asian dragon. The very northern tip of a map of the Philippines could just be seen peeking over the neckline of the shirt. Mindanao, nearer his belly, would be stretched and equal in land mass to China.

He knocked as ordered on the door of the trailer, then looked up to see a dark-haired woman standing behind the screen door, swamped in her clothing.

"Could you tell me where Josephina Valenzuela de Castillo has moved to?"

His Tagalog tongue would have pronounced the names perfectly, and he knew it. But he was in America now, and all Americans mispronounced other people's names. Not one American soldier in the Philippines had ever pronounced his name right or even tried to. Jose Pescado had come to admire that.

"America is the future," his company commander had explained to him, "not the past."

"Who are you?" asked Vernetta protectively.

"Oh, yes," he smiled. "My name is Pescado, Jose Pescado, but I'm changing it to Fish as soon as I get back and hire a lawyer. You can call me Joe Fish. I'm here with Lola. We come to take the boy."

Vernetta ran down the steps past the confused man without saying another word to him.

"And I thought I was a whore," she mumbled to herself.

She ran past Lola and only nodded in her direction. She ran out to the edge of the wash and slid down for the first time without worrying about losing her balance and falling. She raced to the cardboard house, then breathlessly called inside for her friend. There was no answer.

She crossed to the tall weeds that had sprung up since the flood, then stepped lightly on blooming sour grass 'til she reached the newly built home of Silvia and her dogs. There she found Josephina sitting with her friend on a small bench made of milk cartons. Both women were crying.

Without a word Vernetta sat down and joined them. Overhead, pigeons gathered, flashed and canted together from one corner of Buckeye to the next before settling on a direction new to them.

"I've been afraid of this day for so long. What can I do? I have no rights. I have no rights!"

Josephina seemed inconsolable now.

"Why didn't you pray against this?" asked Vernetta. "Why didn't you change her mind?"

Josephina accepted a Kleenex that Vernetta had extended to her. All three women looked up to see the speckled airborne flock bank in unison, then head for the western horizon.

"Some things must be. They just must be. I've got to tell him that I saw a Sikorski today. I saw it fluttering around above the Black Canyon highway. Now I know the dream. I know it all. I've got to tell him. Who else can prepare him?"

"He'll be back," said Vernetta, "or maybe we can go out to Stockton to see him. We can take a Greyhound, all of us, one of those scenicruisers."

"No," said Josephina, breathing deeply in an effort to calm herself.

"No, he reaches for me in his dreams now. He shakes his head at the crazy ironies he sees."

Her soft crying was racking her body. Suddenly she shook herself as if to ward off a chill.

"There's someone on my grave," she said, her dark eyes rolling back into their sockets as if to see into her own mind.

Even Vernetta could not steady her.

"He's honing these days already," she said finally.

"He's honing them sharp now to cut into his own wilderness. I've prayed they're enough to put him in the right place, to keep him in the right place. Oh, *Madre de Dios*, Vernetta, I saw the Sikorski!"

15

For the Blood Inside

He dropped his duffel bag on the sidewalk at the front gate. He had carried it ten thousand miles only to realize that it held nothing that he cared for. He laughed when he understood that he would carry it no farther. The taxi driver wiped the sweat from his brow, then lifted the cardboard box from the trunk and set it down carefully next to the green bag. The man was paid; then he drove off without a word.

He's coming here.

He took off his dress green jacket and hat, then tossed them onto the duffel bag. He removed his khaki shirt and black tie, and finally, his shoes and socks. He sloughed off those skins at the entrance, the olive and the white. He shook them off and stepped out of them. The heat was more bearable now.

He walked through the iron gates and down the narrow sidewalk, following the compass. He slowly walked inside for only the second time in his life—for the first time since before the war and since before the flood. As before, he was blinded by the rigid symmetry of the cement and junipers. There were roses here and there on the plots and an occasional flag. Everywhere he looked, each blade of grass was cut to exactly the same height.

He's coming through the gates.

He walked toward the place that he recalled from years

before, when he and his shaking *abuelita* had stood over small
landslides that fell, striking polished hardwood with a sound
like raindrops on dry ground.

In his arms he carried the cardboard box filled with bunches
of bright orange marigolds, what the *Indios* call *cempazuchiles*
or *maravillas*. The flowers of the dead. Beneath the flowers
there were dozens of long, white candlesticks and several
containers filled with food and drink. In his pocket was an
ancient wad of aluminum foil with dried wedges of the gentle
genius at its core.

The sullen gravediggers and groundskeepers were heading
home for the day. They were *Indios* who removed their hats
when the barefoot man walked by. Mounted on metal grass
cutters and dividing the land into grids, they lowered their
eyes when he passed. When they left, the cemetery was completely silent; not a living soul could be seen. But there was
a twinge tugging even now at his blood, a flash in his sideward glances.

Come this way. My river is here. I can hear the wetness.

Now he was assured of them. There were traces rising up
everywhere, piercing his skull with photons of memory as he
walked—*memorias, recuerdos.*

All those I carried and miscarried are here. All of us on this page.

Through the topsoil, through the enslaved and docile grass
and through the dark dirt, he could see the brass handles
glinting like twin beacons.

There were words about him now. The silence of the outer
cemetery gave way as he walked to the poorer section—soft
whispers in Spanish and every Indian language. The Mexican
graveyard. There were conversations flying now, recipes ex-
changed and letters reread in flashes of energy. There were
love songs hanging as wafts of perfume in the ionized air.
There were curses and flirtations flying like neutrons and
cutting at the hushed center of an airy confessional. There
were chains of morose words here and the spliced couplets
of lovers there. As he walked he passed through pockets of
lives, caresses and slaps, communions and extreme unctions,
haircuts and catheters. There were old voices. Deepest among
them were voices that knew this land by other names. Above

these there was a voice reading a shopping list while another, forever moribund, composed a farewell. The voices dazzled him as he walked—a priest recanting a blasphemy, the giggling of children. And a single, dry, rice-paper voice among them.

In the distance, the lights of the Phoenix skyline came on. The city had pushed upward with more and more cement and mortar. Stone without veins, without grain.

In the distance the sudden flash of rifle muzzles made visible a dry wash in the cemetery where Alberto suddenly saw *Federales* cowering, their frightened horses carrying their ammunition into the dark. The blue-coated soldiers made breastworks of their own dead as arrows flew in by the hundreds from a darkening sky. Side by side with armored Spaniards and feathered Aztecs, they were turned back again and again by the barbarians in Sonora, the *chichimecas*.

"Manuel's dreams."

Over a decade had passed. It seemed to Alberto that most of that time had been an instant and that the least of the time had been an eternity.

Only weeks ago he had stood in another endless place, on metal skids a hundred feet up, watching tracers like metal fireflies rip through the black silk uniforms of North Vietnamese regular troops.

Only days ago he had apologized for the world into the ear of a dying friend who had been lovingly overdosed. A corporal whose brown face was gone but whose windpipe had sucked and wheezed with maddening tenacity. Even with a dozen morphine Syrettes hanging from his skin, the man had lingered on, seeing the end of the world, without eyes. A young Chicano from East L.A., he was seeing *Tlalocán*, the land for those who die by water or liquid.

He had run into Clàude and Louie Perkins in a slit trench north of Chu Lai. The three friends had shared a Thai stick and watched the night sky fill with drifting star shells and the tracers from a minigun. Abuela had been right. The three had been reunited twice. First in California, in a small town where the vineyards provided some families with year-round work.

"I traveled ten thousand miles to find out that the South ain't risin' again in this country either," Claude had laughed. "Manassus and Johnna are fine. Both of them's against the war."

Manuel's *chapayeka* mask had gone with Alberto into the Imperial Valley and north to the San Joaquin Valley. He had carried it with him from labor camp to labor camp, from bunkhouse to quonset hut. *Braceros* had asked about it in Calexico. It had seen the Pinoy bachelor societies in Stockton and San Jose. It had witnessed I.N.S. raids and welcomed a manong's shy mail-order bride.

In Vietnam it had peeked out of his flak vest while he waited in the bush to shoot at a smoking mirror, to hunt dark-skinned, black-haired people. Tenacious, resistant people. It had returned with him to a Buckeye Road that no longer existed. The fringe of the fringe had been swallowed up by Phoenix. The desert had been scabbed over with asphalt, and the poor had been replaced by the impoverished.

Fireballs o' the Eucharist!

Boydeen had typed that Salvador, the old *yoeme*, had finally died of uselessness the day his proud gonads quit on him. It happened as in the dream, in a small house near the meandering Salt River, a two-room house inhabited by a long-haired Maricopa Indian widow and her ancient, toothless mother-in-law. It happened after a dinner of shepherd's pie and frybread followed by fruit cocktail suspended in lime Jell-O.

Compadre is here.

The old hag still had a spark or two left in her, and the double-team the two sweating women pulled on him that last night pushed him right over the edge.

"I'm toothless," the old crone had smiled, implying that there were certain benefits.

The last weary flagellate wiggled halfway up the widow's tube, then gave up.

It was death by humiliation.

He is here, on this page.

Wysteria Silvia Maybelle just couldn't bear to hear about her dear friend Josephina's death. She couldn't bear it and so

she didn't. The day that Josephina fell, Wysteria had spun
up her veil of words again despite all of Vernetta's efforts to
keep her. Even as Vernetta hugged her close, the iambic
shroud had fallen.

Her small, broken body was found up on the soft shoulder
of the Black Canyon Highway by a passing trucker. Her four
dogs had died with her.

"It looked like a goddamn combat zone up there," the
trucker would later say.

She'd been hit by a vehicle of some sort. A haunted driver
somewhere remembers his headlights reflecting red from ten
retinas, remembers the small, reciting woman frozen stiff in
the beams of light.

Vernetta bought her Irish friend a coffin and held a proper
wake at the Mighty Clouds of Joy church. She read aloud
"The Mower Against Gardens" as the curious walked by the
open casket just to see the whirling, dancing woman so still
—as if to see a dead proton. Vernetta then put Silvia's body
on the train west and had her properly buried up in Portland.
The gossips in Buckeye Road claimed they heard that a black
porter in the baggage car tipped his hat to her dapper escort
and his white dog.

Boydeen, below, took it down.

Silvia is here, en esta página, on this page with me.

Someone painted five white crosses on the asphalt.

Vernetta had headed back down to Terrebonne Parish with
her son, her cleavage shrunken down to tiny striated mounds.
Her life was small-scale now and slow, more Newtonian.

She'd put new tires on the Highway Comet and had it
towed southeast along with her books and her memories of
Josephina and Silvia. She bought a size four dress and a suit
for her grown son. Vernetta and Danny climbed into a high
diesel cab to sit next to the driver and to retrace their steps
home.

Boydeen, below, took it down.

"You can bypass Arkansas," she told the driver. "Shitfire,
you can drive right around that state!"

She'd heard from a man in Houma that a man in Boudreaux
had seen her mother living alone on the water.

The old Cajun woman stopped scaling and filleting that *sac á lait* when the lapping waves begged her to be still with her work and to look up suddenly at the trailer pulling in at the bank.

The small-boned woman first cried out in the direction of her daughter, then rushed from the narrow, wooden deck onto the bank to throw her arms around her grandson.

Vernetta had gone limp at the scene, her shoulders trembling as the weight of so many years was lifted. She fell to her knees and held her hands in front of her as if to caress the tender scene.

Her mother, looking up for an instant, saw the seven Piyutes circling and fondling the Highway Comet. She could see that there was a thin, black man inside the trailer with a rope around his crooked neck. He was standing there, forcing his clay muscles into a petrified, encrusted smile in the trailer's rear window.

He said good-bye.

Boydeen, below, wrote that the reverend Willie Drake and his wife had moved back down to Georgia. He'd heard the words of another minister and moved south to better preach against racial hatred. But he had his heart broken by a gunshot fired during a garbage strike in distant Memphis. That very same day he would slide his narrow black behind into a cheap, used wheelchair. To the end, Sister Dora Mae would dutifully lift him onto and off of the toilet seat. She'd change the channel when he looked at television, and she would lovingly spoon-feed him his favorite okra mush. The wheelchair was a gift from the Welcome Wagon, and he would put fifteen miles on it before he slid off.

He's in here.

Alberto stood motionless over the graves, staring downward in shock and anger at his grandparents' final earthly resting place.

He sees the irony now. He sees it.

To the left of his grandfather's gravesite, a suffocating concrete sidewalk had been laid down.

In the plot to his *abuelo*'s right, in the very plot that his *abuelita* had purchased years ago, were the grave and tombstone of a total stranger.

To the right of that is the grave of Josephina Valenzuela de Castillo. Between their headstones is the tombstone of Peter Fat Woo, his photo sealed in plastic above his name. He was seventy-two years old when he died, but his family had chosen a photo of him as a much younger man.

His *abuelitos'* bodies are separated for eternity by a Chinese man with horn-rimmed glasses and a gold tooth.

How could this happen? he railed inside as he carefully placed the box on the grass.

How could this happen? This had been in her dreams! This had always been in her dreams!

He was raging now, and the burning thermals above Phoenix seemed to rage with him.

This had been in her sleeping and waking dreams for so many years! Does she hear Cantonese even now?

Some dull scrivener of a mortician had buried Peter Fat Woo in Josephina's precious plot.

"It's only appropriate," Tía Mona would later say. "They always needed a referee."

He imagined the fury and outrage at the burial services when the huddling family first walked to the dank hole that was flanked by electric winches. He imagined their grief redoubled by the travesty.

Manuel and Josephina were forever kept from closure by the body of a lonely man from Longchuan in Canton Province.

The ancestral headstone would have to be two.

"He never even wanted a marker," whispered Alberto.

He kneeled down in the center of his grandfather's plot.

He pulled out a small entrenching tool and began to dig above his *abuelo's* coffin. A light rain squall came by as he scraped, bringing with it the voice of water-stricken dust, sounding like hundreds of dead butterfly children.

First he removed a square foot of turf; then he dug down about two feet or so. He reached into his waistband and pulled out the old *chapayeka* mask. It smelled of his own sweat and of his grandfather's.

It had been to Quang Tri and Phu Bai and into Laos. Alberto had carried the mask with him every day since Josephina had given it to him. It had gone with him as he left his hooch that sad morning for an assembly on the pad. Somewhere at the same time his *abuelita* was walking out to the clothesline. It had risen with him and fourteen others into the air above Quang Tri just as she climbed the creaking steps of the cardboard house. She had been singing loudly when the warrant officer radioed back that the landing zone was as hot as the coffee percolating on Josephina's hot plate. She had swooned just as they cleared the treeline at dizzying speed. She had seized up just as angry lead buried itself in the whirling turbines.

He'd felt his grandmother's death in its fur somewhere in the air above Dong Ha, the Cua Viet River below. Oblivious to the deadly red tracers coming up to rake the green chopper, he'd heard the spoons and dishes crashing down with her small popcorn-bag body to the porch of the Casita Philco.

It had come to him. He'd heard it clear and sharp even above the whine of the miniguns. His gum-chewing friend Cornelius from Oakland had held his helmet for him under his chin as he had gotten sick with grief.

"Hit the skids!" someone cried out just as her veiled face slammed into the wooden porch. There were splinters everywhere—her cheek, her eyes.

Oh God, oh God, he thought, the memory had such a bitter taste.

Solemnly he placed the old mask into the hole, then covered it with the wet soil.

A shaman's proper burial.

He carefully replaced the tender green turf.

Slowly, he crushed the flowers of half the marigolds, scattering the petals over both graves. He then pushed a dozen long white candles into the grass of each and lit them just as the sun touched the horizon. Between the candles he placed styrofoam cups of steaming *café con canela* and a plate of *pan dulce* for Josephina. There were *carnitas y frijoles* for Manuel and an identical plate for himself.

"Only you," he said softly as he ate a meal with them.

Afterward, he divided the remaining flowers and placed them at each headstone.

As he tamped the turf down again in drying, thinning air, he suddenly saw himself from miles up and miles away, scratching and scraping the skin of the earth for the blood inside.

Dowsing for the blood inside.

He reached out then and there to touch the seam where his *abuelitos* reside.

The tensile margin, the quivering, sensual chaos between water and air, spread out in circles from the point of his fingertip, from the tip of his talon.

Do you dream? What do you dream?

His *abuelitos'* fingers reached to touch his, to mirror his.

One hand with the sliver of a silver ring.

The other with a tiny bottle hanging at the wrist and waxed at the cork.

There was a small cross at the place where the heart echoes.

Then an unseen thing happened.

There swiftly came the sound of *teneboim*—hundreds of tiny bodies beating against crystal lids.

There blithely came sweating, stamping deer dancers and a *pascola* at his back to mock him.

To shepherd him.

They sang to the shaken gourd, to the hard beat of cloven deer hooves hanging from their leather belts, flying up then banging against their sweating thighs.

The *pascola* mocked him, mocked his English and the dog tags around his neck.

The *pascola* led him; with two faces seeing then and now, he sang his song.

"Veo que me están esperando; to see you waiting back there for me is to shoo away the mute from the stones," the *pascola* sang aloud as he watched the other dancers moving around him.

"Sabiendo que me están esperando adelante; to know you are waiting up ahead for me is to throw out the imbecile from this muttering dust."

He stomped his feet now to raise the voice of the cocoons.

"*Los veo desnudos debajo de mi*; to see you naked below this waxen light is to undress the secret and frightening depths."

The three sang to the river, the waves, and to the resounding blood, their feet pounding in a circle about the glowing lights.

Then the dancers moved timorously to the unseen water's edge, their now-stilled voices leaving the world soundless. The quiet deer moved as if to tenderly drink and were gone. From somewhere, just two voices began to glisten words, as gems set in silence.

Who is it that taps upon these deep-veined stones?

It will be you. It was ever you.

Who is it that lingers on this green perch, that gazes down from the bleached balcony of our bones in the parched rain?

Who is it to touch the trough of our mourning dreams, to strike our moon-cold flint with new steel?

Who is it to reclothe our shades?

Who will it be that covets the airborne crests, that retells in flesh the fugue of our mixed bloods?

It is a Yaqui word that Alberto heard.

Em-fiba.

As he streaked overhead in a gyre, above the glowing graves, he seemed to hear its perfect echo.

"*Solamente tú.*"

16

Arquetipos Diferentes

Beneath a canvas awning beneath a burning hot sun the group of old men muttered and cursed in a circle around their murky water glasses filled with anise. The whitewashed buildings around them sprayed the sun onto their lined faces and the red tiles beneath their feet.

They gestured, shrugged and slapped their knees in front of a small, cavelike *cantina* called the *Vascongadas*. Spitting and crying, together they beatified the separatists. Words shot from their mouths like friendly fire. Each one of the old men wore gray pants, a dark blue sweater and a beret of the same color.

One of them, an old man who finished every sentence with *"me cago,"* asked the others slyly why the ETA made better omelettes.

"Porque tienen más huevos!" He laughed hard enough to split his sides.

"Me cago en las bocas . . ."—he bent over in an agony of joy—*". . . de diez santos!"*

Behind him, above him, a pale, saintly woman levitated heavenward wearing white clothing and gloves. Her feet were at least five feet above the red tile. Plainly scandalized by her husband's words, she crossed herself repeatedly, once for each foul curse, while whispering plaintively "*Si Dios quiera,* as God wishes."

It was a phrase that she could not whisper when her older daughter married an Indian so far away in America. She had just managed to whisper it with resignation when her younger daughter married a Portuguese.

Behind her, and gradually materializing into view, were the serene tile walls of the beautiful Moorish temple. The gentle cats would be waiting there, lounging and preening in the shade. Dear Adelita would be there, her perfect skin accentuated by the rough stone pillars.

The children would be there to greet her, pressing closer, then closer, until, *gracias a Dios*, their lost faces were replaced, a mouth at last to say a name, to salvage a memory from the heartless press of time and senescence.

The stratospheric white and amber light of pleasure, of anticipation, grew in her, as swelling as a childbirth. The old woman steadied herself as she sat on the porch of the Casita Philco awaiting her spirit's course. Then her weary brow furrowed and the vision suddenly plummeted, was wrenched downward to a loud line of revelers in the reverie, of people coming for her: little flower girls, ushers and semi-naked best men coming up the gravel wash for her. There were Yaqui dancers, *pascolas* with yellow ribbons on their antlers already mocking the bride and groom.

One of them, a man who looked like Salvador only much younger, smiled up at her as he danced. Out of the midst of them came old Refugio to call her out, to take her ceremoniously by the hand, then lead her to Manuel's hiding place.

There were words everywhere in the air, a hundred different tongues to mouth their marvel at the beauty of the bride.

"Manuel is waiting," a voice said.

"I will go to him," she spoke aloud to end the vision.

"I will go . . . but first there are some important things I have to do."

At the same instant one hundred miles to the southeast a young girl in the Pascua shot bolt upright on her twin bed after a short, fitful nap. She sat sweating in her brown dress,

heaving her labored breaths in and out. The candles next to
her bed flickered.

"*Madre de Dios! Madre de Dios!*" she said to no one.

She had thrown both her hands up to her face. There was
no veil, no wrinkles. There was no mourning dress and severe
shoes. She had somehow touched days and years through a
dying woman's heart. She'd jumped into a full life with a
child's eyes, and the wide horizons there had frightened her
. . . almost drowned her.

"People in Spain . . . a Yaqui wedding," she said
breathlessly.

After a time she understood with a mixture of relief and
sadness that the strange dream would not come to her again
on this day. She pushed her dolls aside, then climbed from
her bed.

She knelt on the floor to pray.

The medicinal bag had been opened on the bed in the *casa
de cartón*. It had been spread out and splayed like a woman,
pushed open on the wedding quilt while the old, dry midwife
by its side plumbed the innards for the splintered wooden
cross and the brown cloth of significance.

After touching each of these things with solemn tenderness,
she placed the two precious objects into her purse along with
some dollar bills and small change for the bus, and she left
for the Pascua.

"Driver," she yelled out as she mounted the steps of the
bus, "take me into Tucson!"

On a seat alone, she arranged her hair, wove it into two
braids under her veil. Then she wiped her brow beneath her
veil.

"Take me out to Tucson, driver. Out to 39th Street. Out to
the Yaqui district. I hear about a little girl over there who has
dreams."

She said it to a bus driver who didn't care, and she was
overheard saying it by passengers who laughed at the bearing

and carriage of her, the black dress and veil and the ancient lace-up boots. In her hands was a purse that might have been fashionable before Prohibition.

"She dreams and her mother is a seamstress."

As the bus rode through Phoenix, she stood up every block or so to point out examples of Manuel's work to the other passengers.

"*Mi viejo* built that house there, the one with the blue shutters. He put the fire escape on that building right there."

When the bus pulled into Tucson, Josephina walked to the front to pay the driver. She had been watching his eyes in the rearview mirror, and she knew he was Senegalese. She had studied him ever since the bus left the city limits of Phoenix.

"Soon your wife will cook a meat loaf for you," she said to him as she paid. "The next day do not drive the bus."

Everyone laughed loudly, except the wide-eyed driver, whose laughter was forced and thin.

In the Pascua she walked the streets until she located the seamstress of the rumors. Her name was Cricket Mendoza, and she was said to be the first *India* in Tucson to dye her hair.

In an adobe building painted blue with magenta shutters, she found the woman squinting into a blind stitch. Her hair, in point of fact, had streaks of red in it and perhaps even some purple. And when she saw Josephina standing in her doorway, her words were blue. The pins in her mouth sharpened the orders to leave, but the old woman had remained steadfast and mute in the doorway.

After three hems and a cuff, the seamstress relented with a sigh. She pierced a cloth tomato with her pins, then rose painfully to her feet.

They had coffee in quiet, looking up now and again to begin a sentence that would be weighed for its true value, then left better unsaid. They sat in the shadow of the windowless living room, the floor strewn with cloth, the sun filtering in through a door.

Finally, Josephina asked for some things that the girl had

touched or some other things that held the girl's spirit, a picture or a toy.

"A photograph is best," she explained, "but a sock or a comb will do. I need to run a check on her."

"Why now?" the seamstress wept. "Why now? *Qué lástima*, she's just a child! She can barely read English."

"If she is the one, she will read intentions," the old woman replied with kindness, knowing full well the responsibilities of the *curandera*.

She reached into her purse and took out the old cross. The seamstress winced when she glanced down at it.

"She will read infections and fix pains. She will see the other world. She will know how life itself is punctuated."

In the end Cricket Mendoza the seamstress minced about in aimless circles in and out of the soft, dusty shaft of sunlight, her small hands pulling anxiously at the darts in her own dress.

Finally, she went whimpering far into her home, into her cherished, saved things for a photograph of her daughter.

A small, young girl named Norma Paz, fertile as her father's jungle in the Yucatán and in a sack dress as brown as her own skin, would take charge of the medicinal bag on Josephina's next trip into the Pascua.

The daughter of the seamstress, she would be barefoot with the red juice of a popsicle streaming down her arm when Josephina found her on the sidewalk playing. The bottoms of her feet would be black with dirt as she wiped her nose with her arm.

The brown, wooden cross that would change hands that day had a small spool of thread glued right next to the tiny trailer and a picture of the girl taped over the postmark from Flagstaff. She'd been located and prescreened in the gaps.

After recounting for the little girl the use and history of all the herbs and mixtures in the bag, she would pull out the Mayo cloth.

"This is the cloth."

Josephina would squat down in the shade but hold it up in a shaft of sunlight for the little girl to see clearly. She would spread her fingers beneath it lovingly so the sunlight reached every corner.

"Its power will be made known to you," she would say, realizing that the very same words had been told to her as a young woman. But this was a child. "Just touch it and you'll know what it does. But don't ever go to sleep on it; unseen things happen. *Cosas pasen que no se vemos*," she would be warned. "*And mi mocosita*, don't use it to clean your nose."

The old woman would hesitate a moment before speaking again.

"There is a bottle down in the bottom. You'll know it when you see it. *El agua de alacrán*."

Josephina would find herself repeating the words of Ana Martinez, passed on so long ago. Those horrible, shameful instructions.

"May it never, ever be used. Resist it," she would say tearfully. The old woman would squat down even lower to be at eye level with the little girl, who now sat on the closed bag. She would put one hand on either cheek and gently frame her small face while looking directly into her eyes. "Your dreams will always be far ahead of your power to understand them. Especially now when the dreams you dream are mine. When I am gone you will have your own. It's a kind of process, a transfer of things. You were chosen because hearts are transparent to you. Sincerity will feed you. Evil will eat at you. *Vaya con Dios*."

She would cross herself, then kiss the cross at her wrist. The little girl would follow suit.

Norma Paz would walk away from Josephina, dragging the heavy bag behind her in the soft dust, like a doll. When she was ten or eleven feet away she would stop. She would let the bag fall; then she would turn to face the old woman. She would hold the old Mayo cloth up to her cheek and smile.

"So many voices," she would say. "So many voices. I just heard the echo of yours."

The car followed Route 10 out of Buckeye Road on a stifling hot evening and drove out into the desert past Tonopah, Quartzsite, and into Blythe in the early morning.

"You know it's best to drive through the desert at night. What do you want to listen to, Beto?" asked Joe Fish.

"It's Alberto."

"Oh, I'm sorry." He smiled at Lola.

"What do you want to listen to, Alberto? How about Pat Boone or Eddie Fisher?"

"What I want to hear isn't broadcast."

Joe and Lola looked at each other.

"Who do you like? Who is it you listen to?" asked Lola.

"I like Son House and Big Joe Turner and the Five Blind Boys from Mississippi," answered Alberto, "y Flaco Jimenez."

"Jesus, that old woman really got to you," said Joe Fish. "Don't she know it's a new world out there? Nobody listens to those people, whoever the hell they are!"

"I don't care what other people listen to," said the boy, without bothering to turn his gaze from the window. "You can play what you want."

Lola turned in her seat to face her son, a stern look on her pretty face. "Look," she said. "You're going to live with me now. You won't be living in the desert anymore. In California, Indians are history and Sunday is for football, not for church. I should've taken you away from them a long time ago. In fact, I'm damn sorry I ever left you there at all. Those two old fools have filled your head with such garbage.

"I know. I know what they try to do. They tried to fill my head with that same shit. But look around, boy. This is the twentieth century and this is America. Nobody believes in their stupid superstitions and dumb stories anymore.

"And Christ almighty that neighborhood! I don't know why you had to say good-bye to all that Okie white trash and those whores and Good Lord, those *maricones!*"

Her face reflected her complete disgust at Buckeye Road.

"You can do some work for a change," Lola said without turning to face her son. "No more maid service in the mornings and *frijoles* whenever you please. It's about time you learned to work for a living. Tell him, Joe." She turned to her escort for support. "Tell him that the best thing to learn is the value of a dollar."

"You can pick asparagus at this place we're going and the money's real good. It's called French Camp. It's just outside of Stockton. We call asparagus grass. You see, we cut grass," he laughed. "It's piecework. You get thirty-five cents for every box you fill. On a good day you can make twenty-five, thirty dollars."

Joe Fish was speaking to the rearview mirror, enjoying the authority of his own voice and the impression he was making on Lola.

"When we finish at French Camp, we go up to San Jose for the string beans. Easy money! No bending. No knee-scraping and you get fifty cents a hamper. Then there's walnuts up near Concord and pears up near Placerville."

Lola turned in her seat to face the back. Her eyes were bright with enthusiasm.

"Your little brothers, Roberto and Miguelito, are in French Camp, you know. We can all be together now. We can all be a family. Christ, I hope those goddamn Flips don't have them eating frogs again."

Joe's eyes flashed at the word "Flips." Lola did not take notice.

"I hate frogs," she continued as she lit up a Kool Menthol cigarette.

"I swear, those Pinoys will eat anything."

"But the best of all is Livermore or the Napa valley," interrupted Joe Fish. "If you can hook on at the wineries, you can work year-round."

"I was so damn glad to get to a motel the other night," said Lola. "I'll tell you. If I never see that desert again, it'll be too soon. Did you see that fire they had over at that Blue Moon place? As we were leaving that pathetic cardboard house the night before last, some crazy old *Negrita* woman over there with a blond wig was running around with her dress on fire. Crazy wino bastards were trying to put her out with hard liquor! She looked like the Fourth of July!"

Joe Fish nodded emphatically with every word that Lola spoke.

"Fireballs o' the Eucharist," said Alberto to himself.

"What did you say?" asked Lola, not particularly interested. "In America you can be whatever you want to be. You can drive an Oldsmobile like Joe." She smiled at the driver.

"I don't want to drive an Oldsmobile," said Alberto. "I want to be a physicist."

"A what?" asked Joe Fish.

"A physicist. You know, study the Yaquis' second law of thermodynamics, all the rules that run the universe and especially the theory of relativity. You know, Albert Einstein."

"Albert Einstein was a Jew," said Joe Fish. "Jesus Christ."

"So was Jesus," answered the boy.

Lola turned quickly in her seat to glare down at her son.

"I never want to hear you say that, never again. Never, you hear."

"But it's true. The Last Supper was a seder."

"Shut up!" she screamed. "You keep all that stuff to yourself while you're in our company. Did they teach you blasphemy too? We're civilized in here!"

"I'm not in your company. I don't even want to be here."

"I don't care what you want!"

She was screaming now. "I don't care what your grandmother wants. From now on it's what I want! Do you hear me? What I want!"

Joe Fish reached out his hand to calm her, but she pushed his hand away and continued her tirade.

"Your father, that accursed man, would rather play eight ball and snooker than buy milk for his own child. You don't remember, but I sure do. Now he's running around with that blondie over in Tracy. He treats that bitch like a queen! She goes *pala-pala* and bats her fake eyelashes and he gives her everything. I hear she's even got a maid!

"Well, he's never, ever going to see you and you'll never see him. Not if I can help it. You're mine. I had you and you'll do what I say."

She turned in her seat and folded her arms in anger.

"I've done everything for these kids. I even switch to filter cigarettes when I'm pregnant. Do you know what that crazy old woman did to me?"

She turned in her seat again, to face the rear of the car. There was a pained look on her face.

"She kept me inside the house on Friday and Saturday nights. Every damn weekend night, even when I couldn't have done nothing! All of my girlfriends would go out, but not me.

"It got worse after the first bloody spots came; she kept me inside like I was a goddamn prisoner. She would slap me even when I just looked at a boy.

"Do you know that when I got my first period we went into Phoenix, just the two of us, and we bought a sanitary napkin belt and a training bra at the Woolworth's. She said nothing to me on the way there. Not a single word. I felt like I had done something wrong! She said nothing to me in the store. And when we got back home she put those things on me like I was some kind of draft animal or a *puta*. I remember this! She jerked on the belt and the bra like I had done something wrong to her, like my coming of age had hurt her personally or something."

She began to cry . . . not the hate tears of her arguments with Abuelita, but a child's tears, the tears of a child with children.

For the first time Alberto saw his mother clearly. He saw her tears and what Buckeye Road and places like it could do to a young girl. The Buckeye Road that had lifted him had only wounded her. One day, a few years in the future, he would see those very same tears again as his mother burst from the washroom of a farmworkers' bunkhouse sobbing that Patsy Cline had died.

"I had you when I was thirteen," she whimpered.

Joe tried to console her again with a touch, but she shoved his hand back to the steering wheel.

"Turn up the radio!" she screamed.

Joe Fish meekly complied. He placed his hands on the wheel of his beautiful car. At least the car did his bidding. He loved its metal skin and the four layers of enamel and wax that enclosed him. He was comforted by its loyalty to him as it dutifully followed the broken white line on the highway.

The boy slept through Southern California. Lola and Joe Fish turned now and again to see that his eyes were closed and his head was pressed against the window. He was clutching a cloth bag to his chest.

"Don't you want to see Highway 99?" she asked.

The boy behind their backs was too far away to hear either of them. He was screeching over *ciudad Moctezuma*, following the sun-silvered *rio* Yaqui south to Cocorit and Bacum.

Here and there along the old highway there were single, solitary people who would stop what they were doing to stare at the dark Oldsmobile with the blinding light in the backseat.

A Cherokee truck driver outside of Chowchilla saw it.

Earl J. Waits and Sue Ann, a young Shoshone couple from the reservation up in Wind River, saw it as they sat in their car necking behind a billboard, Sue Ann's brassiere at her waist.

A young waitress in an empty diner and lost in the words of Billie Holiday looked up and saw it.

Alberto had been playing with Claude and Louie. The three of them had wandered far out into the desert to follow the path of the flash flood and to search through the debris that had been swept down from miles away. They found homemade rag dolls with black faces that must have come from Tar-Paper. Some black migratory family must have lost them. They found letters and clothing and cooking utensils. They even found an Armenian newspaper.

"We were real lucky," said Claude. "Our house is on a small rise. I swear some of the houses below us went over like dominoes."

"The Negroes next door to us had a tree branch come plum through their roof," said Louie. "None of us even heard it coming. And one of the Hindu families down below lost their car, their whole car!"

Claude, who had seemed a bit disturbed all morning, finally confronted the reason for it.

"Ma says we're moving again pretty soon."

"Do you know where you're going?" asked an obviously concerned Alberto.

"California is all we know," said Louie. "Some valley."

"Pa says the picking's better out there and it ain't so God awful hot. And Ma says we gotta go someplace where there's schools. Can you feature me in a school full of city kids?"

Claude wrenched his face into a look of complete disgust.

"I'm gonna miss this place," said Louie, picking up a rock and throwing it as far as he could. The rock sailed across a wash and into a manzanita bush before dropping to the sand.

"The Indian kids tell me that in California that rock woulda hit somebody or landed on someone's property. That don't sound like fun to me."

"I wish you didn't have to go," said Alberto. "But *mi abuela* has told me that we're gonna see each other again, in California and maybe someplace else."

"Well," said Claude, "she ain't hardly ever been wrong."

"Alberto!"

All three boys looked around to see who had shouted Alberto's name.

"Alberto!"

The running form of Vernetta appeared on a small *mesa* about a quarter mile to the north of the boys.

"Jesus," exclaimed Louie, "that's Vernetta! She's running like an antelope. God, look at her go! Let's go see what she wants."

The three boys ran to meet her.

"If any money falls out of her shirt, it's mine!" shouted Claude.

Though none would admit it, all three were frightened by the sight of their friend running at them. The memory of Boydeen was still fresh in their minds.

"Your mother's here," she said breathlessly. "Your mother's here and she's come to take you back to California with her."

Alberto was stunned when he heard those words. Vernetta and the two boys saw it in his face. They saw anger there too.

"Josephina sent me out here to tell you that she doesn't want you to come home just yet, not 'til after dark. Then she'll send Lola and that idiot she's with into Phoenix to stay at a motor hotel.

"Come home when Silvia starts the fire. Then we can all be together one more night."

The three boys came toward the light of the fire. After seeing Vernetta, the three of them had wandered even farther out into the desert. They had done nothing differently than all the other times that they had gone out together to the boarded-up mineshafts or out to the Navajo hermit's hogan, but this time it was purposeful, conscious—for the collection of memories.

They said good-bye to each other in an unacknowledged running ritual of lizard catches and a mad laughing flight from rocks hurled by the old Navajo. When Alberto finally entered the light of the fire, he was alone.

"*Mijo*," said Josephina sadly, "I'm sure I will never see you again, except in dreams. I won't live to see you again. I know *en mi corazón* this is true because I've seen it."

Wysteria Silvia Maybelle covered her ears to block out even the smallest suggestion of her friend's dying. With her hands over her ears, she shook her head slowly back and forth.

"The next time you come here you will be a man, *mijo*, and I will be with *mi* Manuel and we will have settled most of our differences.

"Your mother is here, as you know, and she has demanded that you go with her back to California. I cannot stop her from taking you.

"This is very hard for me, but I have something here for you. Something I have to give you."

Josephina reached behind her, and when she turned she held a cloth bag in her hand. Alberto had never seen the bag before. She handed it to her grandson.

"I buried it right beneath the front doorstep along with

some fetishes that Ana Martinez gave me to protect the house," grinned Josephina. "No one but a Mayo *bruja* could find it."

She arched her eyebrow to emphasize the point.

"Sure, I could feel old Salvador's *nagual* probing for it. Probing here, poking there." She jabbed her finger to illustrate.

The boy reached into the bag, then pulled out a worn leather roll that was tied around its center with a shoestring. Alberto pulled at one bow of the shoestring, which came undone and fell away.

The roll was actually a piece of headgear made of goatskin. The fur in the front had been carefully scraped away and two eyeholes had been cut into the leather. There was faded red paint around the eyes and on the cheeks. It was the *chapayeka* mask. It was a *fariseo* mask, the face of a Jew.

"The *chapayeka* mask, Abuelita, *muchísimas gracias!*" said Alberto, an exultant look on his face.

He held the goatskin face up to his own to look deep into the black of the eyes, the face that sweats from the inside, the skin over a skin. Now, someday, his first promise to his grandfather would be kept.

"A Jewish face. At least that is what the Spanish missionaries so happily believed it had become," Salvador had explained to the boy one day when the two had met in the desert. "To the Yaqui, it was the symbol of the Spaniard's greatest enemy: the persistence of the old beliefs, those that sprung up from the ancient spirits of the land.

"The missionaries said that the *fariseos* sought out the Christ to persecute him, and so the mask is used as such in the Passion plays of the Easter season.

"A mask that once stood for sexual energy and abandon was made evil by the Europeans. It was transformed by the Catholic church into a symbol of base antisemitism.

"Those Catholics are always obsessed and threatened by sexuality, I don't know why. Celibacy is such a mutilation of the spirit much less the body."

Salvador laughed at this notion. His own exploits had continued right into the present. Tonight he had a rendezvous

with a nice round Guerrero Apache widow who could cook
up a storm. He smiled as he imagined her grinning at him,
rubbing the frybread dough across her crotch before tossing
it into the hot oil.

"*Más sabrosa*," she'd whisper.

All them wells weren't dry.

"You see, the Christians and the Catholics in particular are
always worrying about sin. Everything is *siempre* sin this and
sin that. They see the world that way. They're smart, those
white people. First they get to define all the sins. They make
so many sins that practically everybody qualifies as a sinner.
Then they give the poor *pendejos* the opportunity to pay their
way to heaven.

"The Yaquis, the Mayos and even the Aztecs in their beliefs
are concerned only with the idea of well-being, the health of
the universe and the health of the things in it. I tell you, I
wouldn't give you a dime for the Aztecs, but they weren't
completely stupid. A little bloody, *la verdad*, but not completely stupid. They called themselves the people of the fifth
moon. Some say the Aztecs actually harvested the beating
heart like a fruit. And they called us the *Chichimeca*, the sons
of dogs—the barbarians!"

He shook his head with disgust and disbelief.

"You see the true Yaqui language has no word for sin. That
word was forced on us. There was no devil in this land before
the Spaniards brought him. The older Yaquis can still see
beyond the modern meaning of the mask. They see only the
evil Spaniards seeking out the people of the eight cities to
change their lives forever, change their traditions, destroy
them. They see the *gachupines*, the upper castes in Mexico,
trying to steal our lands, trying to subjugate us through the
church.

"The shaman knows what is truly beneath the mask, who
the enemy really is.

"Before there were Europeans the mask existed. Before the
Aztecs the mask existed, and it always transformed men into
clowning, lusting and sometimes gigolo spirits that mess with
people's lives and people's wives. The missionaries deformed
it. They disfigured it."

He winked at the boy. The last conceit amused him. It carried a flood of memories to him. Women in Sinaloa, *la India bonita* who cleaned the bathrooms and changed the bedding at the Motel 6. He imagined her bending over the double beds in room 207, her dimpled, plump thighs rubbing together. He had rutted shamelessly on her tight-stretched bedspreads with their hospital corners in that room, and he had even torn through the sanitary label she had stretched across the toilet seat, but all to no avail on that first evening.

"I can be disrobed with three reasons," she'd said softly as she placed a mint candy on each pillow.

Salvador had to shake his head to dislodge that last memory and return to his present thoughts.

"The *pascola* dances, at their roots, have tapped no Christian visions and they never will. The *pascola* dances to his vision with a *máscara* that recalls the days when the people of the Yaqui basin painted their faces and made war on the Aztecs. The *chapayeka* is a shaman's mask, and in the old days it was always buried with the shaman."

He stopped speaking for a moment to gaze at the sky.

"*Tres razones,*" he muttered with a look of marvel on his weathered face. "A Pima riddle, but shit, I know them all."

He placed one hand on each of the boy's shoulders as a sign of reassurance. He let each hand drop down to touch the boy's hands. Alberto had long ago learned that hand touching was important to the Yaqui. It signified ceremony.

"Our church is higher than all the cathedrals. You will keep your promise."

The old woman reached out her veined hands to touch her grandson's.

"In just a few hours Lola and her *pendejo cabrón con la* Oldsmobile will be coming for you. God must have his reasons," she said, "for taking you away. Keep the *chapayeka* in the bag. Lola will not understand. I'll make sure to give you a couple of burritos to go, so you can eat decent on the road."

When she saw the sad look on her grandson's face, she

resolved to say something to cheer him up, fighting the impulse to leave things forlorn and dolorous, a natural Catholic impulse.

"Me, I can practice my piano and I can cook for the Salvation Army on Thursdays. They have Mexican food on Thursdays. I have many friends here, so I won't be too alone." She looked at Vernetta and Silvia. "Later this very week, I am going back into the Pascua over in Tucson to meet the next one. I found her name last week and I've seen her photograph."

The old woman seemed to lose her train of thought for a moment. "She will move away for a while. She'll toss the medicinal bag into one of her mother's closets and pretend it's not there. She'll be a cheerleader and sell makeup and go to dental-assistant school in El Paso, but she'll move back. *Pobrecita*, she'll have no choice."

Alberto knew she was speaking from experience.

"She is the next one. I screened two others on the old cross, but they only dreamed they were dreamers. She will have my medicinal bag and the cross and the old Mayo cloth. Then I can retire from this business." She smiled. "I will be in the weave."

Josephina could see her own moment of distraction in Vernetta's and Silvia's faces.

"The young girl will learn to live with it," she added quickly. "*Escúchame, hijo.*" Her voice took on a deeper tone. "Now that Manuel has left me I must speak for the both of us. In some things I cannot disagree with him. I know now in my heart that you will never be a very good Catholic."

She looked away toward Silvia, who nodded her head in agreement.

"I guess I haven't been so hot at it either. But I have tried to teach you as well as I can, and though I used to disagree more with your grandfather than I seem to now, I find that I want you to remember also what he taught you. Lola's world"—her face darkened visibly—"the world she wants to belong in is a lonely, greedy and seductive world. You'll see, *mijo,*" she said softly. "Don't be seduced by it."

She looked up at her grandson and seemed dispirited by the small time left to her. She managed a smile and seemed pained beyond words when she hugged her grandson for the last time on their last night. Then for the first and only time since her husband died she lifted her veil.

"The *Mexicanos* and the *Indios* have different *arquetipos* than the *gringos*. Though today, many *Mexicanos* deny their Indian blood. God, how your grandfather hated the Yoris!" The old woman laughed, her body shaking with the value of the memory. "*Arquetipos diferentes*. Remember that, Alberto. Your grandfather said it to you in so many different ways and it is true. I see it now. They have not been suppressed, even after centuries. Even after all of my efforts," she laughed.

"Completely different archetypes flowing from completely different sources. Remember, his strength will always be there for you."

"Like a glove?"

"*Sí, mijo, como un guante.*"

She reached over and ran her fingers through her grandson's *pelo chino*. Vernetta came into the light of the fire with Danny by her side. She was wearing potholder gloves and carrying a large cauldron by the handles. Her son had a stack of Melmac bowls in his hands.

"We have to eat now," she said as she lowered her veil. "Vernetta's made some jambalaya. I tried some earlier. It is a lavish food. The Spanish influence is so obvious in the spices.

"When you go to school, *mijo*"—she rose to walk over to her outdoor dish rack—"and the teacher wants to take a vote, close your eyes when you make your vote." She put a hand over her eyes to demonstrate. It was to be her last lecture.

"Don't look around at the others. Close your eyes, make up your own mind, *mijo*, then you can vote. And when you go to war," she added, almost matter-of-factly, "don't worry. I know you will come back to us."

Somehow she had managed to say the phrase without betraying the dread in her soul.

"Even if I am a fallen Catholic, God has told me this and many other things. Some that I must never say to you. It must mean that I have not lost all favor in His sight."

She walked over to her grandson and placed her hand in his.

"Don't ever take sides against *los desvalidos*, the poor." She groaned. "There's too much to say."

As the car pulled out of Buckeye Road that last sad day, the boy's grandmother ran alongside the car talking to him through the open window, much to Lola's chagrin.

The old woman kept pace with the car down the center of Buckeye Road past Cady and past the Rainbo. She ran past the denizens of the rusted Cadillacs and past the old *sinónimos*. The *maricones* watched tearfully as she ran.

"Keep yourself, *mijo*," she shouted through the window of the Oldsmobile.

Down below, Boydeen's fingers moved with the words.

"You know what I mean," Josephina said between breaths.

"Don't let the *pinche* helicopters make you bitter. Those people will hurt you to your bones and you will hurt some people *también*, but you will come back to yourself. You will know who you are. Don't let the helicopters make you *si amargo*, so bitter."

Boydeen's tears fell onto the keys of her machine.

The old woman ran with her hands on the door of the car, her black shoes flying. She strained for a final look at her grandson.

Her veil pressed against her face, the dark mesh obscuring her wrinkles. Beneath it the boy could see her face as it must've been as a girl.

Below them, her shoulders shaking violently, Boydeen could type nothing more.

In the street above, Lola ordered Joe Fish to speed the car up, and she angrily rolled up her own front window. She turned her pretty face away from the old woman, who was losing her grip on the speeding car.

"If they ever ask you about me," Josephina laughed as the car pulled away from her.

"If they ever ask you about me," she yelled out from the dusty road, "tell them I was a saint."